Once again, Trinket, Bitty, and Divas are headed for trouble . . .

By the time Bitty finally hung up the phone and turned to look at me, I had managed to smear pimento cheese on slices of bread, the countertop, and the back of my hand. She sucked in a deep breath and smiled. It was a feline, satisfied smile.

"Naomi Spencer has been arrested."

In my shock, I nearly spread pimento cheese up my arm. "No! For what?"

Bitty leaned against the counter and propped her chin in her palm. *"Murder.* Her fiancé. Race Champion. They call him Race because he races stock cars."

Bitty and I both silently absorbed the information of Naomi's arrest, each of us from our own points of view.

Bitty broke the silence first. "Just how much pimento cheese are you going to put on that one sandwich?"

I looked down. At least an inch of creamy, yellow-orange deliciousness was piled atop a single slice of bread. "Too much?" I asked.

We ate in silence attended only by the occasional meaningful glance and nod of our heads at one another. I'm pretty sure our inner dialogue ran along similar lines. After all, Naomi Spencer had been heard to say quite a few tacky things about Bitty's arrest for the murder of Philip Hollandale. *What goes around, comes around*, must be the thought uppermost in both our minds.

"Well," Bitty said when we had polished off our sandwiches and licked clean our fingers, "which Diva do we tell first?"

Other Bell Bridge Titles By Virginia Brown

Dixie Divas

DROP
DEAD
DIVAS

Virginia Brown

BelleBooks

B

Bell Bridge

Memphis, Tennessee

This is a work of fiction. Names, characters, places and incidents are either the products of the author's imagination or are used fictitiously. Any resemblance to actual persons (living or dead,) events or locations is entirely coincidental.

Bell Bridge Books
PO BOX 300921
Memphis, TN 38130
ISBN: 978-1-935661-96-2

Bell Bridge Books is an Imprint of BelleBooks, Inc.

We at BelleBooks enjoy hearing from readers. You can contact us at the address above or at BelleBooks@BelleBooks.com

Visit our websites – www.BelleBooks.com and www.BellBridgeBooks.com.

10 9 8 7 6 5 4 3 2

Cover design: Debra Dixon
Interior design: Hank Smith
Photo credits: Shoes -© Ruslan Gilmanshin | Dreamstime.com

:Ld:01:

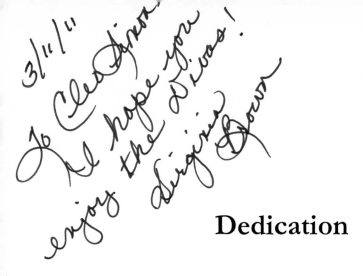

3/11/11

To Cleopatra,
I hope you
enjoy the Divas!
Virginia Brown

Dedication

In memory of Brad Brown—beloved son, wonderful brother, loving father, and happy husband to Cindy. His love and laughter remain in all our hearts.

As always, to the real Dixie Divas of Holly Springs, Ashland, and wherever we gather with wine, chocolate, and good company. We may not solve murders, but we can always kill a couple bottles of good wine.

CHAPTER 1

"Somebody should strangle that slut."

My friend Bitty Hollandale never has been one to mince words about Naomi Spencer. Even in a crowded southern café, where any casual eavesdropper might be tempted to take her words at face value, she managed to be alliterative as well as insulting.

As admirable as that talent may be, in the not so distant past she'd been assigned a caretaker of sorts to slow the flow of incriminating comments that seems to stream ceaselessly from her mouth. But that was when she had been accused of murder and really needed to watch what she said. Now that she'd been absolved, people who know her often nod and agree politely:

"Yes, Bitty, I'm sure someone will."

After I said it, though, I was struck immediately with the realization that we were much too close to other diners who didn't know us, and who might think she—or we—were dangerous. So I quickly added, "Bless her heart."

Bitty lifted a freshly waxed eyebrow at me. "Trinket Truevine, you're just saying that so I won't be tempted to do it myself."

Since the target of her homicidal lust stood only a couple yards away, tossing her hair and batting her eyelashes at a café patron, I thought it best that Bitty be distracted.

"Here." I grabbed the nearest thing at hand and thrust a red plastic basket of corn muffins toward her. "Have one."

"Honestly, Trinket, just look at her. Standing there acting so innocent when she's probably been in the backseat of every car in Marshall County. I have a good mind to—"

Not wanting to hear what she'd do, I snatched up a muffin and stuck it right under her nose. She immediately reared back with a protective hand curved over the small dog she wore in a sequined sling across her chest.

"For heaven's sake, put that down. Chen Ling is on a restricted diet."

The dog—a squashed face, bug-eyed pug—eyed the corn muffin greedily. If Bitty hadn't been holding the animal back, she probably would have swallowed the muffin in one bite.

"Bitty," I said through gritted teeth, "stuff it."

Something in my tone must have alerted her that I preferred discretion in a public place crowded with Memphis tourists who'd come down to Holly Springs, Mississippi for the annual Kudzu Festival.

Bitty leaned forward and lowered her voice. "Well, what I said is true and you know it."

Since her action brought the pug even closer to the muffin I still held in my hand, I quickly dropped it back into the plastic basket. Chen Ling has an occasional lapse of memory regarding proper table manners, and I wasn't about to risk my fingers.

The dog immediately barked a shrill protest.

"There, there, precious," Bitty crooned. "Mama didn't mean to crowd you. Here. Have some chicken."

Bitty scooped up a sliver of chicken from her plate, heedless of dumpling bits clinging to it and broth oozing between her freshly manicured fingers. I pretended it was normal and did my best to ignore questioning looks from patrons at other tables. Although we sat at a small table right in the front by the window and away from others, they must be wondering what kind of service dog was carried in a hot pink baby sling studded with sequins. Most service dogs are much more discreet. Chen Ling sparkled with sequins and diamonds in her collar—yes, real diamonds—so *she* was anything but discreet. Or quiet. Or well-behaved. She also makes porcine sounds when she eats. *Loud* porcine sounds.

"Really, Bitty," I said when I couldn't stand the porky snorts another moment, "why Budgie allows you to bring that dog in here is beyond me."

She didn't even look up. After wiping the dog's mouth with the edge of the bib tied beneath the diamond-studded collar, she kissed Chen Ling atop her furry little head. "Because we happen to be excellent customers, aren't we, precious?"

"*Precious* is dribbling dumplings," I observed. "Is that on her restricted diet?"

"As I was saying a moment ago," Bitty continued, not at all distracted by dog dribbles or diets, "Naomi Spencer will end up in the morgue one day, mark my words."

"We'll all end up in the morgue, Bitty. No one lives forever."

"Don't be morbid, Trinket. Really, I think you may need an anti-depressant. Something strong."

"I have something strong. It's called zinfandel."

"Apparently wine isn't enough. Besides, you don't want to become a wino, do you?"

"Lately, it's beginning to hold a certain appeal for me. We did recently endure a great amount of stress, if you'll recall."

Bitty waved a hand, obviously dismissing the notion that finding her ex-husband, a newly reelected state senator, dead in her coat closet, then being charged with his murder, might be stressful.

"But everything turned out just fine, Trinket. I don't know why you still think about it all the time."

I sat back in my chair to gaze at my best friend—and first cousin— with an emotion close to awe. Mixed with incredulity. I should have been accustomed to her by now, since we'd been in close company ever since I'd come back to Holly Springs a little over six months ago. After my divorce I had returned to care for my elderly parents, mistakenly believing they needed a nursemaid. What I quickly discovered was that what they really needed was a travel agent, not a fifty-one year old caretaker.

Life is full of little surprises. Like Bitty. Of course, if I had pondered it in more detail, I would have remembered that she has always been like this.

Bitty is a true southern belle. Even at fifty-one—and don't believe her when she tells you anything different—Bitty has the power to bring grown men to their knees with just a smile or bat of her eyelashes. She has the full advantage of being born a belle, as does my twin sister, Emerald. Alas, not I. Where Bitty is five foot two, a natural blonde underneath all the stuff her hairdresser uses to "enhance" the color, with a complexion like a California valley girl only partially due to expensive make-up and tanning beds, I am a hair over five foot nine and twenty pounds overweight, according to the doctor's chart in his office. My complexion is somewhere between pale and paler, and my graying auburn hair is only recently all dark auburn thanks to a box of color I bought at Wal-Mart. So it's easy to see where I would be justified in envying Bitty. Truthfully— I don't.

There seems to be a great deal of impulsiveness inherited along with the Belle-gene. At least, there is in my family. My sister Emerald is married with umpteen children and still thinks nothing of coming home for my parents to wait on her hand and foot and take her shopping whenever she decides to get out of bed for a while. She rarely brings her beleaguered husband or any of her umpteen children with her. If Mama and Daddy want to see their grandchildren, they travel to Oregon for a visit. That has become much easier for them now that I'm here to look after Cherryhill and the dozens of feral cats and one neurotic dog that also inhabit my family home.

The cats stay outside in the huge old barn that Daddy has remodeled into a cat-motel. Brownie, their neurotic half-dachshund, half-beagle, lives in the house and sleeps in their bed. Until my parents go out of town.

Then he sleeps in my bed with me, not something I encourage. I must admit, however, that I find it increasingly difficult to resist his canine charms. He does have an endearing quality when he chooses. And besides that, if not for his penchant for consuming indigestible objects like dental bridges and jewelry, I probably would never have met a local vet, Dr. Kit Coltrane, under rather memorable circumstances.

Now, to be frank, I had decided to swear off men. My one and only marriage ended in my one and only divorce, and my one and only child is grown and happily married in Atlanta. So I feel my female duty has been sufficiently satisfied. Bitty has attempted to convince me otherwise. Bless her heart. Her efforts have only complicated matters, but despite her, Dr. Coltrane and I now enjoy a close friendship.

With an unerring instinct for reading my mind, Bitty chose that moment to remind me, "Besides, if not for all that nonsense you wouldn't be dating Holly Springs' most eligible bachelor right now."

"We are not dating," I said primly. "We are friends."

Bitty rolled her eyes. "Good lord, Trinket. You're not in grade school. No one cares if you and Kit are playing doctor in the linen closet."

"Lower your voice, please. Those people are staring at us. Probably because you have twenty pounds of sequins and diamonds eating off your plate, but I'd rather not take the chance they can hear you."

"Oh no, precious. Don't eat off mommy's plate. You might choke on a chicken bone."

While Bitty extricated a piece of chicken from the jaws of an annoyed pug, I reflected on the wisdom of our conversational topic in a crowded café. Discussing my sex life was almost as dangerous as discussing Naomi Spencer, who had flaunted her relationship with Philip Hollandale when he was still Bitty's husband. And still alive. So, a change of topics was definitely desirable.

But then it was too late.

The very topic of our former conversation appeared right next to our table. Naomi Spencer is young, tall, blonde, and the Barbie-doll kind of pretty. She has all the right clothes and looks great from a distance, but up close her facial features are too sharp and there's a vacant look in her eyes that must have something to do with heredity. I won't share Bitty's favorite observation about the Spencer genetics with you here. It's a bit too graphic.

At any rate, Naomi smiled so widely that her newly whitened teeth nearly blinded me. "Why hello, Miz Truevine, Miz Hollandale. I saw y'all sittin' here in the window and thought maybe it's time we called a truce. Don't you think? I mean, what with Philip being dead and all, there's no reason to go on being enemies."

Spots danced in front of my eyes, no doubt caused by a sudden lack of oxygen to my brain. Bitty was right about Naomi. She really is stupid.

Before I could think of anything to say other than *"Uhhhh",* Bitty smiled back at the dumber-than-dog-doo girl. It was not a nice smile. It was a smile full of expensively perfect teeth and venom.

"Why, Naomi. Aren't you just precious?"

Just so you'll know, despite my early years of close proximity to Bitty, I have a horror of public scenes. I'll go out of my way to avoid them. My mother is the same way. It is not a Truevine family trait shared by all, unfortunately.

Regaining some of my wits, I kicked Bitty under the table. She ignored me. A feral light gleamed in her blue eyes. I sensed an imminent beheading. So I began to babble.

"Naomi, is that an engagement ring on your finger? It's lovely. Show it to us. I hadn't heard you were engaged. How nice. Anyone I know?"

Blushing prettily, Naomi held out her left hand. A rather small diamond glittered in a lovely setting. Bitty peered at it over the pug, and squinted enough to make permanent wrinkles between her brows if not for Botox.

"Oh, *there* it is. It's nice, dear. It almost looks real. Where did your brother buy it?"

Naomi looked slightly confused. Being more familiar with Bitty's conjectures on the Spencer heritage and familial bonds, I intervened. "I bet your fiancé bought it in Memphis, didn't he? There are so many lovely jewelry stores up there."

Before Naomi could reply, Bitty said with a puzzled expression, "But Trinket, why would he go up there when there's a dollar store right here on the square?"

Apparently, Spencer stupidity only extends to a certain depth.

Naomi jerked back her hand and glared at Bitty. "Race bought it at Biddly, Banks, and Biddles."

"Do you mean Bailey, Banks, and Biddle?" I asked quickly, but unfortunately, not loudly enough to be heard over Bitty:

"*Race*? Dear god—and I thought your brother's name is Billy Don."

Fists on both hips, Naomi narrowed her eyes. "I'm not marrying my *brother.*"

"Oh. Excuse me. Philip always said . . . but he must have been mistaken about that. He made so many mistakes while we were married. By the way, have you had any more problems with your boobs? So sad about the sag in the left one. And after Philip paid all that money for your implants, too."

Naomi's face turned an interesting color. "I don't have implants," she hissed through clenched teeth. "I'm all natural."

Bitty laughed. "Of course you are, dear. Just not above the waist."

While Bitty hadn't bothered to lower her voice, Naomi sounded like a leaky tire hissing. "That's not true."

"Why, your boob job *looks* perfectly natural except for that left sag. Don't you think so, Trinket? Wait. I'll just ask that gentleman over there what he thinks . . .."

Before Bitty could do more than gesture to a man at the nearest table, Naomi had lifted a half-full glass and poured sweet tea all over Bitty, the table, and the pug. I have to say, Bitty's reflexes are pretty quick. Not, however, quite as quick as Chen Ling's. About the time Bitty managed to sling leftover chicken and dumplings at Naomi, the pug sunk her top fangs—or to be more precise, fang—into Naomi's forearm. She let out a shrill shriek. Naomi, not the dog.

After that, I withdrew to stand next to the brick wall and pretend I didn't know them. Bitty didn't need me anyway. Not only did she have Cujo as her guard dog, the café manager had arrived. Budgie grew up down the road from me. She has lots of siblings and knows how to quell catfights. It didn't take her long at all to disentangle Naomi from Bitty and the pug.

Amidst a flurry of accusations and curse words—all from Naomi—and poses of mystified bewilderment—all from Bitty—Budgie managed to hustle the unattractively raging former cheerleader to the bathroom to clean chicken and dumplings from the front of her dress. The usual lunchtime crowd would relish retelling the episode to everyone and anyone who would listen, of course. Tourists in town for the Kudzu Festival would wonder just what all went on in small towns that they might be missing. If they only knew.

I, however, just wanted to slink home.

"Sit down, Trinket," Bitty said when I continued to make myself part of the brick and mortar. "You're making Chen Ling nervous staring at us like that."

"Chitling doesn't have a nervous bone in her body. And you have no shame."

Ignoring the curious looks in our direction, I disengaged from the wall and sat back down in my chair. The table was a mess. Ice and sweet tea had formed puddles in plates and on the table top. Chicken and dumpling remnants clumped here and there. Chen Ling busied herself with cleaning them up while Bitty cleaned up Chen Ling. To my surprise, my hand trembled slightly when I reached for my tea.

"Why should I be ashamed?" Bitty wondered as she scrubbed dumpling bits from the pug's left ear. "She started it. Only an idiot would come up to a woman whose husband she used to boink at the Motel 6 during recess and ask to be friends."

"She was already out of high school," I reminded as I lifted my tea glass. Just before I took a sip, I noticed half a dumpling floating atop the ice. I set it back down. "Besides, I know your mother taught you to be nice to half-wits. Truevines have always had good manners."

"*My* mother was a Jordan."

My lips twitched. Bitty looked up about that time and laughed.

"See, Trinket? You would have done the same thing."

Probably. But not in public. I had no intention of encouraging her though, so just said, "If you're through bathing Chitling, I'm ready to leave."

"Her *name* is Lady O-ya Moon Chen Ling," Bitty said haughtily, "and I wish you would remember that."

"I'll remember her name if you'll stop making a habit of insulting Philip's former flings in public. My dry-cleaning bill could get steep."

"Sugar, just think how steep it could get if he was still alive. You know how much he loved spreading himself around."

By this time we stood outside on the concrete walk in front of Budgie's café. The cute sign in the window may say *French Market Café*, but it would always be known to the regulars as Budgie's, despite who really owned it now. The new owners had had the foresight to keep the former owner Budgie on as the manager, so not much had really changed over the years, except the décor and a few menu additions.

Bitty caught me by the arm when I started to step off the curb to get into her car. "You've got corn muffin on your rear end, Trinket. Oh. And it looks like dumplings, too. Those pants are washable, aren't they?"

"No. They're unwashable linen. That's okay. I didn't want to wear them more than once anyway."

"Well, I have the dry cleaners on retainer, so we'll just put them in with my stuff. Come on home with me."

"Bitty, you have everyone on retainer. Lawyers. Caterers. Florists. Gardeners. I think I'm the only one you don't pay to hang around. And no, I'll just go home. I have no intention of staying at your house waiting on my clothes to come back from the cleaners. That hasn't worked so well in the past."

"You have a long memory for the wrong things," Bitty said. She pressed the button on her remote, and the car lights flashed, a beep sounded, and the motor started. As soon as cold weather arrived, she'd probably trade in this convertible for a more practical car. If it was still in one piece. Bitty had purchased a stick shift before she learned to drive one. The Miata struggled bravely to outlast her.

After backing out into traffic and hitting no one, we bucked forward on the slope of the street and made a left to go around the square. My parents' house, Cherryhill, lies about three miles outside the city limits of Holly Springs, Mississippi. It can seem much farther when riding with Bitty, depending upon her mood and the weather.

Fortunately the weather was fine, and even Bitty's mood was good. I guess it had cheered her up to insult Naomi Spencer. Elvis played on the car stereo system, a really nice one Bitty had paid extra for, and with the top down, the sun shining, and the wind in our hair, we lurched through the town square at a reasonable speed, the engine only dying twice. Once out on Highway 311, she lowered her foot on the accelerator. I tried not to think about immovable barriers hidden beneath the thick kudzu vines draping trees and telephone poles we passed at seventy miles an hour. And I did my best to ignore the pug sitting in my lap. She pees at inopportune times, and I've found it's usually much drier if I don't upset her. Getting my lunch out of the seat of my nice linen pants was going to be a major feat. I certainly didn't want to extract Chitling urine as well.

"So," Bitty shouted over Elvis and the rushing wind, "have you had that thing you won't let me talk about yet?"

Bitty, I'm sorry to say, discovered that in all my years of marriage, I had never experienced the . . . uh . . . pinnacle of female ecstasy. It's my fault she knows. In a weak moment I'd confessed that my eyes had never rolled back in my head. Not once. She was horrified at the discovery. Since she tends to dwell on the oddest things, and took it upon herself to ensure that I have that special moment before I die—not as that may sound, but by choosing the right man for me—I had quickly decided she was not to mention it to me again. Ever. Bitty nags.

"None of your business," I shouted back.

Bitty glanced at me then made a face. "You forgot to put Chen Ling's sunglasses on, Trinket."

"Why would I wear her sunglasses?"

She motioned impatience, and with a sigh, I took out the pair of doggy sunglasses with the strap to hold them on and slid them onto the pug's head to cover her eyes. Chen Ling bit me in gratitude. It didn't really hurt. She only has one front tooth on top. And an underbite like a Louisiana alligator. She constantly drools. That's why she wears bibs. Bitty has them special-made with embroidered scenes of China, pagodas, dragons, and so on. If not for nice settlements from three former husbands, and alimony checks from her last—and dead—husband, she wouldn't be able to afford canine couture. Fortunately for Bitty, she has rarely been lacking in male attention or alimony.

"What are Aunt Anna and Uncle Eddie doing today?" Bitty asked when the car jolted to a stop in the half-circle driveway at Cherryhill.

I unbuckled my seatbelt and unglued the pug from my chest. She has her own seatbelt, but since I take up all the space in the bucket seat, she has to share mine.

"Probably booking a camel trip along the Nile. I'm sure I saw some brochures with pyramids lying on the kitchen table earlier. It's my job to warn them about sand storms and crocodiles, not to mention bad-tempered camels."

"Good luck with that."

Bitty understood. My parents are enjoying their second adolescence. While I'm glad for them, they can be remarkably stubborn at times. And single-minded. It must be a Truevine trait. After all, Bitty is as stubborn as they come, and her father was Daddy's brother. There is a lot that can be blamed on genetics, I've decided.

Bitty firmly buckled Chen Ling into her own special seatbelt complete with a seat that holds her up high enough to look out the passenger window—a sight bound to have startled more than a few unsuspecting pedestrians—then she tooled off down the driveway with a careless wave of one hand. I went into the house to look for my parents.

Mama stood at the kitchen counter dishing up Brownie's food. I don't know why she bothers cooking special dog meals for him. I believe one of his ancestors had to be a goat. Any dog that can eat metal and expensive jewelry qualifies as a member of the ovine family, in my opinion. I still haven't found one of my emerald earrings he ingested, although I spent a disgustingly long time wearing a plastic glove and looking through piles of dog poop.

"How was your lunch, sugar?" Mama asked over her shoulder. "What'd Budgie have as the special today?"

"Chicken and dumplings."

Mama laughed. That particular dish has been a joke around our house ever since it caused so much trouble a few months back. Trust Bitty to be able to give a household favorite a bad reputation.

"Hey, punkin," my daddy said behind me, and gave me a squeeze around my shoulders. "What have you got all over the back of you?"

I answered dutifully, "Chicken and dumplings."

At that, Mama turned around to look at me. While my father, Edward Wellford Truevine, is six foot four in his socks, my mother is just a little over five feet tall. Once she might have been taller, like five-one. Now she's petite, has nicely coifed silver hair, fair skin that has rarely if ever seen a blemish, and insists on coordinating her clothes with Daddy's. Oh, and with Brownie's. That's only in the winter, though. In the summer he gets to go naked. The dog, not my dad.

Before my mother could ask, I explained. "Naomi Spencer came up to our table to ask Bitty to be friends since Philip is dead and shouldn't mind. It did not go well."

My father guffawed. "She's either crazy or stupid."

"Yes," I agreed.

Mama, of course, had to hear the entire story. She sat transfixed while I related the experience, a hand over her mouth to hide her laughter. Bad manners should not be rewarded or encouraged, she has always felt. When I finished, both my parents expressed their relief that Bitty seems to be recovering nicely from the shock of a few months ago.

"At least she's not grieving anymore," Mama said.

I stared at her. "For *Philip?* Why would she grieve for him? He cheated on her with any bimbo who'd go out with him. He embarrassed her. He gave her nothing but trouble. She's glad to be rid of him."

"Yes, all of that is true. But he hurt her deeply with his affairs, and in public, too. That's not something a woman can easily forgive. Yet she stayed married to him even after he took that girl to Mexico and all the pictures of them drunk in the Acapulco hotel pool made the evening news and papers. She *must* have felt something for him."

I hadn't thought of that. Why hadn't I guessed that real emotion lay beneath all her callous comments about Philip Hollandale? Sometimes I can be so self-centered. I thought about all the gossip, and how I'd listened to what Bitty said instead of how she felt. I should really learn to look beneath the surface, I told myself, and resolved that from now on, I would do my best to recognize what Bitty really meant instead of what she said.

It would not be easy.

CHAPTER 2

"Philip was pond scum," said Bitty, regarding her freshly manicured fingernails with a critical eye. "Do you like this color? It seems too red to me, but DJ says I'm the type who can wear bold colors. Did I tell you I have a new manicurist?"

I tried again to plumb the depths of emotion that must be tightly trapped in her scarred psyche. "But he had his good points, too, I'm sure. There must be times when you really miss him."

Bitty turned to look at me. We sat in her euphemistically named parlor with our shoes off and bare feet up on plush ottomans. Refreshing glasses of sweet tea helped cool some of the heat of midday.

"Eureka May Truevine, have you been drinking? Or smoking something funny? You've done nothing but pester me about that man since you got here. The funeral's come and gone, and now we don't have to pretend there was anything nice about him."

Since Bitty had used my full name, it hardly seemed worth another try. Maybe my mother had misread Bitty. It was possible. Not likely, but possible. Obviously, I would have to be more subtle in my effort to allow Bitty to properly purge her grief.

Subtlety is not my strong suit. Silence stretched until I said, "Well, if ever you want to talk about him, I'm here for you."

"I'd rather eat rocks than talk about Philip. Wait. You aren't thinking of going back to Perry, are you? Is that what this is about?"

Since any discussion of my ex-husband usually summons an instant migraine, I became rather cross. "*No.* I just had the brainless idea your late husband's violent death may have scarred you somehow. My mistake."

"Good god, Trinket. The only thing that got scarred was my expensive rug. By the time I got it back from the police, it was ruined for me. Every time I looked at it, all I could see was Philip rolled up in it like a taco. I donated it to charity, though, so it wasn't a complete waste."

A sharp tap in the region of my sinus cavity suggested that Chen Ling had missed her regular appointment with Bitty's front lawn. It could certainly clear sinuses in a hurry. Since there was no sign of anything unpleasant behind or under the dog sitting next to Bitty, however, I figured it was just Chitling's usual digestive windiness. I put my hand over my nose and seized the moment to change topics.

"What on earth do you feed that dog?" I asked despite knowing the answer. "Gunpowder and pinto beans?"

"Now, Trinket, you know she's on a strict diet these days. I'm still using Rayna's recipe for dog food."

"You mean Sharita is using Rayna's recipe. You don't cook."

Bitty looked at me over the rim of her tea glass. "You're awfully cranky today. I'd ask if it was that time of the month, but you should be past that by now. Maybe you should think about taking Kit Coltrane for a test drive. If you know what I mean."

I knew what she meant. "While your interest in my sex life—"

"You don't have a sex life," Bitty rudely interrupted.

"—is gratifying," I continued as if she hadn't spoken, "we have an agreement."

"I didn't say one word about you not ever having a *hallelujah* moment. You're just being sensitive."

"I tend to get that way when people start prying into my personal business."

"It's fortunate I don't do the same then, because you're always prying into my personal business."

There wasn't a whole lot I could say to refute that. She's right. I have a lamentable tendency to pry into Bitty's personal business at times. There's no good reason for it, since she lives such a charmed life nothing ever really touches her, it seems. Apparently, despite Mama's opinion to the contrary, not even the murder of her ex-husband affected her for long.

"Forgive me," I said, more to end the conversational sidebar than because I was sorry. Bitty, of course, knew what I was doing.

"That won't work every time, you know. I'll let you get by with it now, but you owe me."

I said something rude and she smiled. "Sharita made up a batch of Mama's pimento cheese. Want some?"

Bitty's late mother Sarah made unarguably the best pimento cheese in the entire world, and she'd entrusted her only daughter with the recipe. Eating one of Aunt Sarah's pimento cheese sandwiches is like taking a bite of heaven. Rich, creamy, cheesy, with just the right amount of pimento—I began to drool just thinking about it.

Sharita Stone owns a catering service and also cooks for a few private citizens who were lucky enough to get on her list of clients. Her family owns a diner that makes delicious muffins and other baked goods, and their jams and jellies are superb. Sharita's brother is a Holly Springs policeman, and happened to be the one who arrested Bitty when she was thought to have murdered her ex-husband. All a terrible mistake, of course, and Bitty never held a grudge against Sharita or Marcus Stone for it. She's very open-minded. That's one of Bitty's best virtues, that she holds very few grudges, which makes her hostility toward Naomi Spencer that much more intriguing.

Of course, if my ex had flaunted his mistress right under my nose like the senator did to Bitty, my hostility would have been immediate and flammable. Perry would have been looking for what was left of his . . . well, badly bruised private parts, while I was on the way to my divorce attorney's office. This would have occurred in private, of course, since I really do have a dread of public scenes.

But that's me.

Bitty often utilizes the Southern-belle trick of being a perfect lady in public, yet still manages to convey just what she *really* thinks of the person or their actions. I've never quite figured out how she does it without looking like a complete bitch. If I ever do figure it out, I intend to practice the art until I've got it mastered. There must be some kind of code words belles use. I'm usually so enthralled with their absolute mastery of the art that I don't take notes, and consequently, can never recall exactly what was said or in what tone. It's usually not so much the words as it is the tone of voice, the smile, the tilt of the head and batting of the eyelashes that convey exactly what is really meant, despite even the most innocuous comments. As I said, it's an art form.

As Bitty and I converged on her gleaming kitchen like piranhas in a feeding frenzy, her phone rang. I stuck to my mission and took a bowl of pimento cheese out of the refrigerator while she answered the phone. Chen Ling—abandoned on the floor—looked up at me with a decidedly greedy gleam in her little bug-eyes. I smiled at her, rather relishing the fact that I have opposable thumbs and she—despite her charms—does not. It gave me a rare feeling of superiority, which is usually short-lived.

"Rayna!" Bitty exclaimed in what can only be described as a deliciously shocked tone. "Are you certain?"

Whatever Rayna Blue, a founding member of the Dixie Divas, said on the other end of the line must have been affirmative, because Bitty immediately laughed, then said in a solemn, pious voice, "Well, bless her heart."

My attention was now immediately riveted on the informative phone call instead of pimento cheese. I moved closer to Bitty. "What? Bless whose heart?"

"Naomi Spencer's," Bitty said over her shoulder, and then went back to listening to Rayna.

Naomi Spencer? The young woman Bitty had so recently showered with venom and chicken and dumplings? Oh, this had to be good. I could hardly wait for her to get off the phone and tell me what was going on.

By the time Bitty finally hung up the phone and turned to look at me, I had managed to smear pimento cheese on slices of bread, the countertop, and the back of my hand. She sucked in a deep breath and smiled. It was a feline, satisfied smile.

"Naomi Spencer has been arrested."

In my shock, I nearly spread pimento cheese up my arm. "No! For what?"

Bitty leaned against the counter and propped her chin in her palm. *"Murder."*

She rolled the R and drew the word out like a character in a bad TV show.

I rolled my eyes. "Who did she murder?"

"Oh, that's the best part. Her fiancé. Race Champion."

"Dear god—that's really his name?"

"No, I think it's Rupert or Roger, or something like that. They only call him Race because he races stock cars. Can you believe it? She probably killed him for giving her an engagement ring he got out of a box of Cracker Jacks."

"I don't think Cracker Jacks has prizes anymore," I said, and it was Bitty's turn to roll her eyes. I ignored her. "How did Rayna find out about it?"

"Rob. He's a bail bondsman, remember?"

"Oh, that's right." Rob Rainey, Rayna's husband, is an insurance investigator and writes bonds on the side. Since Rayna would be known as Rayna Rainey if she took his last name, she kept her maiden name. A lot of women do that these days, I've noticed, for various reasons. After my divorce, I went back to my maiden name, too. I'm not really sure why, except that at the time the only memory of Perry I wanted to keep was our daughter. Silly, in reflection, but that's the way I felt then.

Anyway, Bitty and I both silently absorbed the information of Naomi's arrest, each of us from our own points of view.

Bitty broke the silence first. "Just how much pimento cheese are you going to put on that one sandwich?"

I looked down. At least an inch of creamy, yellow-orange deliciousness was piled atop a single slice of bread. "Too much?" I asked.

"Not for me. Slap that other slice of light bread on top and hand it over."

For those unfamiliar with Southern dialect, in some parts of the South *light bread* simply refers to plain white bread, not the low-calorie or low-carb kind. There was nothing low-calorie about our sandwiches.

We ate in silence attended only by the occasional meaningful glance

14

and nod of our heads at one another. I'm pretty sure our inner dialogue ran along similar lines. After all, Naomi Spencer had been heard to say quite a few tacky things about Bitty's arrest for the murder of Philip Hollandale. *What goes around, comes around,* must be the thought uppermost in both our minds.

"Well," Bitty said when we had polished off our sandwiches and licked clean our fingers, "which Diva do we tell first?"

I thought about it. There was no question of keeping it to ourselves, of course. This was big news in a small town. Murder, despite recent experiences to the contrary, was not a common crime in Holly Springs.

"Cady Lee Forsythe," I said, and Bitty smiled.

"Perfect. She's got the biggest mouth in town. It will be all over Marshall County before sundown."

Cady Lee Forsythe, now married to Brett Kincade, whose family owns a chain of department stores, is a member of the Divas as well. A short explanation may be in order here for those unfamiliar with the Dixie Divas.

Sometime in the late 1990s, a group of Holly Springs' female residents formed a club of sorts. It's nothing like the Ya-Yas or Sweet Potato Queens or Red Hat Ladies, but more an informal group of women from thirty to sixty-ish who get together every month to celebrate being alive. Chocolate is a menu staple, as is champagne and/or wine, along with casseroles, and whatever covered dish anyone wants to bring. Membership in the Divas remains at twelve full-time members, with guests allowed on occasion as long as said guest is female. No men are allowed to attend our meetings other than as a deliveryman or form of entertainment. While I shall not go into too much detail about what forms of entertainment they may provide, suffice it to say I still have in my possession a black leather halter top from a transvestite stripper. It was a Mardi Gras celebration, and if you haven't been to one, don't scoff.

At any rate, Divas are doggedly loyal to one another, most recently proven by their belief in Bitty when her ex-husband's body was found in her coat closet. Divas rallied to her cause without question, albeit with the assurance that she had nothing to do with his demise. The aftermath caused quite a few moments of disquiet, to say the least, but nothing that wasn't taken in stride by the members. I'm proud to say I've been officially inducted into the membership of the Dixie Divas. While there is no uniform or gold pin to wear, there is great pride in being among those chosen.

After Bitty called Cady Lee, we sat back and waited for her phone to ring. Within ten minutes, three Divas had called, and the call waiting had beeped in so often Bitty said it sounded like she was in a Roadrunner

cartoon. All we needed was Wile E. Coyote.
****

Within an hour, Wile E. Coyote showed up in the form of Deputy Rodney Farrell, a rather nervous young man with a bristle of reddish hair, freckles, and the efficiency of a Barney Fife. If you are unfamiliar with the bumbling Deputy Barney Fife, watch a few *Andy Griffith Show* reruns, and you'll catch my drift.

"Miz Hollandale?" he said in a questioning tone, although he knew very well who she was since he'd sat on her horsehair-stuffed settee and drank tea and ate cake for a good half-hour a few months before. He shuffled his feet on the porch doormat a couple times and cleared his throat when Bitty nodded pleasantly and agreed that she was Miz Hollandale. "I'm here to . . . uh . . . ask you a few questions. If you don't mind."

"Do I have unpaid parking tickets?" Bitty asked as she opened the front door wider and he paused on the threshold. "Or are you selling tickets to a police benefit?"

Despite her encouraging tone and gesture to enter, the deputy wiped beads of sweat from his forehead and stammered a negative. "No, ma'am. Not any of that."

Now I was intrigued. I'd already formed a pretty good guess as to why he was here, so I wasn't surprised when he finally got out in a single rushed sentence that he had come to ask her a few questions about her relationship with Naomi Spencer.

At that, Bitty's innate southern hospitality took on an edge. She drew herself up into a posture of offended female. As she was just about eye-level with the deputy, even in her bare feet, her glare made him shrink back against the door frame.

Poor man. He hadn't even made it fully into the house yet, and Bitty had him cornered. This was not going to be pretty.

"*Relationship* with Naomi Spencer? Young man, you must be out of your mind. I have no relationship whatsoever with that woman. Why would you even ask me such a foolish question?"

Now sweating profusely, and since Bitty's house was much cooler than it was outside, I was certain it wasn't from the heat, Deputy Farrell cleared his throat. He held his hat in his hands, and his fingers gave the brim a brisk work-out. "Well, several witnesses report that you and Miss Spencer have a long-standing feud, and since Miss Spencer has suggested the police question you about her fiancé's murder last night, Lieutenant Stone—"

"Question *me?*" Bitty's outrage made her seem even taller than her five-feet, two inches. "Is that plastic Barbie doll claiming *I* murdered him?

This is outrageous. I'm calling my lawyer. *And* the chief of police!"

"No, no," Farrell hurried to say as he wiped sweat from his brow with the back of his hand, "no one is accusing you of murder. No one official, I mean. Miss Spencer is so upset by her fiancé being killed that she said you may know something about it. We have to check out all leads, Miz Hollandale, you know we do. It seems pretty clear who killed him since—well, since he was found in a compromising position, but we're bound by law to exclude all possibilities."

Bitty paused and considered the deputy for a moment. Then she smiled. That made *me* nervous. But I knew immediately what she was up to when she took Deputy Farrell by the arm to lead him into her living room and the uncomfortable horsehair-stuffed settee.

"Of course you are only doing your official duty, Deputy, I understand that," she said in a calm, reassuring tone. "It's just the shock of hearing that the poor young man is dead. Such a pity. Here, have a seat while Trinket fetches us some sweet tea. You take lemon in yours, don't you? Yes, I thought I remembered you did. Trinket, dear, do you mind—"

"Bitty," I began in a warning tone, but she flashed me a sugary smile that didn't match her narrowed eyes and insisted that a cool glass of tea would refresh the officer while she gave him her statement.

I gave up, went into the kitchen and fixed a silver tray with glasses, a pitcher of sweet tea, a crystal bowl of lemon wedges already cut up in the refrigerator, long-handled silver spoons, and linen napkins. When I set the tray atop the Turkish hassock that served as a table as well as ottoman, Bitty's glance took in the three glasses. Since she didn't voice a protest, I took my glass and sat down in an antique Louis XVI chair opposite them but close enough to hear every word. This should be theater at its best.

CHAPTER 3

"So, Deputy," Bitty said when Rodney Farrell had downed a glass of sweet tea and stopped looking quite so nervous, "feel free to ask me any questions you like. I am an open book."

While her smile was encouraging, I knew she was just sucking him into her web. Bitty was on a Fact Finding Mission. It's a mission she rarely fails.

Since Marcus Stone, Sharita's brother and a sterling member of the Holly Springs police force, had sent Deputy Farrell to question Bitty, he obviously remembered the last time *he* had been sent to question her. I'm quite certain he had no desire to repeat the experience, but I had to wonder why he would throw such a lamb to the lioness. Stone must know Farrell would be putty in her hands.

Truth was, I was just as nosy as Bitty. I wanted to know all the gory details, too, and if anyone could get them out of the hapless deputy, it would be Bitty.

"Thank you, Miz Hollandale," said the unsuspecting Farrell, and flipped open a small notebook. Sweat stains dampened the blank page when he ran his hand across it to smooth the rumpled paper, but he didn't seem to notice. He had a mechanical pencil in his other hand and stuck the tip to his tongue as if to wet the lead. I watched in growing fascination.

"Now," he said, and cocked his head toward her, "where were you around three this morning?"

"At home in bed, like any sensible person would be," she replied promptly. "I suppose since Naomi Spencer has been arrested, you have proof of her involvement in his death. How tragic. Such a lovely couple."

"Yes. Yes, it is sad." Farrell cleared his throat. "Is there anyone who can confirm your presence in bed between two and three this morning?"

"Really, young man, you must recall I am a widow now," Bitty said in a rather reproachful tone.

I don't know how I kept from rolling my eyes. No matter how often I remind her that, because she and Philip Hollandale had been divorced for over a year when he was murdered, she does not qualify as a widow, Bitty has developed the lamentable habit of referring to herself that way.

Farrell colored to the roots of his reddish hair. It made his freckles stand out on his face like sprinkles of mud. Mama used to call my freckles angel kisses when I whined about them, and maybe Rodney's mother did the same. Mothers are like that.

"Oh . . . yes, ma'am, I didn't mean . . . well, I only meant . . ." Farrell bogged down, and I began to feel sorry for him since we shared the same freckle affliction, though mine are mostly faded now, so I stepped in to help.

"Bitty, didn't you tell me you had to call the vet, last night because Chitling threw up on your bed? What time was that?"

"Oh," Bitty said, "Yes, I did. Dr. Coltrane took the call. He was a bit grumpy about it, too, which I think is very annoying since he should be used to that sort of thing, and after all, he chose to be a doctor and is therefore obligated to take emergency calls, but there you have it. Yes, I called him about . . . oh, I think it was right around two this morning since I was watching some unreasonable man on one of those political cable shows go on and on about—"

"Around two this morning, you said?" Farrell interrupted, jotting down notes in his little book.

Bitty nodded. "Yes. He can confirm that I called him, and if necessary, phone records could prove it, too, I suppose. Do you think all that is really needed, however? I mean, you've already arrested Miss Spencer, so I assume you must have proof she killed Race. Didn't you say she stabbed him?"

"Stabbed him?" Farrell looked vaguely startled. "No, he was shot."

"Oh, I misunderstood," Bitty lied without a blink. "Maybe because I have always thought of her as the kind of person who would stab a man who cheated on her. I suppose the other woman got away without being hurt. Have you found her yet?"

"No, we're still looking for her."

"I see. Ask the management at Motel Six—you did say it was Motel Six where this happened?"

"No, Madewell Courts."

"Yes, of course." Bitty affected a sigh. "So much tragedy lately, and I just cannot keep details straight. Well, Naomi should really have had better sense than to sneak up on him like that, especially with a shotgun. Wait. That's not right. You said it was a . . .?"

"It was a thirty-eight snub nose revolver. Two slugs. He might have survived if not for the second shot."

"Poor dear. I suppose her aim was off. More tea?"

Farrell frowned a little, but since Bitty was already pouring more sweet tea from the glass pitcher and adding a lemon wedge to the rim of his glass, he nodded. Ice cubes clinked softly when she gave him his tea

19

and smiled.

"Well, I can assure you, Officer Farrell, that *I* had no interest whatsoever in Race Champion. He's not at all the kind of man with whom I care to associate. For one thing, he's only a trainer at Gold's Gym—or is it that new gym?"

"And he's twenty years younger than Bitty," I offered helpfully.

She gave me a quelling glance for my effort, then continued, "Yes, he may be a rather well-known drag racer locally, but I would have no interest in a man whose main ambition in life seems to be discovering just how much beer he can drink without throwing up. Besides, he always seemed quite content with an entire string of women on his arm. I hardly think him the kind of man to truly settle down to one woman."

"And he's twenty years younger than Bitty," I reminded.

Bitty glared at me. "He was thirty-one."

"Yep. Twenty years younger. Way too young for you. He'd never be interested."

"I'll have you know men much younger than that have asked me out, Trinket Truevine. It's not like I'm an old crone."

"No, you're just twenty years older than he was."

Bitty doesn't like being reminded of her age. I have no idea what imp of mischief prompted me to bring it out at that particular moment. It just seemed necessary to establish distance between her and the dead man.

Unfortunately, Bitty managed to destroy my effort.

She put her hand on one hip and said, "For your information, Race Champion asked me to go with him to one of his races last year! He said he would see to it that I got a seat on the front row and free beer while I watched him win the cup. Of course, I took my own wine, but he was quite, *quite* taken with me!"

I sighed. So much for establishing distance between Bitty and the dead man.

Deputy Farrell began writing feverishly in his little book, and I could almost see the wheels spinning in his brain. Maybe Marcus Stone had sent the right man to interview Bitty, after all.

Wile E. Coyote had neatly managed to ferret out incriminating information.

****

"Well, really, Trinket, how was I to know what you were trying to do?"

Bitty lay back on the chaise longue in her sunroom with a cool, damp cloth on her forehead and a pug on her lap. The ceiling fan whirred cool air down on us, and outside the screened-in windows crickets chirped and frogs burped. Dusk was settling around Six Chimneys and Holly Springs.

It is usually a peaceful time that I like to hold close around me like a favorite garment.

Not this evening.

Six Chimneys was built in 1845 and has probably seen more human foibles than many other old houses. It was owned by the same family for generations, and until a few decades ago held that distinction. Then the last of the family died out and the younger generation wanted nothing to do with an old house that needed more than a few modern conveniences and upkeep. Enter Bitty, who outbid rivals and took the house under her loving wing and restored it to beauty and dignity. Now the house presides like a grand old belle on Walthal Street and in the annual Holly Springs Pilgrimage every April.

During the pilgrimage, tourists come from all over to view the antebellum homes that graciously open to welcome visitors. Men and boys dress up in ancient Confederate uniforms or costumes, and women and girls wear hoop skirts, corsets, and pantalettes.

Even Cherryhill, my ancestral home, is on the tour, although it had the misfortune to suffer a fire during the War Between the States. Since the fire's cause was a patrol of Yankees, Cherryhill instantly qualified as an attraction on the pilgrimage. There are few things die-hard Southerners appreciate more than rising from any destruction caused by Yankees. At any rate, Cherryhill was rebuilt upon the original footings of the first house right after the war, then completely renovated in 1898. There are still char marks on some of the foundation stones that are pointed out to tourists every year.

None of this, however, was foremost in our minds or conversation.

"It's all right, Bitty," I comforted my cousin. "I'm sure the deputy would have found all that out elsewhere sooner or later."

"Probably. People do love to gossip."

I did not point out that we were among those people who love to gossip. It didn't seem prudent.

"Why didn't you tell me you went out with Naomi's fiancé?" I asked instead, and Bitty immediately lifted up a corner of the wet bath rag draped over her eyes to look at me.

"Well for heaven's sake, Trinket, it was last year. And I've hardly seen you since you started *not dating* Kit Coltrane."

Bitty definitely sounded peevish. It seemed best not to encourage her along those lines, so I merely nodded. "So Race must have gotten engaged to Naomi quite recently, then. What was it—Monday, when we ran into her at Budgie's?"

"I should have run *over* her at Budgie's," Bitty muttered, and let the edge of the wet cloth flop back over her eyes. "The spiteful thing. Telling the police that I probably had something to do with his murder. Especially after all that unpleasantness with Philip. I bet she just smiled like a cat when she said it, too, hoping they'd suspect me instead of her."

"Well," I pointed out, "they arrested her, not you. So they couldn't have believed her very much."

"I should hope not. That girl tells a lie every time her mouth opens. She can't help it, I suppose. Her family never has been known for honesty. Why, her brother Billy Don just got out of jail around Easter after he did a two-year stretch in Parchman for selling cars he didn't own. And her mother is barred from every department store between here and Tupelo because she shoplifts."

Bitty lifted a corner of the bath cloth again and flopped on her side to look at me. "Sukey tried to wedge a microwave oven into her cloth shopping bag at the old Wal-Mart store, can you believe that? Stupid woman. Although if it hadn't been for her forgetting to tuck the electrical cord into the bag, not a one of those clueless cashiers would have noticed. Sukey just sailed on out of Wal-Mart without a soul stopping her. If not for Trina Madewell accidentally stepping on the electrical cord so that the microwave fell out of the bag and everybody turned to look, she might have gotten away with it."

While I tried to envision a shopping bag large enough to hold a microwave, Bitty abruptly sat up and swung her feet to the floor. A smile curled up the sides of her mouth so that she looked just like the Grinch in that Christmas cartoon that comes on TV every year. I figure a lot more people than just me recognize a Grinch smile, because they even made a movie out of it several years back with an actor playing the part of the Grinch.

But I digress.

There sat Bitty with a Grinch smile, ideas churning in her fertile little brain. I didn't know quite what to expect next, but I certainly didn't expect to hear her say, "I must invite Trina Madewell over here for tea."

Stunned, it took me a moment to respond. "But Bitty, you hate Trina Madewell. You call her the Barracuda of Barbecues, the Swamp Thing, and numerous other names I refuse to repeat. Why on earth would you want to invite her anywhere, much less over here for tea?"

"Because, dearest cousin, her family owns Madewell Courts."

When I just stared at her blankly, Bitty sighed. "The motel where Race Champion was shot last night. Trina's family has owned that run-down old ruin since God was a baby. She'll know all kinds of things that the police haven't told."

"Bitty," I said calmly, "forget it. Let the police handle the murder without you."

"Don't be silly, Trinket. I'm not getting involved with the murder. I just want to know all the juicy details. Don't you? Be honest."

Now she'd put me on the spot. To be honest, sure I wanted to know all the juicy details. Curiosity and nosiness demanded it. However, I did my best to rise above such character flaws.

"Remember the old adage about curiosity killing the cat," I said instead of giving her the pleasure of being right.

"Yes, but satisfaction brought it back," Bitty replied promptly.

"Trina Madewell will never accept your invitation," I countered. "You two have been feuding forever. Even the dumbest woman would know you're up to something."

Bitty tapped her chin with a perfectly manicured nail for a moment. Then she smiled. "I'll tell her the Divas are getting together. There's no way she could resist *that* invitation. She's been dying to attend a Diva meeting ever since our very first one."

I was shocked. "You're going to defile a Diva meeting?"

"Don't be silly. I'll just tell her a few Divas are getting together, and ask if she'd like to join us."

Immediately suspicious, I said, "Who is included in *us*?"

"Me, of course, and you. I'm sure Rayna will agree to come. After all, she's the one who called me, so she'll want to hear all the details, too."

"I hardly think two Divas will qualify as a Diva meeting."

"Three."

I narrowed my eyes at her. "*Two*. You and Rayna. I refuse to be a party to this."

"Really. Very well. I'll call Gaynelle, then. She knows a good thing when she hears it."

Silence fell between us. Bitty waited patiently, as if she knew I couldn't stand being replaced. After watching her examine her fingernails for a few minutes, I gave in.

"All right. I'll come. But just to keep you from doing anything too foolish."

To her credit, Bitty didn't gloat. Instead she clapped her hands together and said, "Oh, I'm so glad. What should we serve?"

"Dragon's blood and snake venom soup."

Bitty looked slightly startled at my rather bitchy suggestion, but shrugged it off and said, "I was thinking more along the lines of an English tea, you know, with hot tea served in my Limoges teapot that I bought on my first trip to France . . . with tiny little pastry puffs arranged on that gorgeous matching platter. What do you think?"

"That you're wasting pastry puffs. Trina Madewell is going to see right through you, Bitty Hollandale. You know she is. Once she realizes it's not an official Diva Day, she'll know exactly what you're doing."

"Of course she will. She may look like the south end of a northbound cow, but she's not stupid. Still, she'll get what she wants out of it, I'm sure."

"And what on earth would that be?"

"Well, an invitation to Six Chimneys for one thing. Since I outbid her for it, she hasn't set foot in this house. She told everyone in her Sunday School class that I have atrocious taste in interior decorating, and that a blind mule wouldn't have chosen the antiques I bought. And she also told the entire Holly Springs Garden Club that I cheated her out of her just due for getting The Cedars on the pilgrimage tour."

"Did she ever even meet Sherman Sanders?" I couldn't help asking, thinking back to the rather crotchety old man who had owned The Cedars and had a penchant for greeting visitors with a shotgun loaded with rock salt.

Bitty's smile was a bit smug. "Just once. Briefly. He took a shot at her when she told him he *owed* the town since his ancestors had basically stolen The Cedars anyway. I don't think Mr. Sanders liked her very much."

"Did the shot hit her?"

"Unfortunately, no. Trina's pretty quick on her feet. Must be all that running she does."

"She jogs?"

"Hardly. She runs around from one bar to the next looking for a new husband to replace the last one."

My head started to hurt. This was too much information to absorb all at once. The day had been far too long already, and getting tangled up in Bitty's schemes tends to make time stand still. Or unexpectedly shoot to warp speed. Neither is desirable.

"I'm going home, Bitty. Call me when you have all the details worked out."

"I'll call you in the morning."

"I can hardly wait," I lied shamelessly.

It wasn't until much later that night, when I was lying in my bed staring up at the twelve foot ceilings of my parents' old bedroom, that I convinced myself Trina Madewell would be smart enough to refuse Bitty's invitation. That made me feel much better. After all, the woman would have to be a complete idiot not to suspect something was up if she got a lunch invitation out of the blue from an arch-enemy. At the very least, she would have to wonder what would be in her teacup besides orange pekoe or Earl Grey.

My memory of Trina Madewell was rather sketchy. I'd gone to

school with her, but she had hung out with another set of friends. Even small southern towns can have their own cliques, and can be just as snobby as elite Ivy League communities. Maybe more so in some ways, since the advantage—or disadvantage—of a small town is that it's very easy to know too many incriminating things about your neighbors. Not that the group of friends I hung out with during my formative years were anything close to *elite*, because it didn't matter to any of us who had money and who didn't. What mattered most was who was the most fun to be around. We just naturally gravitated toward those who shared similar interests.

My twin sister Emerald and I hung out in different groups. People tend to think twins are just alike, but Emerald is petite like my mother, blond, dainty, and quiet. I am not. To say the least. I was always the bull in the china shop. Emerald was always the china. In truth, I was much more like our older brothers. Jack and Luke made our old farmhouse rock when we were young. They were loud, boisterous, and so full of life and plans for the future that the military men who came to our house to tell my parents they had both been killed within days of each other could have been speaking Greek for all we could comprehend in that awful moment. I recall my daddy just staring at them without speaking for a long time, his expression disbelieving. It was only when my mother began to cry that we all understood.

Tragedy irrevocably changes some people. My daddy's hair turned gray almost overnight, and my mother didn't come downstairs for nearly a year after their funerals. Emerald and I reacted opposite of one another. Predictably, I suppose. Emerald withdrew into herself, created her own world peopled by fantasies and books.

I threw myself into a frenzy of activity, playing softball, visiting friends, joining school clubs, and as I grew older, even activist causes to protest whatever inequity I considered important at the time. Save the whales, civil rights, stop the war, gay rights, Native American rights— whatever the cause, I protested for or against it. While the 1970s were hardly the same as the turbulent 1960s, it had its moments.

All of which should have prepared me for this time in my life when my cousin Bitty sucked me into her sticky web of insanity. And yet, despite my varied experiences, I still found myself traumatized and, yes, fascinated by just how quickly she can turn the most mundane moments into sheer chaos.

CHAPTER 4

Trina Madewell perched tentatively upon the silk seat of the Louis XVI antique chair in Bitty's living room. She had really dressed up for the occasion; her watered silk two-piece suit was a pale mauve that matched her dyed alligator shoes and handbag. While she was a little younger than Bitty and me, she had not . . . worn . . . well. It could have been that her hair, dyed a harsh shade of black, washed out her complexion, or that she wore enough mascara to lubricate the entire chassis of a medium size sedan. But I think it was more along the lines that she has a hard, brittle look to her despite all her efforts. It was easy to see why she and Bitty have been in competition with one another, and even easier for me to see why Bitty has managed to out-do her. Ruthless people usually step on too many toes.

In her element, Bitty smiled brightly and held up a lovely antique Limoges teapot that must have set her back at least a thousand dollars, even twenty years ago.

"More tea, Trina?"

"Why yes, Bitty, thank you."

A noise to my right sounded something like a snort, but I ignored it. Rayna Blue and I felt much the same way about this latest ploy, but like lemmings, we tagged along behind Bitty toward some distant cliff.

"Another sandwich?" Bitty cooed, and held out a lovely white platter with dainty gilt trim that matched the Limoges teapot, cups, saucers, and small plates. Tiny finger sandwiches were stacked high upon the platter, and Trina chose one delicately. I recognized Sharita's handiwork. Only a talented cook with the patience of Job would be able to pull off twenty cucumber sandwiches, each shaped like a fleur-de-lis.

"I understand that your family property has undergone extensive renovations recently," Bitty said once Trina's mouth was full of bread and cucumber. "I've been just dying to see them. Someone told me your parents turned that lovely old home into a bed-and-breakfast, is that right?"

While Trina could only politely nod affirmation with her mouth full, Bitty went on, "Whatever made you think of such a clever thing? I've been considering doing that with Six Chimneys. Why, I've got all these bedrooms here, and Brandon and Clayton only come home to change clothes during their summer recess from Ole Miss, so it would be just a perfect opportunity, don't you agree?"

I nearly fell out of my chair. Bitty would no more allow tourists free rein of her house than she would invite in a platoon of army ants. Rayna choked on a sip of tea, then wiped her mouth with an edge of damask napkin. Once she was choke-free, Rayna looked over at me.

"Are there any more petit-fours, by chance?"

I knew immediately that what she really wanted was a whiff of sanity, not a dessert cake, so I nodded. "In the kitchen. I'll get them."

Rayna stood up. "I'll help."

"Really," I heard Trina say as I led the way to the kitchen, "it was all my sister's idea. There are specific rules you must follow in order to comply with codes, however."

Rayna said under her breath, "If Bitty opens up Six Chimneys to tourists, I swear I'll book the first room for her ex-mother-in-law. That would teach her a lesson."

"Don't worry," I said when we were safely in the kitchen and out of earshot, "I doubt Bitty would ever risk a single washcloth, much less her Egyptian cotton sheets with complete strangers."

Rayna flicked a strand of her long dark hair back over one shoulder. The motion made her turquoise and silver earrings clink softly. The earrings matched a belt she wore around her turquoise tunic top. An artist, Rayna usually wears trendy clothes with flair, but it doesn't matter what she wears. She looks good in anything. She has one of those slender figures that would make a shapeless potato sack look good. I'm not envious. Much.

"Well, so far Bitty's efforts haven't produced a single detail we don't already know. Did you read the paper this morning?" Rayna asked.

I had. "It said Naomi claims an unidentified person came into the cottage and shot him. Who do you think really killed him?"

"Naomi Spencer."

"Really?"

Rayna nodded. "Who else could it be? Who else would care who Race slept with if it wasn't her?"

"You think he was with someone else and Naomi came in, found them together, and then shot him?"

"It makes sense."

"Hm. She says she didn't do it."

"I would too, if I was her."

I considered that a moment. "True. And it was her gun the police found at the scene. Still, if she's right, shouldn't the police be looking for this other person?"

Rayna looked surprised. "You believe her?"

"No, not really, but still . . . a lot of people thought Bitty killed Philip, you know, and all the evidence was against her, but in the end, it was proven she didn't do it. It's always *possible* that Naomi is innocent."

I don't know quite what made me think that. Maybe it was Naomi's obvious pride in the small engagement ring she'd shown us that day at Budgie's café. She had seemed genuinely happy. Until the food fight, of course.

"Yes, and it's always possible Naomi and Bitty will end up best friends, but I wouldn't count on that either," Rayna said. She flipped open a cabinet door and peered at the neat rows of packaged food, then shut it and opened another. On her third try, she found what she was looking for on the bottom shelf. "If I have to sit out there watching Bitty and Trina dance around what they really want to say to each other, I might as well have something fortifying in my tea. How about you?"

I eyed the bottle of Jack Daniel's for a moment. I'd never had whiskey in my tea, but then, there is always a first time for everything.

"Don't mind if I do," I said, and Rayna smiled.

By the time we drank a few cups of fortified tea and returned to the living room at the front of the house, I was surprised to see Deelight Tillman sitting on the other end of the horsehair-stuffed sofa. She smiled at us brightly. Deelight is a member of the Divas. I wondered if she had just happened to drop by and now refused to leave. Some people do have a sixth sense about where lightning might strike next. Or when something bound to be good is going to happen. I wasn't at all sure which of the two might occur.

It wasn't two minutes after Rayna and I sat back down in the prissy little chairs from Bitty's dining room that had been brought into the living room, that a discreet knock on the front door announced the arrival of Gaynelle Bishop. From the way she said she was just stopping by, I began to think word had gotten out that Trina Madewell was visiting Six Chimneys at last. Of course the Divas would want to be in on this. We had been rude not to consider that.

And really, Gaynelle would be an excellent addition to our group. She may be in her sixties, but she's still sharp as a tack and about as tactful. Now that she's retired, her former attire of matronly dresses, cat's-eye glasses, and gray hair has changed drastically. It was as if the retirement party had unleashed the real Gaynelle hiding inside an old maid spinster costume. Now she wears flamboyant colors, silk, and has her hair dyed a tasteful brown with highlights. Sometimes she doesn't wear eyeglasses at all, and on occasion she wears glasses with no frames, just subtle earpieces. While her outward appearance has changed greatly, she's still the same forthright, no-nonsense kind of person she has always been.

That can be a blessing or a curse, depending upon the situation.

When Cady Lee Forsythe showed up at the door with Cindy Nelson, I knew for certain that word had gotten out. It was a good thing Bitty owned a large dining room set with plenty of chairs. It looked as if the entire membership of the Dixie Divas planned to "drop by" Six Chimneys that afternoon.

Bitty was in a tizzy. She'd only planned a tea for three. When she looked over at me with the wide-eyed stare of a deer caught in headlights, I heard myself offer to bring in more refreshments. It must have been the Jack Daniel's talking.

Fortunately, Jack must have been talking to Rayna as well. She followed me into the kitchen. "Where does Bitty keep the tea bags?"

I pointed, and Rayna picked up the box of Earl Grey and shook it. There were only a couple tea bags left.

"We could use regular teabags," I suggested, but Rayna had a much better idea.

"A little of this should help refill the teapot," she said as she unscrewed the lid to the Jack Daniel's.

"What kind of sandwiches go with Earl Grey and whiskey?" I wondered out loud.

"Not those nasty cucumber things. Does Bitty have any of Sarah's pimento cheese made up?"

It's a testament to the power of great recipes that everyone in the Divas, and probably in Holly Springs, knows that Sarah Truevine had the best pimento cheese recipe ever. I spread what was left of the batch Sharita had made on light bread, cut off the crusts, cut the sandwiches into triangles, then arranged them on the Limoges platter that matched the teapot, cups, and plates. Good thing Bitty had bought an entire set. I'm sure it had set back whatever husband she was married to at the time a pretty penny. Or franc.

When we returned to the living room, Rayna carrying the tray with the potent tea and teacups and me the platter of sandwiches, Bitty seemed to have adjusted to the unexpected. She still sat on the sofa, now wedged between Cady Lee and Gaynelle, but without the presence of Chen Ling. Long before Trina arrived, I'd convinced Bitty it would be much safer to let the pug nap upstairs rather than expose her to possible violence. She'd laughed, but followed my advice, I am glad to say.

Rayna set the tea tray on the Turkish hassock and began pouring, while I passed around small plates with pimento cheese sandwiches. I'd found a can of mixed nuts and poured them into a small bowl that didn't match the Limoges china but fit on the tray better. Bitty eyed it with a frown. She's very particular about how she likes to show off. I pretended not to notice.

About then, Gaynelle Bishop took a big sip of tea and choked. Bitty pounded her on the back as Gaynelle gasped for air.

"It must have gone down the wrong way," Bitty said solicitously, and handed Gaynelle a cloth napkin.

"My," Gaynelle said after recovering her breath, "this is . . . quite *strong* tea."

"It's Earl Grey," said Bitty, blissfully unaware that we had introduced Earl to Jack. "I purchased several boxes while in England last year."

I decided it was best not to tell Bitty she could have bought it in the Holly Springs Wal-Mart as well. There are definitely some things better left unsaid. Rayna just smiled and poured more tea as cups were drained. I must say, Earl Grey has rarely been so popular.

Soon the living room sounded like a grade school auditorium, everyone talking at once. By the time a third pot of tea had been made, I think Rayna didn't even bother to use any kind of teabags. It tasted like straight Jack Daniel's to me. Cady Lee's eyes were a bit glazed as she held out her cup for Rayna to pour more tea, and the usually prim and proper Gaynelle was giggling like one of her former third grade pupils. Deelight Tillman had a smudge of pimento cheese on the end of her nose, but no one else seemed to notice.

Then Cindy Nelson, a young mother from nearby Snow Lake and a fairly new member of the Divas, hiccupped loud enough to stop all conversation. She clapped a hand over her mouth at once as if to stifle the sound, but it didn't help. Another hiccup erupted between her fingers, then another, rolling from her in a tsunami of spasms.

"Give her a teaspoon of sugar," Gaynelle advised, and Cady Lee disagreed.

"No, she should blow into a grocery sack."

"Plastic or paper?" Deelight asked in a rather slurred voice.

"Oh my, not plastic. She would suffocate," Gaynelle said at once. She can usually be counted on to know things like that since teaching a legion of Holly Springs' children to read, write, and not make rude noises in public.

At that point, Bitty leaned forward, her gaze intent upon Trina Madewell. "Were you the one who found the body?"

All conversation ceased. At last we'd come to the real reason Trina had been invited to tea. Everyone leaned forward in their seats, except poor Cindy who kept a hand over her mouth to muffle the tide of hiccups.

"No," said Trina. "But when I heard the commotion I got down to the cottage as quick as I could, of course. It was . . . awful."

We all hung on that last word for a moment before Gaynelle asked, "How awful?"

Apparently Gaynelle still expects detailed answers to test questions, so she can be excused for asking what we were all wondering anyway.

Trina's hand shook slightly and the Limoges teacup rattled in its saucer. Mascara-thick eyelashes fluttered briefly over her brown eyes. Somehow her purplish-red lipstick had smeared from her bottom lip to her chin. With purple eye shadow arched on her lids a bit too high, her face had the rather odd effect of a circus clown in half makeup. All she needed was for her nose to get a little redder and she'd qualify for Barnum and Bailey's.

"When I got there," Trina said in a husky voice, "my sister was hysterical. She was the one who found . . . Race. I suppose she'd gone to wake him for breakfast. That's part of the package we offer, a free breakfast is included in the night's stay."

"What do you serve?" Deelight asked, and I saw Bitty elbow her sharply. "Oof! I was just curious."

In Deelight's defense, she still has children at home and is always looking for new menu ideas.

Bitty patted her on the arm. "I know, dear, but it's rude to interrupt." She looked back at Trina. "More tea? It seems to have an especially energizing effect today."

When Trina held out her cup, I slid a glance toward Rayna, who kept a poker face as she poured from the teapot. I don't know how she did it. Rayna is a woman of many talents.

"It must be the caffeine," said Gaynelle, "but do go on, Trina."

The center of rapt Diva attention now, Trina seemed to swell with importance. She took a deep breath and let it out slowly, prolonging our suspense before she said, "I went into the cottage because I couldn't understand a word Trisha was saying. She was just so hysterical, screaming and crying—well! I got no farther than the bedroom door when I saw him. There he was, lying across the bed just inside the door, naked as a jaybird and with his—*you know*—stiff as a poker and standing straight up. It was so big you could have hung a flag on it."

At that, Cindy Nelson's hiccups stopped.

I think a few of us stopped breathing for a moment, too, and I know all of us were visualizing Race Champion with his *you know* flying a flag. We must have looked foolish sitting there in a circle of chairs with slackened jaws and glazed eyes, and I am very glad Bitty's windows have curtains.

Gaynelle recovered first. "Well then," she asked briskly, "how could you tell he was dead?"

"The hole in the middle of his forehead. It was quite noticeable."

"Oh my," Deelight said in a squeaky voice, "oh my!"

Trina nodded. "It was awful."

An understatement, I thought.

"I heard he was shot twice," Rayna said.

"Yes, so did I, but all I noticed was that hole in his forehead. It looked so big and perfectly round, like someone had used a hole-puncher." Trina leaned forward to set her empty teacup on the tray in the middle of the ottoman. "Of course, I didn't get too close to him. All I could think was that whoever killed him might still be hiding in the cottage and that Trisha and I should get back to the house and call the police."

"I wouldn't have known what to do," Cady Lee said in a horrified tone. "I think I would have just fainted dead away right there."

"Well, I felt like it," Trina said with a light shudder that seemed more put on than real, "but I knew I had to get Trisha to safety just in case."

"Oh, you were so brave!" Cindy said now that she was hiccup-free. "You just never know what you'll do until it happens to you, I guess."

Not too long ago, Cindy had been the victim of a deranged assailant who is now safely in custody, thank heavens. Since I'd also been bashed in the head, I figured she might appreciate a bit of commiseration.

"But we both made it through," I said to her softly.

Tears came into her eyes and she nodded, and so she wouldn't feel alone, I got all teary, too. We hugged each other over Rayna's head, since she was sitting between us, and I heard her mutter, "Good lord!"

Bitty, ever the consummate hostess even after far too many cups of tea, said to ease the sudden downward turn in our conversation, "Would anyone like more tea?"

"Good god," Cady Lee said in a groan, "if I have anymore of this tea I'll need to call Brett to drive me home. I swear I feel tipsy. Am I the only one?"

"No," said Gaynelle, frowning at her empty cup, "I feel . . . odd. What is in this tea, Bitty?"

Looking a bit bewildered, Bitty peered into her cup and then sniffed the contents. I knew the instant she recognized the scent. Her head jerked up in surprise. "Someone spiked our tea!"

All eyes turned toward me.

I said the first thing that came to mind: "Talking about murder requires something stronger than tea."

Heads nodded in agreement, and the moment passed. Rayna smiled at me and I smiled back. Divas always stick together.

"When you found Race dead," Cady Lee asked Trina, "didn't that make you feel just awful? I mean, y'all dated for such a long time."

That information caught all our immediate attention.

I didn't know where to look. Trina seemed caught off-guard by the question, and Cady Lee looked guileless. Of course, with Cady Lee it's hard to tell sometimes. When we went to grade school together she was always voted the prettiest and had all the boys buzzing around her like bees at a sorghum mill. I still don't know how she managed to keep them in order. It must have taken a certain amount of guile, after all.

I've learned through the years that we are who we are no matter how much older we've gotten, or how much life we've experienced. We may learn certain lessons, even if it's not to do *that* again, but we just can't help ingrained personality traits. Cady Lee is still a belle and the prettiest girl at the school dances, even though she's now fifty and her once-brown hair is blond and her once-brown eyes are green or blue, depending upon which set of contact lens she's wearing. She pulls it off marvelously. So you see, she could have dropped that little gem about Trina Madewell dating Race Champion innocently, or she could have said it knowing it would discomfit Trina. It was a toss-up.

Trina's face had flushed to an unflattering crimson. She flapped one of her hands at Cady Lee as if to say *Oh, that*, and remarked, "I hadn't seen him in ages."

"But you two were such a hot item. I always thought you'd end up married to him," said Cady Lee. "Didn't he give you an engagement ring once?"

Now I was pretty sure Cady Lee meant to needle Trina, or at the very least, get her to say something incriminating. Breathlessly, we all waited for Trina's answer.

If she said yes, then it gave her a motive for shooting Race, who had, after all, been found by her and/or her sister in her parents' bed-and-breakfast cottage. We had only their word on that, as did the police, I was pretty sure. Sisters have been known to lie for one another.

Of course, if she said no, it was likely she would still be a "person of interest", as the police like to say. Oh, this was getting good. It may turn out that Naomi hadn't shot Race at all.

There are some people who are lucky in life, and others who are not. Today, it was Trina's turn to get lucky. Or so it seemed at the time.

Just as Trina opened her mouth to say whatever it was we were all dying to hear, Bitty's expensive Limoges teapot exploded off the matching tray set upon the Turkish ottoman. Lukewarm tea—or Jack Daniel's—spewed into the air, teacups shot off the tray, pimento cheese triangles launched onto laps, and mixed nuts peppered the antique carpet and guests like small missiles.

Amidst the confusion, I recognized a familiar porcine snort. *Chen Ling!* How on earth had she gotten out of the upstairs bedroom?

It's amazing what a fifteen pound dog can do to a set of expensive china when it lands right in the middle of it. I suppose we had all been so eager to hear what Trina would say that no one had noticed the pug's arrival in the living room. Not one to be ignored for long, and probably sniffing out forbidden foods, Chen Ling had taken matters into her own hands . . . er, paws.

Chaos reigned. Squeals of surprise and horror filled the air as guests leaped to their feet. While the dog gobbled up pimento cheese triangles and nuts, Bitty scrambled to save what she could of her Limoges teapot and dinnerware. Divas hastily scraped tempting bits of sandwiches and nuts onto the floor, either to keep from staining clothes or to avoid being viewed as possible food by a determined pug.

Crawling around on her antique carpet, Bitty gathered up pieces of china and held them to her chest with one hand as one would a small child. It was rather sad, really, so I got down on the floor with her to pick up what I could.

By the time we'd picked up what was possible to get without a vacuum, Rayna had Chen Ling firmly in hand and the other Divas were fairly composed. Bitty deposited remnants of teapot and cups on the still intact tray and managed a shaky laugh.

"I apologize for this, ladies. Usually Chen Ling is much better behaved."

Since all the Divas knew better, I looked around for Trina to see how she was dealing with the unexpected arrival of a fat pug in the middle of our tea tray. About the time I realized she was no longer in the room, I heard the roar of a car starting and tires squeal on the street outside Six Chimneys.

Apparently, Trina Madewell had made her escape.

CHAPTER 5

Holly Springs, Mississippi has a population of less than ten thousand people, and according to statistical records, that population is fairly even in the ratio of male to female. Considering those facts, you would think there would be enough eligible men for eligible women. Apparently, this is not the case.

Or so I have been led to believe by the inexplicable actions of a few citizens.

In my youth, I was admonished on several occasions about the evils of gossip. My admonisher was nearly always my mother. We children received strict lessons on the proprieties and improprieties in social graces. Gossip was then regarded as harmful to not only the person being gossiped about, but the impressionable soul of the person doing the gossiping. I tell you this only because I now regard those lessons with some regret.

Bitty and I were seated in the garden shade of Rayna Blue's home, the Delta Inn. It's a lovely historic hotel being considered for registration with the historical society. While Bitty and Rayna theorized about motives for Race's murder, I had to bite my tongue to keep from telling them what I'd heard only that morning from my own mother.

Sidebar here: As she ages, Mama regards some information about our neighbors as necessary, and some as just gossip. The catch is that I can never tell which is which, so I have to wait until she asks a direct question or chooses to share a juicy tidbit with me. If she shares, she's quite likely to hang a restriction on it, such as not to pass it on.

Mama had done that very thing earlier in the day after telling me how Trina Madewell had made a huge scene at church last year when she accused her sister of trying to steal her boyfriend. It had been on a Sunday when the minister had decided to try an innovative approach to the entire "confession is good for the soul" thing. He should have left it to the Catholics. Methodists don't seem to be as good at it. Or maybe as used to it. My opinion is that confession is only good for the soul when it is not shared with the wronged party. Anyway, Atonement Day was a disaster from start to finish.

There were two fistfights in the pews, a scuffle in the vestibule, and the screaming match between Trina and Trisha in the church parking lot.

Mama reported that it may have been just coincidence, but two couples from the congregation filed for divorce the week after the Atonement Day event.

Mama had been an unwilling witness to the Madewell hysteria in the parking lot. It wasn't a scene she was likely to forget.

"I thought they were going to snatch each other bald the way they kept yanking at each other's hair," Mama had mused over a second cup of coffee, while Daddy went out to the barn to feed the furry flocks their morning cat chow. As she was battling the start of a summer cold, Mama stayed in to sit with me while I ate a breakfast of sugary cereal and drank coffee with sweetener. There is no rhyme or reason to my dietary choices most of the time.

At any rate, Mama was in a talkative mood, and after I'd told her about the tea at Bitty's house and how it ended, it reminded her of Trina and Trisha's disagreement. That is how I learned they'd both dated Race Champion, and neither of them knew he was still seeing the other one until Atonement Day outed them all.

Mama shook her head and peered at me over the rim of her coffee cup. "None of this should go any further, of course. That would be unkind gossip."

I was flabbergasted. "But how is it considered gossip if you witnessed it?" I had asked. "You cannot have been the only one to overhear them."

"Still, under these circumstances it's best to let them be the ones who tell the police."

Sometimes Mama operates under the belief that all church-going people are always honest. I could tell her a few things. But I won't.

That is how I found myself sitting at Rayna's garden table biting my tongue, while she and Bitty batted around all kind of crazy theories about Race Champion's murder and Trina Madewell's possible part in it. Some of their theories really made me squirm.

"Maybe Trina's pregnant and Race's engagement to Naomi put her over the edge," Bitty said, but Rayna shook her head.

"She's too old to have babies. Besides, she had a partial hysterectomy when she was married to Russell Irons."

"I remember Rusty. Didn't he end up dead in some bridge accident?"

Rayna nodded. "He was an ironworker. Rusty's now part of one of the concrete piers that hold up the bridge over the Tallahatchie. He's on the Oxford side, closer to Leflore County, I think."

A cool breeze wafted the sweet, lemony scent of magnolia blossoms toward us. A huge magnolia tree nearly two hundred years old sits square in the middle of the garden. I tried to focus on how much history this old tree must have seen rather than the discussion going on around me. It was too tempting to jump in and tell what I knew.

How could my normally sweet mother have done this to me? It was torture sitting there and not saying anything. So when one of Rayna's dogs came up to me to be petted, I was delighted to have the distraction.

One of Rayna's extracurricular activities includes the use of her dog as a search and rescue animal. It's a noble endeavor, and quite useful when someone goes missing in Holly Springs National Forest or over at Lake Chewalla. There are vast stretches of real estate in Mississippi occupied only by deer, rabbits, raccoons, and armadillos. It's easy enough to get lost if you aren't familiar with the area. Sometimes, even if you are.

At any rate, when Jinx isn't searching for a lost child or a drunken hunter, he's more likely to be looking for a stray hambone or hot dog. Most dogs I've known are highly-motivated by food. Which can be a very useful bit of trivia to know, by the way.

So while I played fetch with Jinx, Rayna and Bitty continued proposing various scenarios that involved Trina, Naomi, and Race.

"Race could have made a date with Trina, and Naomi just showed up," Rayna suggested. "Surely he wouldn't be dumb enough to take Naomi to Madewell Courts right under Trina's nose."

"I wouldn't count on that." Bitty adjusted Chen Ling in her sling so the sun wouldn't get in the dog's eyes. "The man could be absolutely oblivious to anything but what he wanted. He liked to show off, too. He just loved having lots of women flock around him, even when he was on a date with someone else. I wouldn't stand for that, I'll tell you that much."

"So if he did take Naomi to Madewell Courts, and Trina found out and made a scene . . . would she just stand there and let Naomi shoot him?"

"For that matter, if he was with *Trina* and Naomi found them together and shot him, why hasn't Naomi told the police who the other woman was?"

"Maybe because then Trina would be an eye-witness against her."

"Then why hasn't Trina told the police what she saw? Unless," Bitty said with a sudden jerk of her hand that made Chen Ling bark, "Race was with a *man!*"

"*Trisha,*" I heard myself blurt out, "maybe he was with Trina's sister Trisha!"

I hadn't meant to say it, not really, but the back and forth between the two of them had driven me to it. Or maybe just having that choice bit of gossip was more than my resolve could take. Mama would be so disappointed.

Both of them turned to look at me.

"Trinket Truevine, what do you know that we don't?" Bitty demanded.

I gave up petting Jinx, who seemed to get over my defection quickly, and sat back down at the garden table. Tall glasses of lemonade had been served, and I took a drink of mine before I answered.

"I'm not supposed to pass this on—"

"I hope you don't think for a minute you'll get away with that," said Bitty.

I shook my head. "Of course not. I'm just explaining why I haven't said anything until now. Mama told me not to."

"Aunt Anna said he was with Trisha?" Bitty sounded disbelieving and I couldn't blame her. It's not like my mother to gossip. Or didn't used to be.

"Apparently Mama witnessed Trina and Trisha arguing in the church parking lot on Atonement Day. She must have had a ringside seat, because she heard everything they said."

Bitty rolled her eyes. "That day was a disaster. I think it caused two divorces. But why didn't I hear about Trina and Trisha's argument before now? You'd think someone would have heard it besides Aunt Anna."

"If they did, they've kept it to themselves," I said. "Anyway, Trina and Trisha both found out they were dating Race at the same time, and neither of them were happy about it."

"I'm not surprised."

"Mama said they went so far as hair-pulling."

"Was that a wig Trina was wearing?" Bitty wondered, looking from me to Rayna and back. "Maybe that's why her hair looked so dreadful. And her make-up! She made me think of a circus clown, which was a bit scary. You know I've always been afraid of clowns."

Ignoring Bitty's sidebar, Rayna said, "This is getting even more complicated. If we go under the assumption Naomi is innocent—which I don't believe—then we have not one, but two more suspects who may have had reason to kill Race."

"Heavens," said Bitty as she unlatched Chitling from her chest and lowered her to the grass, "even I had a reason to kill Race Champion. He was obnoxious. There now, my precious, go over there and poo-poo for Mommy."

The last was directed to the dog. I hope.

"Bitty," Rayna reproved, "you shouldn't say things like that. Which reminds me, did you really tell Naomi Spencer that you want to strangle her?"

Startled, Bitty looked up from depositing a reluctant pug on the garden lawn. "If you mean at Budgie's, I didn't get a chance to say it *to* her. I said it *about* her. How did you hear about it?"

"Everyone in the café heard it, no doubt," I said in annoyance. "I told you that your voice carries."

"Are you saying I have a big mouth?"

I considered that for a moment, then shook my head. "Not any bigger than normal, I suppose."

"Somehow, that's not very comforting. I think I've just been insulted."

I picked up a folded napkin and fanned myself with it. "My, my, it's so vairy, vairy wahm out heah," I said in an exaggerated southern drawl, which made Bitty smile in spite of herself. Since we were kids we'd used that trick to change subjects when in tight conversational spots.

Just to keep us even, she said something rude to me, and we both smiled.

Rayna shook her head. "You two are getting scary. Maybe it's all this talk about murder. Let's go inside where it's cooler. I hate to think what the rest of summer will be like if it's already this hot."

Summer in Mississippi is always hot. We just have varying degrees of hot. There is warm, such as afternoon temperatures in the eighties; there is hot, such as afternoon temperatures in the nineties; and then there is scorching, such as afternoon temps at the three-digit level. June had already seen an unseasonable scorcher or two. If it kept up, by July 4th Marshall County would be a red sand desert with no green grass in sight. Except for Bitty's lawn. She has automatic sprinklers.

Rayna's house, the Delta Inn, is a lovely nineteenth century hotel that had fallen into disrepair at one time. As so many buildings and homes, it was scheduled to be torn down and replaced by weeds and forlorn footings, but Rayna and Rob had taken a liking to it and saved it from the wrecking ball. The lobby of the inn still has lots of marble and ornate fireplace mantles, which I'm sure the salvage company still regrets not getting their hands on. Stuff like that sells at flea markets, antique fairs, and on the Internet for incredible prices.

They are slowly refurbishing the interior, and Rayna uses the lobby as her artist's studio since it has plenty of natural light. It has a unique domed skylight on the roof, and floor to ceiling windows on the north, east, and west sides. Potted tropical plants grow to enormous size, and you can usually find a cat or two sleeping under a gigantic leaf as big as a beach umbrella. The former baggage room makes a discreet cattery, complete with litter trays, food bowls, and small dishes with running water. Rob and Rayna have no children, so the animals receive the benefit of their time and attention.

Behind the lobby is an industrial size kitchen with all the amenities.

Rayna cooks gourmet meals when she isn't busy painting and selling canvases of a wide variety of subjects. A lot of the paintings feature her animals or garden and sell quite well locally and at small gallery showings. She really is a woman of many talents.

"How many of the upstairs rooms do you have done?" Bitty asked when we were all sitting at what used to be the check-in counter but is now a breakfast bar of sorts.

"Just two. Rob has been so busy lately investigating insurance claims, and when he isn't doing that, he's busy bailing somebody out of jail. So it's been difficult to put much time into renovation. We'll get it done one day."

"Are you going to do like the Madewells and rent out rooms?"

Rayna shuddered. "Lord, no! Can you imagine me in my painter's smock trying to change beds for new guests? It'd be a mess."

"True." Bitty readjusted Chen Ling in the baby sling she wore across her chest as a constant accessory. I suppose that's why the slings are always in matching colors and suitably fancied up. "I didn't mean it when I told Trina that I've thought about renting out rooms at Six Chimney's, you know," said Bitty as if telling us something we didn't already know. "I just said that to make her feel comfortable."

"Have you heard from her since she tore out of your house like a cat with its tail on fire?" asked Rayna.

"Not even a phone call, much less a written note. Really. People have no manners these days, have you noticed? No one observes the social graces anymore."

"Good god," I said. "Count yourself lucky she didn't take home the silver as she left. You'd be amazed at the things people do in hotels."

"I had forgotten you used to work in the hospitality industry, Trinket." Rayna poured me another glass of lemonade. She makes the old-fashioned kind of lemonade with juicy lemon slices crushed in sugar and ice, and fresh mint added to give it a zing. Her garden is overflowing with different kinds of mint and herbs. Rayna has a green thumb, too. As I said before, a woman of many talents. "I suppose there were a lot of things taken when the guests left. Towels, soap, things like that?"

"If we didn't nail the paintings to the wall, they would be missing. Towels, lamps, shower curtains, silverware, dishes—once a guest took the toilet seat. Don't ask me how he got it off. He must have checked in a tool box inside his luggage."

"Was that at The Peabody?" Bitty asked. "It must have been an expensive toilet seat for him to want it."

"It's been a while since I worked there," I said, "but The Peabody didn't have gold toilet seats or any other reason for a guest to want to take it. Not even a duck motif on it."

For those unfamiliar with "The South's Grand Hotel," The Peabody is a famous hotel in the heart of downtown Memphis, Tennessee. Memphis is about forty-five minutes up 78 Highway from Holly Springs. There is a local saying that the Mississippi Delta begins in the lobby of The Peabody Hotel. It's also said that if you sit in the lobby long enough, you'll see everyone you know and a few people you would like to know.

In the hotel lobby is a gorgeous marble fountain with a gigantic fresh flower arrangement atop the exquisite center and wild ducks swimming in the water. Yes, ducks. Mallards, to be precise. Back in the 1920s, when the hotel owner and a few friends returned from duck hunting in Arkansas, one of the inebriated gentlemen released a live duck into the fountain to swim. While it's normal to bring dead ducks home from hunting, this gentleman apparently got confused. At any rate, the duck in the fountain became a huge tourist attraction, and thus began the practice of live ducks in the hotel lobby. There is a complicated ritual to it now; a red carpet stretches from the fountain to the elevator for the ducks to walk down while the Duck Master accompanies them to the lobby from an elegant and very expensive penthouse suite built especially for ducks. The John Philip Sousa March plays while tourists crowd the strip of red carpet with cameras. The ducks go on duty at eleven in the morning and return to their penthouse at five in the evening, all to great fanfare. While The Peabody has ducks in the lobby, you can rest assured there is no duck on the menus except as photos. It would be just too unsettling for guests to wonder if they were eating a duck they'd seen happily swimming the day before. The Peabody ducks retire to a farm outside Memphis where they live out the remainder of their lives in contented ducky fashion.

So when Bitty asked, "Have they ever served duck on the menu?" I smiled.

"Not officially."

"What on earth does that mean?"

"Well, there was that time a group of college frat boys got drunk, stole a duck from the fountain, and tried to cook it in their hotel room."

Bitty looked scandalized. "No! I tell you, some colleges just let their students go wild. It's terrible. What sleazy college were they from?"

I hesitated, then said: "Ole Miss."

Nonplussed, Bitty fumbled for a response. I could see she was torn between her distaste for bad manners and loyalty to her alma mater, as well as the fact she pays a great deal of tuition money each semester for her twin boys, Brandon and Clayton, to attend Ole Miss. So I softened the blow:

"The Peabody banned that fraternity from their premises for a while, and the boys responsible were sternly disciplined by the school and made to pay restitution. It was dealt with quite well, I believe."

That made Bitty feel better.

"Well, I should hope so. Thank heavens not every university condones such behavior. Then I would worry about my boys being off at Ole Miss."

"When are your boys due back in town?" Rayna asked Bitty.

"This week sometime. They're still in Miami right now, visiting my aunt. They're keeping her pretty busy, I imagine. On the way home they intend to stop by and visit Frank."

While I had my doubts two young, handsome, healthy boys were spending all their time in Miami visiting Bitty's senior aunt, I was intrigued to learn they kept in touch with their father.

"So," I asked rather delicately, since Bitty doesn't always like being reminded of her first husband and the twins' father, "how is Frank?"

"Still in prison. The idiot. Why I ever thought he was smart is beyond me."

"Well," Rayna said, "he was always smart; he just got caught up in something he shouldn't have."

Bitty rolled her eyes. "I know nothing about financial markets, but even I'm not dumb enough to fall for a pyramid scheme. He should have done more research on the men he was working with instead of thinking he was some hotshot investor. Now look. They took off for the Mediterranean with most of the money, and he's doing twenty in a Federal prison. Like I said: Idiot with a capital I."

"At least you didn't spend twenty-odd years following him around the country to different jobs," I said. "It took me a lot longer than you to figure out my husband had problems with dependable employment."

"That's true." Bitty bent down to let a wriggling pug loose in the lobby. Several of Rayna's cats eyed Chen Ling with flattened ears and twitching tails, not a good sign of impending feline friendship. "I always wondered how you could be so stupid."

Before I could say what came first to my mind, she added, "For such a smart woman, you sure did overlook a lot," and I didn't say it. After all, she was right.

Now, to give Bitty credit, even though she's been married and divorced four times, there was always an excellent reason for the divorces. Usually a much better reason, in fact, than there was for the marriage, but since I'm obviously not in a position to judge, I try to refrain from pointing out that detail. After all, I got married because he had great abs. Go figure.

If I haven't mentioned this before, my ex-husband—whom I met at a sit-in for Native American rights—was a jack of all trades. He worked various jobs throughout his career, and still does I imagine, although I haven't kept up with his whereabouts. I wish him no ill, mind you. We just get on much better a continent apart.

Anyway, all talk about ex-husbands came to a screeching halt as two things happened at once: Chen Ling decided to taste a cat, and the doorbell rang. As the lobby is so huge, sound reverberates off the marble, glass, and wood. Jarring echoes of a yelping pug and a deep, repetitive gong made my head vibrate at warp speed.

Since Rayna was helping Bitty untangle Chen Ling and a rather large cat that had been happily napping under a chair before the introduction, it was left to me to go answer the door. Not that I minded. It was much better than getting scratched or bitten.

"Who rang that bell?" I sang as I marched to the double entry doors, mimicking the tone of the doorman/wizard/professor in the *Wizard of Oz* movie. In case I haven't mentioned it yet, I have a habit of quoting from old movies, television shows, and books. I'm not alone in my oddity, as Bitty can match me quote for quote. This talent is a left-over product of our youth. While we were mostly normal children, family rumor has it that we spent a great deal of our time restricted to our respective homes because of some misdeed or other that we had no doubt been unjustly accused of committing, so we used up a lot of time watching television. Don't listen to my mother if she tells you differently. She has memory lapses.

I repeated my demand even louder as I opened the door. Gaynelle Bishop gave me a sharp rap on the arm with a folded newspaper. "Don't be rude, dear."

Rather meekly, I stepped aside to let her into the lobby. It must take a long time to recover from thirty years of teaching bad-mannered children not to shout, swear, or pee their pants in the classroom.

"How are you today?" I asked as I accompanied Gaynelle across the lobby.

"Oh, *I* am fine, but I've been hunting for Bitty to see how *she* is doing."

We both looked at Bitty and Rayna as they successfully rescued Chitling from the sharp clutches of a miffed tomcat. The cat went to work cleaning bits of pug fur from his claws, while Bitty held a recovering dog close to her chest.

"Oh my poor baby!" Bitty said as she examined Chen Ling for damage. "Did that mean ole cat hurt you?"

Rayna hovered close. "I am so sorry. Merlin has little tolerance for strange dogs. I should have warned you. I just didn't think Chen Ling would get too close to him."

"Well, there's no blood so I'm sure she'll be fine eventually. Though I do think she may have been traumatized."

Safe now in Bitty's arms, Chen Ling revealed the depth of her trauma by looking down at Merlin and growling. Then she started barking, shrill yaps that billowed around the lobby all the way up to the domed skylight. I touched my ears to see if they were bleeding yet, while Bitty tried to get the dog to hush.

After a moment, Gaynelle intervened. "Do be quiet," she said to Chen Ling, and the startled pug stopped barking. Not bad, I thought. She could give the Dog Whisperer a run for his money.

"Bitty, have you read *The South Reporter* today?" Gaynelle demanded, and when Bitty shook her head, I had a sinking feeling we were about to hear something dreadful. I was right.

"Here." Gaynelle thrust the paper toward her. "Read *Miranda's Musings.*"

"You mean Miranda's tell-all column. What on earth has she managed to get into print now?"

Bitty took the paper. It had been folded, so the column was on top for easier reading. As she read, Bitty's face took on an odd hue, somewhere between raspberry and purple. It was not a very complimentary shade. When she looked up, her eyes glinted like steel daggers.

"That *bitch!* "

Since she'd crumpled the paper in one hand as she snarled, I snatched it away so I could read it. Rayna crowded close behind me as I read aloud:

"'Trina Madewell reports that she was invited to a Dixie Diva meeting this week. As the Divas rarely invite outsiders to their meetings, Miss Madewell felt especially honored to be invited by the Queen Bee herself, one Bitty Hollandale. Mrs. Hollandale, you may recall, was divorced from the late Mississippi senator Philip Hollandale, who was found murdered a few months ago in his ex-wife's wine cellar. Although arrested for his murder, Mrs. Hollandale was released the same day through the efforts of Jackson Lee Brunetti, her attorney. Brunetti and Brunetti is a well-respected Holly Springs' firm with offices in Memphis as well as Mississippi. Since that time, Mr. Brunetti and Mrs. Hollandale have been seen around Holly Springs enjoying late-night dinners together.'"

I paused and looked up. Bitty had gone quiet. Too quiet. Gaynelle watched her closely as if expecting an eruption, and I noticed that Rayna's cats had all left the room like rats from a sinking ship. This was gonna be bad, I told myself, and prepared for the worst as I continued to read. My voice got lower, not that it mattered. Gaynelle and Bitty had already read it, and Rayna was still leaning over my shoulder.

"But back to the Dixie Divas. Miss Madewell arrived promptly for the meeting, and they were soon joined by other members of this secretive club. For those of my readers who have long wondered if these meetings are just polite socials, let me be the first to inform you—they are anything but polite.

"Instead of tea, Mrs. Hollandale served whiskey in an elegant antique teapot that had to cost a small fortune. Do not be envious, dear readers, for in the ensuing drunken brawl that erupted between the members of the Dixie Divas, that precious antique teapot was shattered, as were Miss Madewell's nerves. When she fled Six Chimneys, all the Divas were flinging canapés and mixed nuts at one another, while a terrible shrieking filled that lovely antebellum home. It is with great sadness that I report the mystery that once surrounded what many of us in Holly Springs assumed was a *ladies* club has now been solved. These women are obviously no ladies. I have some advice for the members of this decadent club: Drop dead, Divas!'"

Silence fell as I finished reading. I swear, not even Chitling made a sound. It was eerie. I folded the paper over again and cleared my throat.

"Oh my," Rayna said faintly behind me.

"At least she didn't name us," I pointed out in a lame attempt to put a better face on it.

Gaynelle shook her head. "She didn't have to. Almost everyone in Holly Springs knows who's in the Divas and who's not. Until now, we've managed to maintain at least the appearance of gentility."

While I hardly thought gentility was the right word, it was no time to argue. The column was a disaster. It was insulting. Worse, if viewed from Trina Madewell's point of view, I could understand that we had probably scared the bejesus out of her. I looked over at Bitty.

She still stood stock still, her eyes glittering, Chen Ling clutched to her chest like some kind of shield. The expression on her face was . . . well, frightening.

"Bitty?" I reached over to touch her arm. "Bitty? Are you . . . are you all right?"

"Of course I am," she said calmly. "I'm just trying to decide who to shoot first, Trina or that malicious Miranda. Maybe Miranda. She's fat and not able to run as fast. Yes, I can shoot her first, then drive out to Madewell Courts."

"Now Bitty," said Gaynelle, "you know you cannot shoot either one of them."

"Oh, I've been going to the shooting range lately. I can do it. My aim is much better than it used to be."

As much as the thought of an armed Bitty terrifies me, I found it rather surprising that she'd been spending time at a shooting range.

"You went to a shooting range without telling me?"

"Well, I don't tell you *every*thing, Trinket. You have a tendency to tattle."

"Only to keep you safe," I defended myself. "Besides, you don't have a permit to carry concealed."

Bitty smiled. "I do now."

"Omigod," Rayna groaned. "Who do you want to hold your bail money?"

"Just call Jackson Lee. He'll take care of it."

"Elisabeth Ann Hollandale, stop talking nonsense this minute!" Gaynelle said sternly. Her use of Bitty's full name got her instant attention. "There are much better ways to deal with this sort of thing than violence. Didn't we all learn that lesson only a scant few months ago?"

Gaynelle's reference to the murders that had taken place shocked some sense back into Bitty. She nodded.

"You're right. I'm sorry, Gaynelle."

"Very well." Gaynelle smoothed a wrinkle in her thin, silk-blend skirt and gave a brisk nod of her head. "We will show Holly Springs and Miranda Watson that the Divas are not only ladies, but *smart* ladies."

"How do you propose to do that?" I wanted to know.

"Simple. Instead of wasting valuable time talking to the suspects, *we* will use our common sense to find out which one of them really killed Race Champion."

CHAPTER 6

At first I didn't really take Gaynelle seriously. I mean, how on earth would we be able to either prove Naomi Spencer killed her fiancé, or that Trina Madewell did it? It's not as if we had access to the same legal avenues as the police. And they have years of experience on their side.

While I understood that Gaynelle feels lingering guilt about one of the murders that occurred a few months back, even though she had no part in it at all, it did seem a bit far-fetched to think we Divas could redeem ourselves by finding out if Naomi or Trina was the one who had killed Race. For one thing, people who wanted to believe Miranda Watson's vicious innuendoes were going to believe them, and nothing we could do would change that. For another thing, my brush with death and danger had led me to the conclusion that staying out of police business was in my best interests. Yes, I can be quite selfish that way.

And finally, I was encouraged to spend my free time doing far more pleasant things. Like going to a movie with Kit Coltrane.

On a nice Saturday night with a breeze blowing hard enough to keep mosquitoes at bay, but not so hard my hair turned me into a punk rocker, we drove up to Southaven. It's a Mississippi bedroom community right below the state line from Memphis, and we went to a Malco theater filled with adolescent girls shrieking over a vampire movie. It took me back twenty years. Okay, thirty or thirty-five, but I can remember going to the movies with Bitty and our friends and doing much the same thing.

Kit, however, seemed to have had a completely different childhood. He was a little horrified by the high-pitched squealing in the theater lobby. I saw him wince once or twice, and had to tease him.

"Doesn't this take you back to your pre-teen years?"

"Actually, yes," he said, surprising me. "They're making the same noise my dad's old Dodge used to make when the fan belt slipped."

I laughed. It's easy being with Kit. Not only is he quite easy on the eyes—over six feet which is always a plus for a tall woman—with dark hair lightly brushed with gray and lovely brown eyes, but he has a great sense of humor and doesn't take life too seriously. I like that. Intense men are nerve-wracking. Maybe it's because I have enough problems of my own to deal with, or maybe it's my age, but I could never be interested in a man who came with emotional baggage. It's rather shocking that I've become interested in any man, really, since as I have said before, a relationship was the last thing I wanted.

When I told Bitty that Kit and I were friends, I wasn't stretching the truth. We are. If we go beyond that, she'll have to drug me to find out about it. A Bitty armed with that kind of information would be impossible to endure.

After the movie, an action-adventure with a light love interest, Kit and I went to eat at one of the dozens of places near the theater. It was crowded and noisy. Rock music blared from overhead speakers, and there was standing room only at the bar.

When Kit leaned close to say in my ear," Let's get out of here," I was only too ready to agree. I had no desire to show my age by asking for earplugs with my entrée.

Since there was a Sonic drive-in in the same area, we ended up parked in one of the slots while cute young girls on roller skates darted around with heavy trays.

"I'd end up two counties over with onion rings in my hair if I had to deliver food on roller skates," I mused, and Kit grinned.

"Oh, I doubt that. You're the kind of woman who can do anything she sets her mind to do."

That intrigued me. "Really? You think I'm competent? Have you been talking to my mother?"

"Not since she brought Brownie in for his rabies shot."

"I don't suppose he gave you a hint as to where he's hidden my emerald earring," I said hopefully, and Kit shook his head.

"Not a word."

"I should just give up on it, I guess. Maybe I missed it in one of his, uh, usual morning deposits. Have you noticed we spend a lot of time talking about dog poop, by the way?"

"It comes with the territory, I'm afraid. We could discuss rabid raccoons if you prefer."

"I'm good, but thanks for the offer."

He smiled at me, and reached out to touch a strand of my hair. It was probably frizzed up from the humidity so that I looked like the bride of Frankenstein, but he didn't seem to notice. It was a really nice moment.

Neon lights flickered across Kit's car and on our faces. We were in his '57 Chevy that he'd restored. It felt almost like date night in the seventies again. If he suddenly suggested going to Make-out Point, I'd probably giggle like a sixteen year old girl.

About that time our food arrived, possibly saving both of us from a bumper crop of mosquito bites at Make-out Point. But onion rings have never tasted quite as good as when shared with a charming man on a summer night.

On our way back to Holly Springs, Kit reached over to hold my hand. It felt nice. Very nice. We sat in companionable silence traveling down 78 Highway with the a/c off, the windows down, and the wind making a rushing sound around the car. My hair blew into what I was sure would be a frightening mess, but I didn't care. Fireflies made sprinkles of light like tiny bobbing lanterns in the darkened cotton and soybean fields we passed, and the sweet scent of honeysuckle filled the car's interior. I remembered why I loved my home state, and thought about how much I'd missed it in my years away. Now I'd come home and everything had changed but my memories.

Land was slowly being gobbled up by investors, home builders, and corporations intent upon paving every inch of grass within commuting distance to Memphis. It would be sad to see that happen. Progress isn't always pretty, and isn't always progressive. In my memories, Mississippi would always be green rolling hills, pine trees, and magnolias. In reality, civilization was making vast inroads on my fondest memories.

One of the delights of my childhood had been trips to Maywood Swimming Pool. The owners had constructed a huge white sand beach around clear blue water in the shape of a small lake. There was a concession stand, trees to sit under, shallow water for the smaller kids, and a slide and deep water for the bigger kids. People drove down to north Mississippi for the day from Memphis, up from Holly Springs, and from places east and west. You could get sunburned, sand in your bathing suit, and sick from eating too much ice cream all in one great location. A kid's paradise.

It's gone now, the lake emptied, the land sold off to build cookie-cutter homes on large lots. In the upstairs closet at Cherryhill there are scrapbooks with black and white and faded color snapshots of me and my sister and brothers at Maywood, moments captured forever by Kodak and Mama's Brownie camera. There are a few Polaroid shots as well, the sixties version of digital cameras. Those haven't survived nearly as well as the wonderful memories.

Just as I decided that this particular moment would go into my mental scrapbook of memories as well, Kit asked, "So what really happened at Bitty's tea party?"

The moment vanished. So far we had carefully skirted the issue that seemed to be on everyone's mind and tongue these days, and I'd mentally congratulated him on his restraint. I suppose curiosity can only be stalled for so long.

"Chen Ling happened. I'd put her in the upstairs bedroom before Trina ever got there. She must have chewed her way out. Or maybe Bitty has secret passageways in that house only old ghosts and dogs can find. At any rate, we'd run out of Earl Grey tea and so Rayna and I supplemented with a little Jack Daniel's. That part is true. But there was no *drunken brawl* like Miranda and Trina claim. Chen Ling jumped up onto the hassock with the tea tray, and everything went everywhere. Bitty tried to save her teapot. The rest of us were just trying to save our clothes and fingers. Chitling has a tendency to forget people aren't edible. Raw, anyway."

Kit laughed. "I don't know about that last part. I read in a National Geographic magazine about this native tribe that—"

"Don't go one word further with that story," I warned. Kit likes to try and gross me out on occasion. Men never really get over that entire fifth grade boy mentality on some levels. "I've had enough traumas this week."

He squeezed my hand. "I know."

"All I need now to make my life perfect is for Naomi Spencer to show up dead in Bitty's coat closet."

I don't know why I said that. Maybe because I haven't quite gotten over the trauma of being the one to discover Bitty's ex-husband dead in her coat closet.

"Naomi got out on bail, you know," Kit said, and I nodded.

"So I heard. Rob posted her bond. Rayna said if Naomi tries to leave the state, she'll go after her with a search dog and a pitchfork."

"She probably would, too."

"Oh, I know she would. Naomi was making big eyes at Rob the entire time he was writing out her bond papers. Rayna was ready to strangle her. I guess the poor girl just can't help herself. Her fiancé isn't even cold yet and she was flirting with Rob, one of the deputies, and an old dog sitting on the jailhouse steps. Why doesn't Miranda Watson write about *that?*"

Kit laughed. "Everything will work itself out, Trinket. At least none of the Divas are accused of murdering anyone. People will forget all about this mess soon and be on to a new target for gossip."

Didn't I know it. And I had a feeling the new topic would have something to do with Gaynelle's grand plan to redeem the Divas. Call it a premonition, or call it recent experience, but I just knew that once any kind of plan was enacted, it would not go well.

Maybe I'm psychic.

****

When I arrived at Bitty's house the next morning she was dressed in white linen capris, a silk blouse, and pug hair. The last she was trying to remove with a brush, but as she wears the dog as an accessory all day, I thought it rather time-consuming and futile.

"Don't bother," I said. "Chitling will just deposit more the moment you pick her up again."

Bitty looked up at me. Her gaze scanned my faded Lee jeans and short-sleeved tee shirt, ending at my rather scuffed white tennis shoes. "I hope you don't mind if I don't take fashion advice from you," she said.

"And if I do mind?"

She looked a little surprised. "Oh. Do you?"

"No. Not today, anyway."

"Really, Trinket. Sometimes I have to wonder about you."

I just smiled. Teasing Bitty is always an amusing pastime, though frequently not without its dangers. But since I'd been coerced, nearly blackmailed, and had my arm hypothetically twisted to join this merry little group on their latest excursion into insanity, I was willing to risk it.

"Is the meeting location still top-secret?" I asked out of idle curiosity. Not that I truly cared where the Divas intended to meet. Since almost everyone we knew in Holly Springs would be at church, an emergency meeting had been set up in an undisclosed location. Only one Diva knew the final destination. The rest of us were to meet at Bitty's house, Rayna's hotel, or Gaynelle's neat little cottage on College Street. I had no idea who else would show up at Bitty's. She was being very secretive and it annoyed me.

Soon Cady Lee Forsythe arrived. She came in Bitty's back door, which meant she had to go through the sun porch and kitchen to get into the living room. I just looked at her. Even though Cady Lee has more money than most people ever see in a lifetime, she had on washed-out jeans with holes in the knees, a tank top with glitter on it, and a knit cap pulled down over her hair. I thought Bitty was going to have a stroke.

"What in the name of all that's holy are you wearing, Cady Lee?"

"My daughter's clothes. Why? You said not to wear anything too noticeable."

"I didn't mean you should dress like a wino, for heaven's sake. You and Trinket look like bag ladies."

I nodded. "Thank you."

"Should I go home and change?" Cady Lee wondered as she frowned down at her jeans.

"No. Where we're going it doesn't really matter. I just hope no one saw you come in. You look like you've been ravaged by dogs."

I looked at Bitty. Since she owns a dog prone to ravaging guests, I thought it rather tacky of her to say that last. Apparently Cady Lee didn't mind, because she just asked if she had time to use the bathroom before we left.

While Cady Lee was off in the powder room, Cindy Nelson arrived. I like Cindy. She's pragmatic and seems much more mature than thirty-one. Maybe it's because she has three or four kids and a menagerie of dogs, cats, hamsters, and whatever else might have fur or feathers and require lots of feeding and cleaning up after. That tends to age people, I've noticed. Or at least, it ages me when I'm left with my parents' cat colony and neurotic dog to feed and care for.

Cindy is a very attractive young woman. Her light brown hair is cut into a short style that looks tousled and chic at the same time. She always wears casual clothes to our meetings, and looks good in anything from faded jeans to walking shorts. Today she wore a pair of knee-length khaki shorts, a bright red sleeveless blouse, sandals, no makeup, and managed to look cool and pretty. It must be an inherited talent.

Since Cindy and I share a love of books and writing in our personal journals, we get along famously. If anyone ever reads our journals, we both plan to plead dementia. If hers are anything like mine, I'm quite sure we'll end up with adjoining rooms down at Whitfield, the Mississippi state insane asylum. They call the asylum something else now in this new age of being politically correct, but it means the same thing.

Once Cady Lee got out of the powder room and everyone hugged, Bitty said in a brisk tone, "We can all ride in my car since I know where we're going."

"We won't all fit in your car," I pointed out. "It's a two-seater. The back seat is just for insurance purposes."

"Don't be silly, Trinket. We'll take the Franklin Benz."

In case I haven't mentioned this, Bitty had gotten very nice settlements in her four divorce cases. With each lump sum, she'd purchased something expensive as a sort of consolation gift to herself. Her divorce from Frank Caldwell had paid for a brand new house. That had been before the pyramid scheme collapsed and Frank was left with nothing but debts and criminal charges against him. Her next divorce, from Delbert Anderson, had paid for a trip around the world. The Mercedes Benz had been from her divorce from Franklin Kirby, III. Philip Hollandale's settlement had helped purchase the Miata she usually drove.

"Do I have to sit up front with the dog?" I asked as we headed for her garage. "I'd much rather sit in the back."

Bitty toted Chen Ling sans baby sling for some reason. The dog wore a pink bib that matched her collar, and some kind of garment on her rear that looked suspiciously like a diaper. If Chitling was having digestive troubles, I definitely did not want to sit by her. And there was no way in hell Bitty would ever convince me to change her diaper.

"Just for a few minutes, Trinket. I don't want to leave her alone, so

I'm taking her over to Luann Carey's while we're gone."

Spots danced in front of my eyes. Hope sprang anew. I hardly dared breathe for fear she'd change her mind and we'd end up carting Chitling with us to our mysterious rendezvous location. Then it occurred to me that if we were going to a place so remote or dangerous that Bitty wasn't willing to risk her dog, I wasn't willing to go either.

"Bitty Hollandale, you tell me right this minute where we're going or I won't get in this car," I said, and she stopped by the driver's door of the black Benz and glared at me. I glared back.

"Fine," she said after a minute of us glaring at each other, "we are going to meet the others at the junction of Liberty Road and Highway Five."

I blinked. "That's in the middle of nowhere."

"Not really. It's between Ashland and Hickory Flat."

"Like I said, the middle of nowhere!"

"Don't worry, Trinket. We're just meeting the others there so they can follow me. I'm the only one who knows our final destination."

"If that's supposed to be reassuring—it's not."

"Oh for heaven's sake, have a little faith. Have I ever gotten you lost?"

While I stood there with my mouth open and a dozen different scenarios zipping through my brain, Bitty got into the car and started the engine. Cady Lee and Cindy got into the back seat rather quickly, I thought, and I was left to either get in or be run down as she backed over me. I almost decided upon the latter, but gave in and got into the roomy passenger seat. Chitling looked up at me with a smirk.

I really hate it when dogs know more than I do.

We stopped in front of Luann Carey's house. She lives on Higdon, a nice street off Highway 4 that runs to Ashland. She has one of those Tudor style homes that looks like an English cottage, complete with a front garden that billows with roses, lilies, and every kind of blooming or green plant you can name. The garden also teems with pugs. Luann sat in a wooden swing under an arbor festooned with snowy white roses, smiling as peacefully as someone can who has a dozen smush-faced dogs under their feet. I began to suspect she may be another candidate for Whitfield, but she seems fairly sane when you talk to her.

With Chitling safely stowed in the loving arms of her former caretaker—Daddy still says Luann saw a good thing coming when she "loaned" Bitty that dog—we drove off in the Franklin Benz, headed for parts unknown.

Believe it or not, there are parts of Mississippi with mountains, all under a thousand feet. While the flat delta is mainly along the Mississippi

River, in Benton County hills run up and down pretty steeply in places, and the Holly Springs National Forest climbs ridges that break off sharply into kudzu-choked ravines and barren red dirt. Liberty Road winds through flat farmland and rolling hills studded with small houses, large houses, and house trailers here and there. It comes out on Highway 5 right above Abel's Store Road. An old country store used to stand on the side of the highway, gone now since the new fork signals the end of old Highway 5 and the start of the new section. A new bridge has been built over Tippah Creek, too.

I recognized Gaynelle's old blue Cadillac at the side of the road, and right behind her was Rayna's black SUV. I couldn't see how many passengers each vehicle held, or if all the Divas had reported for active duty. We are three down right now, two having left our membership at the same time, and one inactive for a while.

Bitty's cell phone rang. I usually recognize her ring tone. It plays a short refrain from *Dixieland*. Not this time. A theme from the 007 movie franchise lit up her phone. It was all I could do to keep from rolling my eyes and saying something tacky. It would be a waste of my time anyway. Bitty does love her intrigues.

"Yo," Bitty said crisply into her pink jewel-toned cell phone. "Red Dog here."

This time I just could not help myself. I rolled my eyes and laughed out loud. As I suspected, it was wasted on her. She didn't even acknowledge me.

But when she said, "Phase one complete. Phase two initiated," my hysteria set in.

It was not intentional on my part. For one thing, I have a tendency to snort when hysterically laughing, and it's a bit embarrassing. For another thing, when Bitty is in one of her role-playing modes, as she obviously was, it only annoys her.

In the midst of my snorting, cackling, and wheezing, I heard Bitty say, "No, I don't have live chickens with me. That's Trinket. She's choking on something. Or will be in a minute."

I have a healthy respect for personal threats. I did my best to muffle my snorts. In the back seat, however, could be heard giggles. That set me off again. My jaws began to ache from trying to hold in my laughter, and my ribcage hurt. I even pinched myself in an effort to bring it under control, but nothing worked. Tears ran down my cheeks and over the fingers of the hand I clapped over my mouth as I tried to regain composure.

It took Bitty slamming on the brakes so that I lurched forward and cracked my knee on the dashboard before I could finally stop laughing long enough to breathe. Red dust boiled up around the Benz. It hung in the air outside the car for a moment before dissipating back along Liberty Road. Through the haze I saw Rayna's SUV window glide down and her head poke out.

"Are y'all all right?"

"Use your cell phone!" Bitty yelled back, and held up her pink spy phone.

Rayna must have complied. 007 theme music played again a second or two later. This time I was able to maintain. I thought about sad things to keep from laughing again.

While I focused on the huge hole in the ozone layer, the Mid-East situation, the price of a small loaf of bread, and how the price of oil had skyrocketed during vacation months, Bitty finished her code word conversation and took the lead position in what must have been a really strange looking caravan of vehicles. We traveled down the narrow ribbon of Highway 5, then she turned onto Renick Hill Road. It winds up a rather steep grade, and after turning onto Autry Road, she made so many turns I felt like Alice in the Queen of Hearts' garden maze. If we'd come upon a croquet court, complete with flamingo mallets and hedgehog balls, it would not have surprised me.

Lately, I often feel much like Alice in *Through the Looking Glass.* Everyday things have a way of turning round about so that they make no sense. I tell you this only because the rest of our day seemed to go that way.

By the time we'd been driving around the wooded hills for a half hour on a gravel road that felt more like a dried up creek bed, I was ready to reach wherever we were going, if only to stop my intestines from being jarred completely out of my body. If the ruts in the road could make a Mercedes Benz feel like riding in a log truck, I could only imagine how the passengers in Gaynelle's old Cadillac must feel.

Finally Bitty stopped the car. Right in front of us on a small rise sat a rather nice-looking cabin. Pine trees clustered around it, and fallen debris and deep green moss made a soft, thick front yard. In that front yard sat a Volkswagen Beetle. I spared a moment's awe for the power of German engineering that had enabled that tiny yellow car to get up the road we'd just traveled.

Bitty, however, seemed shocked to see it.

She scrambled for her cell phone. Since Rayna and Gaynelle had parked on each side of us, I thought it a waste of battery. But apparently, we were so far back in the boonies no cell tower was close enough to provide service. Bitty cussed and slammed the phone to the leather seat, then opened her car door.

"Did you tell anyone where we were coming?" she demanded of no one in particular as she stomped toward the cabin.

"How could I when I have no idea where we are?" Rayna answered reasonably. She looked around a moment. "Wait. Didn't there used to be some kind of lodge near here back in the nineteenth century?"

"Oh, I know what you mean," said Sandra Dobson, whom I hadn't seen since our last Diva meeting the month before. "That was over on Beck's Springs Road, I believe. It was a resort of some kind, wasn't it? People used to come here all the way from Memphis back before there were cars. Maybe they took the train to the railroad depot, and a horse and buggy from there. I think I saw some old photos in the museum."

While we leaned up against the cars and chatted about the old resort and whether or not it would really be worth such a long buggy ride up what looked like logging roads and felt like mountain goat tracks, Bitty banged on the cabin door.

"Whoever is in there, you are on private property! You are trespassing! Come out here at once!"

Deelight Tillman looked from the cabin over to me and asked, "Do you know where we are, Trinket?"

I shrugged. "Only Bitty knows, apparently. And she doesn't sound pleased that someone else beat her here. Whose car is that?"

Rayna looked at it with a slight frown. "I've seen that car recently, but for the life of me, I cannot think where."

Keys rattled, and Bitty shouted that she was coming in and they'd better be getting out. Wherever we were, Bitty had keys to it. The cabin didn't look old; in fact, it seemed to be fairly new. It had obviously been here a few years, but not so long it would qualify for the historical register or even a new tin roof.

The window glass in the cabin door shuddered when Bitty flung it open, and it banged against the frame with a loud crack. Birds roosting in the pines shrieked and rose up into the air en masse. Crows. They're terrible scavengers, worse than buzzards in my opinion, because if their chosen meal isn't dead, they'll still eat it. At least most buzzards have the decency to wait.

I began to feel a bit uneasy. Bitty had disappeared into the cabin and I could hear her yelling at someone. She sounded furious. Whoever she was yelling at didn't do much shouting back. At least, I couldn't hear them. After a moment it got quiet. Too quiet.

Then an unearthly shriek that sounded worse than the crows came from the cabin, and we all burst into action. I started toward the cabin in a gait somewhat similar to that of a crab on a pier, since my knee throbbed from having hit the dashboard earlier. Beside me, Rayna ran much more gracefully—and faster—to leap up on the cabin porch ahead of me. Gaynelle and Cindy weren't far behind us, while Deelight huddled in a crouch on the ground next to Marcy Porter and Cady Lee. Sandra had disappeared.

Rayna, going into the cabin at a run, met Bitty coming out of the cabin at a run. They collided just inside the doorway. The impact knocked them both backwards. Bitty landed inside on the floor, and Rayna sprawled on the porch.

I had a stitch in my side from trying to run the hundred yards or so to the cabin and arrived out of breath and holding a hand to my ribs. Rayna looked dazed but okay. I lurched toward the still open door. Bitty had landed on her rear end, hard. It had obviously knocked the breath out of her. I hovered over her, hair straggling down in my face and my hand to my side, trying to talk but still struggling for breath. Gasping, I held out my other hand for her to grab.

She looked up at me and recoiled, then seemed to recognize me and took my hand. As I helped her to her feet, I heard Gaynelle call from outside, "Is it a bear, Bitty?"

Rayna sounded edgy "How many bears do you know that drive a Volkswagen Beetle?"

"It smells funny in here," Cindy commented as she sidled into the cabin.

I looked around. It was a nice cabin, as cabins in the woods go. It was open plan, with living room and kitchen on opposite sides, and a well-stocked bar dividing the room. Beyond the living area I could see a huge bed in a back room, but no sign of an intruder.

Bitty, still breathless from the impact with Rayna, clutched at me with her other hand. I could see she had smacked her mouth in the collision; blood dripped from her bottom lip. She said something unintelligible, and I shook my head.

"Catch your breath, honey. You've just got a split lip. We'll deal with whoever is trespassing."

I still sounded a bit wheezy myself, but apparently Bitty understood me because she shook her head vigorously.

"No! Me!"

"No, no, you need to rest and catch your breath," Gaynelle said in her best teacher voice, but this time it didn't work on Bitty.

She jerked away from me, but caught my wrist and dragged me toward the room with the bed in it. "No . . . me!" she got out again. "No . . . me!"

It wasn't until she had me all the way inside the bedroom that I saw what she was really saying.

A body lay lifelessly atop a comforter spread over the bed. Blond hair spilled atop white pillows, and the face turned toward me was purple and contorted. A silk scarf was knotted tightly around the neck.

Someone had strangled Naomi Spencer.

CHAPTER 7

Not all outings with Bitty end this way, though lately her ratio is rising. Sandra, who had gone back to the car to get her first aid kit, something she usually carries with her when traveling with Bitty, checked Naomi's vital signs and agreed that she was, indeed, dead. Since Sandra is a registered nurse, I tended to believe her.

Unfortunately, none of our cell phones worked on this hilltop thick with pine trees and crows. Rayna offered to drive down the hill until she could get a signal, and we all thought that was the best thing to do. The police would have to be called, of course. Since we were now in Benton County instead of Marshall County, the nearest sheriff would be from the county seat of Ashland.

Dazed, Bitty just nodded to everything that was suggested. That was how I knew she must be in shock.

"Should I make her some coffee?" I asked, but Gaynelle quickly said for me not to touch anything in the cabin.

"Fingerprints or evidence, you know. I don't have any coffee with me, but I do have something in the car for emergencies." She headed for her car, picking her way carefully down the rather steep slope covered in pine needles.

We were all out on the front porch, not really knowing where to sit or look or not look—it seemed incredible that Naomi Spencer was dead. Deelight echoed my thoughts.

"It's a Sunday," she observed in a soft voice as if afraid to disturb anyone. "It's not even noon yet. She can't be dead. Why, she's . . . she's so young."

I don't know what Cindy must have been thinking, especially with Bitty sitting right there on the porch with us and all, but the moment Cindy started to say, "Well, the good always die young," Bitty leaped up from the porch with an angry shriek.

"Good? *Good?!* That little harpy shouldn't even know about this place, much less come here to be killed! *Ohhhhh!*"

The last was uttered with a frustrated, furious gritting of her teeth. She looked and sounded like a mad cat. If she had fur, it would be standing straight out. As it was, she stomped a foot and clenched her fists.

"Damn Philip Hollandale! This is all his fault!"

Thankfully, Gaynelle returned about that time with her emergency "coffee" and unscrewed the top. "Here. This should help."

Bitty took the bottle she held out and downed a healthy swig, then gave it back. I recognized the familiar scent of Jack Daniel's. Gaynelle took a drink then passed it to the rest of us. It's amazing what just a tiny bit of whiskey can do to calm the nerves.

Since Bitty seemed much calmer, I couldn't help asking, "How is this all Philip Hollandale's fault, Bitty?"

She sat back down on the porch, this time picking a bent-willow rocker despite the cushion being dirty and strewn with leaves. "Philip must have brought her here. She wouldn't know about it any other way, I'm sure."

"This is—was—his cabin, then?"

"No. This is my cabin. I had it built right before Philip and I married. It was where he and I could 'get away from it all' when we wanted to be alone. It was supposed to be our hideaway, and no one else was to know about it. This is where we spent our . . . our wedding night."

I remembered what Mama had said about Bitty grieving over Philip. If she loved him, this must be terribly painful for her. Although I was sitting on the porch floor with my legs hung over the side, I reached up to put a hand on her foot. It was the only part of her I could reach to offer comfort.

"And now those lovely memories have been ruined for you."

"Lovely? Hardly. The man was drunk as a sailor on leave and about as romantic. I had to hold his head while he puked in a bucket. And after I'd gone to so much trouble, too, with candles, and champagne, fresh flowers and silk sheets—good god! I hope those aren't my silk sheets on that bed!"

Ah. Bitty must be feeling better.

It was a good thing, since about the time we heard Rayna's SUV coming back up the goat track road, distant sirens could be heard as well. Ashland police were certainly on the ball.

Ashland, Mississippi is the only town in Benton County that has a traffic light. It's not a large town. It has a lovely old court house with a clock that doesn't work, a small library, a grocery store, a dollar store, a motel/Laundromat built sometime back in the 1940s, and various other small businesses scattered here and there. Since this is the South, and we believe strongly in salvation, there are several churches in town, of course.

Brunetti and Brunetti has an office located on the court square there, too. That turned out to be a really good thing.

Across a vacant lot from the grocery and dollar stores sits the Ashland police station. It is a gray concrete block building. The new court house is on the other side of the police station a short distance and has all the modern amenities.

While we didn't have to travel with the police in handcuffs, our immediate presence at the police station as possible *witnesses*—which I translated to mean *suspects*—was greatly desired. On our way back down the steep hill from the cabin, the coroner's van pulled over to the side of the narrow road to let us pass. That was when the enormity of it all had really hit me.

Not only had we found a body, but it was the body of a young woman who used to date Bitty's husband, and with whom Bitty had publicly quarreled just the week before. Those were the unpleasant facts.

Déjà vu all over again.

As there were nine Divas in all and the station was rather small, we were parceled out to several officers for our interviews. It was disconcerting to be separated and seated in a very uncomfortable chair directly across from a uniformed officer and a tape recorder. I don't know which cop got the short straw and Bitty, but my interviewer must have had a terrible headache. He was decidedly grumpy.

"Let's hear it," he said, leaning back in his chair to glower at me from under eyebrows that resembled large black centipedes. "Wait a minute. The damn thing isn't working."

That was in reference to the tape recorder, I think. He punched a button and that must have fixed it, because he leaned back again and stuck his thumbs into his armpits. I just stared at him. Wasn't he supposed to ask questions?

"Name!" he shouted, and that made me jump a little.

"Whose name?" I asked somewhat frantically.

I'm not normally obtuse. In fact, I can usually grasp a situation fairly quickly. If not frightened out of my wits by having just seen the dead body of a murder victim I knew, I might have already picked up on the fact he wanted my name.

The officer heaved a great sigh that sounded disgusted and rubbed at his eyes with thumb and forefinger. I heard him mutter, "Why do I always get the crazies?" but I pretended he was talking about someone else.

"My name," I said with what dignity I could muster, "is Trinket Truevine, and I'm from Holly Springs. We, my friends and I, went for a Sunday drive out to my cousin's cabin, where we found . . . Naomi Spencer. She was dead."

The officer scribbled something on a notepad. Apparently a tape recording wouldn't be enough to try and hang me. I assumed that was what he intended to do. And really, I couldn't blame him. Much. After all, Ashland is only fifteen miles from Holly Springs. They get *The South*

Reporter, too, and would know all about the death of Race Champion and Naomi's arrest. And if the police read Miranda's gossip column, they'd know all about the Dixie Divas as well.

"Why were you going to the cabin?" he asked without looking at me.

"It's a nice day, and we decided to have a get-together."

"In a remote cabin?"

This time he looked up at me. His brows crowded his eyes like fuzzy caterpillars. This camouflage didn't fool me. I knew he was watching me carefully.

"Sometimes we just like to get out of town for a while."

"Right." He sat back in his chair and studied me until I began to feel like a bug under a microscope. Since my roots needed a touch-up and I'd just pulled my hair back with a barrette, I probably looked somewhat like a bug. Not that it mattered. I've learned that the police don't care who you are or what you look like if you're suspected of being involved in a crime.

"How well did you know the victim?" he asked next.

"Not well at all. I've met her a few times here and there, of course, but we were not friends of any kind."

"Would you say you were enemies?"

"Of course not!"

"What was your relationship?"

"Acquaintances. None of us know her well."

He squinted at me. "She must have known you well enough to join your day out at the cabin."

"No, we had no idea she would be there. It was a complete surprise. In every sense of the word, I might add."

"Who found the body?"

"My cousin, Elisabeth Hollandale."

"Were you with her at the time?"

"I was just outside the cabin with the others."

"Name the others."

I reeled off the list of names as best I could. By now my palms were sweaty, my all-day deodorant had expired, and my knees had gotten shaky. It was obvious he was doing the math: Bitty plus Naomi equals trouble. Bitty plus friends plus Naomi equals a lot of trouble.

"You're part of this club, the Ditsy Divas, right?" he asked out of the blue, and I got a little indignant.

"It's the *Dixie* Divas!"

"Hunh," he grunted, which I took to mean he apologized for his mistake, so I said he was excused.

At that he sat back in his chair and stared at me for a long, long moment. I began to fidget. Really, he could be quite unnerving. Not just because he was gruff, but because he wore a badge. Not to mention a gun. It was the gun that could be most unnerving. I did my best to look not only innocent, but harmless.

But he only asked me where I worked, if my address was current, did I have a cell phone where I could be reached, and then stood up.

"We may have more questions later. If we do, we'll be in touch."

"So I can leave?" I said hopefully.

He stepped to the open door and motioned me through it, rather impatiently I thought. "Please," was all he said, and I was relieved.

It could have been worse. Much worse. That was why I'd argued for telling the truth. Not the *complete* truth, mind you, but the simple facts. We'd discussed it on the ride down that rutted road, and called Rayna and Gaynelle to be sure we were all on the same page. We were to tell the truth. With a caveat: No one need know all the details about a secret meeting to make plans on investigating if Trina Madewell had a hand in the murder of Naomi's fiancé. That would only complicate matters.

So imagine my surprise when I was finally returned to what must have been the holding area for deranged witnesses to find Cady Lee chatting up a complete stranger and telling all the details of our excursion. The complete stranger wore a tan blouse that said *Ashland Police* on an arm badge, but she looked quite nice and sympathetic to what Cady Lee was telling her.

"Yes, I read that article," she was saying as she smiled at Cady Lee, and I knew then we were all dead ducks.

"Well, it was just *awful*," Cady Lee said with a mournful shake of her head, and I felt like pushing her out of the chair and onto the floor. "It wasn't at all like Miranda made it out to be. Bitty's dog jumped in the middle of the tea tray, and food went just everywhere—have you ever tried to get pimento cheese out of white linen? It never comes completely out, you know."

"So that is when you all decided to have a secret meeting at the cabin?" the officer prodded tactfully.

"Oh no, not right then. That came later, after the article came out. Bitty was just fit to be tied, you know. I thought for sure she would shoot either Trina or Miranda, but—"

"But Bitty would never do anything like that," I put in from the doorway, and both of them turned to look at me. The police woman frowned, but Cady Lee looked a bit relieved.

"Trinket, tell this lady just how it came about that we decided to meet secretly. I can't recall."

As I got close enough, I smelled the strong odor of Gaynelle's emergency "coffee" on Cady Lee's breath. Ah. That explained it somewhat. Cady Lee had ridden back down the hill with Gaynelle while Sandra Dobson rode with Bitty, Cindy and me. Since Sandra is a registered nurse and we thought Bitty just might come unglued, it seemed the best thing to do at the time. So much for best-laid plans. At the best of times Cady Lee has a big mouth. With it well-lubricated by Jack Daniel's she had probably told this woman everything and anything she asked. Time for damage control.

"Oh Cady Lee, you know how Bitty loves to keep us all guessing what she's up to most of the time. Going out to her cabin was just a surprise for all of us."

And how! I added silently.

"Are you through interviewing us, officer?" I asked sweetly in the hopes that she would say yes.

Cady Lee turned a rather surprised gaze toward the woman, as if just figuring out she'd been talking to an officer of the law. She must really be bombed. Stress and whiskey don't always combine well.

Before the officer could respond, a familiar drawling voice behind me ended my suspense. "Hey there, Lucy, you through talking to my best clients?"

Jackson Lee. Thank god! While I had no idea how he'd gotten here so quickly, I had no doubt that we were now in good hands.

"You representing *all* these ladies, Jackson Lee?" the officer named Lucy asked with a wry smile.

"You know I have lots of clients, especially the pretty ones," came his easy reply.

Jackson Lee Brunetti is one of the most charming southern lawyers anyone could ever meet. Bitty has always said he can charm the bark off trees when he sets his mind to it, and after having seen him in action a time or two, I became a believer. He's one of those big men who can look elegant in an Italian suit, and just as good in a flannel shirt, Levi's, and cowboy boots covered in cow manure. In fact, the latter was just how I'd met him a few months ago. He hadn't impressed me at first, but that changed quickly.

So I gave a sigh of relief when he slid one arm around my shoulders, helped Cady Lee to her feet with the other, and headed us toward the hallway.

"We'll be glad to answer any more questions you may have once I've conferred with my clients," he said to Officer Lucy on the way out, and I wasn't at all surprised when he got all nine of us "sprung" within five minutes.

We gathered in the gravel parking lot outside the white concrete block building for a few minutes while Jackson Lee gave us instructions on what not to say and who not to say it to. Then he looked at Bitty and back at me. I tried to avoid what was probably coming my way by turning to squint across the street. An old dog ambled across the road toward our group or the garbage cans, I wasn't sure which.

"Trinket, you know how much I trust you," he began charmingly, and I started to back away as if I hadn't heard. He forestalled that option by quickly looping his arm through mine and drawing me closer to Bitty. "I think it's best if you go on home with Miss Bitty to make sure she's all right."

I knew exactly what he meant. The last time Bitty had been accused of murder I'd been given the unenviable position as her guard dog. Not to keep her safe from harm by some skulking criminal, but to keep her safe from her own mouth. You may have noted that Bitty has a tendency to say . . . unusual . . . things. It's even worse when she's under pressure.

"Jackson Lee," I said after taking a deep breath, "I am not a miracle worker."

"Sure you are, honey," he said, giving me an encouraging squeeze on my arm. "I have faith in you."

Great. Just great.

As I opened my mouth to tell him that his faith in me was misplaced, church bells began to ring loudly. Apparently Sunday morning services were over, which meant church-goers would be leaving church, getting in their cars, and quite a few of them would pass by the police building on their way home to Sunday dinner. Did I really want to be seen arguing with a lawyer while in the company of possible "felons" like myself?

It seemed my fellow felons felt the same. A rush toward the cars ensued, and I was right along with them. Since my car was still in front of Bitty's house, I got into the Franklin Benz with her, Cindy, and Cady Lee. When we passed Jackson Lee, where he still stood in the parking lot, I waved at him.

I was feeling like I'd just escaped a bullet when Bitty said, "Ashland police must be idiots. They actually asked me if I killed Naomi. Not that I wouldn't if I'd the chance, of course. I just didn't know where she'd gone after she made bail. Do you think Billy Don paid her bail? I know he's her brother, but I still think those two were a bit too close, if you know what I mean."

I knew what she meant. So would anyone else with half a brain cell left.

"Bitty, do you ever stop to think that the things you say might be misunderstood by some people?"

She looked at me, startled. "Did you understand what I just said? I thought so. If you understood me, Trinket, so can anyone else. Why do you think I said it?"

"Because you have a death wish. Stop sign."

"Really, you say the damnedest things sometimes. Then you go and accuse me of not being—"

"Stop sign!"

"—clear enough when I speak. I'll have you know that I took elocution classes—"

"Bitty!" I shrieked, *"stop sign!"* A blast of noise from an air horn cut through the air much too close to our car.

"—at Ole Miss—omigod!" Bitty wrenched the wheel of the Benz hard to the left and stomped the brakes, but the heavy car kept hurtling through the stop sign, across the two-lane highway and into the gravel parking lot of an antique and junk store. Dust rose in a cloud, and a passing log truck laid hard on its air horn as it barreled down the highway. A millisecond faster and it would have clipped the rear of our car.

It being a Sunday, no cars were in the parking lot. We'd come to a halt only a couple inches from the edge of a front porch filled with old dressers, bed frames, and cast iron stoves. I sat quietly while Bitty held on to the steering wheel and breathed hard through her nose. In the back seat, someone whimpered, but nothing was said.

I may have mentioned that Bitty has amazing powers of recovery when she chooses. She gave a brief shake of her head, cleared her throat, and said, "I'll have to remember to start carrying emergency coffee with me when I leave home."

We wheeled out of the empty parking lot, back up onto Highway 5, and tooled past the abandoned nursing home and the health clinic, on down to the junction of Highway 4. As we headed west and picked up speed, I knew that whether I'd actually promised Jackson Lee or not, *some*one would have to stay with Bitty to keep her from talking herself right into jail.

Maybe I could talk Mama into it.

CHAPTER 8

Normally, my mother is one of the most cooperative, sweetest individuals you would ever want to meet. Occasionally, however, she reveals that beneath her sugary exterior beats the heart of a mule.

"I said no, and I meant no, Trinket."

As usual, Mama did not raise her voice. She sounded perfectly reasonable and calm, while I felt the wings of panic beating against my ears.

"But Mama, Bitty always listens to you. She respects you. She regards me as a co-conspirator and thus foists impossible schemes on me."

Mama bent a stern gaze toward me. "That is because you are usually quite agreeable to her impossible schemes. It has always been this way. I thought by now you would have learned better, but it seems Bitty is still able to coax you into overriding your natural common sense."

While at the same time I appreciated my mother thinking—or saying—that I have some natural common sense, I cringed at the implied rebuke that I'd still not learned any better than to go along with my dear cousin's nutty antics. So I resorted to wheedling.

"If you'll share Bitty-duty with me, I won't say one word in complaint when you and Daddy take your next trip."

Wheedling works no better now than it did when I was fifteen.

"Thank you, dear, but your father and I aren't planning any trips in the near future."

Foiled again.

I flopped down in a chair at our kitchen table and slumped over my cereal. Snap, Crackle and Pop had gone silent. My coffee was probably cold, too. What had seemed such excellent argument while lying in bed the night before had fallen flat. I was consigned to fulltime Bitty-duty.

Now, I love my cousin dearly. She is wonderful and witty and fun, and all good things—in small doses. Enforced Bitty-time, however, can be hard on my ears. And my nerves. Not that Six Chimneys isn't a lovely antebellum home with all the modern amenities, and within walking distance of Rayna's if I feel energetic enough. It is. I always enjoy visiting. Boarding there, however, is less enjoyable.

Besides, Mama is right. I always end up joining in whatever idiotic thing Bitty does, whether I'm right under her nose or in my own bedroom at Cherryhill. There must be a twelve-step program for people like me. Holly Springs probably has its own chapter; Bitty Hollandale Anonymous. Most likely, however, the Ashland police officer had it right: Ditsy Divas.

About the time Daddy came in the back door from feeding cats, saw me gazing glumly at my cereal and asked if I was getting a summer cold, too, the kitchen phone rang. Mama answered it, and Brownie took the opportunity to nudge my knee in hopes of getting a piece of toast or the rest of my cereal. I gave him half a slice of buttered toast. I had lost my appetite anyway.

"No, I'm not getting sick," I answered my father. "Nothing that minor."

His brow rose as he crossed to the kitchen sink to wash his hands. "All that mess from yesterday is on your mind, I guess."

"Oh yes. Is it just me, or has Bitty become a magnet for murder?"

Daddy grinned. He shook his hands free of water and reached for the towel that hung on a small hook over the sink. "Bitty has always been a magnet for trouble. Maybe she's branched out since you came home."

"Lucky me. It does not bode well for the rest of my life if in the first six months I'm home, four people we know end up dead."

"Well," Daddy said thoughtfully, "it's not as if *you* knew any of them well. Or at all."

"But I seem to get mixed up in it anyway. Imagine, I've gone all my life without people dropping dead around me, and I come back here and they hit the dirt like flies."

"Look at it this way, punkin. Holly Springs is not a huge town. Not like Memphis or New Orleans. People you know are bound to die eventually."

"Yes, but not by gunshot or strangulation. You must admit the murder rate has probably tripled in the last six months."

"Probably. But this last one won't be counted in Marshall County. It happened in Benton County."

"Well, there's a ray of sunshine," I said gloomily. "The Marshall County police must be ecstatic."

Daddy just laughed and hugged me around the shoulders, then wandered into the living room to watch TV. Morning news, no doubt. Hopefully none of this had made the national media like last time. Bitty and I had been beamed all across America and eight foreign countries when we'd attended Philip Hollandale's funeral. The fact he had been a United States senator was reason enough, but the scuffle in the church between Bitty and the late senator's sister had been prime-time newsworthy. Afterward, Bitty had received several marriage proposals in the mail, most of them from men incarcerated in American prisons, but a few from overseas. Apparently, being a rich widow and still lively enough to trade licks with another woman entices a certain male element.

Mama hung up the phone and returned to the kitchen with it. Even though it's a cordless phone and quite capable of service if not returned to the cradle after every call, my parents treat it as if it is one of those old black box phones with a rotary dial and a long cord.

"That was Bitty," Mama said. Then she stopped in the middle of the kitchen and looked down at her dog. He looked back at her. His tail thumped happily against old pine floorboards, and a piece of crust hung crookedly from his jaws. "Did you feed him people food, Eureka May Truevine?"

Without waiting for my denial, she scolded, "You know he's on a restricted diet and should eat only proper dog food."

"Yes, ma'am."

Anytime my mother uses my full name I know I'm on her bad side. I looked down at Brownie. He has a dachshund head and coloring, but the body type of a beagle. And the loud bay of a bloodhound in full hunting mode when he spots a squirrel or bird trespassing in our yard. He is also a treacherous little beast when the occasion calls for it. As it did now, apparently.

He dropped the toast crust, his ears lowered, and looked up at my mother with a mournful gaze. Then he lay down on the floor and put his head between his paws. He really knows how to get to her. I would have tried it myself if I thought it'd work for me. However, I have my own methods.

"What did Bitty want?" I asked. "I take it she's home from staying the night with Rayna and is expecting me, right?"

"She said not to come."

Hope danced before my eyes. "Not come? Okay. Did she say why?"

"Yes. Brandon and Clayton are home from Florida."

"Why doesn't that comfort me?" I wondered aloud, and Mama patted the side of her leg to tell Brownie that all was forgiven. He immediately jumped up, barked, and did a circle dance as if reprieved from a long prison sentence. Maybe I should try that next time I get reprieved from babysitting Bitty. It expresses so much without words.

"You're still going, of course," Mama said once she had rewarded Brownie with a special dog treat for his dance of joy.

"No, I'm not. Not if her boys are there. They're grown now and fully capable of watching her mouth."

I got up from the table, put my dirty dishes in the dishwasher, wiped crumbs from the table, threw away the toast crust still on the floor, then looked at my mother. She wore a small frown.

"Still," she said slowly, "it might be best if a real adult were there."

"If you're sure you want to go," I said cheerfully, "I'll be glad to drop you off on my way to town."

To demonstrate my newfound joy in the day, I mimicked Brownie's dance of joy around the table, complete with the little hop at the finish. Mama laughed, and I got out of there before she could wrangle me into sacrificing my sanity. Or what's left of it.

Once up in my bedroom, I chose my attire for the day rather carefully. Someone had recently mentioned that there was an opening for a clerk at the lingerie shop in the town square. Normally, I wouldn't be interested. After all, I'd been a rather nicely paid glorified secretary in my former career, working in the hospitality industry all across the continental United States. I'd done everything from reception desk clerk to personnel, to filing insurance claims on Workmen's Comp. I'd conducted employee initiation days, tours, and worked in banquet departments or for executives, depending on what part of the country and how desperate I was to work. I was usually pretty desperate since my ex—Perry Berryman—was a charming rogue with great abs but the work ethic of a sloth. Well, maybe not that bad. I'm just bitter. Or so Bitty tells me. She could be right. Bitter or not, Perry always found work several hundred miles from wherever we were living at the time. Staying in one place too long bored him. And the next place would be "the one" he'd always swear was our perfect paradise.

After living in the middle of the desert, where even the wind was hot and the rain non-existent, we moved to the top of a mountain where we were snow-bound all winter. I worked at a nearby lodge and Perry taught skiing on the Bunny slopes, and when the spring-thaw came, we headed back down the mountain. Once he got a job logging in the wilderness of Idaho. I got a job at a motel in the valley, and we saw each other every other week-end when he'd stagger down from the mountain with his paycheck. Since I worked at the motel, we had a room there rent-free. That was good, because the pay was nothing to write home about. That had been not long after Michelle was born, and it worked out okay until she started walking.

Thankfully, Michelle is now grown, married, and living in Atlanta, and I am free to work wherever I please, as long as it's within reasonable commuting distance from my parents. After all, they're the reason I came home. Or so they like to remind me when I find out they've planned another trip that will leave me with the cats and Brownie.

But I digress.

It seemed that Carolann Barnett had put a sign in her shop window advertising for help. While it's a lovely lingerie shop, she also sells gifts and books. Most of the gifts are the usual things, like pretty little jewelry boxes, bath sets, soaps, and so on, and the books are almost all romance novels. There's a certain rationale that lingerie and romance go together.

I would have to take a refresher course on that. My idea of romance—until lately—has been going to bed in a tee shirt three sizes too big and a pair of loose boxer shorts, with a good book and a box of Junior Mints. Now I'm a bit confused as to what my idea of romance is, because Kit and I are still dancing around the edges of that. Like me, he prefers to take things slowly. Thank heavens.

At any rate, a part-time job would fulfill two main requirements: I would earn a bit of extra money which I definitely need, and it would also fill up my free time. Seeing as how my parents and Bitty are determined to keep me busy schlepping after dogs, cats, crazy and/or dead people, I'd decided that it would be to my advantage to say quite truthfully, "I'm working."

This would also keep me from being involved in any of Bitty's schemes, and give me a great excuse not to be included in any secret meeting where a body might pop up. It sounded perfect.

So I showed up in front of Carolann's shop wearing a nice, cool cotton blouse and pair of freshly-pressed pants. I stood there a moment looking in the window that faces the courthouse square. Exquisitely designed nightgowns, robes, slippers, and teddies draped over headless mannequins. Sheer silk, embroidered satin, lace, ribbons, and all manner of feminine nightwear and underwear could be glimpsed beyond the artfully arranged front window. Taped to the lower part of the window was a 'HELP WANTED' sign. I took a deep breath, pushed open the front door, and entered the shop.

It was crazy, but butterflies fluttered in my stomach as if I was a teenager again applying for an after-school job. A pretty blond girl met me not far inside, coming to where I stood gazing in awe at the racks and shelves filled with gorgeous garments.

"May I help you?" she inquired in a soft voice that would be right at home in a library.

"Yes," I answered in a voice that automatically lowered to match hers. I don't know why. It just seemed appropriate. "I understand you have a position open for a sales clerk." She stared at me blankly, so I added helpfully, "There's a sign in the window."

"Oh, why . . . let me get Miz Barnett."

As she retreated to the rear of the store, I wandered around. One look at the price tags let me know these things were probably out of my price range. I have a dollar store budget these days. Gift items were arranged here and there atop glass tables or tucked between stacks of lingerie. A lovely fragrance filled the air, probably from all the lit candles and potpourri. Off to one side, blue velvet curtains swagged over a doorway, and I went through it to see if maybe this would be the bargain side of the shop.

Instead of bargains, I found myself in . . . well, a very interesting section. Discreet arrangements of penises sat perkily upon a black velvet covered shelf just to my right. It took me quite by surprise, and I jumped back and said something that sounded like, "Eek!" in a louder than library tone of voice.

"Are you unwell?" someone behind me asked, and I whirled around as if I had been caught peeping in a stranger's window.

"Oh no . . . well, this is . . . I think I came in here by mistake."

Tall, composed, elegantly dressed, the owner of the voice just smiled. "Indeed?"

While I floundered around for something to say that wouldn't sound too foolish, the cool blond stepped aside as another woman hurried toward me. Dressed like a hippie from the 70s, this woman had wild, curly red hair that made an A-frame around her head.

"Good god, Rose, don't tell me you've frightened another customer!" she shouted. Lunging toward me, the woman stuck out her hand. "Carolann Barnett. Heather tells me you've come in to apply for the sales position?"

I took her hand and nodded. Carolann Barnett certainly did not speak in a library voice. In fact, her voice was so loud I think I saw one of the penises fall over. I didn't want to look, though, so I could be mistaken about that.

"Yes," I began, but she shook her head.

"Sorry. I filled it two days ago. Don't I know you?"

I hesitated. Relief that the position was already filled was somewhat startling, but in light of the, uh, decorations in the room where we stood, I didn't think I was qualified to be a sales clerk. Common wisdom demands that one must know something about the merchandise being sold, and I'd never seen anything quite like those fully erect rubber penises in my entire life. Not once. Thank god. They're frightening.

Carolann snapped her fingers. "Wait. You're Trinket, aren't you? Emerald's twin sister?"

Since Emerald and I look nothing alike, I was rather surprised she knew that, but I nodded. "Yes."

"Emerald and I were best friends in junior high. My maiden name is Lewis. I moved away for a while, then moved back here after I got married. I heard you were back in town. Aren't you one of the Divas?"

Feeling rather like I'd stepped into a minefield, I slowly nodded. The woman she'd referred to as Rose looked at me with a lifted brow. She had a cool expression that let me know she didn't approve of the Divas.

Carolann said, "I thought you were. You're Bitty's cousin. Bitty used to come in here a lot when she was married to the senator, but I don't see her much anymore. Rose is my business partner. It was her idea to add the Blue Room. What do you think?"

The Blue Room must be where we were. I turned away from the shelf holding the row of penises standing at attention like little soldiers wearing hats, and tried to focus my gaze elsewhere. It was difficult. Crotchless panties in red satin trimmed with black lace were pinned to the opposite wall. Bras with a portion of the cups cut out hung right above the panties. A matching set. How nice. If you lived in a brothel. I tried to think of something tactful to say.

Books were stacked here and there, some on a shelf within my reach. Blindly, I grabbed one of them. "Romance novels are my favorite. I read them all the time. I'll take this one."

"That's the *Kama Sutra*. Rose keeps the romance novels over here." Carolann pointed to a shelf attached to the wall below the penises.

I froze. I just couldn't look. If I went to that shelf and one of those penises fell on my head, I would run screaming out of the shop and everyone would know I'd been in there. Or in the Blue Room, anyway. *How can a woman who looks so cool and elegant and acts so snooty stock a room with rainbow-colored penises?* I wondered wildly.

As if sensing my predicament, the young girl, who'd met me when I first came into the store, stepped from behind Rose and took the book from my hand. She gave me a big smile, and I noticed again how pretty and young she was.

"I read romances all the time," she said in that same, soft voice, "so let me pick one out for you, okay?"

"Sure you're old enough?" I joked, and she laughed.

"Old enough to vote, thank you. Here you go. It's a historical romance. I think you'll really enjoy it."

"Do you mind checking her out, Heather?" Carolann boomed. "I'm still opening boxes of new merchandise."

"Sure thing, Miz B. I'll take care of the front while you take care of the back."

"Good girl! Glad I hired you. Oh." Carolann gave me a guilty glance, and I shook my head.

"I can only work part-time anyway, so it's just as well."

Carolann looked relieved. She was pretty in a flamboyant sort of way, with her mass of unruly curls waving all around her head and shoulders as if having a life of their own. She was almost my age, but somehow she had never left the 70s. She wore a tunic and long skirt, and several strands of beads around her neck. One strand held the emblem for a peace sign. Another held a glittery rainbow.

"That's good. Come back again, Trinket. Get something for Emerald. I'll pick it out for you, if you like. She'd love this room." A loud burst of laughter followed that comment, and made me wonder if there was a lot I didn't know about my sister.

Then Carolann leaned a bit closer to me and said in a loud whisper, "Maybe you can tell me the real story behind what I read in the papers next time we meet, too. I bet it's a lot more interesting than what I've already heard."

I mumbled, "Uh, yeah, sure. Next time. Maybe."

"Good!" she said.

With a wave of her hand, Carolann disappeared back into the main part of the store and the room seemed much quieter. At some point, Rose had slipped away, and I was rather glad. She couldn't have been forty, but she gave me the impression of an old-maid schoolteacher. Or a nun. With a peculiar penchant for penises.

Heather checked me out. I left the store with my romance novel, got into my car, and drove straight to Bitty's house. I had questions about the Blue Room and its merchandise that needed answers only she could provide.

As I rather expected, Bitty's house was rocking. I sat in my car for a moment. If Six Chimneys had been a cartoon, the house would literally be bulging at the sides and rocking from side to side. Since it's not a cartoon, only the doors were swinging. It looked like a conga line of kids coming in and out the front door. Cars were parked in the double driveway all the way up to the garage, resembling a used car lot.

It occurred to me that getting Bitty's undivided attention wasn't going to be possible unless I dragged her into one of the bathrooms and locked the door. Even then it might not work. As always when Brandon and Clayton are in residence, they attract friends in large numbers. Like packs of dogs, they scavenge Bitty's house for food, then leave a mess behind when they go. I find it amazing that she allows it, but she's just so happy when her boys are home.

Maybe Bitty is one of those people who has to have a lot of distraction in her life. Me, I could go for a month alone on a desert isle and still be miffed if I saw a rescue boat coming my way. The solitude would be heavenly. Bitty always has people around her. So I guess for her it's just normal and fine to allow roaming packs of wild young people run around her house. My head had already started throbbing and I hadn't even gotten out of my car yet.

While I debated the wisdom of going inside, one of Bitty's boys came up from behind and opened my car door. Since I'd already unbuckled my seat belt and was leaning against the door, I nearly fell out, but he caught me under the arms.

"Whoa there, Aunt Trinket! Have you been drinking?"

"No," I said a bit crossly since I was embarrassed, "but I think I'll start right now. Which one are you?"

He grinned. Brandon and Clayton are identical twins, both blond like their mother but tall like their father, and very handsome young men.

"Brandon. Want me to fix you a drink?"

I thought about it for a millisecond. "Yes. Something strong. Whatever Bitty is drinking."

"Mama is drinking sweet tea."

That stopped me. I turned to look at him with what must have been an incredulous expression. He nodded.

"It's true. Nothing but sweet tea. Except for some pretty strong coffee earlier."

"Is she sick?"

What I really meant was, *Is she hung over*, but as it's rather rude to ask him that about his mother, I used tact.

"No, ma'am. She's just fine." Brandon is an astute young man and knew exactly what I had asked him, and as we walked through the iron gate and up to the front porch, he said, "We got in late last night and called her to find out where she was, and she told us what happened. She was staying the night with Rayna, but came right over when she found out we're home. We stayed up late talking."

"How is she doing after . . . everything?"

"Pretty good, considering the shock of finding Naomi's body. I think she feels a little guilty. You know, after saying all those mean things about her."

Guilty? Bitty? I doubted that, but then, stranger things have happened.

Not that Bitty is mean or malicious. There's not a truly mean bone in her body. If she has been wronged, however, she feels it keenly and is not shy about telling people what's on her mind. While it's not nice to speak ill of the dead, Naomi Spencer did do Bitty terribly wrong.

It was a point I was certain the police would investigate, unfortunately.

To my surprise, Gaynelle was sitting in the parlor with Bitty. They both had their shoes off and feet up on ottomans, and looked totally relaxed. Since I was anything but relaxed, and not at all sure I wanted to ask Bitty questions with anyone else around, I sat down on the edge of a sofa to indicate I wasn't staying long.

"Aunt Anna said you were really stressed out," Bitty remarked. "Are you feeling better now?"

"A little, yes." How nice of my mother to run interference for me. And she hadn't even said anything to me about it. "How are you doing? And you, Gaynelle?"

Bitty waved a hand dramatically. "It's been dreadful! The phone hasn't stopped ringing—how many people have called, do you think, Gaynelle, just since you've been here?"

"At least ten or twelve. I stopped counting after eight. Nosy gossips, all they want is information they can spread around town."

Gaynelle looked downright disapproving. I completely understood. Friends and family members you haven't heard from in ages always seem to remember your phone number when you come into money or are involved in scandals. Like murder.

"It was just the same way when Philip and I were getting a divorce," said Bitty. "And of course, when he went and got himself murdered, it was even worse. So many people called—Trinket do you remember our cousin Jobert? Well, he's my cousin on my mama's side, but he always showed up at the family reunions and we had to be nice and play with him. He was the one that talked me into climbing up that big ole oak tree and then took away the ladder."

"Oh yeah, I remember him. Skinny kid who always wore suspenders. Everybody was out looking for you for hours, and he never said anything about you being stuck up in that tree. If not for my daddy hearing you pitching a hissy fit up on that tree limb, we might never have found you."

"I was so mad! And Mama wouldn't let me hit him or anything. She said we had to feel sorry for anyone mean enough to do that sort of thing and pray for him." Bitty slid me a wicked smile. "I prayed he wouldn't come back to anymore of our reunions. It worked, too."

"Not that prayer doesn't work," I said, "but he didn't come back because your daddy threatened to whip him with a hickory switch if he ever did anything like that again."

"Oh. Well, anyway, Jobert had the nerve to call me after Philip died. Said he knew I must have come into a lot of money and asked if I'd be interested in investing in some new invention of his."

"I hope you told him no," Gaynelle said.

"You bet I did. I told him I hadn't just fallen off the watermelon wagon, and he wouldn't ever get another chance to trick me again."

Bitty sounded quite satisfied with herself. I waited patiently for whatever this waltz down memory lane had to do with the present. Surely, there must be a reason for her bringing this up now.

"So what on earth does your cousin Jobert have to do with anything?" Gaynelle wanted to know. "Or are we just wandering through past injustices to feel better?"

Chen Ling, who had been sitting in Bitty's lap, sat up with a yawn. She has a really long tongue, and it curls up over her face when she yawns. Kind of cute, in a doggy sort of way.

"Even Chitling is bored by that story," I said to prod Bitty into connecting the dots. "Did Jobert call you again?"

"No, of course not. He may be about as bright as a burned out light bulb, but he's not completely stupid. No, Jobert just made me think about Trina Madewell, that's all."

Gaynelle and I looked at each other. Then I asked, "Bitty, what's in your tea?"

"Lipton and sugar. Really, don't you see the connection? Jobert fooled me once, and even though it had been a long time ago, he still thought I'd be just as naïve. The same thing with Trina. She came to my tea thinking I'd still be as unsuspecting as I was when we were in the garden club together, and she'd be able to put one over on me."

After a moment of silence, I said, "Well, she seems to have done a pretty good job of it. Miranda's column was quite nasty."

Bitty waved a hand as if that didn't matter at all. Which made me quite certain she had spiked her tea.

"Even if Chen Ling hadn't knocked over the tea tray and you hadn't put whiskey in the teapot, she would have found something ugly to say. That's just her nature. But why did she come here? It couldn't be just curiosity, could it? I mean, I know I said that her curiosity would get the better of her and she'd want to go away and say mean things—although I had no idea she would go and have them printed in the paper for everyone to see—but thinking back on it, Race was found in her parents' cottage. Maybe Trina knew I'd dated him recently and thought I had something to do with his murder?"

She'd said the last as a question, and I shook my head. "That doesn't make any sense. What, did she think she'd show up here and you'd suddenly feel guilty and confess to killing him?"

"Trinket's right," said Gaynelle thoughtfully. "There must be more to it than that."

"Or it could be as simple as Bitty first thought. Trina hasn't been inside Six Chimneys since losing the bid and she wanted to be able to tell everyone Bitty has atrocious taste. Then Trina actually got here, saw that Bitty's taste is impeccable," I quickly added when Bitty made an indignant sound, "and so Trina had to go and exaggerate about what happened."

Somewhat mollified, Bitty nodded. "That could be it, of course. Still, now that I think about it, it seems odd that Trina would show up. She was so pleasant on the phone when I called to invite her, though she did sound shocked at first, that it was probably to cover up some deep, dark reason for accepting."

I looked at her. "Bitty, *you* had a deep, dark reason for inviting her."

"Not really. I mean, yes, I did have a reason, but just so we could all find out what happened when Race was shot. And we do know more details now than we did, you have to admit."

My thoughts went immediately to the image Trina had conjured up of how she'd found Race lying naked across the bed with his . . . business . . . standing at attention. That mental image brought back the recent shock of seeing a dozen rubber soldiers in all their erect glory. I had to fan my face, my cheeks burned so badly.

When I glanced at Bitty and Gaynelle, they had the same glazed eyes I figured I had, so I knew we were thinking along the same lines. I leaned forward and lowered my voice so none of the hundred or so kids running in and out of the house could overhear me.

"Bitty. Have you been . . . in Carolann Barnett's shop?"

She looked at me. "Of course I have. Wasn't I the one who told you she has a sign in her window looking for help?"

"Probably. But that's not what I mean. Have you ever been all through her shop? Lately? You know, in every room?"

"Every room? She has rooms? I don't know. I suppose. Why?"

I glanced at Gaynelle, who looked as clueless as Bitty as to where I was going with this, so I knew neither of them had been into the Blue Room. I briefly debated my choice of words.

"I was there today about the open position for clerk. It's been filled. But while I was there, I met her business partner."

"Rose Allgood. Yes, I'd heard they joined business ventures."

Allgood didn't seem quite the suitable name for Rose, but I ignored that and went on. "Rose seems to have stocked the shop with . . . ." Here I stopped. I couldn't think how to go on without either laughing out loud or cringing. No proper word came to me.

"With what, Trinket?" Gaynelle asked sharply, and I could imagine her doing the same thing to legions of school kids. It produced similar results. I blurted out the answer immediately.

"Dildos."

"What?"

"Dildos. You know. Imitation . . . man things."

"Imitation *man things*?" Bitty echoed, then started laughing.

I felt my face flush even redder, and heat beat its way down my neck to my chest and probably all the way to my toes. I should have listened to my better instincts and kept my mouth shut. I gathered what was left of my dignity and stood up to leave.

"Wait . . . Trinket . . . don't leave . . . ." Bitty gasped out between bouts of laughter. She put out a hand as if to stop me, and Chen Ling started barking. Even Gaynelle, who had to have heard almost everything in her years of teaching, was giggling.

I gave them my coolest glance and stuck my nose in the air. Definitely time to go. If even the dog was laughing—

"No . . . wait!" Bitty leaned toward me with her hand still outstretched, and her foot nudged Chen Ling. The dog fell off the ottoman and onto the plush rug spread over the wood floors. She barked even more furiously and seemed to blame me for her fall. Before I could move, the pug grabbed my pants leg with her three teeth and shook it like a rat.

"Call off your mutt," I said.

"Promise you won't . . . won't leave."

"I'll do no such thing. Chitling can go along for the ride if she doesn't let go."

"C'mon, Trinket, it just sounded so . . . so funny! Especially coming from you."

"I do live to entertain."

"Oh, lighten up. Or I'll . . . I'll smack you with . . . with . . .."

"A *man thing*?" Gaynelle chimed in, then dissolved into hysterical laughter. That set Bitty off, and she rolled to her back and drummed her heels on the ottoman. They both shrieked with laughter, while Chitling mauled my pants leg and I stood there with my hands on my hips glaring at them.

They must have been making more noise than the pack of wild co-eds down in the basement playroom, because Brandon and Clayton appeared in the parlor doorway right behind me.

"Is everything okay?" Clayton asked. He hooked an arm on the door frame and leaned in to look at his mother. She was still beating her bare heels against the ottoman upholstery and laughing. It was very annoying.

"No," I said. "Your mother is having a seizure of some kind. She needs to be doused with a bucket of ice water immediately."

Clayton gave me an uncertain look while Brandon just grinned. Chen Ling still had hold of my pants leg, and I briefly considered lifting my leg high enough to give her vertigo. Or punt her back over to Bitty.

I did neither. It took great restraint.

Brandon nudged me. "What's so funny?"

"Your mama's face," I said, reverting to my grade school days. If Bitty heard me, she let it pass. She was still laughing and holding her sides.

"Want me to unhitch the dog from your pants?" Brandon asked instead of getting upset at my insult. He was used to Bitty and me by now. We trade insults a lot.

"That would be nice. Thank you."

Brandon bent down to untangle Chitling from the ruined hem of my slacks, and I saw Clayton slip away. Smart. He had no intention of remaining close enough to get in the line of fire.

"There you go, Aunt Trinket," said Brandon and stood up with the disgruntled dog under his arm. He grinned. "I think she needs to go outside, so I'll take her."

"Good idea. Careful. She pees randomly."

He stuck his arms straight out and carried Chitling toward the back door. I could hear her still growling all the way down the hall.

Gaynelle wiped tears from her eyes and shook her head. "Do stay, Trinket. You know it wasn't anything personal. You just had this *look* on your face when you said that—well, it was funny!"

I tried to sound as cool and composed as Rose Allgood. "So glad I can entertain you both."

"Get the stick out of your rear," said Bitty and patted the ottoman at her feet. "Then come over here and tell us about the, uh, merchandise in Carolann's shop."

"You don't deserve to know. You are both wicked, wicked people."

"So? You're one of us, my dear. Now come on. You know you're just dying to tell us all about it."

Because she was right, I made her coax me some more before I gave in, but I sat down in a chair just so she didn't get her way entirely. After I relayed the episode as best I could without going into too much detail, Bitty put a hand over her mouth.

It was Gaynelle who asked without laughing, "So, what book did you buy?"

"I have no idea. Heather—the girl Carolann just hired—picked it out for me. It has a half-naked man on the cover, that's all I know."

"Well," Bitty said after a moment, "I see that I must make a trip soon to buy some lingerie."

"You have more lingerie than Macy's," I said. "You just want to go look at . . . at the *man things*."

That started them off again, and this time I laughed with them. Really, thinking about it, it was kind of funny. As I got into the spirit of the moment, I said, "You should have just seen them, all lined up there like little soldiers in helmets, in all these different colors—"

"Different colors?" interrupted Gaynelle in a hushed tone, sounding shocked. "Well, I *never!*"

"Like a rainbow."

"Well, *I* never!"

I knew what Gaynelle meant. "Me neither."

"You ladies need a trip to the French Quarter," said Bitty, sitting up in her chair to reach for her tea glass. "Or out on Summer Avenue in Memphis."

"Why am I not shocked that you would know where to buy things like that?" I mused aloud, and Bitty just smiled.

"I am a woman of many interests. And I don't tell all I know, either."

Gaynelle snorted. "Yes, you do. Just not all at once."

Bitty nodded thoughtfully. "You're probably right. I could tell you things—"

I decided it was time to change the subject since it looked like Bitty was about to expand upon the nature of her many interests:

"Has anyone talked to the others since yesterday?"

"If you mean our cohorts in supposed crime, I have. They all called this morning to see how I'm doing. Really, just to see if I got arrested since Naomi and I haven't been the best of friends the past two years." Ice clinked in Bitty's tea glass. "Good thing I have an alibi."

"You do?" I asked, rather relieved to hear it. "What is your alibi?"

Bitty paused with her tea glass in front of her mouth. "I was with all of you, of course."

Gaynelle broke the bad news to her. "Bitty dear, that alibi will only be good if she was killed right before we got there."

The tea glass quivered slightly. "Oh. Well. I didn't do it, so I'm sure everything will be fine."

Gaynelle and I looked at each other. We were probably thinking the same thing: it wouldn't be the first time an innocent person was charged with a murder they didn't commit, and Bitty was a prime example.

Would lightning strike twice in the same place? I wasn't at all sure I wanted to know the answer to that.

CHAPTER 9

Fortunately for Bitty, Jackson Lee had already done some investigating and learned that she'd been on her phone quite a bit the night of the murder. That didn't definitely exclude her, but it made it unlikely she could have gone out to the cabin, murdered Naomi, and gotten back to Holly Springs between calls.

Unfortunately, it didn't remove her from the list of prime suspects, either. Police, I have discovered, are naturally suspicious creatures. They may not have been born with that skill refined, but their chosen careers definitely hone that particular personality trait to a fine edge. It can be very disconcerting.

Pinpointing the time of death—TOD, Sandra called it—is a delicate procedure. Naomi's body had been sent to the state medical examiner's office in Jackson, our state capitol, for more exact information. While none of the basic details were expected to alter a great deal, a final report would be delivered to the Ashland police. If the TOD was narrowed down to the hours during which Bitty slept, and thus had no record of being in her own home, that would greatly complicate her life. To say the least.

Like I said before, *Déjà vu all over again.*

"So what we have to do," Gaynelle said matter-of-factly, "is help the police find the real killer."

Most of the Divas sat in Gaynelle's living room, a rather small space decorated in cottage chic. It surprised me a bit, since I'd always figured Gaynelle for the minimalist kind of person, but it was a pleasant surprise since this was the first time I'd been inside Gaynelle's home. I appreciate the comfort and at-home kind of decorating much more than those modern homes that are all sleek lines and hard surfaces.

Anyway, there we were drinking sweet tea and eating chips and dip, and trying to figure out a way to get Bitty off the hook. I personally thought Gaynelle's plan unlikely to work and said so.

"It has come to my attention that police aren't necessarily grateful for help," I pointed out. "In fact, they tend to tell you to butt out if you offer suggestions."

Gaynelle gave me a stern look. "I never suggested going to the police, Trinket. I said *we* will have to find who killed Race, and that will most likely be the person who also killed Naomi."

Since I couldn't figure out how to say what was on my mind tactfully, I just said it bluntly: "I realize you feel you have to make it up to Bitty for what happened a few months ago, but you had nothing to do with killing the senator or Sanders."

"I know that. But I should have guessed what was happening instead of being so blind."

"We all should have, for that matter." Rayna leaned forward to pat Gaynelle on the arm. "Unfortunately, none of us are psychics."

Bitty sat up straighter in the big arm chair. "Oh! That's a great idea, Rayna! We'll go to a psychic!"

Sandra Dobson laughed, then apparently realized Bitty was serious and reached for the tortilla chips and cheese dip instead of saying what obviously had come to her mind.

To forestall Bitty's enthusiasm, I said quickly, "No, Bitty. No psychics. Maybe Gaynelle's right. Maybe we can figure out who killed Race and Naomi, but I want to make one thing clear: I will not be a part of it unless any information we get we turn over to the police at some point. If there's a deranged killer on the loose, I certainly don't want to end up alone with him somewhere."

"Now that's an angle I hadn't really considered," said Rayna. "I just assumed it was a woman who killed Race. You know, the whole love triangle thing. What if it was a man? Someone in Naomi's past who was angry because she got engaged to Race?"

"Then why would he kill *her* after Race was out of the way?" asked Deelight. She shook her head slowly. "That would defeat the whole purpose of killing Race."

"What if Naomi was there and saw him kill Race? She'd be a witness against him. Maybe she told him she was going to the police so he killed her." Cindy leaned forward. She sat on the comfortable sofa next to me, and I felt her tension as she gestured with a half-eaten chip. "He lured her out to the cabin with a promise of a night of passion, maybe, or to tell him he would leave, or wanted to beg her forgiveness—whatever excuse he used, she went out there and he strangled her!"

"You watch too many soaps," Cady Lee observed. "If Naomi knew he was a killer she'd be stupid to meet him anywhere."

"Well," said Bitty, "she *was* stupid." When we all looked at her she said, "What? Just because she's dead doesn't change the fact she was dumb as dirt. Bless her heart."

"Cady Lee's right," Gaynelle said after a moment. "Naomi wouldn't have gone to meet someone in such a deserted location if she was afraid of them. Fear trumps stupid every time."

"So either she went out there to be alone and hide, or she trusted this person." I thought about that a second and then added, "Or he followed her and surprised her."

"Yes, that last part makes the best sense, I think," Gaynelle said. "Whoever killed her must have snuck up on her and surprised her."

We all went silent for a few minutes, mulling over the options and no doubt thinking about how horrible Naomi's last minutes must have been. In something like this, it didn't really matter what kind of person she'd been; no one deserves to be murdered.

"Well," Bitty said after a moment, "she didn't put up much of a fight. I mean, the cabin looked pretty clean. Nothing broken, no chairs overturned, or anything like that. She was just lying on the bed with her face to the wall like she was asleep. It wasn't until I grabbed her shoulder to turn her toward me that I saw . . . saw she was dead."

To keep Bitty from dwelling on what must have been a horrible shock, no matter how she felt about Naomi, I said quickly, "Then she obviously didn't feel threatened by this person. Or they killed her while she was asleep."

Rayna leaned forward. "Bitty, think a minute. Did it look as if she'd tried to fight off anyone? I mean, were her nails broken or did she have cuts or bruises?"

Bitty gave Rayna a blank look, so it was Sandra who answered. "When I checked for a pulse, all I noticed was that she had a couple broken fingernails. She was lying atop the blankets, and if I remember correctly, she had on a nightgown. Not lingerie, but a plain cotton one, like you buy at Wal-Mart. It was sleeveless, I remember that."

"Wal-Mart sells *clothes?*"

Bitty's question let me know that she wasn't as traumatized as I'd feared. I gave her a reassuring smile. "Yes, dear. If you're a good girl, one day I'll take you there."

"Oh, I've been in Wal-Mart," Bitty lied. "Lots of times."

"Not shopping for clothes, I bet," Deelight said, and we all nodded in agreement. Even Bitty.

"Back to the murders, please." Gaynelle is really good at keeping us on track. "I've thought this over, and I have some ideas on how to proceed."

"Wait. Let me get some more tea," I said.

My conversational detour to the kitchen took us all in there, where we refilled tall glasses with sweet tea, replenished the chip bowl and dips, then returned to the cozy living room. White slipcovers drape over big comfy chairs, and the long sofa is one you just sink into so that it's hard to get up if you're pregnant or just have a big tummy. Thankfully, my stomach isn't quite that big yet, or I would have had to homestead Gaynelle's sofa. Blue and yellow are her predominant colors in the room, with wainscoting painted white and a soft yellow on the walls. Since it's an antebellum cottage, it has wonderful wood trim, also painted white, and dentil-detailed molding at the ceiling. Very clean and fresh looking, and not at all what I'd imagined Gaynelle would like. Just goes to show you, you cannot judge people by their appearances.

Gaynelle sat in one of the fat chairs with white slipcovers and blue toile pillows. She crossed her legs at the ankles, looking very much the prim and proper school teacher in her loose silk blouse, straight fitted skirt, and snazzy espadrilles. Well, maybe not so prim.

"Here is what I think we should do," she said. "We'll divide into groups of two or three. Each group should focus on one area of investigation only. Once a day we'll compare notes. Whatever has been discovered will be discussed and dissected, then we'll decide what's important and what's not."

She looked at me, and I knew what was coming.

"Trinket, you and Rayna will be with Bitty. Your plan is to talk to Trina or Trisha Madewell and see what you can find out about their relationships with Race Champion."

"Good god!" Bitty burst out. "Are you nuts? Trina Madewell? After what she did? I would rather just shoot her than have to talk to her."

Gaynelle pursed her lips disapprovingly. "That is one reason I decided you're to remain in the company of Rayna or Trinket most of the time. You have a lamentable tendency to act upon emotion rather than reason. You and Trina have a history. She'll most likely talk to you, and perhaps betray herself in the process."

Bitty muttered under her breath *Who died and left you in charge?* But I ignored it, as I'm glad anyone else who heard her did, too.

"Cindy," Gaynelle went on, "you and Deelight and Sandra live fairly close to one another, so I think you three should find out what you can from Naomi's family. If she had any ex-boyfriends with a temper who might stalk her, that sort of thing. Sometimes people will tell friends or neighbors what they would never tell police, so listen for any kind of off-the-wall comment that might be important."

"What do you consider an off-the-wall comment?" Deelight asked in between licking cheese dip off her fingers. It does have a tendency to drip, and no one wants to waste good cheese dip, especially when it's Pancho's.

"Oh, something along the lines of, 'Well, I told her not to date Leroy or whoever, but she didn't listen.' That sort of thing."

"So that leaves you, Cady Lee, and Marcy Porter," Bitty said. "What are you all going to do?"

"We will talk to Race Champion's family and current—or ex—girlfriends. That should keep us pretty busy. By the way, does anyone know how Marcy is doing? She's missed the last two Diva meetings. Not counting Sunday's excursion. Is she all right?"

"Yes and no," said Cindy. "Morning sickness."

"Ohhhh," most of us said in unison, but from different perspectives, I'm sure. My perspective is more like *Thank god it's not me.* I'm pretty sure Cindy and Deelight think it's sweet, but they've still got kids at home and haven't yet experienced the heady taste of freedom that comes with knowing you don't have to wipe dirty bottoms or deal with surly teenagers. Not that my daughter was ever surly. Well, not for long, anyway.

Gaynelle, ever the mistress of any and all situations, merely said, "I'll make sure I have plastic bags in the car."

"So when do we start this?" Rayna asked. "Some of us work or volunteer."

"We start tomorrow. Each team will choose their own times, but at ten each night we should be able to phone in our reports. Just write down things that you find out, and one of you call it in."

It sounded too much like high school to me. I wasn't at all sure I wanted anything to do with written reports. But when Rayna stood up and said, "Everyone agree?" we all stood up and lifted our tea glasses at the same time, bumping them together.

"Agreed!" I heard myself say in unison with the Divas.

It occurred to me that we may have all just agreed to put ourselves in danger of being run out of town on a rail. After all, some people get belligerent when asked nosy questions. Guns are prevalent in Mississippi. A lot of people carry, whether in their purse, pocket, or a rack in the back of their truck. Maybe Sherman Sanders had loaded his shotgun with rock salt pellets, but most people use live ammunition. Did I really want to go around knocking on doors and asking rude questions?

I would just have to do a Scarlett, I told myself, and worry about that tomorrow.

****

It didn't take Rayna, Bitty and me long to find out that Trina and Trisha Madewell did not regard our visit as polite. Or necessary.

We stood in the lobby of the large house turned bed and breakfast and did our best to appear non-threatening.

"Really," Rayna said, "we just wanted to correct the impression you must have gotten of us at Six Chimneys. We feel terrible you were frightened. It was all just a big misunderstanding. Wasn't it, Bitty. Bitty?"

A little belatedly, Bitty muttered, "Yes. Terrible. Misunderstanding."

I just stood there with a big fake smile on my face since I could think of nothing to say that wouldn't sound like a lie or ridiculous. Not that white lies and silliness have ever slowed me down before, but this was important. I didn't want to screw it up.

Trina Madewell looked at us with suspicion. Without all that make-up she'd worn to Six Chimneys, she was much nicer looking. She'd reminded me of Mimi, the overweight, over-made-up secretary on the Drew Carey show. I told you I watch a lot of TV, right? Anyway, with just the barest of foundation on her face, the wrinkles were less apparent, and she didn't look quite so . . . hard. Trisha must be "the pretty one" in the family. Every family of more than one child has one of those, it seems. The one who is prettiest, or smartest, or more athletic. Emerald's the one in my family who always stood out. Maybe that's why I felt I had to outdo her in other ways; not always the best ways, mind you, but I felt it my duty to be noticed. I had usually succeeded, much to my mother's dismay.

But I digress again.

There we were, standing in the lobby of Madewell Courts trying to schmooze bits of information out of the sisters. Surprisingly, it was Trisha who helped the most.

"If you're here to talk about the murder, just ask me what you want to know. I've already told the police everything that matters."

Since that was indeed why we were there, I appreciated her bluntness. Apparently her sister did not.

"Be quiet, Trisha!"

Trisha shrugged. She was about the same height as Trina, somewhere around five-four, I'd say, but much slimmer. And her hair hadn't been dyed lifeless, but was a soft brown, shiny, and cut in a flattering style around her face. She wore jeans and a pretty blouse and looked stylish, whereas poor Trina in her overdone silk dress seemed like a dollar store mannequin. It was a startling contrast in a way, because my understanding was that the Madewell family had money. At least, once upon a time. I know the house is antebellum and probably costs a pretty penny for the upkeep, as old houses often do, and I'd heard the whispers about the Madewells turning it into a bed and breakfast because of necessity, not choice. But hadn't someone recently said that Trina Madewell had lots of money? I'd have to ask Bitty and Rayna later.

"It's not like it won't soon be public information anyway," Trisha said to Trina. "I just want all this over with."

"It won't ever be over with!" The ferocity in Trina's voice was shocking.

I looked over at Rayna. As usual, she appeared calm. Bitty just looked annoyed.

Trisha ignored her sister's fury and said, "Race was supposed to meet me in the cottage. We'd been seeing each other for a while. I had no idea Naomi claimed to be engaged to him until I heard about the scuffle at Budgie's café. I was furious with him and intended to have it out. But when I got down to the cottage he was already dead."

"I heard Trina and Race were still seeing each other," Rayna said boldly. "Is that true?"

Trina's chin jutted into the air and she crossed her arms over her chest. "Not after I found out he was dating my sister, it wasn't!"

"Bet that made you mad when you found out," Bitty put in. "It would make me pretty damn mad."

Trina's dark eyes narrowed. "Yes, it made me mad. Trisha and I had a big fight over it. I was angry enough to kill both of them at that moment. But I didn't. Now. Are you happy?"

"No. But I am satisfied. Thank you."

That seemed to take Trina back, and she just looked at Bitty. Then she said, "You dated Race. Did *you* kill him?"

"Of course not. I thought he was an obnoxious drunk. Not at first, of course, or I wouldn't have agreed to go out with him, but he quickly proved that he was a womanizer of the worst kind. Having been recently divorced from one of those, I had no desire to get tangled up with another one."

Bitty's frankness silenced Trina, and she nodded. When she looked at me as if to ask if I had any questions, the only thing I said was, "May we look at the cottage?"

It wasn't what I had intended to ask. Looking at the murder scene was the last thing I wanted, so I have no idea why I said it. Sometimes my mouth comes out with things my brain has no part in.

After a moment of stunned silence, Trisha said, "Why not? It's not as if the police haven't been over every inch of it already. Help yourself. I'll get the key."

She went behind a small desk and reached under the counter, then held out a key attached to a small disk printed with the words '*Cottage One*' in a very fancy script. No one else moved, so I stepped forward and took the key from her.

"Don't you want to go with us?"

Trisha shuddered. "No. I don't think I'll ever be able to step in there again without seeing . . .no. I don't want to go."

"I'll bring it back," I said, and turned to look at Bitty and Rayna. They stared at me with widened eyes. Maybe they felt like I did about it, but we had the key and should not let this opportunity pass.

Madewell Courts is rather plain on the front, with only a small portico and narrow white columns, but the back yard is a jewel. It's obvious someone here loves gardening. The original structure built in the early 1800s has been added on to, and a Victorian style sunroom looks out over sunny stretches of green lawn bordered with flowerbeds. Every kind of flower imaginable fills sun-drenched beds. Beyond those, magnolia trees spread out like gigantic umbrellas, some with their branches all the way to the ground, some trimmed to reveal shaded flowerbeds beneath. Tall ash and spruce trees strategically form a windbreak at one side of the house and lawn.

Four structures form a semi-circle at the far side of the lawn. They look a lot like quaint English cottages. They're small, and perhaps had been sheds or servants' quarters at one time in the past, but each is unique and has a tiny courtyard in front. Paving stones lead from the main house out to each cottage.

The remodeling alone must have cost a fortune, I thought as we made our way to Cottage One. It was at the far left of the lawn, shaded by a magnolia, and with flowers foaming over the low bricked courtyard walls.

Rayna sounded impressed when she remarked that the gardens were gorgeous. "I cannot imagine how much money all this cost," she added.

We were obviously thinking along the same lines.

"And they have rooms inside the house they rent out, too," Bitty said. "Wonder how much they charge and if they can really make any money way out here?"

"It's not so far from Cherryhill," I said, "and very close to Strawberry Plains. You know how many tourists show up every year to see the hummingbirds come to fuel up on their way to South America. People show up in just as many droves as the birds."

"Flocks," said Rayna. "Birds fly in flocks. Except geese. They gather in gaggles."

"Horses run in herds," I said, "but sheep are in flocks, too. Right?"

"Termites fly in swarms," Bitty observed.

"Witches gather in covens, dogs have litters, dolphins swim in a— pod," I finished as I remembered the right word.

"But a gathering of hummingbirds is called a charm," said Trina Madewell, who had come up behind us. "What do you call a gathering of Divas?"

"A delight," Bitty said promptly.

Trina raised her eyebrows. "Hm. I had another word in mind."

Where this came from I had no idea, but the minute I said it I knew I shouldn't:

"A gathering of crows is called a murder."

Everyone stopped dead in their tracks and looked at me. No doubt Rayna and Bitty were remembering the crows in the pines at the cabin, but I had no idea what Trina must be thinking. Nothing nice, I'm quite certain.

I gave a little shrug. "Sorry. My mind was still on collective nouns."

"I'll give you the fifty-cent tour," Trina said after a moment, and led the way through the cute little iron gate and into the cottage courtyard. I handed her the key and she unlocked the door, then stood back to let us file inside.

Still mulling over unusual collective nouns for animal gatherings, I thought a *file* of Divas would be appropriate in this instance. Sometimes my brain goes off on a tangent without my permission. I do the best I can at those moments.

Traces of police presence were evident everywhere. Fingerprint powder dusted all surfaces, from door frames to furniture. The cottage has a front room, a bedroom, and off to one side, a bathroom. The front room is large enough for a small sofa, a big chair, and a wall cabinet that holds a TV and DVD player. Shelves on each side are filled with books and magazines. It's decorated in much the same style as Gaynelle's house, that cozy, shabby but still chic look that's been so popular.

Standing in the front door, it's easy to see straight into the bedroom. The small entry alcove holds a rack with four hooks for coats and an umbrella stand. Step from the alcove into the front room, take about ten more steps and you're in the bedroom. The bath adjoins the bedroom. Trina followed Bitty and Rayna into the bedroom. I remained in the alcove. I get a bit squeamish about murder scenes, even the ones without a body.

I heard Bitty and Rayna asking questions, such as where had the body been, and how did the police know someone else had been there with him.

Trina said in a calm, flat voice as if she had already repeated this a dozen times, which I had no doubt she had, "He was lying right there with his body half off the bed. A pair of crotchless bikini panties were left on the floor."

"Really? What size?" Bitty asked.

"How would I know? I didn't get close enough to look," said Trina in an irritable tone. "I just saw them lying there close to where his feet were, and I knew they weren't his. They had lots of black lace."

"Did he . . . look as if he'd been facing the doorway or the bathroom?" Rayna asked after a short silence.

"As far as I could tell, maybe the doorway."

I saw Trina indicate the front alcove where I stood. Since it was easy to see all the way into the bedroom, it was probably just as easy to see the front door from the bed. It was a straight line of sight for anyone. But if it had been at night, would someone in the bedroom be able to see a person standing in the alcove? If the lights had been left on, maybe. If not, it would be difficult, I would think. It was shadowed even in daylight.

So I asked from where I stood, "Were the lights on when you found him, Trina?"

"Just the bedroom lights. Why?"

"No reason." That I wanted to say out loud right then. No wonder Naomi had said she didn't see the person shooting. They would be pretty well hidden if they remained in the alcove. Whoever had killed Race must have been either a really good shot, or really lucky. Especially if he was moving around and trying to get off the bed. Naomi was lucky she hadn't been shot . . . well, partially lucky, anyway.

When we left a few moments later, Trina shut and locked the door behind us, then pocketed the key. I couldn't help but wonder if there were master keys to all these cottages. If so, that would allow any of the Madewell family access to the cottage. Or any of the employees.

"How many do you have on staff?" I asked as we walked toward the house. "It must take quite a few to keep this place up so beautifully."

"Not as many as you might think. Trisha does most of the booking reservations, and I check behind housekeeping. We only have two outside people employed. My parents prefer keeping this a family-oriented business."

"Who does the meals?"

"We only serve breakfast, and have the croissants delivered daily. Someone from Sharita Stone's catering does all that, the jams, jellies, muffins and so on. Mama cooks the eggs, bacon, sausage, oatmeal, and makes the coffee and tea."

Bitty looked a bit ruffled. "Sharita comes out here?"

"No, someone from her catering service does the deliveries."

"Oh. That's better."

There was a note of relief in her tone. Sometimes Bitty can be a bit selfish.

"Do you know who does the deliveries?" Rayna asked next.

Trina gave her a strange look. "No, it's usually some young man. They deliver every morning between five and six. Why?"

"I just thought that if someone was angry with Race, perhaps they might use the excuse of delivering baked goods as a cover to be out here," Rayna explained. "Have you thought of that?"

Trina shook her head. "Since Race was killed between three-thirty and four in the morning, I doubt it would be one of Sharita's nephews or cousins."

"How do you know the time so closely?" I couldn't help but ask. "I thought it'd take the police a while to find out the results."

"Because I heard the shots. Didn't you read the newspapers? It was all in there. I heard the first shot and thought it must be a hunter getting too close to our property, but after the second shot, Trisha came running up here to get me, all hysterical."

"Oh," I said.

By this time, we'd reached the house and gone through the sunroom into what must have been formerly a living room but was now the lobby. Most of the furniture must be family antiques. Some of the antiques looked a bit shabby in places, but not very chic. Upholstery was worn, and I noted pieces that should have had all their handles and chair rungs, didn't.

Trina walked to the front door and opened it, then stood there. We immediately understood that our tour was finished. After saying our thank-yous and good-byes, we got back into Rayna's SUV parked under a white oleander. She paused, looking at the tall tree.

"How on earth did they get that tree to that size?" she wondered. "I have to bring mine inside in the winter."

"Maybe it's protected by the windbreak," I suggested, and she nodded.

"Could be. It's obvious someone has a green thumb. Oleanders do best farther south."

Bitty, sitting in the front passenger seat, gave Rayna an exasperated glance. "Do you mind? While this botanical lesson is fascinating, I'd rather you turn on the AC!"

"Yes, Your Majesty." Rayna started the vehicle and the AC blasted cool enough even for Bitty, I'm sure. "So, anyone have any ideas we can write down?" she asked as she wheeled the car out of the driveway and onto the narrow blacktop road that led to Highway 311.

"I do," Bitty said promptly. "Trina killed him."

Since I was sitting safely in the back seat and she couldn't see me, I rolled my eyes. "You said that about Naomi, too."

"Did I? Well, I'm probably right."

"About which one?"

"Both of them. Maybe Naomi shot him the first time and Trina shot him the second time. Or maybe they were in on it together." Bitty turned around in her seat to look at me. "It's possible, you know."

"But not probable."

"Pfft!" said Bitty with a wave of her hand, and she turned back around and adjusted the AC vent. "What do you think, Rayna?"

"I think someone should be writing all this down. Just the facts, though. About their relationships with Race, how the cottage looks, where he was found, the panties left behind—what was on your mind about the lights, Trinket?"

She glanced up at me in the rearview mirror. I wasn't sure if I was imagining things, but decided it wouldn't hurt to verbalize my theory.

"Well, standing in the alcove, I could see into the bedroom pretty well. It occurred to me that at night with the lights off, someone in the bedroom wouldn't be able to see me well, or at all. Maybe Naomi was telling the truth when she said she couldn't see who shot Race."

Leather made a snicking sound as Bitty turned around in the seat again to look at me. "Are you defending Naomi?"

"No. I'm just presenting an alternate theory of how things might have happened."

"Write down the facts," Rayna said again, and I reached for the notebook we had brought with us. The ballpoint pen stuck in the notebook's metal rings took a moment to produce ink, and I made several scribbles before getting it to flow correctly.

"So what should I start with?" I asked when I was ready.

"Describe the cottage interior," Rayna said at almost the same time Bitty said, "Tell how shifty Trina and Trisha were being."

I paused. Then I decided to go with Rayna's dictation. It was no contest, really. I wrote down the details of the alcove, living room, and bedroom, including the panties on the floor. I also included that the night of the murder, there had been no lights on in the front room, just the bedroom. Then I read it back to them.

"You didn't include about Trina and Trisha being shifty," Bitty complained.

"I just didn't get to that yet," I lied. "What else?"

"Maybe note that the only outside help they have come in are two employees. Oh, and the deliverymen from Sharita's catering."

"Sharita's really building up her business," I said while I wrote down Rayna's suggestions. "She's likely to turn into a corporation one day."

"Like that Mrs. Fields," Bitty said. "Sharita's baking makes Mrs. Fields' cookies taste like they're made from sawdust."

I agreed. Then I looked up at Rayna and waited for her next suggestion. It took a while. All of us went quiet as we mentally replayed our time at Madewell Courts in an effort to pick out anything unusual. Or "off the wall" as Gaynelle had said.

Something struck me while I went back over all that happened, but I couldn't quite put my finger on it. There had been something said that didn't ring true. But what was it? Ah. I hate it when that happens. I'm always afraid it's a sign of impending senility. Usually it's just imbecility.

"Did you write down that Trina and Trisha were acting shifty?" Bitty asked after a moment, and I sighed.

"I'm doing that now," I said, and started writing.

Just as my pen hit the paper, the SUV jerked forward on the road and I made a long black line across my notes and nearly bumped my head on the front seat headrest.

"Hey," I started to protest when the SUV bounced forward again. I threw my arms up to keep from hitting the back of the front seat, lost paper and pen, and gagged as the shoulder strap of the seatbelt yanked hard across my neck and throat.

Rayna started cussing, and I saw her yank hard at the steering wheel as we were tossed around inside the vehicle. Bitty's head bobbled like one of those dolls on a spring people stick to their dashboards. I grabbed hold of the handle above the door as the SUV rocked from side to side, then it suffered another seizure in a lurching jump forward.

"Someone keeps hitting us in the rear!" Rayna screamed as she tried to keep the top-heavy car upright. "Who is that?" I craned my neck as best I could with the seat belt restraining me and caught a glimpse of a black truck. It looked huge. Chrome everywhere. Tinted windows. Dust a haze in the air. Engine roaring, sounding like a train engine, noise and fear all jumbled up together in a passing collage of images. My body jerked every time the truck hit us, and I held on for dear life.

"They're trying to knock us off the road!" I shouted back at Rayna. "Pull over!"

"I can't! We'll go in a ditch!"

I looked out the window. My stomach turned over. Steep red banks fell away from the narrow road, cushioned here and there by kudzu-covered trees and bushes. There was no shoulder, nowhere to go but down an abrupt drop to a wooded creek. If we stayed on the road, maybe we could outrun the maniac behind us. If we went over the side—it wouldn't be good.

"Duck, Trinket!" I heard Bitty yell at me, and even as I ducked I wondered why. In the next instant I heard an ear-shattering *boom!* and the crackling sound of breaking glass. Another boom immediately followed it, then another. Tires screeched, rocks and gravel shot into the air, and the big black truck fell back. The smell of sulphur and cordite was suddenly strong, and my ears rang.

When I glanced up, I saw why.

Bitty had a gun as big as a small rifle held in one of her hands and braced on the back of the front seat. With her other hand, she held on to the headrest for dear life. She had the most determined expression on her face I've ever seen; I saw her lift the gun again and automatically ducked for cover.

Kaboom!

This time it worked. I peeked over the backseat. The black truck braked to a stop in the middle of the road.

"Yee-haw!" Bitty hollered so loudly I could hear her even through the ringing in my ears. "Come get some more, you sonuvabitch!"

"*Oh noooo,*" Rayna screamed loudly, and I turned back just in time to see a big wall of kudzu loom right in front of the SUV. She jerked the wheel hard left, and the SUV went to the right, dipped, back wheels spinning, and the engine died. Kudzu leaves pressed hard against the windows as we smacked into whatever was hidden behind the tangled vines. My body slammed hard against the car door. Then it got very quiet.

I drew in a deep breath. Dust and smoke rose up around the vehicle. Bitty had been tossed to the floorboard. Rayna sat like a statue behind the steering wheel. I saw her nostrils flare in and out.

"Are we all right?" I asked in a loud whisper. My ears still rang, and all sound was barely audible. I saw Rayna's head turn and her lips move.

"Don't anyone move. Stay on the floorboard, Bitty."

"I dropped my gun," came a muffled voice from the front floorboards. "Do you see it?"

"Yes. Be still."

"Like this?" Bitty snapped. "My ass is on the floor and my feet are hanging over the backseat!"

It was true. I saw her Aigner flats dangle near my face.

"Listen to me, dammit! The rear end of this truck is hanging over the edge of the road and if you—oh!"

A low rumbling beneath the SUV made the entire vehicle quiver, and slowly, slowly, it began to slide backward. As if in a made-for-TV movie I saw the kudzu leaves shudder and fall away as we began to slide down and down, it seeming to happen in slow motion.

"Hang on!" someone screamed, then there was nothing but chaos, red dirt, an ear-splitting shrieking of metal, and the smell of fear thick in the air. With a nauseating roll and drop, we bounced down the side of the ravine like a child's toy. I remember thinking that this wasn't a nice way to die, then we slammed hard against something and everything went dark.

CHAPTER 10

I don't know what woke me. It could have been that I was hanging upside-down from my seat belt like a vampire bat and all the blood had rushed to my head. Or it could have been the strong smell of gasoline. Or even that my seatbelt was cutting into my boobs and making it hard to breathe. Whatever it was, I knew I had to get us all out of that SUV.

The vehicle was tilted at an odd angle, kind of nose-down and leaning to the driver's side. Red dirt and crushed kudzu were all I could see out that side, so that left the passenger side as a possibility. If I could get my window open, maybe I could unfasten my seatbelt, then unfasten Rayna's, and get us both out. Rayna slumped over the steering wheel, her face turned toward me, her eyes closed. A fine white glow covered her, and for a moment I panicked. Was she dead? Could it be that people . . . glow . . .right after they die? Then I saw her deflated airbag. It cushioned her head against the steering wheel. When her nostrils flared slightly I knew that she was breathing. But Bitty?

My heart lurched. Her door was ajar. Had she been thrown out and . . . and been rolled over? *Ohgodohgodohgod,* I started praying in a kind of moan, let her be okay!

I fumbled around for the latch to the seatbelt, but it was really difficult. Since I was sort of just hanging there, I had to do it blindly, feel around for the latch by twisting my arm backward. It took forever, but finally I found it. Then it took another forever before I could get the blasted thing to free the metal latch that held me suspended. When it finally slid free, I immediately dropped like a stone.

Now I was half-on, half-off the seat and in the floorboard. My right arm bent at an odd angle, and when I tried to use it to push up, sharp pain shot up all the way to my shoulder. I yelped.

Maybe my yelp woke Rayna. She stirred slightly, her eyelids fluttered, and from my awkward position, I could see her try to push away from the steering wheel.

"Wha—?" she muttered in confusion.

"We ran off the road," I said, only it came out all smushy for some reason. That was when I realized I must have smacked my face on something, because my lips were swollen and I'd bitten my tongue. I tasted blood. It was not nice.

Rayna shifted position slightly. Then she seemed to really come to, because she immediately leaned forward and turned off the SUV's ignition. It must have been an automatic reflex.

"Bitty? Trinket?" She sounded hoarse.

"Trinket here. Bitty not. You okay?" It was the best I could manage with my lips all puffy and my tongue uncooperative and painful.

"Yeah . . . I think . . . so."

I tried my door, but the handle didn't budge. Nor did my window roll down since the engine was off. I would have to get out the front door, if possible.

"Must find Bitty," I got out, and managed to scoot slightly so I could loop my left arm around the back of the front passenger seat. Pain shot through me every time I tried to use my right arm, so I decided to listen to my body and desist. It was clumsy using just my left hand and arm, and took a lot more effort than it should have, but finally I managed to pull myself up so I could get my legs under me.

By this time I was sweating. Perspiring is too gentle a word for the stuff that poured off my body in rivers. Heat shimmered beyond the wrecked SUV, coming up in visible waves off the red dirt rock scraped free of kudzu. The inside of the vehicle was an oven, and we were slowly being baked to a crisp. I didn't want to be crispy. I wanted to be my familiar soggy self.

"Come on," I said to Rayna as I worked my way toward the opening between the two front seats. "We need to get out."

Rayna shook her head. "I . . . can't. My arm is trapped . . . my left foot is stuck."

"I'll try to get you free."

"No . . . my foot is wedged in by the wheel well . . .. It will need . . . to be cut free."

"Where's your cell?" For the first time I regretted not having my own cell phone. It would certainly come in handy about now.

"Don't know. Somewhere."

Rayna still sounded hazy and slightly confused. Even through the white powder coating her face and arms, I could tell she was pale. Her eyes looked like huge smudges in her face.

With my left arm I grabbed the front of the passenger bucket seat and pulled until I inched forward down to my waist. Getting my hips through the opening would be the trick. Maybe I should have refused that last muffin at breakfast. Or the countless muffins I'd eaten in the past few months. Not to mention the one cup of sugar ratio to two quarts of sweet tea that I drank regularly.

None of which helped at this moment.

I huffed, I puffed, I wiggled and squirmed. I panted and swore, then prayed for a miracle. Lo and behold! Just as I was giving up on ever squeezing thirty-eight inches of hips through a twelve inch opening, I shot through like I'd been greased. I landed with my face on the passenger floorboard. A crumpled airbag cushioned my landing. It tasted awful. I didn't care.

I rested a moment after my exertions, and then tried to free Rayna. It was futile. As she had said, her left foot was wedged tightly into the damaged wheel well of the vehicle. It would take the jaws of life to free her, I was pretty sure.

I contorted my fifty-one plus body into an aching position no human has ever tried before. While I do not recommend it, I did succeed in slithering very close to the open passenger door. It's amazing what determination, desperation, and downright idiocy can do. My body would never be the same. But at last I launched myself free of the SUV and into a patch of nettles.

"Ouch, ouch, ouch," I said. Then I added a few obscenities I shall not repeat here. It took a minute or two of sticky, stinging effort to get to my feet, but I did it. By that time I was really breathing hard and fast. I had a stitch in my side, my right arm was useless, and I'd lost a shoe. I limped over to the SUV still leaning heavily to the left, and reached up into the floorboard. Maybe Bitty's cell phone was there. Or Rayna's. At that point, I would have borrowed a cell phone from Jack the Ripper if he'd ambled past.

No such luck. Rayna looked at me and smiled weakly. That cut straight to my gut. *No!* By god, I was going to get us all out of here, even if I had to drag Bitty from under this damn SUV myself! We were all going to survive this. And when we did, next time Bitty went to the pistol range, I was going with her.

"Hang on," I said to Rayna. "I'm looking for a cell phone. And Bitty. She might be . . . be under the car. So I'm going to duck down and look, okay? Don't make any quick moves or you might end up toppling this thing back over on me."

"I won't." Rayna sounded so faint I could barely hear her. Or maybe I was still deaf from Bitty firing a cannon right beside my head. Whichever, it spurred me to greater effort.

It smelled awful under the SUV, like burned motor oil and grease— and gas. That last gave me pause, but I had to make sure Bitty wasn't trapped. There was so much kudzu everywhere. I swear the vines had already started to grow around the car. If we didn't get Rayna out of it, she would probably be covered up by the next day.

Broken tree branches, brambles, nettles, and every other unpleasant botanical nightmare you can think of was tangled up in the SUV's undercarriage. I saw that the driver's side was hooked pretty firmly on some kind of tree trunk that had snapped in two and held it fast. That might keep the vehicle from rolling the rest of the way down the hill if we were lucky.

A glance down the hill was not at all comforting. It ended in a creek that wasn't very deep, but was far away. Those red banks could wash away pretty fast during flash floods.

Crouched down, I studied the undercarriage and the stout tree that held the SUV in place. It looked like it would hold, so I worked up my courage and crawled under the SUV looking for sign of Bitty. I couldn't go far, so I took a broken limb and poked it into any spot that looked like it might harbor a person. No yell greeted my pokes, but I didn't find any lifeless body, either. Satisfied at last that Bitty was at least not under the SUV, I started backing slowly out from under it.

"Are you *sleeping* under there?" a voice right behind me demanded, startling me so badly that I shrieked and tried to leap up.

Not a good idea. Not only did I bang my head against the undercarriage of the car—contrary to popular opinion, manufacturers do use materials harder than plastic in today's autos—but I forgot about my right arm being useless. It collapsed under my weight and I shrieked again, landing face first in what was probably poison ivy. Spitting dead leaves, debris, and green stems from my mouth, I rolled over and looked up.

Bitty stared down at me. "You're having a seizure?"

"No," I said more calmly than I felt, "I'm pitching a hissy fit. Where have you been?"

She held up her cell phone. "I couldn't get a signal down here. I had to climb up to the road while you two slept."

Exasperation and relief make an odd combination, but that is just how I felt. I didn't know whether to kick or kiss her, so I did neither one. I just held up my good hand.

"Help me stand."

"Good lord, you must be kidding. You've got at least fifty pounds on me," Bitty said, but since she leaned down to take my hand as she spoke I didn't say anything really nasty to her. Not until I was on my own feet again, anyway.

"Are you hurt?" I asked, and she shook her head. That figured. The only one not wearing a seat belt was the only one unharmed. But seeing as how it was Bitty, it made perfect sense. She's always unscathed by disasters. "Good," I said. "You only weigh a few pounds less than me. Twenty at the most."

"*Twenty* pounds? You're dreaming!"

No. I was lying through my teeth. But why let her know that? She'd scared the hell out of me. She deserved to be irritated at least a little bit.

"Suck it up, cupcake."

"Why do you sound like Elmer Fudd? And your face is a mess. You've got dirt all over you."

"That's blood," I said, and since my ears were still a little stopped up I could tell I was lisping so that it sounded more like *That'th bluth.* "My mouth ith blithink," I heard myself say next .

Really, I was so relieved we were all alive and reasonably unharmed that I didn't care who I sounded like, or that I apparently had so much blood on my face it looked like dirt. Now Bitty looked concerned. She peered at me more closely.

"Oh my! It is blood! Give me your shirt."

"Wha'?"

She motioned impatiently. "Your shirt. Take it off and give it to me. I'll make you a tourniquet or something."

Since I had no desire to take off my shirt or have it ripped into shreds to use as a tourniquet around my neck, I politely declined. "Hell no."

Bitty threw her hands up into the air. "Try to help some people—"

"Rayna," I said in my interesting Fudd-voice, "let's help Rayna."

"Is she still in the car? Why on earth didn't she get out?"

Bitty had already started picking her way to the side of the SUV to look inside. I noticed she was barefoot as I followed along behind her. That meant she'd climbed that steep hill to the road to use her cell phone, then came back down again to find us without her shoes. Her feet were probably a mess. And suddenly I thought how wonderful she was to do that without complaint. My earlier irritation disappeared.

"Rayna," Bitty called, "why are you still in the car?"

I couldn't hear exactly what Rayna replied, but guessed from Bitty's reaction that she had said she was stuck.

"Oh, I can get you out; give me a minute. Do you see my shoes by the way? They should be in the back seat. I don't know where my gun went. I dropped it—ah, there it is."

"Bitty," I asked as she reached inside the vehicle, "who did you call to come get us?"

"Jackson Lee."

I've had experience with Bitty's emergency phone calls. She tends to leave out important details. "What did you say to him?"

She looked over her shoulder at me. "I *thaid* we'd been run off the road by a maniac and fallen over a cliff close to Highway 311. He said he would come right away."

"Did you tell him what road we're on?"

Bitty seemed startled by the question. "No. Should I?"

I sighed. "It would help speed things up."

"Well, I'll walk back up the hill and see if he can't *thpeed thingth* up, then."

"You're gonna hurt my feelings if you keep mocking me."

"I doubt that," she said. "If your *feelingth* aren't hurt by now, you're used to me."

That was true. I changed the subject.

"Can you really get Rayna out of the car?"

"Yes, I think so. Why?"

I held out my hand. "Give me your cell phone. I'll call Daddy and see if he can get someone to pull Rayna's car out of this gully."

"I know you're just checking up on me," Bitty said, but she put the cell phone in my hand anyway. "Boost me up into the car before you go. I'll get Rayna unstuck while you call the Mounties."

At first I didn't know how to give Bitty a boost. For one thing, my right arm was near useless, and for another, it's not as if she's light as a feather, no matter what she claims to weigh. Finally I ended up bending over with my good hand braced on my knee, and let her use my back as a stepping stool. It worked.

"Find your shoes while you're in there," I said. "And give me my shoe. It should be in the back seat."

It turned out that Bitty's shoes were in the back seat and my shoe had wound up under Rayna's feet. Go figure. The cause and effect of aerodynamics has never been my strong suit.

"Here's your *thew*," Bitty said as she handed me my tennis shoe, and only the sight of her cut-up bare feet kept me from bonking her on the head with it. She still hadn't complained. I was pretty sure she was saving that for later.

Climbing back up that steep hill was a lot harder than it should have been. I may have shoes on, but trying to grab hold of a tree or vine to pull myself up was awkward. I slid back down a few times before I figured out that if I planted my feet firmly, then got a good hold on a limb or vine and pulled slowly, it would get me up a bit farther. I angled across instead of straight up, and finally, after a lot of sweating, swearing, and sobbing, I got to the road. Since by that time I was practically on my knees and crawling, I just sat there for a minute to catch my breath.

My useless right arm hurt like the very devil. It felt like flaming needles went the entire length of it. I hoped for a sprain instead of a break. I'm an awful patient. Mama and Daddy just have so many years left, and I'm sure they wouldn't want to hear me whine through their final decade.

Sunlight beat down with a vengeance, and I had to close my eyes against it. I felt a bit dizzy, no doubt from climbing Mount Kudzu. I waited for it to pass, and after a few moments, opened my eyes. Spots swam in front of me. They were very pretty, purple centers with yellow rings around them, and shaped a bit like Pac-man. My ears rang, my eyesight faltered, and I could barely see the cell phone I pulled from my shirt pocket. I had to squint to see the numbers. Why had I thought I would be better at this? I have a terrible tendency to overestimate my abilities, it seems.

Holding the phone in my left hand, I managed to press the 9 with my thumb, then the 1, and then the last 1. It took a lot more effort than it should have. For some reason my entire body was shaking like I was cold. That was ridiculous. It was hot as blazes out there. Why was I shivering? Would any cell tower relay this call?

Bitty's cell phone probably has its own satellite, so after a half dozen rings, I heard an impersonal voice say, "Nine-one-one, what's your emergency, please?"

All I could say was, "Help."

Then I keeled over on the gravel shoulder like roadkill.

****

They told me later that the operator was able to help the rescue team find us by our satellite coordinates. Since Bitty probably has a 600 volt battery in her phone, it led them straight to us. While I don't understand all the technicalities, I was just glad others knew what the heck they were doing. I don't remember a whole lot about the rest of the day. Images come back occasionally but are disjointed, like in a dream. All three of us were loaded up into ambulances and taken to the hospital in Desoto County. It's the largest facility within fifty or so miles, and apparently we made it there pretty quick once they got us on board. I would have loved to have been awake for that trip.

None of us were badly hurt. Bitty had the fewest injuries: bruises, aches, and bad cuts on her feet. Rayna suffered a broken collarbone and sprained left wrist as well as the same bruises, aches, and pains. I ended up with a broken right arm and concussion. My teeth had bitten my lower lip pretty badly, but no long-term damage. The SUV, however, was a total loss.

After an overnight stay at the hospital, Rob came to take Rayna home, Jackson Lee and the twins came for Bitty, and Mama, Daddy, and Kit came to take me home. We were all just one big happy family in three separate vehicles.

Kit sat in the back seat of Mama's big old Lincoln with me, and

Daddy drove. He went more slowly down the congested main road than all the other cars, until finally Mama said, "For heaven's sake, Eddie, if I'd known you were going to go this slow, I would have packed us a lunch."

Daddy sped up some after that, but I could see him watching me in the rearview mirror as if to check and see if I'd broken yet. Actually, it made me feel special. I was still Daddy's Little Girl, even if I weighed nearly as much as he did.

"Did they find out who ran us off the road?" I asked when we were finally on 78 Highway headed to Holly Springs. "It should be pretty easy. Just look for a black truck with cannon ball holes in it."

Kit grinned at me. "Did Bitty really shoot out Rayna's back window?"

"Afraid so. My hearing will never be the same."

Mama looked at me over the front seat. "She's pretty proud of herself about that."

"So I hear. She'll be insufferable now. Too bad she didn't hit the guy chasing us. I wouldn't feel a bit bad about it if she had."

"Road rage?" Mama asked. "Do you think that was it?"

I thought about it a minute. "I don't see how," I said finally. "We didn't even see the guy until he rammed us. We were talking. It just came out of the blue."

"People these days are crazy," said Daddy. "It's all those different drugs they take."

"You don't mean Viagra makes—"

"No, no, Anna," Daddy cut Mama off. "Nothing like that. It's all the other drugs like Valium and cocaine. You know. Street drugs."

At last the secret of my parents' newfound libidos was out. I didn't want to think about it. So I said, "Valium isn't necessarily a street drug. I don't know why people take it when there's a liquor store on practically every corner. A glass of wine works just as well and is better for your heart."

Kit laughed. "Yeah, and there are people who take that too far as well."

My head lay on the back of the massive rear seat, and I turned to look at him. "I hope you aren't referring to me as one of those people."

Since he had his arm around my shoulders, he gave me a slight squeeze, not enough to hurt, just enough to reassure. "Nope. Not at all. You don't drink yourself into oblivion."

"Unfortunately, no. I must give it a try sometime, though. Oblivion sounds pretty good right now."

"You in pain, sugar?"

I just love southern men. They call you "sugar" and "honey" and "baby', and you know they know your name so they're just doing it as a form of endearment. Except the construction guys on the street when you pass them. It's been a while since it's happened to me, but those guys are the same everywhere. It doesn't matter if you're in Washington State, California, Pennsylvania, Indiana, or Georgia. They're going to shout, whistle, call you "HeyBabyLookin'Good" and other appreciative names. I never minded it so much, but I've known women who find it offensive. Now I'm just glad they don't do the flip-side of that and shout unkind things like "WideLoadComin'Through". It would really hurt my feelings.

"Not really hurting," I said to Kit, "just a little uncomfortable."

The doctors had set my arm and put it in a cast. Now I had a baby sling, but not one that looked anything like those Bitty used for Chitling. It was bright blue and black, colors not especially appealing, but very appropriate for the rest of me. I was bruised from head to toe, my slight concussion was nothing to worry about, and my dehydration had been fixed up with a few bags of IV fluids. I asked for wine instead, but the nurse only laughed. She had no idea I was serious.

Mama turned around in the front seat again to look at me. "I'll fix you up a bed on the couch. Just until you feel better. I can look after you if you're downstairs. I don't think I can manage all those stairs, though."

My current bedroom was my parents' old bedroom. Once they figured out that all those steps up and down every day were not contributing positively to their arthritic aches and pains, they made the old parlor their bedroom. It's right off the living room and much easier on them. I love the new arrangements. Their bedroom has what used to be a sleeping porch back in the old days before air conditioning made life in the South livable from April to November. When I was still a child and we kids were all at home, Daddy had turned the sleeping porch into a sort of sunroom/sitting room connected to the bedroom by French doors. It's lovely, and I still like to sit there and watch the day turn to night or listen to the rain.

"Oh Mama," I said, "don't go to all that trouble. I can get up and down the stairs just fine." As I said that, a pain shot through me from my toes right up to my eyebrows. I think my body went into detox at even the thought of all those stairs. But I didn't want my mother fussing over me, either. I'm a terrible patient, usually cranky and frustrated at being held prisoner by my own body. Also, I did *not* want to be asleep on that couch right next to my parents' bedroom if they got frisky. That would send me screaming into the night, I was quite sure.

Sometimes, fate is quirky. Really.

Kit's cell phone rang while Mama was telling me it would be *fun*, just like the pajama parties we had when I was ten or eleven—ignoring the fact there had been a few other ten and eleven year olds present—and so I just nodded and smiled and tried to think of a way to kill myself so the insurance company wouldn't know it was suicide. It would be preferable to the alternative.

Then Kit held out his cell phone. "It's for you."

"Me?" I looked at it a bit warily. Transferred cell phone calls are unpredictable. I have rarely had one turn out to be good news. He waggled the phone in front of my face and I took it just to make him stop. I knew the moment I recognized the voice that my convalescence was going to be fraught with peril.

"Yes, Jackson Lee," I said politely, "I'm doing just fine, thank you."

"Good, good," he said a bit too heartily. "You ladies had quite a scare. Scared the hell out of the rest of us, too."

"Unh hunh." I had to watch what I said and not accidentally commit myself to something. Jackson Lee can be tricky.

"How's your family doing? Parents okay? They were mighty upset when I called to tell them what had happened."

"They've recovered nicely."

"That's good, that's good. I know you came back home to take care of them, and here the shoe is on the other foot now. But I'm sure your parents can manage. They take care of all those cats very well, and your mama keeps up the house and cooks—I'm sure it won't be *too* much extra effort at all for her to nurse you back to health."

I had a sudden vision of Mama trudging from the kitchen to the couch with trays of food, bringing wet cloths for my forehead . . . .

"It's not like I'm an invalid," I said to banish the vision. "I can walk. Slowly, but I get there sooner or later."

"Oh, I know, Trinket. Just like I know you always take good care of family. It's what we do. Family is everything to most of us. I doubt we'd get along nearly as well as we do without our kinfolks helping us out."

I saw where this was going. Maybe I'd known as soon as I heard his voice on the phone, but now I knew what I'd say.

"I'll do it, Jackson Lee."

"Do what, Trinket?"

"Stay with Bitty. That is why you called, isn't it?"

He gave one of his warm, lawyerly chuckles. "I had you figured for the smart one, and I see I was right. You know how she is, always busy doing something and talking to her friends . . . sometimes she just forgets herself. The boys are a big help, but they're young and get distracted easy. I knew she could count on you to be here for her."

"Of course. Where else would I rather be? Maybe Whitfield, but I hear they no longer take reservations."

Jackson Lee laughed. I was sure he was just humoring me since he'd gotten his way. I was equally as sure that I'd be an excellent candidate for Whitfield by the time I'd been at Bitty's for a half hour. But, patients don't always get to choose their insane asylum.

CHAPTER 11

While I've been told a couple of times that "insane asylum" is no longer politically correct, I could not imagine Six Chimneys being referred to as anything else at the moment. It looked like the inmates were running it, too. Not an adult in sight.

Oh Bitty was there, all right, in plain view. But she was hardly being the adult. Her feet were bandaged up to her ankles. Instead of a wheelchair or crutches, she sat in a sturdy leather office chair with arms, while one of the kids pushed her hither and yon. I wasn't in the house thirty seconds before I considered opening the front door and giving that chair a pretty good shove out onto the porch. Let the chips—or wheels— fall where they may.

Using my good arm, I snagged the first kid that happened past. He was a rather tall, gangly young man who seemed horrified when he got a close look at me. I smiled, which must have terrified him since my lips were swollen and cracked, my face a rainbow of bruises and cuts, I had a black eye, and I still lisped a little.

"I want everyone out," I said as clearly as I could. *"Out!"*

Kids scattered like roaches under a sudden spotlight. Evidently my lisp carries. I stood by the front door with it left open in invitation, and before Kit could even get my overnight bag up the front porch steps, the house was cleared. Blessed silence fell around us. It did not last long.

"Trinket!" Bitty said, and shoved away from a Regency table to roll toward me. "I thought you'd never get here. Good god. You look awful."

"Thank you. I feel awful."

"Poor thing . . . come on in here and lie down. The boys made up a bed for you in the parlor, so you don't have to go upstairs. Jackson Lee told me you insisted on coming to stay with me. You shouldn't have, really."

Jackson Lee owed me. Big time.

"Where *is* our illustrious lawyer?" I asked as I followed the leather desk chair down the hallway. Kit tagged along behind, and I thought I heard him laugh, but when I turned around to look at him, he had a straight face. I must have been mistaken.

"In court," Bitty sang out gaily. "Or doing something legal. I can't remember."

Bitty powered the chair by pushing herself away from walls and furniture, or kicking her heels against the floor. It worked just fine until she hit a carpet. The chair balked, teetered, and she spun around in it trying to keep it upright. She looked like a toy top gone berserk. If I hadn't been so wobbly on my feet, I might have tried to stop her mad spin, but with my luck we both would have ended up on the floor.

Kit came to her rescue just before she pitched out of the chair. He caught her as she launched toward the parlor carpet, and kept her from landing on her face.

"Oooh, ouch, oooh!" she said.

"That's Bitty-speak for thank you," I interpreted when Kit looked concerned. "She has stitches in her feet. Just put her in that chair over there. The one without wheels. We're all safer that way."

True to her word, Bitty had a bed for me in the parlor. Really, it was just one of the oversized chairs and oversized ottoman put together, but it looked inviting with soft blue Egyptian cotton sheets, a light summer quilt, and fat goose feather pillows stacked up so high I'd have to take away at least two if I wanted to sleep lying down. Bitty knows how to treat guests. I was lucky she considered me a guest this time instead of just family.

"Brandon and Clayton are going to take good care of us," she said from her spot in the matching chair-turned-bed. "I've given them their orders."

"Did those orders include inviting half of Ole Miss to homestead your basement?" I asked. "Why on earth were all those kids here?"

"Oh, Trinket, they were just having fun. I kinda enjoyed them."

I looked at her more closely. Her eyes were a little too bright, and she was a little too mellow.

"Bitty Hollandale, have you been drinking?"

She blinked. "No. Well, nothing but sweet tea. Why?"

Kit set my overnight case down by the small sofa against the wall. "Excuse me, but I think I'll be running on now," he said. "Bowel re-section waiting on me."

Bitty turned toward him with a big smile. "Tell Mr. Recession I said hello, will you?"

For the first time since I met him, Kit seemed at a loss for words. Then he nodded and said, "I sure will, Bitty. You two take care now. Trinket—" He came to where I sat on the edge of my little bed, bent and kissed me on probably the only spot that didn't have a big bruise—the tip of my nose—and whispered, "Valium. Percocet. Morphine. One of those, I bet."

He was probably right. Bitty did have a glazed look in her eyes, and she was too happy for someone who had gotten stitches in both feet. And—the biggest clue—she was not wearing a pug. There was no sign of Chen Ling.

I squeezed his arm with my left hand to let him know I agreed, then he left. Bitty sat back in the chair and regarded me with that same smile. It did look a bit sloppy. But maybe it was best if she was dopey. I mean medicated.

While I was contemplating my options, Brandon appeared in the parlor doorway. "What can I get you ladies to drink?"

Before Bitty could answer I said, "Sweet tea. Lots of it. We're both on antibiotics so shouldn't drink anything else."

It was true. Especially if taking pain killers. My prescription had been filled at the drugstore, but so far I hadn't taken anything. I needed to get the antibiotics in me, and I'd see how quickly I'd need something for pain.

A funny thing about me and medications: I often have adverse reactions. During my divorce from Perry, my doctor had given me Xanax to sleep. Let me tell you—Xanax does anything but put me to sleep. I was as wired as if hooked up to a car battery. It got so bad I couldn't even stand to be in my own company, and that's when I knew I was in no danger of ever getting addicted. Same thing with Valium. After that, I discovered I can have a glass of wine or two and get nearly the same effect. I've been cautious about pain medication ever since. It may not be exactly the same thing, but why take chances?

When Brandon returned with our tea, he was accompanied by a girl who looked vaguely familiar to me. Blond, petite, pretty, I knew I should know her. When she smiled as she handed me my glass, it suddenly came to me: "Heather?"

"Yes, ma'am. I'm surprised you remember me."

I turned to Bitty. "Do you remember me telling you about applying for a job at Carolann Barnett's lingerie and gift shop? Well, this is the lucky young lady who got there first."

Ice clinked in her glass as Bitty took it from Brandon. "I don't know about lucky. Do you have to have experience with dildos to sell them?"

"Mama!" Brandon said, sounding scandalized.

"Well, that's what Rose Allgood is selling in there. Isn't she, Heather?"

Laughing, Heather nodded. "Yes, ma'am, she sure is."

"Do you sell lots of them? And who to? I know—I bet I can tell you just who comes in to buy those!"

Heather held up her hands palms out as if to ward off Bitty's guesses. "No, no, I can't rat out our customers. Miz B would fire me."

"That's okay. I pretty much know who some of them are. Trina

Madewell, for one." Heather got a funny look on her face, and Bitty laughed. "See? I knew it, I just knew it! Can't fool me all the time. Or some of the time. How does that go?"

"Let it go," I said, and surprising me, she did.

"So," Bitty went on, "how do you and Brandon know each other? I'm pretty sure he doesn't shop at Carolann's."

Brandon grinned at that. "Not lately," he said in the same dry tone his father used to use, and I wondered suddenly if he and Clayton visited Frank much. "Heather and I both go to Ole Miss. She's in my psych class." Bitty looked sharply at Heather. "Who are your people, dear?"

"Oh, I'm from Pass Christian, near Biloxi."

"Really? I have friends there. Do you know the Granville family? No? Perhaps you know the Fontaines? Well my goodness, they're very well connected, so I thought you might know them."

Since Bitty seemed to be exercising her snobbery gene at Heather's expense, I took the conversation in another direction:

"You're taking *psychology?*" I said to Brandon. "I thought you were going to be a lawyer."

"Yes, ma'am, but good lawyers have to know psychology. It's one of the basics of figuring out which clients are lying."

"Oh," said Bitty with a flap of her hand, "they all lie. It's just what people do. If they've been charged with a crime, I usually figure they're guilty. Otherwise, why would the police arrest them?"

Coming from Bitty, who had been arrested just a few months before on a murder charge, and who was even now under suspicion for another murder, it should have earned a lightning strike on her roof at the very least. Of course, nothing more happened than me and Brandon shaking our heads at one another.

When I glanced at Heather, she was still staring at Bitty with that strange look on her face. I knew how she felt. Dealing with Bitty can be trying for anyone, but especially those unaccustomed to her.

"It's okay," I leaned forward and said in a loud whisper, "we don't let Bitty near courtrooms."

Heather looked at me, then smiled. "Oh, I think she'd make a formidable defendant."

"Not any time soon, I hope." I lifted my tea glass in a salute to Bitty. "I propose we do our best to keep us all out of courtrooms—at least, as clients."

Brandon laughed. "I'd drink to that if I had anything. Come on, Heather. Let's go back downstairs before Mama and Aunt Trinket find anything else for us to do."

"Turn your cell phone on," Bitty called after them. "Just in case I think of something I need."

"You're going to phone him?" I wondered aloud.

"Well, I'm certainly not going to walk downstairs to get him." She put her feet up into the air. "My size fives aren't up to it."

"Size *five*? Aren't you thinking of your SAT score instead of your shoe size?"

"No, honey, that would be the score you got on your Civil Service exam."

We both smiled at each other. Things must be all right if we were able to trade insults as usual. Maybe coming to stay with Bitty wouldn't be so bad after all. If nothing else, we could annoy each other and save our friends and family a great deal of stress.

The next few days really tested that theory to the max.

First, I had truly forgotten what it was like to live in the same house with young people. True, it is an exceptionally roomy house, but unless the parlor moved to the next county, I could still hear every footfall on the stairs, every slam of the refrigerator door in the kitchen, and the *thump thump thump* of music in the basement vibrating the parlor floor. Bitty, who had insisted upon being carried upstairs to her own room at night and downstairs to hold court in the morning, aided and abetted the culprits.

I suspected her pain medications rendered her insensible to the irritations of loud noises at two in the morning, and after that first sleepless night, I decided to take matters into my own hands. Or hand, since my right arm was in a sling that made using the plural impossible.

"Brandon, Clayton, would you mind joining me for a moment?" I went to the kitchen door and asked. About six or seven young people sat at either Bitty's small round kitchen table, or had pulled up a stool to the Corian worktop where Sharita Stone made her magic with flour, milk, and a Cuisinart. Unfortunately, kids were there and she was not. I crooked the index finger of my left hand at the twins.

They came immediately and went back into the parlor with me, the unsuspecting, trusting lads that they were. I gently closed the door, then leaned back against it so they couldn't get out until I had finished.

"Boys, you know I love you," I began, and they exchanged glances. I heard one of them mutter, "Uh-oh" but ignored that for the moment.

"However, you have befriended a herd of buffalo that stampede regularly up and down the stairs—stairs that are, coincidentally, very close to my head. Perhaps you can see how that might be irksome. Since being bounced down a hill in a box of metal and plastic a few days ago, I find I'm not as . . . *nice* . . . or patient as I normally am. My head hurts. My arm hurts. Everything between my toes and scalp hurts, actually, and I'm doing my best to stay away from mind-altering drugs. That poses a problem. Can you see where I'm going with this?"

"Yes, ma'am!" they said in unison. Such polite boys. Loud, occasionally inclined to forget, but polite. Bitty raised them well.

"We'll tell our friends to hang out over at Heather's place," Clayton said. "She has the cottage all to herself, so it shouldn't bother anybody."

"Now that you're here to watch over Mama, though," Brandon said with a smile designed to charm and coax me into agreement, "we don't need to be here *all* the time, do we?"

"Just make sure I have your cell phone numbers before you go." I moved away from the parlor door. They charged it at the same time, bumping into each other in their haste to leave. "Boys?" I said right before they managed to get through it completely; "I expect you to answer when I call."

Brandon turned and gave me an impish grin. "We'll anther, Aunt Trinket, I promith."

"Get out of here," I said sternly, but wasn't really perturbed at them mocking me. The prospect of peace and quiet was too alluring to get upset about anything so minor.

For the next two hours it was blessedly peaceful.

Then Bitty returned from wherever she had been. I heard them come in the front door, Jackson Lee laughing at something she'd said. I debated getting up from my cozy spot on the couch-bed, then decided against it. I was comfortable, and if they wanted me in on their private moments, they knew where to find me.

As luck would have it, Chen Ling found me first. So that was where Bitty had been, to Luann Carey's house of pugs to retrieve her dog. One more night was too much time away from her, apparently.

Jackson Lee was not far behind Chitling, and he had an armful of Bitty with him. I started to lift my eyebrows, remembered that it would hurt, and settled for saying, "I guess years of wrestling steers and cows have given you plenty of experience in carrying a two-legged heifer."

"Aw, she's just a little thing," Jackson Lee said promptly. Bitty gave me a smug look that reminded me of her dog. Maybe that saying about people beginning to resemble their dogs really is true.

Rolling my eyes wouldn't be nearly as painful as lifting my brows, so I did. I thought they were kinda cute, though. I mean, there's Jackson Lee, a big Italian-looking guy, with petite blond Bitty held in his arms as carefully as if she was made of glass. Anyone can tell just by the way he acts around her that he's crazy about Bitty. It's written all over his face. He has no self-control when he's with her, that's plain.

When he had Bitty settled in the other chair with a pug on her lap, he sat on the wide, rolled arm next to her and smiled. "Now ladies, I took the whole day off just so I can be of service. What is your pleasure?"

"Jack and coke," Bitty said promptly, and I cleared my throat and gave Jackson Lee the evil eye. He understood what I meant.

"Sugar, how 'bout something else? I know you don't want to upset your stomach with all that stuff the doctors are making you take."

"Oh honey, aren't you the sweetest thing to worry about me? I'll be fine, though. A little drink won't hurt me at all."

Jackson Lee paused. I recognized indecision in his face. I didn't envy him. It would be difficult for him to refuse Bitty. He patted her on the arm and Chen Ling nearly took a plug out of him, so he jerked back.

"You just wait here, sugar," he said, "and I'll surprise you."

"Make it a good surprise," I said as he stood up, and he nodded in my direction. I had no faith that Bitty didn't have him wrapped around her little finger so tight he'd do exactly what she asked. So it was indeed a surprise when he brought us both tall glasses of sweet tea.

He made up for disappointing Bitty by saying, "I know you wanted something else but I'm not about to risk your health even to make you happy, sugar. You're too important."

Now, that would make any woman happy, I thought to myself. It worked on Bitty, too. She beamed up at him and batted her eyelashes, ever the southern belle.

All of a sudden I felt like the third thumb or fifth wheel. It didn't help that I felt so bad, and that my arm had been hurting like the dickens. Maybe I was being stupid for not taking a pain pill. So what if it made me crazy? Crazy was better than hurting.

"Where are the boys?" Bitty asked. "It's awfully quiet."

"They went to a friend's house. We're to call if we need them, but I gave them the afternoon off."

I was proud of myself for not quite lying without having to confess that I had put them out of their own house.

"Well, that's probably best," Bitty said. "When they're here we've got half of Ole Miss here as well. It does get tiring."

I nearly fell off my bed. "Bitty, are you feeling all right? Is it time for another one of your pills?"

"Oh, I'm fine, Trinket. But I know you aren't used to having young people around so much. I suppose I'll feel that way when I'm older, too."

If my right eye hadn't already been swollen shut and my lips nearly the size of water balloons, I would have glared at her and blown a raspberry. As it was, I said, "Yes, I suppose my being six weeks older than you makes a big difference—in dog years."

"Six weeks? Honey, you know you're quite a bit older."

"Eight weeks. Tops. But I don't blame you for forgetting. I was so far ahead of you in school and all that it must have felt like I was much older."

Jackson Lee threw himself into the breach. "Ladies, ladies—let us have civility, please."

Bitty laughed. "Oh sugar, we do this all the time. See how much better Trinket looks now? She was real peaked when we got here, but now she's all perked up."

That was probably true. I hadn't felt like getting off the couch when they arrived, but now I felt like getting up and thumping Bitty on her head. Since I had no intention of doing anything like that, I started laughing. It was silly, really, but Bitty could almost always get me out of feeling sorry for myself.

We were still laughing when the doorbell rang and Jackson Lee went to answer it. He seemed relieved to get out of the parlor, and I couldn't blame him.

"You made everybody get out, didn't you," Bitty said to me like she knew the answer, and I started to nod.

"Yep."

"Good for you. Don't nod, Trinket. It looks like it hurts."

"It does."

"Take a pill," she advised. "It's better than being noble and suffering."

"I'm not trying to be noble. I'm just trying not to be crazy."

Bitty sighed. "Take a chance. If it makes you crazy, at least you won't be in pain."

"What makes you crazy?" Gaynelle Bishop asked from the parlor door. "Being an invalid? Can't say I blame you there."

"Trinket's always been a bad patient. She gets all mopey and irritable, and the rest of us have to put up with her. Have you been to see Rayna yet?"

Gaynelle came in and sat on the small sofa against the wall. "I just left there. She said she'll go nuts if she has to just sit around all the time, but Rob is fussing over her like she can't do a thing for herself. She said she sends him to the store just to get him out of the house for a while so she can get something done."

That sounded like Rayna. She's one of those people who has to stay busy all the time.

"Here." Gaynelle produced a folded newspaper from her purse. "Y'all got a write-up in the Memphis paper about the accident."

"We did?" Bitty sat up a little straighter, but I reached over and took the newspaper from Gaynelle's hand. If it said something tacky, there was no way I'd let Bitty read it. My patience would not deal well with her reaction.

Fortunately, it was a brief paragraph next to a photo of Rayna's crunched SUV, and said only that Holly Springs' police were investigating the accident. It listed our names and ages—a practice I personally think should be abolished since giving out a woman's age is not always polite— and that we were all from Holly Springs. I gave it back to Gaynelle, who handed the paper to Bitty.

"Look at this," Bitty exclaimed a moment later, "they put our ages in here! That is outrageous! I have a good mind to call up the editor and—"

"Here you are, Miss Gaynelle," said Jackson Lee, and he handed her a tall glass of sweet tea. "If you take lemon, I'll get you some."

"No, this is fine, Jackson Lee, thank you."

"Who are you calling, sugar?" Jackson Lee asked Bitty, and she sat there for only an instant with her mouth still open before she shook her head.

"Oh, no one. I was thinking about Rayna's car. I guess it's totaled, isn't it."

"Not even the door handles can be salvaged. Too bad. You know they have pretty good insurance on it, though."

"I imagine so," Gaynelle said. "Not having insurance these days is foolish. Or downright stupid. You never know what might happen."

As we launched into a discussion on the dozens of different evils that had befallen the uninsured, Bitty's doorbell rang again. My head clanged along with it, so I decided to take Bitty's advice and a pain pill. If it made me crazy here, no one would ever notice. I'd fit right in at the Six Chimneys Lunatic Asylum.

My plastic bottle of pain medication had a long name with letters like X and Y in it, and I shook one of the round pills onto my lap since I was working left-handed. It said in the directions not to half the pill as the medication was time-released, so I popped the entire pill into my mouth and swallowed it with sweet tea. Delicious. Soon, I should feel much better. Or at least, bearable.

Jackson Lee returned to the parlor with a thick envelope. It looked like FedEx or UPS had delivered it instead of the post office. That probably meant Bitty had ordered more toys or clothes for Chen Ling. That dog has her own chest of drawers upstairs, an antique Bitty keeps stuffed with outfits from rain slickers and snow boots to designer doggy sunglasses and bikinis. It's ridiculous what too much money can buy.

"Hm," Jackson Lee said, looking at the envelope, "this is from the senator's law firm. Want me to open it for you, sugar?"

Bitty waved a hand. "Heavens, yes. They're always sending me stuff to sign since Philip died, loose-ends that need tidying up, I suppose."

For a moment Jackson Lee paused in opening the envelope. He looked down at Bitty with a frown. "Sugar, you do bring everything you get from his lawyers to me to look at before you sign anything, don't you?"

"Why, most of the time. Unless it's a check."

"Have you gotten any checks recently? Other than the alimony checks?"

"Yes, I think I did. A dividend or settlement check or something like that."

Jackson Lee drew in a deep breath. "Settlement check? Do you still have the paperwork?"

"Of course I do. I put it with the other things to be taken to your office. You know I don't come by there every day, so I put things in a basket to bring to you. Sally is always real nice about reminding me once a month to bring in stuff. Why are you asking me all these questions?"

"I'm not sure, but I'm about to find out, I have a feeling," said Jackson Lee as he finished opening the thick envelope and took out a sheaf of papers thick enough to choke a mule.

As he scanned the cover letter, then flipped it over to read the next page, I saw his face turn colors. He normally has a nice warm complexion given him by heredity and the Mississippi sun, but it began to turn an unhealthy gray. Uh-oh. This may be unpleasant.

After a moment he looked up at Bitty with a grave expression. "We need to talk privately, I think."

"Privately? You can speak freely in front of Trinket and Gaynelle."

"No, Bitty. This is a private matter."

Before she could offer another protest he moved forward, scooped her up from the chair, and carried her out of the parlor. Apparently surprised by the swift decisiveness of his action, Bitty put her arms around his neck and held on.

Chen Ling, however, barked furiously, jumped down from the chair to the carpet, then chased them down the hallway, her toenails clicking furiously against the bare wood floors. The tone of her shrill barks said there would be hell to pay for this outrage.

Gaynelle and I looked at each other.

"Well," she said after a moment, "what did you find out at the Madewells?"

It took a moment for me to remember. Time had ceased to exist since the SUV took a dive into kudzu, it seemed.

"For one thing," I began, "Trina and Trisha were both dating Race. That much is true, although Trina claims to have stopped dating him once she found out he was seeing her sister. Trisha was pretty blunt and honest, and just seemed to want to get this all behind her. Trina, though . . . " I paused. She hadn't seemed forthright, just angry. But angry enough to kill Race? I didn't know that, and didn't know if I should say it, either.

"Trina is still angry, isn't she," Gaynelle stated, and I nodded. That made my head throb, but I still heard her add, "I thought as much. But the question is—is she angry enough to commit murder. We don't know that. We can only guess. Did you see the murder scene, by chance?"

"Trina took us to the cottage. I stayed in the doorway, but Bitty and Rayna went in to the bedroom. Oh, while I was standing in the doorway, I noticed that it's in shadow. If the killer stood in that alcove at night, he or she could see straight into the bedroom from that position."

"And could anyone in the bedroom see into the alcove?"

"Maybe, but not unless they were looking. It would be very easy for someone to sneak in the front door when the living room lights were out and see exactly who and what was going on in the bedroom."

Gaynelle lifted an eyebrow and nodded. "I see. That means—"

A piercing shriek from somewhere down the hallway penetrated walls and my skull to reach my brain. I recognized it immediately as a Bitty-shriek. An *angry* Bitty-shriek. "*Noooooooo!*" the shriek said.

Since I put up my left hand to prop up my head so it wouldn't fall off into my lap, I didn't see Gaynelle jump. I did see her land, however, and she sprawled back into the soft cushions of the sofa with one hand to her chest as if having an attack.

"Are you all right?" I asked, and she gave me a wild look.

"What in God's name was that?"

"Bitty. I think she got some bad news. We'll find out soon, I'm sure." My voice slowed down. How strange. It was an effort to speak, even to focus as Gaynelle faded.

It was the oddest thing, but as I sat there on my couch-bed facing the parlor door, the light coming through wood-shuttered windows took on a fuzzy glow. The parlor walls are painted a deep rose that's almost maroon, but grew brighter and brighter. I tried to think if the sun rose in the east or west, but the answer escaped me. Since these windows faced east, maybe the sun was setting. Or rising. Really, it ceased to matter. I just felt this tingly warmth spread through me, and closed my eyes and thought of that song by Uncle Kracker about fish swimming through my veins . . . or was that him swimming through veins like a fish in the sea? The melody went round and round in my head, and my ears stopped up as if I had soared to a high altitude. Maybe I was flying. That would explain the light. How nice it was to fly. I just drifted and drifted along on the wind and clouds . . .somewhere, far, far, away, I heard someone talking, but they must have been still on the ground while I was high up in the sky. So high. So very nice and high, just floating . . . floating . . ..

"Up, up, and *awaaaayy*, my beautiful, my beautiful *balloooon*," someone close by me sang as I drifted on puffy clouds of light and air.

CHAPTER 12

Someone kept calling my name, and it was very annoying. Over and over, like a broken record, "Trinket! Trinket! Trinket!"

Not only that, but my balloon must have landed pretty hard because I felt the ground shaking beneath me. I tried to open my eyes, but not much happened. So I just let myself drift, and the balloon took off again.

The next time I opened my eyes, the light was gone. A fuzzy darkness blanketed the room, and for a moment I couldn't remember where I was supposed to be. Then it came to me that I hadn't been in a balloon at all, but in Bitty's parlor. Thin slits of light made bars across the floor and up the wall. I blinked, the light wavered, then steadied so that I knew it was real.

My throat and mouth were terribly dry, and I pushed myself up on my left arm to peer at the table beside me. My tea glass was still there, though all the ice had melted long ago. I didn't care. It was wet, and my parched throat soaked it up.

It came to me what had happened. The pain pill, of course. At least I knew it did its job, because I wasn't hurting anywhere, just a residual ache or two. It also knocked me out. Not that I considered that to be a necessarily bad thing. Maybe being knocked out for a while helped. The house was quiet. Not even an annoyed pug could be heard snorting for her dinner.

Thinking of dinner made my stomach growl. The power of suggestion is an odd thing. Bitty always has lots of food in her refrigerator. Perhaps even some of Aunt Sarah's pimento cheese.

I sat up, determined that I was still a bit wobbly, and stood very slowly. When I didn't fall over immediately, I figured I was good to go. So I began my trek to the kitchen. It isn't too far, out the parlor, across the wide hall and entry, through the living room and past the coat closet, then pass under an arch of white-painted molding, and into the kitchen. I knew the path well. That's why when I found myself in the downstairs powder room, I had a momentary pause. I'd obviously made a misstep somewhere. But since I was already there . . . .

When I left the powder room, I felt my way along the walls by touching the rail of wainscoting for a guide. It led me straight to the kitchen doorway. Blinding light flooded the kitchen, and I blinked a few times as I moved cautiously forward. Using my left hand to block out the light some, I managed to find the refrigerator. It was already open.

"Are you hungry?" Bitty asked from somewhere behind me.

"Yes. Room service sucks here. Why didn't you tell me you were in here?"

"Well, for heaven's sake, can't you see me?"

I squinted in the direction of the elusive voice. "I can't see squat. You've turned on all the strobe lights."

"God, Trinket, you really are a wretched patient." There was the sound of motion, then the lights dimmed so that I could open my eyes without risk of having my retinas burned to a crisp. "Is that better?"

"Yes. What is there to eat?"

"We have enough food for about six days, tops. After that—we're down to beans and taters."

Since Bitty sounded glum, I peered in her direction again. "I like beans and taters. Don't you?"

"Not when that's all there is to eat day after day."

I snorted. "Since when have you ever been reduced to eating just beans and taters, may I ask?"

"At your house when we were kids. Don't you remember? It was when Uncle Eddie had just changed jobs and y'all didn't have much money, I guess. I stayed with you while Mama and Daddy were on a trip, and all we had to eat every day was grits and gravy for breakfast, and beans and taters for dinner."

"Hm. I don't remember that. All I remember is we always had enough to eat." I looked back at the well-stocked refrigerator, then what she had said soaked into my rather fuzzy brain. "Why do you think you won't be able to get any more food after six days?" I asked as I found a small plastic container that looked like it might hold pimento cheese. "Did all the stores close down?"

"They might as well have for all the good they'll do me."

It wasn't easy opening the plastic container, and when I got it open with my one good hand, it held what looked like really old lasagna. I put the lid back on it and renewed my search. "Why do you say that?" I asked distractedly, my search for pimento cheese overriding my curiosity.

"Trinket Truevine, pay attention to me instead of food!" Bitty demanded in a tone that got my complete attention. "Did you even hear a word I said earlier?"

"How earlier?" I asked after my brain came up with no instant replay.

Bitty sat at the kitchen counter on one of the bar stools. She looked frazzled. Her hair stuck out at odd angles as if someone had been yanking on it, and her always pressed shirt looked like she'd slept in it, and she had a mysterious stain on the knee of her Capri pants.

"Never mind. You were probably so drugged you didn't hear a thing. I'm broke. Ruined. Cut off. I have no money. Do you understand any of that? *No money!* My life is over. I have to give up everything. I'll end up in a gutter somewhere, me and poor little Chen Ling, eking out an existence by begging for bread crusts on corners . . .." She began to cry then, big tears that slid from her eyes, over her cheeks, and plopped into her lap without her even dabbing at them with an expensive handkerchief.

I tried to absorb what she had just said, but could find no good reason for her to be broke that would happen with such cataclysmic swiftness.

"Did the stock market go bust?" I asked. "Did Wall Street finally steal every bit of money and disappear to some tropical island?"

"Worse than that. Much, much worse than that." She sobbed more loudly.

I straightened up, alarmed. "Did Congress sell America to the highest bidder at last? Do we now belong to China? India? Vanuatu?"

Bitty briefly stopped crying to ask, "What does Vanna White have to do with any of that?"

"Vanuatu. It's an island near Fiji, I think. So answer me. Why are we broke?"

"Oh, *you're* not broke. Just me. Just me, because . . . because I was in a hurry and did something stupid!" Tears flowed freely again.

I was understandably skeptical. To Bitty, being broke means having less than six figures in her mad money checking account.

"Unh huh," I said. "How broke?"

"Ruined! I have only a few thousand left after paying the bills, and no telling *how* long that will last, and with nothing else coming in—I'm ruined!"

I sorted through that for a few seconds. "Why won't you have any money coming in? You always have money coming in: dividends, oil lease payments, alimony, interest on bank accounts—what's changed?"

Bitty sniffed, coughed, and wiped her wet cheeks with the heels of her hands. It was plain to see she was genuinely distressed, not just being melodramatic for a change. Or not being melodramatic for the sake of drama, I suppose I should say.

"Well," she said after composing herself, "since Philip is dead, his attorneys said he's no longer liable for alimony payments every month. Jackson Lee anticipated that he would one day try to get out of paying, and included a clause in our divorce agreement that stipulated that should he die, I would continue to receive a percentage of his estate every month up to but not exceeding our agreed-upon alimony payments. Should I choose to do so, however, I could always accept a lump sum payment in lieu of continued alimony."

Poor thing. She sounded like a sixth grade student reciting a book report. I nodded at her encouragingly, and she took a deep breath, her voice only slightly quivering when she continued.

"So instead of sending a settlement proposal to Jackson Lee's office like they're supposed to do, they sent it directly to me. He didn't even get a copy of it."

"And you signed it without reading it," I said when she gave me a wretched look that spoke volumes.

"Oh no. I didn't sign the agreement at all. I put it with all the other stuff I save to give Jackson Lee once a month. It was the check I signed. It came in a separate envelope, you see, so when it said it was from the Philip Hollandale Estate, I figured they'd just moved the money into another account. I signed it and deposited it as usual."

"So if you haven't signed the agreement, what's the problem?"

"Well, you know I can pretty well follow all that legalese talk lawyers use, but after I read the first page or two, I put the whole thing into the Jackson Lee basket. Since I didn't finish reading it, I didn't get to the part where it said that signing the included check would be construed as signing the agreement, and once the monies were deposited, it would end any further financial obligation on the part of the Hollandale estate. Damn them! You know it was that Patrice and Parrish who put the lawyers up to this trick!"

I didn't doubt that for an instant. Philip's mother and sister had always disliked Bitty. Parrish Hollandale had spoiled her son rotten in childhood, and even if all the stuff Bitty said about him and his sister didn't have an ounce of truth to it, they were really unpleasant people. Parrish Hollandale was rumored to have given a ten thousand dollar garden party in celebration of the event when Philip and Bitty's divorce became final. I also heard that Naomi Spencer was an honored guest at the affair. Talk about spite.

I closed the refrigerator door and joined Bitty at the breakfast bar. While I had no intention of trying to heft my aching body up onto the kitchen stool, I did lean against the counter right beside it.

"Bitty. Jackson Lee is a really smart attorney. You know he will go through those papers with a fine-tooth comb, and if there is even as much as a suggestion of a loophole, he'll find it. You still have investments, you still have property, you still have loads of money in savings. There is no need for you to worry about starving to death or ending up homeless. Six Chimneys is paid for, isn't it? Isn't it? Well, see then, you'll be just fine."

"Taxes. State, city, federal . . . sales taxes, property taxes, all those taxes will eat up every penny I have in a very short time. You know they will." Bitty sucked in a deep breath. "But I'll hold on as long as I can. I'll make up a new budget and get rid of every expense that's not necessary. I'll cut coupons. I'll shop at Wal-Mart. I'll pump my own gas. I'll do my own cooking. I can read, so I can figure out a recipe, surely."

I blinked. If Bitty did even one of those things the earth would probably wobble on its axis.

"You can't cook," was all I said, however. "You can't even boil water without ruining a perfectly good pot."

"You'll teach me, won't you, Trinket?"

I stood there with my mouth open. Then I said weakly, "Teach you to cook?"

"Sure. You can cook, can't you?"

"Not with one hand."

"But that will be perfect. You just tell me what to do, and I'll do it. See? I'll have to let Sharita know I won't be needing her for a while. Maybe a year or two. For however long it takes to get through this."

The prospect of Bitty learning to cook was daunting enough, but doing without money for a year or two? It would kill her. She wouldn't know what to do. She'd be like a baby duck learning to swim in the middle of the Atlantic.

I didn't have the heart to disappoint her, so I said without meaning a word of it, "I'll teach you to cook, Bitty. Everything will be just fine. You'll see. Jackson Lee will be able to figure something out before you have to start shopping at Wal-Mart, I promise."

"Do you really think so, Trinket?"

God, I hope so, I thought, and said aloud, "I really think so. Now. Is there any pimento cheese left?"

Since all the pimento cheese was gone, I ended up eating Sharita's homemade chicken salad. It's delicious, with pine nuts and small cut up grapes, big chunks of chicken and minced celery all mixed up with some kind of seasoned mayo that gives it an excellent flavor. I ate two sandwiches, then felt too full to have dessert, so limped back to my bed in the parlor.

Bitty was already there. She was walking much better, I noticed, and wondered if she'd taken another pain pill. Maybe her pills were less powerful than mine. She stayed awake and alert, if fairly goofy when taking them. I should probably call the doctor and ask for something not quite so strong. Not that my balloon ride hadn't been fun, but I had obviously missed out on important events while flying high in my dreams.

"Where are the boys?" I asked. "Have they come home from Heather's yet?"

Busy spreading a newspaper over her lap, Bitty nodded. "Oh yes. They're all in the basement watching a movie. I said they had until midnight, then everyone needs to go home."

"Well, they are certainly being quiet," I observed. "I wouldn't even have known they were here." Bitty just nodded, and I noticed she had a huge pair of scissors in one hand. She wielded them across the newspaper in her lap with soft snicking sounds. Pieces of paper fell away in neat squares. I watched for a few moments before I couldn't stand it any longer.

"What on earth are you doing?"

Bitty kept snipping, her focus on the paper. "Clipping coupons. I thought I might as well get started on saving our pennies. You eat hot dogs, don't you?"

"Yes. You don't, however."

"Well, I will now. They're like bratwurst or Polish sausage, right?"

"It depends on the kind you buy. Bitty. You have no idea how to make out a grocery list. You have no idea what you have in your pantry. Or your freezer. Wait until tomorrow. Sharita will be here and she can tell you what you need."

"I'm going to need an envelope for these. So, when I go to Wal-Mart all I have to do is pay for stuff with these coupons, right?"

I rolled my eyes and sank back onto the cushioned comfort of two fat goose-feather pillows. "They also require green ones. You know. With the faces of presidents on them."

"Oh." Bitty looked up at me. "Then why am I clipping coupons?"

"Damned if I know. If you go to a Wal-Mart, I want to be there with my camera."

"Trinket, you know I've been to Wal-Mart before."

"Not to shop, Bitty. You go there with someone, not get a cart and go up and down the aisles looking for bargains, price-checking, comparing size to brand—that isn't your style."

"I can't afford my style now," she said, and there was something so vulnerable about her at that moment I couldn't pick at her anymore.

"All right," I said. "I'll show you how to shop at Wal-Mart. Just don't blame me if it turns out wrong."

"How can it turn out wrong?"

I hated to even consider the many ways Bitty could get into trouble at a Wal-Mart store.
****

It was the fire alarm that woke me. At first I thought someone was shrieking, but even in my sleep-fogged and still slightly drugged state, it quickly became apparent that it was much more than that. For one thing, it had a *whoop whoop* sound like no shriek I've ever heard. For another thing, it was continuous, and even Bitty would have to draw a breath every now and then.

I leaped out of my bed too quickly, got dizzy, and stood there a moment before I decided I could walk without falling. So I lurched from the parlor into the hallway. A thick cloud of smoke drifted from the direction of the kitchen. It smelled suspiciously like burnt bacon. I expected a small grease fire, not an inferno. Foolish me.

In the kitchen, it boiled up from the state of the art stove like a black mushroom backlit with orange-red flames. Bitty beat frantically at it with a towel while it spread over the stovetop and licked a path toward the counters. Chen Ling came out from behind the breakfast bar like a pug missile, and shot past me toward the front of the house. Even the dog knew when it was time to abandon ship.

"Bitty!" I yelled over the alarm, "Where's your flour or cornmeal?"

"Are you mad?" she yelled back. "This is no time to be baking!"

There was no time to explain the dynamics of a grease fire. I jerked open a couple of cabinet doors and found something that looked like flour. At the moment I managed to toss it over the worst of the flames, the fire department arrived. A good thing, because whatever was in the plastic canister flared up and shot sparks into the air.

Two firemen wearing helmets, boots, and asbestos jackets and pants barged into the house through the front door. One of them grabbed me and shoved me toward the still open door, while the other one attempted to remove Bitty. She bopped him on the helmet with a metal spoon and said something I was glad I couldn't hear, but he merely picked her up and carried her out onto the front lawn where Chen Ling sensibly sat and barked at the big red fire truck. Bitty was unceremoniously dumped next to her dog.

I stood in the bushes next to the house and regretted wearing just a tee shirt and panties to bed. Thank heavens it was one of those really long tee shirts, but still—there I was, once more outside without proper clothing. Dreams can come true, it seems.

At any rate, moments later Brandon and Clayton were escorted downstairs and joined us on the front lawn, where they looked at their mother in bewilderment.

"What happened?" one of them asked.

"There's something the matter with that stove," said Bitty. "It started a fire!"

"They can do that when they're turned on," I said from the hydrangea bushes, and Bitty shot me a disapproving glare. I didn't care. It didn't take a genius to figure out she had been trying to cook. If nothing else, the charred sticks of bacon were evidence enough against her.

The boys were still confused. "Who turned on the stove? Was it an accident?"

"Your mother was trying to cook," I said as I artfully arranged myself behind the thickest limb of blue snowball flowers. "I think she burned the bacon."

"Trinket, I can speak for myself, thank you," Bitty said in a very shrewish tone. "I do not need you to make up stories."

"*Were* you trying to cook?" I demanded, and when she didn't answer, I added, "See? I was right."

After a moment, one of the boys—Clayton, I think—asked, "Aunt Trinket, why are you standing in the bushes?"

"I didn't have time to dress. What took you boys so long to come downstairs? Didn't you hear the alarm?"

"Oh, we heard it, but thought Mama had just forgotten the code again. She does that sometimes. A lot."

Bitty sat down on a garden bench near a flowerbed that held dozens of pink vinca flowers and a huge blue gazing ball on an elaborate stand. Of course, she was clothed in a dressing gown and silk pajamas, so she didn't have to hide in the hydrangeas like I did.

By now neighbors were out on their front lawns, too. Mrs. Tyree, who lives next door to Bitty, stood at the iron rail fence between their yards and peered over at us. "Are you all doing all right?"

Bitty, ever the gracious hostess, nodded and smiled. "We are doing just fine, Mrs. Tyree, thank you for asking. Lovely morning, isn't it?"

"Yes, quite lovely. Not as quiet as usual, however," Mrs. Tyree responded in a dry tone that made me laugh. She's lived next door to Bitty for years and years and has seen just about everything in that time, I'm sure. Mrs. Tyree is elderly, dignified, and the epitome of a well-educated black woman. She reads voraciously, and in her spare time conducts tours through the Ida B. Wells Museum. I suspect she has more fun keeping up with Bitty's antics than she does watching cable TV.

Across the street beyond the front of the fire engine, I recognized more neighbors. Richard Simmons—no kin to the bouncy gentleman with the exercise videos—wore a bathrobe, slippers, and carried his morning paper in his hand. People craned their necks to see what was happening on their street. It was still so early no one had left for work yet or gotten ready for the day, and they milled around in the brittle early sunlight that hadn't had time to heat things up. Except for a few bugs and the inconvenience of the fire, it might have been as lovely a day as Bitty pretended.

Just about the time the firemen got the fire put out in the house, Bitty's automatic sprinklers came on. I usually forget about those things, since they come on before I get up, and apparently, so had Bitty.

She leaped up from the garden bench as jets of water shot up from the ground like Old Faithful. They're the kind of sprinklers that send out sprays of water in a rapid flow as they make a 360 degree turn to cover as much ground as possible. Since they're every six feet along the water line, there is practically nowhere to escape them if you happen to be standing in the front yard.

Brandon and Clayton made a mad dash for the front porch. Since they were wearing some kind of athletic shorts like basketball players wear, it didn't really matter if they got wet. Bitty made frantic circles looking for a way out, holding her hands in front of her as if to keep the pulses of water at bay. Chen Ling snapped at the water coming from the ground a few times, then beat a retreat to the shelter of the porch.

There was no way I was moving from behind the hydrangea bushes, not with all those people standing in the street. Besides, the water wasn't so bad where I stood since the bushes formed a barrier of sorts. I'm tall enough that the water didn't hit me in the face, either. Poor Bitty.

She staggered drunkenly around the lawn with her eyes closed against the water jets, her hands out in front of her like a blind person might do to keep from running into obstacles. I couldn't stand it.

"Bitty!" I shouted. "Over here! Come over here!"

"Where?" she shrieked, and opened one eye in an attempt to find me. She looked nothing less than a drenched Cyclops in a lovely pink dressing gown, silk pajamas, and with bandaged feet stuck into white fluffy slippers.

That was the picture that made the front page of *The South Reporter*.

CHAPTER 13

Sometimes the worst days in our lives turn out to be not so bad in retrospect. I thought about that a lot in the days following the fire. Bitty's insurance picked up the costs of repairs as well as clean-up, and she and I went to a hotel in Memphis to stay until it was over. Her insurance paid for that, too. Good insurance is essential, we agreed.

That was how we ended up at The Peabody Hotel. Since I'd never stayed there as a guest, but had worked there for two years, I figured it was about time I was treated as nicely as they treat all their guests. We ordered room service in the mornings for our breakfast, spent a leisurely time eating Eggs Benedict and drinking mimosas, then dressed to go downstairs and sit in the lobby.

Bitty, of course, had refused to leave Chen Ling behind no matter how many times I pointed out that dogs aren't welcome in most hotels, but no one said a thing about the ugly baby in the sling. It must be a new part of the employee training that has been implemented since I left their employ. Not that I minded.

No, after the stress and horror of the previous weeks, this was a vacation for both of us. We deserved to be pampered, we said over breakfast mimosas, luncheon Bloody Marys, and supper's White Russians. Well, I had the White Russians and Bitty drank the Jack and Coke. My system is less tolerant than hers, and even though I had gladly left my pain medication behind, I was still taking antibiotics.

So on our sixth day at the hotel, we sat near the marble fountain and watched the ducks paddle around while we drank a Bloody Mary. It was my first, Bitty's second. I had talked her into giving up her pain medication by promising not to say a word about the photograph in the paper. I think it was one of the reasons she was glad to leave Holly Springs behind for a week. Quite a few people had called her about it. If I say it was a bad picture of her, that is a mild statement. It was atrocious. Poor Bitty had her head tilted to the right, her mouth open in a lopsided scream, and one eye squeezed shut while the other eye looked as if it was about to pop right out of the socket. Silk dressing gowns and pajamas have a habit of clinging to the body when drenched, and there was Bitty on the front page of *The South Reporter* with both arms out, one foot lifted, fingers splayed, and silk clinging to her like a second skin. Fortunately for me, all the photographer got of me in the photo were my feet and head. Of course, it looked like I was wearing a bush, but I can overlook that. Nothing important showed.

Anyway, her feet were much better, and she'd removed the bandages and wore shoes again. I still had my right arm in a sling, but since Bitty wore Chen Ling across her chest in a discreet sling, we matched. The casual passersby might assume we had recently been in an auto accident, which was completely true.

"So who do you think ran us off the road?" Bitty asked while stirring her Bloody Mary with the celery stick. "I told the police I think it was Trina Madewell."

"Does Trina drive a black truck?"

"Well, how should I know that?"

"It will be rather important to the police, I'm sure." I took a sip of my drink and briefly reflected on how a bit of vodka can improve the taste of tomato juice, then said, "I don't think it was Trina, somehow."

"Why not?"

Bitty sounded indignant, so I thought about it a moment before I said, "She's angry, but I don't think she's particularly angry at you. She has no reason to be angry with me or Rayna, so why would she want to hurt or kill us?"

"Maybe because she's a bitter, malicious person. She always has been. Have you forgotten how she tried to steal The Cedars away from me? And after I went to all that trouble, too, taking muffins and jams out there to Mr. Sanders all the time."

"But you did get The Cedars on the pilgrimage," I reminded her. "And maybe she really did want to end your feud, or she wouldn't have come to your luncheon no matter how much you begged."

"Sometimes, Trinket, you think everybody has good motives just because you do. It isn't that way anymore. If it ever was."

I sighed. Really, she was right. It isn't necessarily that I always have good motives, it's more like I'm not clever enough to think of all the different ways people can trick each other. People do things that would never occur to me in a million years. I'm always amazed at how many different ways they can beat the system, cheat their friends, family, and the government, and still go on just as happy as a lark. There has to be something wrong with their internal wiring for them to be able to do that. Or maybe I spent too many years listening to Mama explain to us kids why and how we had to behave so that we would be acceptably social human beings. "No one lives as an island," she used to say. "Everything we do has ripples of consequences that reach far beyond our own lives."

I had only to look at the murder of Race Champion to realize the truth in that. He'd been murdered by someone angry at him for some misdeed. Then Naomi had been murdered because she was engaged to Race.

That thought struck me as important. It was that simple: Naomi died because of Race. He died because—he had cheated on the wrong woman? Despite what Bitty thought, Naomi wouldn't have killed Race. I was sure of it. There had been genuine pride in her face when she'd shown us that engagement ring. But someone was angry enough and dangerous enough to kill them both.

Who else had Race Champion been dating?

"Give me your cell phone," I said to Bitty, and she looked startled.

"Are you all right?"

"I'm fine. I just thought of something. Give me your phone. I want to call Gaynelle and find out what the others have discovered."

Bitty dug into her purse and pulled out her phone, and said as she handed it to me, "I don't think I want to know. I'm out of the mood to care about all that now."

"You better care," I said as I dialed Gaynelle's number, "because you may end up the prime suspect in Naomi's murder. As far as the police are concerned, you're the only one known to have a feud with her."

"If you're trying to brighten my day, it's not working."

I made a face at her, and surprisingly, it didn't hurt. My body was healing, and so was my brain. I put it down to the reviving effects of vodka and tomato juice. A miracle cure for the blahs has been found at last. I should really alert the medical community.

"Gaynelle," I said when she answered, "we need to talk."

****

"I was having fun," said Bitty in a wistful tone. I looked over at her from the passenger seat of her Franklin Benz. We were almost back to Holly Springs. Bitty hadn't wanted to leave The Peabody. Neither did I, really, but unless we had our driver's licenses changed to reflect our new addresses, we would have to return eventually.

When I said as much to her, she sighed. "I know. It was just that we didn't really have to do anything or think about anything but whether to have the Eggs Benedict again or the fresh croissants and fruit. Or if it was cool enough to go on the roof to listen to the band."

"Bitty, that describes your entire life," I said. "Your most difficult decision is usually something along the lines of which color car you want to buy."

She looked over at me. "Not true. I have had lots of hard decisions to make, and you know it."

"You're right," I said, because she was. "But you must admit that most of the time now you have very little to worry about except your boys." A porcine snort from the wide front seat made me add, "And Chitling."

"You sound like you want me to have to make hard decisions."

"Of course not. I just want you to remember that no matter how difficult things might get at times, basically you are very well-prepared."

"Oh. Well, I used to be prepared. Now I'm broke. Unless I can figure out a way to get my homeowner's insurance to support me until Jackson Lee finds a loophole in those damn papers, I'll have to stand on street corners and beg for spare change."

I patted her on the arm with my left hand. "I'll buy you coffee at Budgie's every day." To my surprise, big tears rolled from her eyes. "Hey, I was just joking. You know everything is going to be fine. Don't cry, Bitty. I can't stand to see you cry."

"I can't help it. These past few days have been so nice because I could pretend it was like always, but now I'm going home where I'll be reminded every minute that I'm as poor as Job's whiskey."

Her metaphor perplexed me, but I said, "You are not poor. You are just having a temporary cash flow . . . er . . . blockage."

"That's *it!*" Bitty suddenly put on the brakes and swerved to the shoulder of 78 Highway. A semi behind us laid on his air horn and rattled our car windows as he passed us at seventy miles per hour. The movement of the passing truck made the heavy Benz rock like a baby cradle.

I'd grabbed hold of the dashboard with my left hand and braced for a crash, and when it didn't happen, I let go of the breath I had been holding. "Fawww!" I said.

Bitty ignored me. She unbuckled her seatbelt, grabbed her purse and pug, and opened the car door. "Don't just sit there, Trinket. Come on."

Come on? Where? We were on the shoulder of 78 Highway, not at a mall. It took me a moment to figure out what she was doing; then I saw the neon sign above a house trailer that backed up to the highway: *Psychic*. It glowed in a bright red, and on a painted yellow sign next to it: $5.

When I didn't open my door and get out of the car, Bitty came around and opened it for me. "Get out and come with me. You might as well, because you know I'm going to do this."

She was right. I knew Bitty would visit the psychic come hell or high water. I still had to protest: "How good can she be if she lives in a house trailer on the side of 78 Highway?"

My protest went unheeded, as I figured it would. I got out of the car only because the quicker I cooperated, the faster we would get home.

Grass was knee-high on the verge and in the ditch that lay between the shoulder of the highway and the backyard of the house trailer. I had on sandals. By the time we got up to the wooden porch off the back of the trailer, I had cockleburs between two of my toes. And probably a family of deer ticks nestled happily in the cuff of my Lee jeans. Hello, Lyme disease.

Bitty knocked on the door, and we waited for someone to answer. "If she was any good at all," I muttered as I dug at the cockleburs, "she would have known we were coming and met us at the door."

"Be quiet. I hear someone coming."

I'm not quite sure what I expected, but it certainly wasn't the ordinary looking woman who answered the door. "Come in,' she said, and motioned us to follow her, so we went into the trailer that smelled like tomatoes and oregano. We'd entered the small kitchen, where she had a huge pot on the stove and something simmering.

When she gestured, we sat at the round kitchen table flanked by four chairs. She went to the stove and stirred the pot a couple times.

I couldn't help myself. I put two fingers of my left hand to my forehead, closed my eyes for a second and said, "I see . . . spaghetti sauce in your future."

Bitty was irritated and tried to kick me, but I'd anticipated her and moved my feet. Fortunately, the woman at the stove looked over her shoulder and laughed.

"You must be psychic."

"Not in the least. But thank you."

"You may call me Gypsy," she said when she pulled out a chair to sit down with us at the small table. "It is not my name in this world, but I prefer it."

In this world? Great. We were sitting in an ordinary house trailer with perfectly ordinary furniture, and talking to a crazy person. I felt right at home.

"First I must tell you," said Gypsy, "that the regular psychic was called away today. I will be glad to answer your questions and give you a reading, but if you prefer to come back, I will not be insulted."

"So, you're a substitute psychic?" I looked over at Bitty, who narrowed her eyes at me. "It's up to you," I said. "I'm just along for the ride."

Gypsy smiled. When Bitty said she would be honored to have a reading by her, the psychic got up to lower the window blinds and light candles. With it darker in the kitchen, it seemed less prosaic and a bit more mysterious. She crossed into the living area and dimmed the lights, then disappeared into the room beyond.

Bitty leaned forward. "Don't ruin this for me!"

"God forbid. I'll behave. Witch's honor." I made a solemn sign in the air that earned a bark from Chen Ling. Until then, I'd forgotten the little beggar was still with us. She was in her usual sling, peering out from Bitty's chest like some wayward gnome.

Gypsy returned, wearing a shimmering shawl over her head and around her shoulders. For some reason, it seemed to change her entire appearance. Before, she'd been an ordinary looking woman with brown hair and regular features; now she looked suddenly exotic and other-worldly. Maybe I'm just suggestible. I'm positive Bitty is.

She had a pack of badly worn cards with her. Strange symbols were on them, like nothing I'd seen before. She shuffled them expertly, halved them, then set them out in three separate stacks of almost equal size. Without speaking, she motioned for Bitty to re-stack them. Bitty did, unusually silent as if caught up in a spell. Even Chen Ling was quiet, and I thought that if nothing else, that was remarkable.

Then Gypsy picked up the cards and dealt them on the table in an intricate pattern like a gigantic cross. She started talking in a different language, more to the cards than to Bitty or even herself. I couldn't understand a word of it, and I doubted Bitty could either. After a couple minutes, Gypsy reached out in an abrupt movement and scattered the cards. She looked up at Bitty with a frown.

"The cards are not talking today. There is no charge."

Bitty looked as confused as I felt. "What do you mean? I don't understand."

Gypsy stood up, then bent over and blew out the candles. "I am not the regular person who does this. Perhaps I do not do it well. Come back another time."

"But—maybe I can ask some questions first? There are things I need to know that you can help me with, if you—"

"I cannot help you. You must help yourself." Gypsy looked straight into Bitty's eyes. "But I tell you this—One who is good, is not. There is darkness inside the light."

In what seemed like only an instant, we stood outside on the wooden porch off the back of the trailer. The door shut behind us with a firm click. Bitty and I looked at each other.

"Well," I said, "I think that was her way of telling you to carry a flashlight."

"Funny," Bitty said, and went down the stairs and out into the grassy yard. "Now what do I do? I was just sure she could tell us who killed Race and Naomi. And I wanted to know some lottery numbers, too."

"Bitty, if she knew the winning lottery numbers, do you think she'd be living in a trailer?"

"But she doesn't live there. She said so. She was just filling in."

"She probably lives in the trailer next door. I knew this was a bad idea, but you never listen to me. You're so hard-headed and always have to be right—"

Bitty hit the remote on her car keys and the horn beeped, engine started, and lights flashed. "It's not that far to Holly Springs from here, Trinket. If you walk fast, you should be there before dark."

"Have I ever told you how pretty you look in that color pink? It really sets off the tone of your complexion. Peaches and cream. Yep. Very flattering."

"That's better. Do get in, dearest cousin, and I'll turn the air up just for you."

We both laughed. I love the way Bitty gets over some things so easily.

By the time we got to Six Chimneys and took in our overnight bags, the workmen were quitting for lunch. It was amazing what they'd gotten done in such a short time. There was no trace of the smoke that had darkened white molding and painted walls, and no burned smell in the air. While it did have the scent of fresh paint and sawdust, it wasn't unpleasant. New granite countertops replaced the ones scorched by fire, and there was a new vent and stovetop as well. Only the floorboards in front of the stove had been charred, and Bitty had chosen to have them sanded and refinished rather than taken out, since they were original to the house. She was lucky the entire house hadn't gone up in flames like a paper airplane. Antebellum homes are hardly flame-retardant.

All the furniture had been removed to be cleaned, and canvas drop cloths lay over the floors. The house looked odd without the furniture, like it belonged to someone else.

"I'll be glad when the furniture comes back," Bitty said with that instinct she has for knowing what I'm thinking. "It looks so empty in here."

"Well, there's still the basement and upstairs. There's furniture there."

"Bless Jackson Lee. He took care of getting all this done for me, handling the insurance company and all."

"Don't forget that your boys helped, too."

"Oh, I haven't. I've been thinking about them a lot, and thanking my lucky stars that their trust funds weren't affected by my stupidity. They'll be fine. They can still go to Ole Miss, still have everything they need. I just won't be able to help them any."

"Bitty, I'm sure they don't care about that. They love you, not what you buy them or give them."

She nodded. Even though she sounded a bit sad, she didn't look distressed, and I was glad about that.

"Well, speak of the devil," I said when I saw Brandon open the door coming up from the basement. "One of my two favorite nephews."

"Hi, Aunt Trinket, Mama," he said, and grinned. "I take it y'all were talking about me?"

He came to his mother and gave her a hug and kiss, not at all embarrassed to be doing so in front of Heather, who followed close behind him.

"I'm always talking about you," Bitty said, and smiled at Heather. "Did he rope you into helping?"

"No, ma'am. I offered. I'm pretty good with a broom and dustpan. It was the least I could do since he helped me move."

"Ho," I said to Brandon, "you *have* been busy while we were gone."

"A lot busier than Clayton. He's been lazy as a hound dog. I can't get him off the video game long enough to do anything."

Bitty smiled. "Don't worry about Clayton. I'll be sure he does his part. Is he by himself down there?"

"For now. If you want to talk to him, better unplug the PSP first."

"Oh, he'll listen to me," Bitty said as she headed for the basement door.

Left alone with Brandon and Heather, I handed him my overnight bag. "I think I'm staying in the guest room now that I can walk without whining."

He grinned and took my bag. "You got well pretty quick. How did you manage that?"

"Vodka and tomato juice," I replied promptly. "They have amazing healing powers, I've discovered. I recommend it to anyone."

"I think Mama's out of vodka, but I do have some julep syrup in the refrigerator if you're interested."

"Interested? Any more interested and I'd be wagging my tail and barking."

Heather laughed, and she climbed the staircase to the second floor with us, making small talk as we went.

"Miz B got in some new merchandise yesterday. You should come see some of the lovely things she ordered."

"Um, I don't know—did Rose Allgood have anything to do with the orders?"

"No," Heather said, and giggled. "She has her own catalogue."

"Ah, a Frederick's of Hollywood, I presume."

"Ma'am? I don't think I know who that is."

"It's all right. I'm probably way behind the times."

Frederick's of Hollywood was popular when I was young. Or younger. It was a catalogue filled with . . . *unusual* . . . garments. Panties without a crotch, for instance. Strap-on dildos. Lingerie so sheer that wearing it would be like wearing nothing but lace around the throat and on the wrist cuffs. Nowadays you see stuff like that on cable TV, so I guess Frederick's went out of business. Or is thriving on the Internet.

I had stayed in Bitty's guest room before, and was relieved to see that nothing important had changed. It was still filled with antiques, still comfortable, and still light and airy. The high antique headboard has a lovely canopy, and a light summer quilt was spread atop the overstuffed mattress. Bitty loves antiques, but she's practical, too. No one wants to sleep on an antique mattress, I don't care how into antiques they may be.

Brandon set my overnight bag on a chair, and he and Heather paused in the door to look back at me. "Do you want your julep on the sunporch or up here?"

"The sunporch, please. I'm sure your mama will find me out there. Especially if she knows you're making juleps. Extra mint in mine, please."

"I always do, Aunt Trinket."

Heather looked puzzled. "Aunt? I thought you were Miss Bitty's cousin."

"Oh, I am. We use it in the southern sense. You know." When Heather still looked puzzled, I explained, "Any relative that's a second cousin, third cousin, or not related at all but still included in the family is called Aunt or Uncle. You're from down here. Doesn't your family do that, too?"

Heather shook her head. "No, I guess not."

"Well, it's what we've done all my life, so I suppose we're used to it. I'll be down soon to join you. I think I want to freshen up a bit first."

I closed the door behind them and went into the adjoining bathroom. It had been two days since I'd had the courage to look at my face, and now that I was on familiar turf, I wanted to see if I looked less like a Halloween poster and more like a human.

Bitty should really change the lights in that bathroom. They're awful. For one thing, they're far too bright. For another, they shine down on a person's face so it looks like you have two chins. The shadows are terrible. But, all in all, I was healing nicely, I decided. My black eye had faded to only a faint bruise, my lips were back to their normal size, and the cut on my forehead was a pale pink line. It was important that I look fairly decent since I expected Kit would be coming over soon for a visit.

He had wanted to come see me in Memphis, but I begged him to reconsider. My purple and blue bruises had turned a very ugly yellow and my lips were still puffy. I wanted to wait until I could put on makeup. Yes,

I guess I am vainer than I ever thought I'd be. Still, what woman wants a man she likes to keep seeing her at her worst? Not many I know of, that's for sure.

When I got downstairs at last, Gaynelle and Rayna were on the sunporch with Bitty. They already had mint juleps in their hands, so I knew I was behind before I got started. Within thirty seconds, Brandon placed a sterling silver cup in my hand. To keep my fingers from freezing, the cup was inside a small, intricately wrought holder with a handle like a coffee cup. Very nice. Juleps are mostly ice anyway, flavored with just the right amount of bourbon, sugar, and crushed mint. Bitty keeps the sugar syrup in a pitcher in the refrigerator year-round. Just in case.

I listened to Gaynelle and Rayna while I sucked the ice against my front teeth and enjoyed the exquisite pleasure of bourbon and mint-flavored sugar syrup. It is a most refreshing drink for a hot summer afternoon, I can tell you.

Stretched out on one of the lounge chairs with fat cushions, a ceiling fan whirring overhead and a cold drink in my hand, I appreciated the moment for what it was and let their voices fade into the background. I already knew most of what they were discussing anyway, since I had picked Gaynelle's brain clean of information before ever starting back to Holly Springs.

The Divas assigned to question Naomi's family had learned that since meeting Race, she'd dated no one else. Not even once. She had been head over heels for him. So that ruled out any jealous man from her past; or almost ruled it out. There could always be some nut lurking out there like a stalker, I soon discovered.

The most interesting information had been gained by Gaynelle's group when they questioned Race Champion's family. It was pretty well known that Race was a terrible womanizer, and no one in his family argued that point. However, his younger brother claimed Race was being stalked by someone, and it had spooked him pretty bad. That information was helpful and fascinating. No, the brother didn't know who it was, but he knew she'd made a habit of following Race around. She'd even come to their house in Ashland once, but no one had seen her. The only way Race had known about it was the note she'd left in the cab of his truck.

Too bad the brother couldn't find the note, or that would have been a great help. As it was, however, the information gave us a bigger picture of what might have been going on. Maybe Naomi hadn't had a stalker, but Race had.

I pondered the likelihood of a man as big and beefy as Race being afraid of a female stalker. Had it been a woman connected to an ex-boyfriend of Naomi's, perhaps? Someone jealous of her that her family didn't know about, or pretended not to know about? But if they did know who it was, they'd be more likely to tell so suspicion wouldn't smirch the memory of their daughter/sister. They'd want to clear her name of any kind of suspicion about murdering Race—wouldn't they?

"Trinket. Trinket! *Trinket*—don't you agree?"

I blinked and looked over at Bitty. "Agree to what?"

"I knew you weren't listening. I can always tell you're off in the ozone when you get that glazed look in your eyes. We should just let the police handle everything. Don't you agree?"

Normally I would have immediately agreed. It's always best to let professionals handle matters, especially when one of the matters is murder.

This time I wasn't so certain. For one thing, I had a personal stake in it now. Someone had tried to kill us. Whoever it was hadn't cared that we had family, or that none of us were guilty of anything more than snooping—they'd decided to be judge, jury, and executioner. I didn't like that.

When I shook my head, Bitty's mouth fell open. She'd obviously been sure I would agree with her. "No," I said, "I think this time it's personal, and I intend to find out what I can. Not that I intend to go snooping where I shouldn't, though. I'm not brave enough to do that. Or stupid."

As usual, Bitty recovered quickly from her surprise. "Well," she said, "*I* do not intend to do any more investigating. Especially not after what Gypsy told me."

"What gypsy?" Rayna immediately wanted to know. "You know a gypsy?"

"Her name is Gypsy," I explained before Bitty could. "But she could be a gypsy, I suppose. I'm not sure of that."

"As I was saying before Trinket so rudely interrupted," Bitty continued, "I was told by Gypsy to beware. So beware I shall be.. Besides, I have troubles of my own that demand all my attention right now."

"Yes, Bitty is to beware of a flashlight," I interrupted cheerfully. "Or carry one. Gypsy didn't specify, so we're not sure which it is."

"Trinket Truevine, you know very well that's not what she meant. She said I must watch out for the darkness behind the light."

"That could mean anything, Bitty. She could have meant you need to watch the street lamps come on for all we know. She just acted strange, that's all."

"Since when did acting strange upset you? We all act strange."

"We all *are* strange," I corrected. "But she's on a different level of strange. It's not the same thing at all."

Even Gaynelle agreed with that last comment. "Psychics operate on another frequency entirely, Bitty. An interesting phenomenon. But we are straying from our main purpose, and that is to figure out who is behind the murders of Race and Naomi. Find the killer, and we find out who tried to kill you, too. I'm sure of it."

I was sure of it, too. Normally, I'm not a vengeful person. Oh, I can be bitter and bitchy, certainly, but I don't go out of my way to right a slight or perceived slight. I prefer to let time and fate do it. It usually settles matters long before anything I could do would have an effect. No, I do not consider myself vengeful at all. Yet something about the cold, calculated murders and our attempted murders got to me. It took a truly warped individual to commit such acts.

"Do you think Trina and Trisha Madewell are capable of killing Race?" I asked Gaynelle. "Either separately or together?"

She thought about that for a moment, tapping her fingernail against the silver rim of her mint julep as she pondered my questions. Then she shook her head. "Not really. I think in a heat of passion, yes, threatening to shoot him would fit their personalities. But the actual deed? Not unless it was accidental."

"Well, you're dead wrong about that," Bitty said decisively, not even seeming to recognize her pun. "Trina Madewell is quite capable of murder."

"On what do you base that belief?" Rayna asked.

Bitty blinked at her. "Well, look how vicious she was about getting the winning bid on Six Chimneys. And getting The Cedars out from under me for the pilgrimage. Not to mention what she went and told the garden club, and now that horrid Miranda Watson at *The South Reporter*. If she doesn't have a murderer's soul, I'll eat my Sunday hat."

"You better have a Sunday hat made of bread and cheese, then," said Gaynelle. "I don't think Trina did it."

"What about Trisha?" I couldn't help reminding them. "Do you think she could do it?"

Gaynelle frowned slightly, and contemplated that question while she sipped from her julep. "Trisha is largely an unknown quantity to me. I know Trina mainly because we sat together on the social committee at church. So I cannot say for certain if Trisha is capable or incapable of murder. It does not seem to fit her personality, but I could be wrong, of course. I have been wrong about people before, you know."

We tactfully let that last comment lie unremarked. It was obviously still a painful subject for Gaynelle.

"There does seem to be a lot of animosity between the sisters," I said. "Especially when it came to the subject of Race Champion. Trisha seemed much more forthright to me about matters, while Trina—and here I'm going to contradict myself and sound just like Bitty—sounded defensive and secretive."

"*Aha!*" said Bitty.

"That doesn't mean she's hiding anything more deadly than a secret wish to smack her sister in the head with a loaf of bread," I continued as if Bitty hadn't *aha*-ed me at all. "And she's probably defensive because she's been asked dozens of questions by the police, and invited to tea just to find out gory details, and now she suspects the entire town of having ulterior motives."

After a moment of silence, Bitty commented, "You come up with great scenarios and then shoot them down. Why do you do that? Can't you just stick with one theme?"

"I'm thinking out loud, Bitty. I trust you three to pick apart my theories and find the flaws. What we end up with should be pretty much solid facts without any kind of personal emotions coloring them."

Bitty flapped a hand at me and yawned. "I'm tired of playing Law and Order with the rest of you. I have to figure out how to save myself from complete ruin, so I shouldn't be wasting my brain cells on things we already pay the police to do."

I looked at Gaynelle and Rayna, who both kind of shrugged as if to say, *Well, that's Bitty for you.*

A little irritated by her attitude, since I thought she should care more about some nut running people off the road, not to mention killing two others, I said, "Of course, we should have thought of that, Bitty. Why on earth would we want to think of anything but your lack of enough money to buy a dog more diamond collars?"

I told you I can be bitchy. I'd like to put it down to pain or exhaustion or some other reason, but that would be dishonest. I confess, it was pure bitchiness that made me be so mean. Fortunately, Bitty didn't take great offense. Instead, she crossed her legs at the ankles, lifted her sterling silver cup in my direction, and said:

"My, my, it's so vairy, vairy wahm in heah."

Since I recognized her ploy immediately, I countered, "Well, turn off the heat" in my thickest Southern drawl so that it came out more like, *Wail, tuhn awf th' heet.*

Then we both laughed. Thank heavens Bitty is reasonable and forgiving, even if she is a little scatty at times. You can see why I love her, I'm sure.

Gaynelle and Rayna wisely decided to ignore us both.

"Are you going to the funeral?" Rayna asked me, and I blinked at her.

"Whose funeral?"

"Race Champion's," said Gaynelle. "His body was sent back from Jackson this week and the funeral is tomorrow."

"Oh. Well, I never met him, after all. Are you going?"

They both nodded, and Rayna leaned forward a little to peer at Bitty. "We thought the three of us should go and see what happens."

"What happens?" I echoed while Bitty frowned at them; or tried to frown. Too much Botox can be risky.

"Yes," Bitty answered me, looking away from Rayna and Gaynelle. "It should be interesting since Race's father is Naomi's uncle's first cousin. I don't care. I'm not going."

While I tried to figure that out, ticking through the family relationships to see what that would have made a marriage between Naomi and Race, I heard Rayna say, "But isn't that just through marriage or something?"

That put a new wrinkle in my deciphering, so I stopped trying to figure it out. It would likely give me a headache.

"Bitty," said Gaynelle rather sternly, "you must go with us to Race's funeral. You knew him. It wouldn't look right if you didn't go."

"I knew him, but I didn't like him. Therefore, I shouldn't have to go."

"But no one knows you didn't like him," Rayna said. "Besides, we really need a good reason to go, and you're it. We don't want to look like ghouls just showing up to gawk."

"You *are* ghouls just showing up to gawk."

"Not at all. It's been my experience that funerals often bring out the worst in the bereaved," Gaynelle said. "It would be to our advantage if that happens tomorrow, since we would be right there to hear it."

"Hear what?" Bitty demanded. "How Race drank too much and ran around with any and everything in a skirt? That's common knowledge. You don't have to go to his funeral to hear that. Just ask anyone in town. They'll tell you."

I decided to intervene. "Bitty, I think what they're trying to tell you is that it's not only possible, it's likely that Naomi's family and Race's family will have words if they're both at the funeral. See? Race's family probably thinks just like everyone else does, that Naomi killed him. So if—what's her name?"

"Sukey," Gaynelle supplied the mother's name for me.

"If Sukey," I continued, "shows up at the funeral as family, there may be hard feelings. Loud and hopefully overheard hard feelings."

"Well." Bitty flounced around on the longue, took another sip of julep, patted Chen Ling atop her grumpy little head, and then said, "All right. I'll go. But I'm not happy. And I'm not going to the cemetery, either. I have no desire at all to get pushed into the dirt."

The last made me reflect on the funerals I'd attended in the past. Oddly enough, the only ones that really stick in my mind are those in the South. Maybe because I hadn't really known people well enough in other parts of the country to attend their family funerals, but really, it is probably because the Southern funerals seem to come with grand theatrics and high emotions. If not during the funeral itself, at the wake or the gathering of family and friends afterward. Of course, I've always assumed it was my family alone that has relatives prone to, shall we say— *awkward* outbursts of emotion at times of great stress.

Although recent events have given me the comforting notion that other families might also be demonstrative in certain situations, I'm still not certain there are many families who can completely qualify as candidates for Whitfield's caring embrace. Proof remains to be found.

"May I come, too?" I heard myself ask, and before the enormity of what I'd said aloud penetrated my stupefied brain, Bitty looked over at me.

"You have no other choice."

"I bet Trina and Trisha Madewell will be there," Rayna mused aloud, and we all looked at each other.

Ever practical, Gaynelle said: "Wear something washable, ladies."

CHAPTER 14

Funerals are really for the living, I've decided over the years. The dead aren't actually there to appreciate how many people dress up and show up, except maybe in spirit. Nor are they there to hear the eulogies spoken on their behalf.

That can be a good thing.

It turns out that Roland "Race" Champion wasn't a frequent church-goer. Nor was his family. In fact, it was doubtful any of them had seen the inside of a church except for funerals in their entire lives. So the minister who was drafted to perform the services had to separate gossip from fact and try to come up with a polite, gracious speech about how wonderful a man had been taken away far too young from the bosom of his loving family.

Ministers are probably grossly underpaid.

It would have made more sense to me to just have the funeral home take care of all those details and have the service in their own chapel, but I wasn't consulted. And apparently there was some kind of scheduling conflict at the Ashland Methodist church, so the services were to be conducted graveside in the Ashland cemetery on School Street.

A long, solemn procession of cars filed behind the black hearse as it rolled up and down the hilly highway between Holly Springs and Ashland. The twenty miles had never seemed quite so far. I sat up front with Bitty—sans pug—and Rayna and Gaynelle sat in the back.

"Where will the wake be held?" Rayna wondered aloud, and I turned to look at her.

"If you're referring to the gathering after the funeral, I hope you don't expect me to go *there*."

"Why not? If you're going to the funeral, you might as well get to eat some good food later."

"That's only if you know who's doing the cooking," I said.

"Trinket, remember where we live. Since the Champions don't really belong to a church, I can almost guarantee you there will be Baptist and Methodist ladies' societies trying to outdo each other with covered dishes and desserts."

I reflected a moment, then nodded. "That's probably true. Then it depends on where the wake is being held as to whether or not I go."

Rayna and Gaynelle both nodded understanding. At least once in our lives I'm sure we've all found ourselves at someone's house for an after-funeral gathering that included family pets walking on counters, tables, and the stove, and hosts of insects lined up greedily at food platters. There are bathrooms in this world so dirty that I prefer to go outside behind a bush rather than risk my bare behind on a toilet seat occupied by hordes of bacteria. In fact, I prefer an old-fashioned outhouse to some of the bathrooms I've been unfortunate enough to see in my lifetime. It's enough to scar people forever.

At any rate, with the matter of the wake settled, we discussed odds and ends of gossip rather than what was really on our minds. The motive for Race's murder still hung in the air like a giant question mark. We'd been back and forth over it a hundred times and none of us had come up with a reason that seemed good enough.

It occurred to me that perhaps we were looking at it the wrong way. For us, there was no good motive for murder. But for the person who had shot him, obviously they thought there was reason enough. Maybe we should stop looking so closely for a clear motive, and look for someone capable of murdering two people in cold blood. It had to be the same person. Nothing else made sense.

But who did we know who would be capable of such a thing?

Anyway, there we all were, Bitty, Rayna, Gaynelle and I, comfortably seated in Bitty's Franklin Benz and driving slowly over broken asphalt, red rock and loose gravel as we followed the hearse and long line of cars to Ashland. Two motorcycle cops led the procession. When we turned off Highway 4 onto Ripley Street, the line slowed to a crawl.

There are two cemeteries in Ashland. This one is on School Street across from the brick high school and a couple of Headstart metal buildings. Smaller cemeteries sprawl on church grounds throughout Benton county, as well as family cemeteries, but this cemetery has been in use for a century and a half or more. Some of the headstones are moss-covered and leaning and some are brand new, a glistening white that speaks of new grief. A few ancient trees provide some shade here and there, and on the far side could be seen the bright green of a funeral tent erected for those who had come to pay their last respects to Race Champion.

Cars snaked around the cemetery toward a distant goal, until finally we got to the gravesite. The awning had been erected over strips of green artificial grass that made a square around the grave. Folding chairs were set up on three sides, some of them in the bright sunlight that beat down mercilessly. Tripods of flower wreaths ringed the entire area, and I could see NHRA on some of the ribbon banners. Apparently the National Hot

Rod Association was well-represented. Red carnations, white lilies, gladiolas, red, yellow, and pink roses; even sunny daisies filled the air with scent. As soon as I opened the car door I could smell their fragrance on the hot breeze.

Gaynelle carried an old-fashioned parasol, and popped it open as we gathered by Bitty's car. I recognized a lot more people than I'd thought I would, seeing as how I had been away from the area for so long, but Bitty quietly pointed out the ones she thought important.

"That's Ashland's mayor over there, and see that woman with the frizzy hair? We used to go to school with her. Her name's Jewell Hopkins. Or was back then. I think it's Jones now. Or maybe Smith. One of those. And over there is—"

"Trina and Trisha Madewell," I interrupted. Bitty caught her breath and I gave Rayna a nudge with my elbow and then bent my head in the Madewells' direction. She in turn nudged Gaynelle, and we all stood gawking from under the scant shadow of a pink polka dot parasol for a moment. We must have looked like idiots.

I broke away from the others before people turned to stare, and started toward the gravesite, angling in the general direction of the Madewell sisters. They both wore black. I mean jet black, too. Even their stockings were black. The thought of wearing pantyhose in this heat made me itch. I don't know how they did it. I had worn nice cotton slacks so I didn't have to even think about hose. My mother would be horrified if she knew. She still believes in the old ways of wearing white cotton gloves and hose to any function that is remotely public. Fortunately, though I'd never burned my bra, I had burned all the old-time civilities during my rebellious teenage years and never looked back. I felt no guilt whatsoever.

In the heat of a Mississippi summer, black is not the coolest color to wear. I'd thought ahead, so my light cotton slacks were a tan that matched my short-sleeved black and tan shirt. It was cool and somber at the same time, I'd thought when I looked at my reflection in Bitty's antique mirror. My sensible black flats matched my cheap pleather purse, and all in all, I thought I represented Southern womanhood respectably.

Trina and Trisha both wore long-sleeved black dresses, black hats with flurries of black netting that half-hid their faces, and carried black handkerchiefs in their hands. I really felt sorry for them, as much because of the heat as their obvious grief. It's always sad to lose someone you care about, even if that someone cheated on you. There has to be several dozen country songs dedicated to just that very theme.

Behind me I heard Gaynelle whisper, *"Is that Sukey Spencer I see over there?"* and it was quickly followed with Bitty's, *"Omigod, it is! I just knew she'd show up!"*

Rayna caught up with me. "Hold on, Trinket. If there's going to be trouble, I want to stand by you." Just as I was feeling flattered, she added, "You're tall enough to block anything coming my way."

"Thank you" was all I could think of to reply.

The arrival of Naomi Spencer's mother portended trouble. This is the woman who is banned from every major store between Holly Springs and Tupelo because she's a kleptomaniac, so perhaps it's understandable. I looked around the growing crowd to find her.

"Which one is she?" I finally asked Rayna, and she bent her head in the direction of a line of wreaths set up on tripods. I looked. Searing sunlight was blinding enough, but all the wreaths had banners with messages written in glitter that reflected light in broken refractions. I squinted. "I can't see anyone."

"The blond dressed in sequins," she replied in a loud whisper.

For a moment I had a difficult time telling what was sequins and what was glitter, then I distinguished the wreath banners from the woman when she moved toward the line of chairs set up under the funeral home awning. Sukey Spencer wore a dark navy dress with a flirty chiffon skirt; the bodice was made entirely of blue sequins. Sunlight bounced off her chest in a dozen different Morse Code messages, and I had to really squint to keep looking at her. I should have worn sunglasses.

"She looks like she's on fire," I whispered back to Rayna, and she nodded.

"Sukey always looks like that. I heard she even wears nightgowns with glitter and sequins sewn on the front."

"Maybe she's kin to Chen Ling," I murmured, and Rayna giggled. We were both pretty nervous. I could tell she was by the way her bracelet bangles kept clinking together, even though she had her hands clasped in front of her. It's pretty easy for people to tell when I'm nervous. I say stupid things.

My focus was on Naomi Spencer's mother as she walked slowly across the uneven ground toward the funeral tent. She wasn't quite what I'd expected. For some reason I'd envisioned a much older woman, the kind who went out in public with foam rollers in her hair and flip-flops on her feet. I hope I never get to the age when I feel comfortable at the local Wal-Mart or Sears store wearing house slippers, hair rollers and no underwear. Not that there's anything intrinsically wrong with people who do feel comfortable doing that, I guess; it's just that Mama spent far too many years investing her time and advice into me about always wearing clean underwear in case I was involved in a wreck for me to flout her rules on social etiquette at my age.

At any rate, Sukey Spencer didn't look at all the kind of person to flout etiquette rules, either. While she was rather gaudy in her sequins, satin, and chiffon, I cannot say she looked slovenly. Just the opposite, in fact. Her blond hair had been teased and curled into submission, her navy blue stockings matched her navy blue dress and shoes, and even the huge purse she carried was a dark navy blue. It looked like a diaper bag, with pockets and wide straps, and seemed to weigh her down a bit as she struggled over a rut in the ground.

"I wonder if she could get a microwave into that purse?" I must have said aloud, because Rayna dug her elbow into my ribs and shook her head. I looked around and realized a kind of hush had fallen over the crowd, even though moments before everyone had been talking almost normally.

The black hearse had stopped several yards away, and the doors opened. It was easy to tell the funeral home people from the pall bearers; they all wore dark suits and had stoic faces. The pall bearers were dressed in what was probably their best clothes, but hardly looked like suits. Two wore casual jackets; most wore shirt sleeves and ties. One of them wore a NHRA jersey and blue jeans. Probably a family member. They were all stout young men, with the oldest no more than forty, maybe. The pall bearer wearing the National Hot Rod Association jersey looked grim. He had a buzz cut that showed pink scalp, and big ears like jug handles.

A tall, cadaverous looking man stood beneath the tent, a Bible in his hands. He held his head up, gazing out at the crowd as people trickled into place and a cleared path was made for the pall bearers and casket. The brittle sound of metal on metal cut sharply into the silence as the casket was pulled from the hearse and the men each grabbed hold of the long handles on the two sides. They carried it to the waiting metal frame behind the bright green fake grass and settled it into place. The man with the Bible moved to stand right in front of Race's casket. Apparently, he was the minister.

He launched into an obviously rehearsed eulogy, listing the virtues of the deceased as a wonderful son, brother, and friend beloved by all who met him. While he listed all the accomplishments of Race's life, I let my gaze wander. Sukey Spencer stood as rigid as a pole, her eyes fastened on the pallbearers still gathered around the coffin with their heads bent. Not far from her, Trina and Trisha Madewell sobbed softly into their black lace handkerchiefs. Really, I had no place being at this funeral. I felt awkward, and made up my mind to slip away just as soon as I could do so without being noticed.

Finally, the minister asked if anyone else wished to say something. No one spoke. It looked like the funeral was over when the minister bowed his head for the final prayer. A nice service, and blessedly brief, I thought to myself when the minister ended his prayer.

I didn't realize I'd been holding my breath until the pallbearers stepped back and I let it out. The cinnamon scent of Big Red chewing gum wafted away on the hot breeze. In stressful situations my throat gets dry. I chew gum to grease my jaws. Or at least, that's how Daddy puts it when he sees me smacking away on a tasteless wad of gum.

"Greasing those jaws, girl?" he'll say, and that's when I realize I'm probably making too much noise.

Since Daddy wasn't there to make sure I stayed quiet, I decided to tuck the gum up into my cheek until I'd made the ritual progression through the tent to speak to the family seated beneath its green shade. While I worked it up there with the tip of my tongue, my peripheral vision caught a flurry of motion off to the side. Naturally, I turned to look.

Sukey Spencer had a big old gun pointed right at the NHRA pallbearer's head. It didn't waver even though it was a really big gun and she didn't look strong enough to hold it up that way for too long. Sunlight gleamed along the length of the wicked-looking barrel. She said something to him I couldn't hear from where I stood, and he slowly turned around to look at her.

By that time, several mourners had moved hastily out of the way so that NHRA stood there virtually alone, only a couple yards from the minister and the coffin. The rest of us stood there as if nailed to the dirt, watching the scene play out like it was on-stage.

"*Ohmygod*," I heard Gaynelle say in a shocked whisper, "that's Race's brother! Why would Sukey want to shoot *him*?"

Sukey started yelling at Race's brother, using the gun to emphasize her points as she jabbed it toward him. People had scattered, but he stood still, just looking at her with a face scrubbed clean of any kind of emotion. She could have been giving him a grocery list for all it seemed like at the moment.

As if drawn by an invisible rope, the four of us moved closer so we could hear what she was saying. If Bitty hadn't been behind me pushing, I probably would have stayed right where I was, but she somehow managed to herd the three of us toward the danger zone despite our reluctance. Since we were behind and to the left, I felt pretty sure we were out of Sukey's sight and range. Of course, that was subject to change at any moment.

Still, when we got close enough to hear, I wasn't that surprised to hear Sukey talking about her daughter. Frankly, I would have been more surprised if she hadn't been talking about Naomi.

"She was too young . . . and beautiful . . . she didn't have to die," Sukey was saying to him, and the young man just kept still and silent, although his eyes were watchful. "It was you, wasn't it? I know it was.

You told Artie that you knew she'd killed your brother and you'd get her if it was the last thing you ever did!"

Safely tucked out of sight behind the three of us, Bitty stood on her tiptoes and whispered in my ear, "Artie is Sukey's older brother."

Sukey started poking the pistol toward the NHRA guy a bit erratically. I thought she looked about to completely lose it and braced myself for the sound of a gunshot. She took a step closer to him, wobbled a bit on the uneven ground, then halted.

"I want to hear you say it. I want you to tell everyone here just what you did to my baby!" she shouted.

Finally he spoke, his voice low and his words terse: "No. I never did nothin' to Naomi."

"You're the only one who had a reason!" Sukey screamed at him "Almost every other person 'round here loved her!"

Somehow I knew what would happen next, and I straightened to my full height and squared my shoulders to shield Bitty from sight.

"Not *her*," NHRA said, and jabbed a finger in our direction. "Not Miz Hollandale. She hated Naomi and you know it."

All of a sudden being a human shield got really risky. Sukey Spencer swung her eyes—and gun—toward us as we stood there in a little knot of Divas. She looked really wild. Saliva had gathered at the corners of her mouth so that spit flew when she spoke.

"You're lyin'! I don't see her. She ain't here."

To forestall the inevitable, Gaynelle took three bold steps toward Sukey. Using her schoolteacher tone, she said sharply, "Sukey Lee Spencer, you know good and well that what you are doing is wrong. Stop it this instant."

Sukey's eyes widened slightly. "Miz Bishop," she started to say, then stopped as she apparently caught sight of Bitty standing behind me and Rayna. Anger replaced the look of surprise on her face and the gun barrel lifted. Hot air shimmered in a haze freighted with apprehension. My heart beat so hard and loud it could have been heard all the way back to Holly Springs. It occurred to me that this crazy woman's gun could blow a hole the size of a baseball through any one of us.

"*You!*" she shouted. "Miz High-and-Mighty Bitty Hollandale! Was it you that killed my baby? Did you? Just because of the money? Is that it? Why should you care now if the senator left my girl all that money! You got what you could off him, why begrudge her a little bit?"

An indignant Bitty popped around from behind me before I could stop her. "What do you *mean*, Philip left her money? Are you crazy? He wouldn't do that!"

Sukey acted offended. "Well, why shouldn't he? She spent damn near two years puttin' up with all his wishy-washy crap. She should'a got something for her trouble!"

Bitty made a hissing sound like a snake, and for an instant, I was afraid she was going to do something really stupid and lunge toward Sukey Spencer. But then Gaynelle took a quick step forward and brought the end of her folded pink parasol right down on Sukey's gun so that it flew from her hands. Apparently her action also activated not only the latch of the parasol so that it popped open with a snap, it caught the trigger on the gun somehow. Or maybe Sukey had it cocked. I don't know. All I know is that it went off with an eardrum-splitting *BANG!*

All sound temporarily ceased, while around me things seemed to happen in slow motion.

Somehow the pink parasol went airborne like a polka dot butterfly, and just beyond its unmanned flight the minister and NHRA both jumped a few feet into the air. NHRA landed on his feet a good yard closer to where we stood, but the poor minister toppled backward into the open grave. I saw the Bible fly into the air and his legs go up, feet pointing skyward for a brief moment before he disappeared into the dark, earthy space between the coffin and the Astro-turf. For a moment no one else moved.

Then Gaynelle's open parasol landed atop the funeral tent, the curved handle caught on a rope, and it swung upside down from the tent-edge to rock to and fro. That seemed to jar people into action. Two men leaned over to peer into the grave, while two men ran toward the gun lying on the ground; I could tell they were shouting by the way the veins bulged in their necks, but fortunately, my hearing was still blissfully gone. I could imagine what they were saying, and I didn't much blame them. That didn't mean I wanted to hear it, though.

By the time my hearing returned with a snap, crackle, and pop, most of the loud shouting was over. Just an occasional sharp word rose above the small crowd gathered in the cemetery. Apparently there was a disagreement about how best to rescue the minister flailing about in the grave, and another quarrel erupted between the two men hovering over Sukey's pistol. Neither one of them seemed inclined to actually pick it up. Their objections wavered between disturbing any fingerprints or keeping it away from the crazy lady. Since she was moving closer to the gun, I leaned toward the latter option.

Fortunately, several uniformed men got to Sukey before she got to her gun again, and one of them grabbed her by the upper arm and held her tight.

"Now, Miz Sukey, you don't wanna do that," he said calmly.

She argued with him, but it didn't matter since he just kept shaking his head and telling her he'd warned her before about shooting at people. He gestured to one of the motorcycle cops with him, and the man picked up the gun, broke it open and removed all the bullets, then snapped the cylinder shut. The sheriff took the pistol and Sukey Spencer, and headed back across the cemetery toward Ripley Street. I could hear her still arguing with him as he put her into his patrol car. He just nodded his head and patted her on the back before he shut the door.

It was a bit deflating. I'd expected something straight out of *Law & Order*, maybe, with rights being read, handcuffs used, and so on. Apparently the Ashland police have other methods for maintaining peace, because there aren't too many murders that happen in the area.

When I looked back at Bitty, I saw that she was positively furious. Her blue eyes glittered so bright it was hard looking at her, and I put up a hand as if to shield myself.

"Whoa! If looks could kill—" I stopped talking right there. It seemed best.

Gaynelle retrieved her wayward parasol, manhandled it until it was neatly folded again, and came up and took Bitty by the arm. "Come on, dear. I brought some emergency beverage. It's in the car."

"Did you hear that?" Bitty complained angrily. "Philip left that twit something in his will! I can't believe it! How dare he—"

Gaynelle gave her arm a little shake. "Bitty. Calm down. People are watching and listening." So Bitty shut up as Gaynelle escorted her to the car to be refreshed.

Rayna and I stood there in the searing sun without speaking for a moment. Then we looked at each other and shrugged. Whatever else happened this summer, it couldn't possibly beat the bizarre antics at this funeral.

CHAPTER 15

As I'd feared, we attended the wake. It was held at the Champion home, a nice little Craftsman bungalow-style house in Ashland. Next door sits an antebellum home of the type most popular in the 19th century. Across the street is a third-story Victorian era home, complete with a pineapple fountain in the front yard. The house had been painted a nice shade of pink.

Cars lined the street on both sides, and Bitty ended up parking at the end of the street where it dead-ends in green and brown furrowed fields. We sat for a few minutes in her car. I occupied the time trying to think of an excuse good enough to get us all back to Holly Springs without invading a wake I was sure we hadn't been invited to attend.

Bitty occupied that same two and a half minutes dabbing pressed powder on her nose and re-applying mascara to her lashes.

"Are there going to be photographers at the wake?" I asked a bit shrewishly. "If I'd known, I would have worn my best pearls."

"You lost those things thirty years ago," Bitty said without pausing in the sweep of the mascara wand up her lashes. "I remember that only because you said at the time that without them you would never be able to look like Laura Petrie."

For the unfamiliar, in the 1960s TV program *The Dick Van Dyke Show*, Laura Petrie was married to Rob Petrie. Her real name is Mary Tyler Moore, and no matter how hard I tried, the pearls would not have been enough; I would have had to lose fifty pounds and have cosmetic surgery to ever come close to looking like her.

"Mercy, Trinket," said Gaynelle, assessing me from the back seat, "pearls would not help at all. Why did you think they would?"

I was getting pretty irritated by the trivia that seems to compose my life. "Because every TV housewife wore pearls, even when they wore slacks and sweaters, and I thought that was the way it was supposed to be in suburbia, that's why."

"Yet you married Perry." Bitty snapped her compact closed. "Whatever made you think he would settle down in a house in the suburbs?"

"Probably the same thing that made you think Frank Caldwell would ever be an honest businessman," I retorted. "Idiocy."

Instead of being insulted, Bitty just nodded. "Can't argue with the truth. Are we ready, ladies?"

"Ready to go home," I said. "We can't just walk in where there's grieving family, Bitty. We don't even know these people!"

"Of course we do. Or I do. You don't think I'd go if I thought I wasn't going to be welcome, do you?"

Yes. I certainly did. Bitty assumes she's welcome everywhere. Maybe she usually is welcome, but this was a wake, not a fund raiser. I tried to think of a way to say that, and ended up trailing behind as Bitty and the others started up the blacktop road. It occurred to me that if Rayna and Gaynelle weren't that worried, I was probably wrong in thinking we would be out of place. I just wasn't used to barging in without being expressly invited, I told myself.

"Now listen," Rayna suggested as we walked up the tree-lined street toward the Champion house, "we need to find out what we can. The best way is to just keep our ears open and our mouths shut, unless the perfect question comes to mind. Bitty, why don't you and I stay together?"

I was rather grateful that Rayna would have Bitty under her wing. That left me free to hide in the bathroom until the madness of our scheme became clear to the rest of our happy little group. It would eventually, I was sure. After all, entering the home of a grieving family just to find out possible information about their loved one seemed—well, just plain wrong. It helped that our motive was to find his murderer, but somehow the police or relatives rarely saw it that way.

Despite my certainty that people would immediately gawk at us and demand to know why we were there to pay our respects to the bereaved, Bitty was greeted warmly by the deceased's father. He grasped both her hands in his and leaned forward to give her a peck on the cheek.

"It's nice of you to come, Miz Hollandale," he said while he still held her hands tight in his big paws. "Especially after the mess at the funeral. We're honored. I mean, you bein' a senator's wife and all."

"*Ex*-wife," a female voice said from behind me, and I wasn't a bit surprised to see the Madewell sisters when I turned to look. Trina Madewell didn't even flinch when I lifted my eyebrow at her. Instead she stuck her square chin up into the air, and her tone was harsh. "She dated Race one time, then never returned his calls after that, so don't go thinking she had any big love for him."

Mr. Champion turned his head to look at Trina. "Don't matter none, missy. She's here now, and we're honored to have her in our house."

Since the elder Champion still held fast to Bitty's hands, even though I saw her try to pull away, I figured he must be the only family member to feel that way. That notion was cemented by a woman's appearance at his elbow, and the expression on her face was guarded.

"Husband," she said in more of a question than comment, "I've been waitin' on you to come help in the kitchen."

"Somebody's got to be out here to greet folks nice enough to show up for our boy's funeral," he replied. "Meet Miz Hollandale. The Miss'ippi state senator's wife."

Before Trina Madewell could speak up again, I said quickly, "I'm her cousin, Trinket Truevine. We are so very sorry for your loss, Mr. and Mrs. Champion. I never met him, but I understand your son was a famous race car driver."

Finally the elder Champion let go of one of Bitty's hands to gesture to the wall in an adjoining room. Even from the front room it was easy to see that trophies lined wood shelves; they gleamed dully in the light that came through multi-paned windows.

"Three hunnerd and forty-two trophies and ribbons he won doing his racing. Got most of 'em in the first few years. That was before he got hurt a couple years ago. If it hadn't been for Cliff Wages, he'd of won the national championship that year."

He turned his head to look back at Bitty. "It was your husband that promised to see justice done for that, and I reckon he would'a done it if not for goin' and gettin' hisself killed. 'Course, now that Race is gone . . . well, I guess it don't matter much anymore."

Since Bitty had been uncharacteristically silent, I glanced at her face to see if she was paying attention. Her eyes were open; a good sign, I thought. But her brows were tucked down in a slight frown despite the Botox.

"I think I remember hearing Philip talk about that," she said. "Something about a deliberate sabotage on Race's car."

As she spoke, she pulled firmly away from Champion's grip; her hands were a bit red from how hard he'd held them. When he reached for her again, she deftly avoided his grasp by turning to put her hand on Rayna's arm.

"Don't you remember, Rayna? There was a big fuss about it for a while, but no one could ever prove Cliff Wages messed with that alternative thing."

"Alternator," Champion corrected. "Buck Sewell saw Wages messin' around the car and hollered at him to get out of the garage. They checked ever'thing out, but he'd been so sly they never saw what he'd done 'til after the wreck. It was Wages that runned over my boy, even though ever'one was hollerin' at him and wavin' flags and all after the danged car quit on the track. Sent him to the hospital and kept him out the rest of the year gettin' over it." He shook his head. "Race wasn't the same after that.

Wages got plumb away with it, too. Police wouldn't press charges or nuthin'. 'Course, he took off like a scalded cat after that race, and last I heard, he's out in California or Mexico."

By that time, several others had joined our little group standing in the middle of the plain living room. Some of the men nodded their heads like they knew what was said was true. Then the conversation switched to engine sizes and horsepower, so I looked around for the bathroom. Maybe I could hide until this was over. Especially if they had any good magazines.

Gaynelle nudged me and whispered in my ear, "See what you can find out about Cliff Wages."

I whispered back, "Okay" without any intention whatsoever of questioning the mourners. As soon as Gaynelle moved on, I went off in search of the bathroom.

After our greeting and acceptance by the family, no one seemed to care if we were there or not. The bathroom was right off the hallway to the kitchen. It was very clean and neat, a little old-fashioned with a flowery shower curtain and what were obviously the "good" towels put out for guests. Unfortunately, the only magazines were about hot rods. Still, I spent as much time as possible in there, washing my hands, looking out the window at the brick house next door, and thinking how easy it was to get mixed up in uncomfortable situations when I hung around with Bitty. She attracts weird people and circumstances. I seem to always get caught in the fall-out, which must say something about me, too. But Bitty's a Leo; she gets away with it. My horoscope usually has dire warnings about getting involved in risky situations.

While I stared out the window at the neighbor's brick wall, I thought about the man who'd sabotaged Race's hot rod. If he was guilty of doing a mean thing like that, was he also capable of murder? It was a distinct possibility. Maybe Race's murder had nothing at all to do with Naomi or jealous women, but with a rival hot rod driver. But if that was true, why had Naomi been killed? It was always possible that her murder wasn't tied to Race's, but also highly unlikely.

Truthfully, I still suspected the Madewell sisters of *something*, if not murder. It was just too much of a coincidence that we had no sooner left their property than a mystery truck ran us off the road. Police had yet to find the truck. It could be anywhere.

Rayna had driven Rob's old Jeep up and down back roads, hills, abandoned properties, and as close as she could get without trespassing on the Madewell property. No luck; there had not been one sign of the black truck with a shattered windshield and Bitty's bullets. There were dozens of abandoned barns in Benton and Marshall Counties; the truck could be sitting right in Holly Springs, and unless we knew where to look, we'd never find it.

So many irritating clues, so little progress. All any of the Divas had been able to discover so far were bits and pieces of interesting information that still didn't form a pattern. That I could see, anyway. Naomi being in the late senator's will was definitely an intriguing fact that should be important. But how? I just couldn't see the Hollandale women paying someone to knock her off, regardless of how much she might have gotten. Besides, they would have paid well to get rid of Bitty first.

While Bitty wouldn't put it past Trina Madewell to have killed both Race and Naomi, I wasn't quite so sure. Trina was certainly an angry person and she'd been engaged to Race. She had motive and opportunity. The police had interviewed her several times, I knew from Jackson Lee. But they'd interviewed us more than once, too, and I knew none of us had killed either one of them. Or was pretty sure. Recent experience convinced me that it's not always possible to identify someone capable of murder. People can hide things about themselves pretty well.

After the second person rattled the glass doorknob, I decided my time hiding in the bathroom was at an end and I would have to join the mourners. As I made my way out the door and past the rather irritated looking gentleman in the hallway, I chirped Bitty-style, "Thank you for being so patient with me. It must be the beer."

The man looked startled, then nodded agreement and a comment that "beer is only rented anyway" as he went into the bathroom and shut the door. I hoped he remembered to put the seat back down. Most men never do. It had been an on-going battle with my ex about that, until he'd pointed out quite reasonably that if men should remember to put the toilet seat back down, women should remember to look before sitting.

The long hallway started in the living room and ended in the kitchen, with doors opening to other rooms. I chose the kitchen instead of the den, where evidence of Race's hot rod career lined all the walls. Of course, it would have been rude not to eat, and since I've never been one to refuse a plate of southern pit barbecue, I heaped a pile of chopped pork onto an open hamburger bun, garnished it with a generous dollop of coleslaw and a hefty squeeze of dark red vinegary-sweet barbecue sauce, and ate two of them along with a scoop of baked beans and a handful of potato chips. Maybe invading a wake wasn't as bad an idea as I'd first thought. I could eat and pretend to mingle at the same time.

All kinds of pies, cakes, and other desserts lined the clean kitchen counters. Other dishes crowded table tops. Certainly, the generosity of neighbors and churches was well-represented. Not to mention the generosity of friends who had brought six-packs on ice.

It's a strange thing about wakes. Even though a loved one is being honored for passing from this life, the things people say about the deceased is often as funny as it may be sad. Maybe it makes family feel better to know so many people have fond memories of the dearly departed, or maybe, it's just that laughter—even through tears—helps lighten even the heaviest heart. It's an unspoken rule that people should try and find just the right balance for an amusing story about the deceased, and not go off into some other direction.

Of course, in the case of murder, some rules just fly right out of the windows.

Race's brother obviously had trouble with the rules. He came in late, then drank beer and glowered at people from a corner of the den instead of mingling. Most people wisely stayed away from him.

Not Bitty.

She stopped right in front of him, put both hands on her hips, and said, "I want to know what you meant at the cemetery about *me* having a reason to kill Race. You know better than that, Ronny Champion."

For a moment he didn't say anything back. He took a swig of his beer and looked away from her. Then he sucked in a deep breath. "Aw'right, I'll say it: You had more reason than anybody I know to kill Naomi, and from what Race told me, you're probably the one who was stalking him."

Bitty's eyes narrowed, and I was really glad she wasn't armed.

"For your information, I have never had to stalk *any* man, much less a man like—well, an engaged man like Race."

At least she hadn't ended that sentence the way it started out. No point in insulting the deceased to his brother's face.

"Well, somebody was stalking him," Ronny said harshly. "I found a note stuck in his truck windshield."

I couldn't help asking, "You don't still have that note do you?"

He looked at me and shook his head. "Naw. Gave it to the police. They'll find out who wrote it."

"Why do you think it wasn't Naomi who left the note?" I asked. "That would seem more likely, wouldn't it?"

"Yeah, but she pitched a hissy fit when she saw the note, so we pretty much figured she didn't write it. Besides, why should she when they were engaged and all? I couldn't believe it when Race said he was gonna marry her, but then it got easy to figure out why."

"What was in the note?" I asked at the same time as Bitty asked, "Why was he going to marry Naomi?"

He looked from me to Bitty, then shrugged. "I've already told all this to the cops. There's no point in going over it again, especially with people who don't really care."

"You're wrong," Bitty said before I could think of a reason besides the truth. "I do care about what happened to Race. Maybe not for the same reason Naomi cared, but he should never have been shot down like he was. It's wrong."

Ronny suddenly grinned. "Funny, you saying that when if it wasn't for you, he probably wouldn't have been with her anyway."

"Because of *me*?" Bitty looked stunned. "He was with Naomi because of *me*?"

"Not so much you, as your husband's money."

By now I was thoroughly confused, but I could see Bitty was beginning to understand. She sucked in a sharp breath and then let it out slowly before saying, "Are you telling me Race got engaged to Naomi because he thought she was inheriting money from Philip's estate?"

He laughed. "Something like that. She talked about it all the time, about how the senator had promised to put her in his will, and how after the divorce he'd even shown her some papers that said she'd get a couple million dollars if he died."

"That's preposterous," Bitty snapped. "Most of his money was tied up in family holdings. If anyone had been able to get their hands on it, it would have been his sister, not that twit with plastic boobs!"

"Did you read the note?" I asked in the sudden silence that fell in our part of the room. A few people had turned to gawk at us, but it didn't seem as important as finding out what had been in the note left on Race's windshield.

Ronny shrugged. "Yeah. It didn't say much. But it sure spooked Race, I know that."

"Did he tell you who he thought wrote it?" Rayna asked, and I realized she and Gaynelle had joined us.

Another shrug, and he lifted the beer bottle to his mouth. "Just said it was some crazy chick that wouldn't leave him alone. Followed him from Biloxi to Oxford and then here."

That didn't sound like Naomi. Or either of the Madewell sisters, either. Who else had Race Champion promised to marry?

When I looked away from the beer-guzzling brother, I happened to catch Trina Madewell's eyes. She had a look on her face as if she was wondering the same thing.

It was Trisha, though, who asked, "Did Naomi promise to invest in Race's new hot rod so he could get more sponsors?"

Ronny nodded. "She said she'd pay whatever it took to get him back on the track."

Trisha and Trina exchanged glances. It wasn't long before they left the wake, and thankfully, we left soon after them.

After we finally left Ashland, we ended up at Rayna's where we rehashed the day's events. Since Gaynelle had fortified Bitty with beverage at the funeral, she was still going strong, despite nearly getting shot by Naomi's poor crazed mother.

"Really," I said, more to myself than to anyone else sitting out in the sunroom, "I feel sorry for Sukey Spencer. I can't imagine what I'd do if someone hurt my child."

"I can," said Bitty. "I'd shoot whoever was responsible."

"Now see," Gaynelle chided, "that's the reason we can't take you anywhere, Bitty. You keep saying incriminating things."

"Oh for heaven's sake, I'm among friends, aren't I? Well? Aren't I?"

We reassured her she was, but Rayna added the warning, "You aren't always so sure of other people, though. Keep in mind that not everyone we know wishes us well."

"I should say not. Miranda Watson is still on my list. Why do you suppose Trina Madewell thought it would help anything to go and talk to that gossipy woman? Did you hear Race's aunt ask me if it was true that we cast spells and talk to the devil at our Diva meetings? I almost said yes, just so she'd stop asking stupid questions about the Divas."

Bitty can have a very long memory about some things. Not that I blame her. For a week after Miranda's nasty column came out in *The South Reporter*, Mama kept asking me questions about what we planned for our next Diva meeting. It was most unsettling.

"That might be a fun theme," Rayna said after a moment. "Maybe for Halloween we could dress up like witches, create some kind of brew, and get a psychic to come tell all our fortunes."

"That's still four months away. We need a psychic now," Gaynelle said.

Bitty flapped her hand. "I tried that, remember? The woman wasn't at all helpful. Just said I should carry a flashlight or something like that."

I started to disagree, then thought better of it. Why go into that again? There are times when explaining things to Bitty can be very wearing on the nerves.

"So where do we go from here?" I asked the group at large. "We have information the police already have, and since they haven't made any arrests, I'm assuming none of it is very important. Or strong enough evidence against any one person or persons."

Bitty dug into her purse and brought out her car keys. "I don't know about the rest of you, but I have an engagement this evening. So I'm going home to get ready. Trinket? Do you want a ride to your car?"

My car was parked in front of Bitty's house, so I nodded. All of a sudden I was very tired. The thought of going home sounded wonderful. We left Rayna and Gaynelle still discussing possibilities and walked out to Bitty's car. It had gotten a lot cooler than it had been earlier, but the leather seats were still hot to the touch.

"You need cloth seat covers," I remarked, and Bitty blew out a derisive raspberry.

"You're just spoiled by mediocrity. What are you doing tonight?"

"With any luck, sleeping until tomorrow night. I take it you and Jackson Lee are going out?"

"Why do you think he's the only man in my life?"

"Because he is. Isn't he?"

"Yes. Do you think Philip really left that—Naomi—any money?"

"It's doubtful, Bitty. Besides, you didn't leave him with any money to give her, did you?"

"Oh, he had money stuck in all kinds of different accounts, the crook. I'll bet he had money the IRS couldn't find in a million years. Offshore accounts or something like that."

"Well, don't brood about it. Even if he did leave her money, she can't spend it where she is now."

For some reason Naomi's face as I'd last seen it suddenly came to mind, and I winced. Poor girl. No one should have to die like that. Not even Bitty's mortal enemy.

Not surprisingly, Bitty echoed my thoughts: "Poor girl. I didn't like her, but it was a horrible way to end."

Since Brandon and Clayton were obviously having a party when we got to Bitty's house, I was even happier I was going home to the relative peace and quiet of my parents and their menagerie. At least their neurotic dog and feral cats don't play loud music and eat all the good food. Yet, anyway.

"Honestly," Bitty muttered as she pulled into the already crowded driveway, "it's not like I can afford feeding all these kids anymore. Now that I'm broke and have to beg for food, you'd think the boys would understand."

I rolled my eyes. "You don't have to beg for food yet, Bitty. Before it gets to that point you can sell a car or two. Or one of your houses."

She gave me a horrified look. "Sell my house? Then where would I be? A poor widow out on the street with nowhere to live and no one who cares . . . ."

To my consternation she burst into tears. Real tears, too, not just Bitty trying to get sympathy tears. So I refrained from reminding her that she was not technically a widow and gave her an awkward pat on the back.

"Everything will turn out all right, Bitty. Really it will. Jackson Lee will figure it all out, and you won't have to worry about money or where to live."

"You really think so, Trinket?"

"I do. Stop worrying so much."

She sniffed pitifully and used the edge of a tissue to dab at her tears. "I try not to think about it all the time, but you know, it's always there in the back of my mind. What would I *do* if I had to live like you?"

I knew what she meant so didn't take any real offense. Bitty has never had to do without money. Her daddy married into a wealthy family and made tons of money on his own, and Bitty married men who had a knack for making money, even if they didn't quite figure out how to do it legally. I married Perry. He was legally lazy.

"Don't worry," I said. "You won't end up like me. It just seems that way now."

"I hope not. I don't know how you do it. I go crazy just thinking about having to watch every penny at the grocery store, or not being able to buy things I like . . . I'm really spoiled, I guess."

"I hope you aren't expecting me to argue," I teased, and she smiled.

"That would be too much to expect. Well, Jackson Lee won't let me starve. He's smart and he'll figure out a way around all that legal stuff."

Bitty really is good at bouncing back.

Brandon appeared at the driver's side of her car, and his cheerful grin made us both smile. "About time you got back," he chided. "Chen Ling is wearing me out. Why do you keep spoiling that dog?"

"Because she appreciates it," Bitty replied with a wag of her finger. "I'm not so sure about you boys."

"Oh, Brandon appreciates it, Miz Hollandale," said Heather, who had followed him out to the car. "He's always saying how much you do for them."

"He better," I put my two cents in, "or I'm putting in my application to take his place. I wouldn't mind being back in school and carefree again."

Heather looked at me with a faint smile. "It's not as carefree as some people think it is."

"Time has a way of erasing the worst memories," I agreed. "But I do seem to have a good memory for all the wrong things. I'm always amazed at the trivia that sticks in my mind. It does come in useful at the oddest times, though."

Bitty slanted her eyes at me. "Trinket is much older than me, you know. Don't be thinking *I'm* getting senile yet."

Heather laughed. "Don't worry, Miz Hollandale. I would never make the mistake of underestimating you."

"Smart girl," Brandon said, and slid his arm around Heather's shoulders to give her a squeeze. "See why I hang around her?"

Heather flipped the ends of her long hair and affected a sultry smile. "And here I thought it was my beauty that intrigues you."

"Oh, that's just the icing on the cake, sugar," Brandon returned easily, and I was somehow reminded of his daddy. Frank Caldwell had been just as charming, but not as sincere. Fortunately, their sons seemed to have inherited their father's charm but their mother's moral center. Bitty may seem shallow at times, but she's intrinsically honest, and a generous-hearted, loving person.

"I'm off," I said as I got out of Bitty's car. "Y'all are piling it too high for me."

I stuck my head back into the passenger side to say to Bitty, "Next time there's a funeral for someone I don't know—don't call me, okay?"

For a minute she didn't answer, just stared at Brandon and Heather; then she gave a shrug and turned to me and said, "You know you enjoyed it."

I straightened up. "I enjoyed the barbecue sandwich, not the gunfire. And no," I held up my hand and said at the question already forming on Brandon's lips, "I have no desire to rehash it. Ask your mother. She just loves sharing information."

True to form, as I walked down the driveway to my car, I heard Bitty launching into what promised to be a long retelling of everything that had happened that day. That should keep her busy and her mind off other problems for a while, I thought. And it saved me having to repeat it when I knew I'd have to go home and tell Mama and Daddy about it. They would never forgive me if they heard it from someone else first.

As usual, my mother continuously surprises me. When I went in the kitchen door, she had a frosted pitcher of lemonade and a glass ready. She poured lemonade over ice, while I tried to avoid Brownie's lukewarm greeting. The dog has finally decided that I'm a permanent resident, I suppose, so treats me as one of his rivals. His greetings now constitute a showing of teeth accompanied by a low growl. Mama shushed him and pointed to an empty kitchen chair.

"Sit. Drink. Then tell me everything."

"I fondly remember the days when you refused to gossip," I said as I pulled out the old ladder-back chair. "Now you insist upon knowing all kinds of details."

"Don't be too sassy," Mama said as she sat down. "Or I'll tell everyone in my Sunday School class about your refusal to wear clothes until you were two. The postman will back me up. He still remembers pulling your training panties out of our mailbox."

"Blackmailer," I said. "Besides, he's retired and in a nursing home carrying on long conversations with doorknobs now. No one would believe him."

Mama just looked at me, and I knew she wasn't bluffing.

"Well," I began, "it was the first funeral I've been to where the preacher ends up in the grave before the deceased . . . ."

I finished reciting the day's events by saying, "So that's how Race Champion got shot a third time."

Mama's eyes were wide. "You're kidding."

I shook my head. "Nope. Race's brother said a bullet went right through the casket."

By this time Daddy had joined us. He shook his head and continued to stroke Brownie's head since the dog was sitting in his lap at the table like he belonged there. "It amazes me just how many folks get so riled up about money," he said. "Especially when it's not their money in the first place. Why did Sukey think the senator owed her daughter anything?"

"You've got me," I said. "Bitty was fit to be tied, of course. She doesn't doubt for a moment that Philip promised Naomi money. She just doubts he kept his promise to really put it in his will."

"I can't see the senator doing that either," said Mama. "After all, he carried on so loud and long about having to pay Bitty a settlement as well as alimony, and his mother and sister are still fighting it."

"They may win," I said. "Unless Jackson Lee can come up with some legal tactic to override Bitty's signature on those release papers, she's liable to lose both alimony checks *and* the rest of her settlement."

"She'll still be well off," Daddy said. "It's not like she was penniless when she married Hollandale."

"Tell that to Bitty."

Daddy looked at me and nodded understanding. While Bitty hadn't yet sunk to the financial level of Scarlett O'Hara and been reduced to eating raw turnips left in the field, she considered herself penniless. Since I've never had more money than what was necessary to pay bills and put some by for the rainy days that were pelting me now, it was difficult for me to comprehend her panic. After all, it's hard to miss what you've never had.

"A shame you had to miss the wake," Mama said, and I paused.

Should I admit we'd shown up where we weren't invited, even though Race's father had welcomed us? Or should I tell the truth and end up going into infinite detail for another thirty minutes?

I did a Bitty: I opted for the coward's way out and pretended I hadn't heard my mother's comment about the wake.

"I'm tuckered out," I said in as weary a tone as I could muster—which was a lot easier since I really was tired. "I'm going upstairs to take a nice long bath, and then curl up with a book."

Daddy leaned over and gave me a peck on the cheek before he left the kitchen. He still had Brownie in his arms, and the dog took the opportunity to lick the make-up off my chin before I could jerk away.

"ACK!" I said out loud. Wretched beast. Payback for some of the things I said about him, probably. He actually grinned at me over Daddy's arm as they left the room.

I went upstairs and scrubbed my face before taking a bubble bath. While soaking, I had a horrible thought. Bitty might decide to attend Naomi's funeral. That horrible thought was quickly followed by my determined vow not to be anywhere in the state of Mississippi when Naomi Spencer was buried. And to take Bitty with me. Otherwise, the funeral might be like the splitting of the atom—instant and deafening annihilation.

CHAPTER 16

"I figured it out," Gaynelle said, and before I could ask what she'd figured out, she added, "I think I know who murdered Race."

That was pretty astounding. Especially since I had no clue.

"Are you sure?" I asked. I held the phone tightly to my ear as if afraid someone would overhear us.

"Well, of course I'm not *certain* about it, but all indications are that she did it."

"She?"

"Rose Allgood."

"Rose All—good lord! You don't mean the penis merchant?"

Gaynelle laughed. "Yes, the very one. It seems that she came here from Biloxi not long ago, and rumor has it she followed a man here, but he dumped her. She's pretty bitter, I understand."

"But . . . Rose Allgood? I mean, she hardly seems the type of woman Race would go for, does she?"

"Rumor also has it that she's very well off. Old money family. Carolann was delighted to get her as a partner."

"Oh, that changes things. Race did seem to follow the money, didn't he?"

"That's another thing. He was deeply in debt and desperate to get sponsors for his races. After Cliff Wages caused the accident that wrecked his car, he needed new money in to keep him in the game. Apparently, he thought marrying it would be the best solution."

"Huh." I pondered this new information for a few moments. "I suppose Rose has motive, but how about opportunity and means?"

"You cannot expect me to do everything. I figured out who, so it's up to you and Rayna to find out how."

"I note you're leaving Bitty out of the equation. Good call."

"Yes, she has enough to think about these days, and besides, she can be a very disruptive complication."

True enough.

When we hung up, I immediately called Rayna. It took her several rings to answer and she sounded out of breath.

"Did I catch you at a bad time?" I asked.

"Oh, no. Not really. Merlin found a mouse, and I had to rescue it from him."

"Eew."

"Not that I want mice in the house, I just don't want mice portions all over the lobby. What's up?"

"Gaynelle has an important lead."

"Did she give it to the police?"

"You're kidding, right?"

Rayna sighed. "Never mind. I keep forgetting they don't want to hear from us again."

"Sergeant Maxwell made it quite clear we are to stay out of police business and take up needlework."

"I wonder if Linda Maxwell knows her husband thinks women should stick to needlework and cooking instead of using their brains?" Rayna mused. "It would be most interesting to hear *her* take on that topic."

"Do we really need to heckle the police? Think of the fall-out. We wouldn't be able to drive down the street without being stopped for something. Men can be quite vindictive when there's trouble at home."

"True. So, what's the lead and just how much trouble is it going to cause us?"

"Rose Allgood." Since Rayna was just as surprised as I'd been, I gave her a quick recap of Gaynelle's theory. "She just doesn't seem Race's type, but as Gaynelle pointed out, his type seemed to have money."

"Then explain to me why he dated both Madewell sisters. They don't have a spare dime. Not that they weren't well off years ago, but bad investments took a toll."

"Hm. Maybe Race didn't know they were broke? After all, Trina especially puts on a show of having more money than Wall Street. Trisha isn't so showy, and he dated her as well, though."

"That could explain it, I suppose. If you consider that his reasons for dating certain women depended upon the size of their bank accounts. It happens," Rayna said.

"Still, I find it very difficult to visualize Race Champion—a redneck stock car driver and admitted booze-hound—romancing the Rubber Penis Lady. But come to think of it, maybe there's a lot of fire under that icy exterior."

"You never know," said Rayna, and we both got quiet for a minute, our minds probably drifting in a parallel direction. Any woman who sells dildoes and crotchless panties must know quite a lot of things that would make a man happy. And she was attractive, albeit far too cool and reserved for a woman in her line of work. But what did I know?

"And then there's Naomi," I said after banishing the image of rubber dildoes and silk panties sans a crotch from my over-burdened mind. "She obviously had no money, but expected to gain from Philip Hollandale's will. Maybe he heard about it and asked her to marry him."

"Naomi wasn't exactly a person who kept her thoughts—such as they were—to herself," Rayna agreed. "I imagine she'd told anyone who'd listen that she was coming into money. Which leads me to the question, Why didn't any of us hear about it?"

"It's not exactly like we traveled in the same circles."

"Yes, but this was gossip. *Good* gossip. It should have gotten to everyone within a fifty mile radius within twenty-four hours."

"Someone along the line squashed it. I wonder who and why?"

After another moment of silence, Rayna said, "I think I may know who, but I'm not at all sure about why."

"Who?"

"Miranda Watson."

"Miranda—the gossip columnist from *The South Reporter*?"

"You do remember what she did, right?"

I did. "How could I forget? Bitty was fit to be tied and threatened to sue the paper for slander."

"Since it was basically the truth, I don't think even Jackson Lee could have pulled that one off. Anyway, Miranda generally knows all the gossip around here. And I mean *all* the gossip. If anyone knew about it, she would. So why wouldn't she pass along the info she got from Naomi, or Sukey, or whoever her sources were? This was good stuff. Yet not even a hint of it got around town. Why not?"

Rayna had some good points, but I wasn't so sure. Naomi definitely had been the type to tell all, but even Jackson Lee hadn't been aware of the late senator leaving money to a girlfriend. And he was usually up on all the attorney gossip.

"So where do we start asking questions?" I foolishly inquired.

Before the day was out, I found myself standing next to Rayna at Miranda Watson's front door.

I met Rayna at her house first. Rob was there, and he didn't look at all happy about his wife poking into official police business.

"You could get arrested," he said with a warning shake of his head. "Police tend to get territorial about a case, and don't usually appreciate amateurs messing with possible witnesses or tampering with evidence. Remember what happened last time."

"How could I forget?" Rayna continued looking through her purse for car keys. "I thought you'd never let me go to the cemetery again."

Rob, a tall, handsome man with silver-frosted black hair, shook his head again. "I won't bail you out this time," he threatened, and Rayna just laughed.

"Yes you will. You don't like cleaning cat boxes."

Rob sighed. "Just don't do anything illegal, okay? It doesn't look good for a bail bondsman to have to post bail for his wife too many times."

Having found her elusive car keys, Rayna slung her purse on her shoulder and gave him a quick kiss. "We aren't meddling in anything dangerous or liable to prosecution. We're simply going to talk to the village chatterbox."

"And yet, I sense possible complications," he said as we went out the door, calling after us, "Don't get arrested!"

That rather worried me. In the twilight of my years, I've discovered an aversion to being arrested or in police custody of any sort. I'm funny that way. In the days of my public protests, getting arrested for misdemeanors was a badge of honor, a signal that I had achieved my purpose. While my parents were certain my purpose was to embarrass them, I had a more noble goal in mind. Calling attention to injustices, for example. I still feel that way, but prefer now to adhere to caution in the pursuit of justice.

Or so I told myself.

Anyway, once Rayna and I were standing on Miranda Watson's front porch and ringing her bell, I began to question our methods.

"Are you sure she'll tell us anything?" I whispered.

"Of course. She won't be able to help herself. She's a gossip. She does it for fun as well as money."

Since Rayna seemed so certain, I smothered my doubts. And almost swallowed my gum when the front door suddenly swung open with a vengeance.

Miranda Watson—or who I assumed to be her since we had never met—barred the entrance with a thunderous voice and bulky body.

"Just what are you doing skulking around on my front porch?" she boomed so loudly several mockingbirds in the magnolia tree on her front lawn took flight with startled squawks. "I should call the police!"

"Calm down, Miranda," said Rayna. "We rang your bell. Didn't you hear it?"

"It's broken. Has been for years." Miranda stared at us suspiciously. While she is quite overweight, she has a lovely face. Her complexion is flawless, and her large brown eyes are slightly tilted, giving her an exotic appearance. It was rather offset by her flowery cotton muumuu, however. "What do you want?"

"Information," Rayna said bluntly. "Everyone in town knows you're always up to date on the latest events, public and private."

"What on earth makes you think I'd tell you even if I had any information you might want?"

That sounded just like what I'd expected, and I took a backward step to return to our car sitting at the curb.

But Rayna had an answer for that, too: "Because you're dying to get in on the action."

Miranda lifted an eyebrow. "How do you know I'm not already working with someone else?"

"Because the only someone 'else' there is working, is the police. And I happen to know for a fact they do not want your help. Or ours, for that matter."

Maybe it was the last admission that swung Miranda around, since she opened the door wider and stepped aside. I followed Rayna inside.

Cool air blew from a window air unit, ruffling a stack of papers teetering on a flat surface. We had apparently interrupted Miranda at her desk; her laptop sat open with some kind of word processing program blinking until she moved to close the lid. Blocking the view of the desk with her body, Miranda crossed her arms over her chest. I recognized her body language as resistant to suggestion. Rayna may have gotten us inside, but she still had to work to bring Miranda around.

"So, just what do you want to know?" Miranda asked abruptly. "Not that I'll give you an answer. It depends."

"May we?" Rayna said, gesturing to a loveseat nearly covered by newspapers and cats. Without waiting for consent, she proceeded to pick up a cat and take its place on the furniture. I, however, hesitated. Two cats occupied the other cushion, and looked at me with eyes narrowed malevolently. I sensed retribution if I tried to move them. Rayna took charge and swept them from the cushion with her free arm. The two cats hissed and fluffed out their tails as they darted in opposite directions. I sat down immediately.

Miranda plodded to a nearby overstuffed chair and eased into it, taking her time to think, no doubt. She must have a pretty good idea of the questions we wanted answered. It wasn't exactly a secret that Divas were snooping around town trying to find out who had killed Race and Naomi; and in particular, who had tried to kill Rayna, Bitty, and me.

Eying us for a moment, Miranda smiled. "You want to know if I talked to Naomi before she died, don't you." She said it more as a statement than a question, and we both nodded.

"Yes, that would be a good place to start," Rayna said. "Someone killed that poor girl, and they must have had what they thought was a good reason for it. If Naomi said anything that might give you an idea who hated her—and Race—enough to kill them, it would definitely help if you would tell us."

Miranda shrugged. "I already told the police everything I know, or heard. They're competent enough to find the killer, I'm sure."

"Then if the police already know, telling us won't hurt anything."

"It might. After all, I seem to recall dangerous blunders the last time Divas got too involved in things they should stay out of. And from what I hear, someone has already tried to kill you this time, too."

Her gaze shifted to me, and she lifted a brow.

"I take that rather personally," I spoke up. "I didn't appreciate being run off the road into a gully."

"I'm sure you didn't." Miranda paused, then said, "Bitty Hollandale made a few enemies when she divorced Philip, you know. All the nastiness, the scandal, the possible legal complications . . . ."

"Philip caused the nastiness with his public affairs, especially with Naomi since she was still underage when he first started messing with her," I defended Bitty, "and he caused his own legal difficulties by his underhanded business dealings. Bitty had *nothing* to do with any of that."

Miranda steepled her hands and gazed at us over the tips of her fingers, which I noticed had long, curved nails painted a bright blood-red. How did she type on that little laptop with those talons?

"True," she said. "But it's not like she was the only woman hurt in that affair. For all her youth and—well, shortage of intellect, Naomi was a sweet girl. There were so few people she could really talk to, people who wouldn't *judge* her."

I got a little mad at her sanctimonious tone. Was this the same woman who had written scathing snippets of gossip about us in her weekly column? All without asking us if any of it was true? The same woman who'd said, quite literally, "Drop dead, Divas"?

As I opened my mouth, Rayna grabbed my wrist and said quickly, "I'm glad you were able to be there for her. But she was happy at last, wasn't she? I mean, Philip may be gone, but she was engaged to Race and really loved him, right?"

"Yes, I believe she did," Miranda replied slowly, as if thinking it over. "Or at least, she'd convinced herself that she did. She was very lonely, you know."

I knew what Bitty would have said to that, but kept my mouth closed since that seemed to be the wisest course at this time. If Miranda was going to share with us, I should just shut up and let her.

Rayna clucked sympathy. "I'm sure we all know how it feels to be lonely that way."

Miranda nodded. "For someone like Naomi, being without a man in her life made her panicky."

While Rayna nodded in agreement, I thought about my life without a man. Lonely? No, I didn't feel that way at all. Liberated was more like it. Until meeting Kit, I'd decided never to rely on the company of a man again, for anything in my life. Not that I relied on Kit now, but it was nice to have male companionship without a feeling of dependence in any way, whether financial or emotional. Very nice.

Besides, I had Bitty and my parents to worry about. Not to mention the zoo in my parents' barn. When did I have time to get lonely?

Miranda leaned forward in her chair. Her full lips twitched and her eyes dilated. Her voice was low. "Naomi was afraid of more than being alone, poor thing. She came by to see me right before . . . before she was killed, you know."

Rayna made all the appropriate replies to that bit of information to encourage her to continue. I just sat quietly and tried not to look as uncomfortable as I felt. Prying good gossip out of someone was not really my strong suit. Apparently, I had a lot to learn.

Miranda Watson rattled on about how Naomi confided in her quite a lot during the past two years. Miranda was the "only one in the world" who Naomi had felt would understand why she clung to Philip Hollandale for so long. That part was a bit intriguing to me, but since Miranda chose not to embellish on Naomi's motives, I had to listen instead to how people might think Miranda gossipy and mean at times, but really, she was more of a free psychiatric therapist.

Rayna was right. Miranda Watson couldn't resist gossiping. It was a personality characteristic that came in very, very handy.

Finally she came back around to a big reason Naomi was afraid before she died.

With her tone lowered theatrically, Miranda said, "Someone had threatened her life!"

Rayna retained her composure, but I got pretty fidgety. This wasn't going to be one more accusation against Bitty, I hoped, because I might just ruin everything and give Miss Miranda Watson a piece of my mind.

"Whoever would have done that?" asked Rayna, her voice lowered to match the theatric tone.

"Well . . . let me just say that this certain someone claimed to be engaged to Race Champion instead of Naomi, and not only that—she moved to Holly Springs to be closer to him!"

It was like pulling teeth from an alligator, but Rayna persisted politely and quite skillfully, to draw the entire story from Miranda. Then Rayna sat back on the loveseat and drummed her fingers on the cushioned arm.

"Let me try to put this into perspective, and you tell me if I have it right, okay?" she said to Miranda, who also leaned back in her chair.

After a moment's hesitation, Miranda nodded. I wondered if she already regretted her lapse of confidentiality.

"So, Naomi confided in you that she was being followed and was afraid. Also, that someone was following her and leaving notes not only on her car, but also on Race's truck. That right so far?"

Miranda nodded again.

"And Naomi was certain it was a woman stalker who left those notes?"

Miranda looked a little surprised by Rayna's question. "Well . . . no, she never said she was *certain* it was a woman. We both just assumed—you know, that the notes were left by—by *her*."

"And she had no idea who 'her' was."

Here Miranda pursed her lips, then shook her head. "Well, yes. She thought she knew who it was, but as a legitimate journalist I don't like making false accusations without proof, you know. It's unethical."

I could not contain myself. I blurted out, "Too bad you didn't feel that way when you wrote that article about the Divas! You made wild allegations without knowing all the facts *then*. What's the difference now?"

Rayna's elbow in my ribs indicated I had made my point and should shut up now. So I did. It was difficult, but I clamped my lips together so I probably looked like I had just bit into a lemon.

Miranda's face had gone an interesting shade of purple, and her lips opened and closed a couple of times as she apparently fished for just the right curse words. I braced myself for it.

But then she surprised me by saying, "You're right. I should have checked all the facts. My editor said almost the same thing after receiving several phone calls defending y'all. I intend to say so in my weekly column."

My irritation shifted to suspicion. She gave up too easily. What was she up to, I couldn't help but wonder. At the same time, I was a bit surprised by my pessimistic and suspicious turn of mood. I just hadn't been the same lately, I thought as I studied Miranda Watson. Maybe that was a good thing. Maybe even my usually cynical outlook needed sharpening. Or smothering.

While I hung between the two worse sides of my nature, Rayna, fortunately, had no such hang-ups.

"I'm very glad you reconsidered that article, Miranda."

"I didn't say I was wrong," she defended herself again. "I got my facts about the Diva luncheon straight from an attendee."

"Trina Madewell, perhaps?" I asked, even though I was pretty sure I knew the answer.

"Perhaps."

"I'm sure Trina thought the worst when Bitty's dog barged into the room and upset the tea tray," Rayna said. "It did get a little crazy after that."

"The *dog* upset the tea tray?" Miranda repeated slowly, then nodded. "Well, that does make more sense. I did wonder about the food fight, though."

"As you may imagine, it didn't happen exactly like you were told." Rayna paused and smiled before directing the conversational detour back on track. "Did Naomi tell you anything about the person she suspected of stalking her, other than that she'd also been engaged to Race?"

"Just that she works on the square now. In a nice shop."

Since there are only a few clothing stores still open on the court house square, it was pretty obvious that Rose Allgood had to be the person Miranda was reluctant to name.

"Of course," Miranda was saying, "whoever it was could have left town by now. I mean, why would she stay here if the man she followed is dead?"

"Unless she already lives here," Rayna said.

"Or if she has just moved here," I said.

Miranda said nothing, obviously determined to hold onto the identity of the person. Maybe it was time to give her a not-so-gentle nudge.

"Rose Allgood has recently moved here," I said as if thinking aloud, "and she works in one of the clothing shops on the square. She's a business partner, in fact. She came from Biloxi, I understand."

Miranda waved a plump hand as if dismissing me. "A coincidence, I'm sure."

Rayna shot me a quick glance of frustration. Miranda smiled mysteriously at both of us. Then she stood up and indicated the front door with one hand.

"If you ladies have finished asking questions, I need to finish writing my column. Deadlines wait for no one, you know."

As she stood up, Rayna said, "I hope the Divas see that apology in your column this week."

A broad smile curved Miranda's mouth. "Oh, believe me, this week's column is one that will have *the entire town* talking."

Somehow, I thought as Rayna and I walked down the pathway to the curb, that sounded a bit ominous.

****

Of course, the minute Bitty found out we had a new lead, she was bound and determined to investigate it.

"Why not?" she said, looking from me to Rayna and back. "It's the least we can do."

173

"No," I said, "the least we can do is nothing. You want to barge into Carolann Barnett's shop and accuse her business partner of murder. That's the *most* we can do."

"Gaynelle is usually very accurate," said Bitty. "If she told you Rose Allgood has a good motive for killing Race, then we should check it out."

"What she said was that Rose was once engaged to Race," Rayna pointed out. "That's quite a bit of difference."

Bitty dismissed that notion with a flick of her wrist. "I say we march right up there and ask her about him."

I was intrigued by her appeal for tact. "Really? And how exactly shall we do that? 'Excuse us, Miz Allgood, but we understand you were once engaged to the dead man, and we'd like to know if you killed him.' Is that your plan?"

"Don't be silly. We don't have to be quite that blunt."

Rayna looked at her wrist and said, "Oh my, I need to go home and feed the dogs before they start gnawing on furniture. I'd love to go with you, but . . . ."

When her voice trailed off, and it became obvious she intended to get out while the getting was good, I said, "How can you tell the time on that watch?"

Bitty clapped her hands and called for Chen Ling, and Rayna parried my question about the watch she wasn't wearing by leaning toward me and whispering, "Don't tell her we went to Miranda Watson's house. She won't take it well."

Since I'm well aware of Bitty's attitude toward people who humiliate her in print, I whispered back, "Coward!"

"Bye, Bitty," Rayna called toward the back of the house, where Bitty was no doubt dressing Chen Ling in a pink tutu, and to me, "Wear dark glasses. Maybe Carolann won't recognize you."

I shook my head at her departing figure. "She knew my sister. She'll recognize me."

We parked in the square and walked across the street to the lingerie and book store that had forever changed my idea of what to expect from such establishments. Bitty was a little too eager, in my opinion, and I wondered if that was because she wanted to question Rose or sample some of her merchandise.

Wisely, I didn't ask. There are some things it's best not to know.

Once inside, Bitty and Chitling pretended to browse the racks, while I hung close by the door in order to make my escape should it be necessary. There was no sign of Rose, Carolann, or Heather. After a few minutes Bitty got impatient and walked to the desk and rang the old-fashioned little bell that sits atop the counter by the cash register.

Carolann bustled out a few moments later, and looked surprised and pleased to see us. I figured that would change quickly enough, so just waved and made sure my sunglasses still covered half my face.

"Bitty!" she greeted my deceitful cousin, "I'm so glad to see you again. It's been forever since you came in. I have a new shipment of things that we're still putting out. I know how you love the special laces and silks from Vera Wang. Do you want to see them first?"

Chitling barked when Carolann got too close, and she jumped back. "Oh, this is the dog I keep hearing about. Isn't it?"

I understood why she might be doubtful, and chuckled to myself. Since there was no sign of Rose Allgood, I might be spared the awkward scene of Bitty being tossed out of the shop on her curvaceous little rear.

"Why yes," Bitty trilled, "this is my Chen Ling. Isn't she precious? I don't know what I would do without her. She's been my constant companion these past few months of trials and tribulations. I know you've heard all about Philip, and of course now those horrible murders—I wonder, is Rose Allgood in today?"

Carolann seemed momentarily confused. I empathized. Sometimes Bitty can switch conversational gears so fast it's hard to keep up.

"Why yes, she is in. She oversees the merchandise in our new department. Have you seen it yet? It's quite nice. Rose and Heather have been working away in there."

"New department? Oh, I hadn't heard," Bitty lied without a hint of shame. "I'll have to check it out, of course. You know how I like to keep up with the latest fashions."

Carolann laughed at that. I found myself snickering and following behind them at a safe distance as Bitty was led to the Shangri-la of crotchless panties and paraphernalia. Still chattering away, Carolann sounded quite enthusiastic about what she referred to as the "Blue Velvet Room."

"There was a movie with that title, you know," Carolann added, "and I just thought it was so appropriate, and Rose agreed with me, so that's what we call it, and—well, this is Rose. Rose, this is Miz Bitty Hollandale, and she's asked specially to see your stock today."

Stock didn't sound like quite the right word to me, but then, I've always had a bit of trouble figuring out what exactly one should call sex toys. They don't really seem to fit the innocent name of "toys" to me. That word brings up visions of kids at Christmastime or in the schoolyard, not whips, chains, handcuffs with fur, and odd-looking things that seem to defy logic as well as physics. But then, I've been told I'm quite naïve in those areas, too. Thankfully, that's true.

Chen Ling set up a deafening racket as soon as Bitty stepped into the

Blue Velvet Room, and I was pretty sure I knew why. All those little soldiers standing at attention had probably scared the bejesus out of her. They had me.

Irresistibly drawn closer, I stood in the doorway under the velvet drapes and got a bird's-eye view of the proceedings as Bitty pretended to browse among the shelves of upright rubber penises while she talked animatedly to Rose Allgood. Fascinated, I had to admit Bitty kept her focus pretty well while standing in a forest of rainbow-colored erections.

"So you see," Bitty was saying as she idly picked up a massive rubber penis complete with testicles and an on/off switch, "as soon as I heard you were new in town, I had to come right down and introduce myself. It's so important for a community to welcome newcomers, don't you think?"

Rose regarded Bitty with cool appraisal, and I knew she wasn't a bit taken in by my cousin's blather. She was obviously just waiting for the punch line.

"You're very kind,' she said. "This is our newest model, the JetBlaster 600. Do you like it?"

"Like what? Oh, this? Heavens, what on earth—stop it, precious, you mustn't do that. No, no, don't bite it—let *go!*"

Chitling, accustomed to rubber toys that bounced and jingled, had a tight grip on the head of the penis with all three of her fangs. Bitty did her best to pry the dog loose. It was a losing battle.

In the struggle, the switch went from Off to On, and the entire penis began to vibrate at warp speed. Chen Ling was delighted, Bitty was horrified, and Rose Allgood was worried about ruining her "stock." I was laughing too hard to notice what Carolann was doing.

About the time Bitty set Chitling down on the floor to try and retrieve the rubber dildo, a customer entered through the separate outside door into the Blue Velvet Room. It was Fate.

Chen Ling took off at a pace matched only by a roadrunner fleeing a coyote, and was out the door and down the sidewalk in a flash, dragging the still vibrating dildo that was nearly as big as she was. By this time I was near hysteria. I collapsed on the small step under the blue velvet drapes and tried to keep from wetting my pants.

Rose Allgood drew herself up into a tight knot of disapproval and announced that the charge for that item was $59.99 plus tax, and Bitty threw her hands up in the air and took off after her wayward pug. I just lay back on the nice carpeting and screamed with hysterical laughter, while Carolann Barnett seemed torn between following Bitty, waiting on the newly arrived customer, or finding a glass of water to throw in my face.

I heard later that she did none of those things, but just turned around and walked to the back of the store. At the time, I took no notice. I was just too busy pounding my fists on the carpet and cackling like an old hen with a nest full of eggs.

Some days, it's good to be alive.

CHAPTER 17

Maybe it was the exhaustive thinking I'd been doing lately, or maybe it was just that I had finally reached the point where my brain would not absorb any more abuse, but I went to bed early that night and slept late the next morning. Not even my mother's call up the stairs had gotten me out of bed. No, I burrowed farther beneath my handsewn quilt like a rabbit going down a hole and pretended I didn't hear anything. It must have worked pretty well, because by the time I finally opened my eyes again and looked at the clock, it was nearly one in the afternoon.

The overhead fan whirled cool air down on me to help the central air that Daddy had put in a decade or so ago, and the quilt was just enough to keep me from being too chilled or too warm. I'm one of those people that prefer it cool at night so I can pile on the blankets and snuggle under them. I'm sure psychiatrists would have a lot to say about my quirk, but in the grand scheme of things, it's one of my minor ones, so I'm sure they'd focus more on my bigger quirks.

Like tagging along behind Bitty no matter what madness she drags me into. There was no doubt that for the next few weeks the talk of the town would be the runaway pug dragging a flesh-colored vibrating penis with a magnificent erection down the sidewalk right at the Holly Springs rush hour. There had been two wrecks caused by people halting in the middle of the street to stare disbelievingly, one fainting spell from an elderly lady who happened to be exiting the bank when Chen Ling trotted past, and a close call with a patrol car called to the scene by someone on a cell phone reporting that dogs had savaged someone and were dragging body parts all over the downtown area.

Bitty got a ticket for violating the leash law, but on the bright side, she now owns a magnificent rubber penis to keep on her bedside table. It may have a few teeth marks in it, but it survived the ordeal in remarkably good shape. Of course, Bitty was mortified by the entire incident and refuses to discuss it.

Fortunately, she also abandoned her intention to interrogate Rose Allgood about her previous relationship with Race Champion. Life should always be so easy.

This time, however, Bitty had been thrust into the middle of two murders by no fault of her own. It was almost as if someone had planned it that way. So who—besides the two Madewell sisters—would hate Bitty enough to try and incriminate her? But maybe I was looking at it the wrong way, I mused as I watched the ceiling fan blades blur shadows on the walls. Maybe it was someone who thought Bitty was a good scapegoat because she had an alibi, or because she could afford the best attorney in town.

Bitty's alibi was okay, but not the best. Jackson Lee Brunetti was—in my opinion anyway—the best attorney in town. So even if the police should charge Bitty with murder, she'd have little trouble being acquitted. Only circumstantial evidence at best tied Naomi to her in any but the most innocuous way.

After about a quarter hour contemplating whirring fan blades and the vagaries of murder suspects, I felt refreshed enough to actually get out of bed. Really, I was getting slothful lately. It must be the heat. Days were scorchers, and even the nights muggy and too hot to sit comfortably outside.

By the time I showered and went downstairs to the kitchen, Mama and Daddy had finished eating a light snack and were still sitting at the table discussing their next trip. That was enough to make me consider going back upstairs to bed, but my stomach was empty and growling.

Empty saucers with what looked like chocolate cake crumbs sat in the middle of the table, surrounded by colorful brochures. CANADA leaped out at me from the page as I headed to the refrigerator. I held open the refrigerator door a little longer than I should, while I considered asking to go along with them if they actually went to Canada. It sounded very nice, and very cool.

What I said though, was, "I don't see any cake in here."

Mama turned in her chair to look at me. "For heaven's sake, Trinket, chocolate cake should be served at room temperature. It's on the stand. Are you having cake for breakfast?"

She said "breakfast" with special emphasis. Obviously a reminder that I had slept far too long.

"No," I said as I pulled out an egg carton. "I'm having eggs first. Then cake. Are you planning another trip?"

Daddy answered, "We're thinking about it. It's so blamed hot here. We thought about going up north. Maybe seeing Niagara Falls."

Since that sounded a lot closer than the brochure on Egypt and the Nile, I said it was an excellent idea. I felt Mama watching me as I broke two eggs into a cup, stirred them up with salt, pepper, and a slice of American cheese, then covered the cup with a paper towel and stuck it in the microwave.

"Are you all right?" she asked me a minute and a half later when I pulled my eggs out of the microwave.

"Uh-huh. Just hungry. Why?"

"You didn't say anything about our trip."

"Yes, I did. I said it's a good idea. Didn't you hear me?" I scooped the eggs out of the cup onto a small plate, and then cut a nice slice of cake to go along with them.

"Yes. I just thought you said something else."

"Oh. No. That was all."

Since my eggs were a little too hot, I took a bite of the cake. It was moist and delicious, gooey with lots of creamy frosting. As I licked my fingers, I looked up to see them both watching me.

"What? Can't I have breakfast without an audience?"

Daddy smiled. "Sure you can, pumpkin. Mama and I are just—well, a little worried about you lately."

"About me? Why?" I was dumbfounded. "I'm just fine."

"Are you sure?" Mama asked. Her normally clear brow was furrowed in a slight frown. For a woman her age, she has great skin and very few wrinkles. I probably looked like that once. Back before I came home to Holly Springs and started hanging out with Bitty again. Before too much longer I would no doubt look like a dried apple doll, all deep, pruney ridges and my eyes nearly lost under my eyelid folds.

Rather concerned that my recent activities had hastened the inevitable, I pulled the toaster toward me and peered at my reflection. Was it just the curve of the toaster top or was my face really that shape? At least my wrinkles weren't that bad yet. I could still see without much trouble.

"No," I answered, "I'm not at all sure, now that you mention it. Do I look sick? Am I running fever, do you think? Maybe I'm contagious."

Mama raised her eyebrows at me. "I do not mean *that* kind of all right, Trinket. It seems to your father and me that you're keeping really odd hours lately. And half the time you're not here, and when you are here, you get a phone call and rush out of the house like your tail feathers are on fire."

"Ah. No, my tail feathers are fine, thank you. It's just all that business about the murders, and the Divas, and Bitty's money, and whoever it was who tried to kill us, that's on my mind."

"Sugar," Daddy said, "what you need is a vacation from your head."

"Is this an invitation to go with you to Canada?"

Mama looked startled. "Oh no, dear. Not at all. We just think you need a night in. Some rest."

Actually, a night in didn't sound bad at all. A day without dressing or thinking of anything more strenuous than whether to eat cake or pie would be most welcome.

"You're right," I said. "If anyone calls, take a name and number. Tell them I'm in the barn, or just out of my head for the day." I waved my fork in the air like a baton. "I'm giving in to pure laziness!"

It was a luxury just to do nothing. After about an hour of catching up on growing my hair, however, I decided to clean out the jumbled up drawer of my nightstand. It had gotten really junky the past few months, and I hadn't taken time to put it to order. So I pawed through shreds of used tissues, anti-diarrhea pills, a few Benadryl, TV remote, the cable remote, the DVD remote, post-its with ink scribbles, three pens without ink, a paper clip, a peculiar green rock, gum and wrappers, and a jar of face cream.

I looked more closely at the green rock. It had something attached to it, some kind of wire—wait! This was my lost earring! It had been missing since Brownie's indulgence in a snack of jewelry and my watch, and now here it was, mangled but right here! I was thrilled. My daughter had given me those earrings for my birthday years ago, and they are very special to me. Michelle had been so proud of giving them to me, too, and if I closed my eyes I could still see her sweet face beaming at me.

This rated an immediate call to Atlanta.

Talking to her always lifts my spirits. Even though she's a young adult with a life of her own, a job and a husband and a house to care for, she'll always be my little girl. I don't know if it's because she's my only child, or because I've never let go, but the years roll away once I hear her voice. We talked for fifteen minutes or so, just about mundane things like the high price of gasoline, the summer heat, and her vacation plans, and then she asked, "So what's going on with Aunt Bitty?"

I tried to play dumb. "What do you mean?"

"Mom, Grandma already told me about the murders and Aunt Bitty being broke. I just hope she'll be all right."

"Bitty is always all right. She has a lucky star hanging over her head, and probably a four-leaf clover tattooed on her butt. Things always turn out good for her. Thank heavens. I don't think I could stand the drama if they didn't."

Michelle laughed. "Well, she does have friends in high places."

"If you're referring to Jackson Lee, he's been working overtime to keep her out of trouble and in the money. He probably needs a month's vacation in a padded room by now. But then, so do I."

"There's a lovely sanitarium in Atlanta if you decide to check in for a rest."

"I'll keep that in mind."

When we hung up, I took my mangled earring to the bathroom and put it in my cup to clean later. I'd probably have to take it to a jeweler before it would resemble the other one, but at least the mystery of the missing earring was solved. Brownie could be forgiven. Not that the dog would care. He had my parents wrapped around his little brown paws, and that was all he needed.

The rest of my lazy afternoon hummed along nicely. I tidied my closet, rearranged the furniture in the glassed-in screen porch off my bedroom, listened to music from the seventies, and drank enough sweet tea to float a medium size sedan. It was excellent therapy.

By the time the sun set, I was neck-deep in a bubble bath and watching light fade outside the bathroom window. Three Dog Night sang about a bullfrog, and I hummed along quite contentedly. It was one of my favorite songs from the past, and when it got to the part about *Joy to the World*, I used my bar of soap as a microphone and belted out the lyrics right along with my stereo. I mean, I really got into it, sloshing water over the edge of the old clawfoot tub, my eyes closed as I acted out my fantasy of being a famous rock star.

I ended up with a flourish, slapping the water with my free hand and singing—or shrieking as my voice is sometimes called—*woooo!* at the end of the song. Brief silence fell.

Whatever I expected, it certainly wasn't a male voice asking if I was all right. I shrieked for real and dropped my soap microphone into the bath water so I could cross my arms over my chest.

"Trinket! Are you okay?" came the insistent question, accompanied by a rattle of the doorknob.

Before I could say I was okay, the bathroom door swung open about a foot and Kit poked his head inside. I immediately slid down further in the tub so that only my head and knees could be seen above the bubbles.

"Fine, I'm fine!" I yelled through billows of bubbles. Several took flight and rose into the air like tiny balloons before popping. "What are you doing in here?" I demanded with as much dignity as I could muster in my situation.

"Your mother said I should just come on up, that you were cleaning and wouldn't mind. I didn't think she meant you were cleaning . . . well, bathing."

Even if the water hadn't been pretty warm, it was steaming by then since my face was so hot. Kit just grinned. He leaned his shoulder against the door frame and looked as if he had no intention of doing the proper thing and getting the hell out of there.

"As you can surely see," I said primly, "I am in no danger of drowning. I'm just fine."

Kit shook his head. "I don't know," he said slowly, "you *seem* to be just fine, but I can't really see . . . ."

"You can see all you're going to see right now, Buster, so back out and shut the door! *Go!*" I punctuated my demand by sloshing more water over the side of the tub with my foot, and he laughed.

"This is a very interesting situation, Trinket. On one hand, the polite thing to do would be to back out and shut the door."

I glared at him. My face was on fire and even worse—the bubbles were starting to pop. "So what's the problem?"

"Ah, the problem is that I'm not always polite. I know that must shock you."

"Not really."

Ignoring me, he went on, "So I find myself torn between courtesy and curiosity at this moment. Can you see what a dilemma this is for me?"

"I can see a worse dilemma for you if I yell for my daddy. He may have trouble getting up the stairs, but he's still pretty good with a shotgun."

Kit was still grinning at me wickedly, and my heart did one of those annoying flips that usually leave me breathless, even at my age. Then he shook his head and did his best to look disappointed.

"Since you've dragged your father into this, I should tell you that he's out back feeding the multitude of cats. However—I'll wait for you downstairs. Better hurry. Bitty sent me out here to get you."

Once he'd backed out and closed the door, I pulled the plug and stepped out of the tub to the bath mat. Of course, the first thing I did was lock the door. Then I said through the wood, "I'm taking today off. Bitty will have to do without me."

"Bring a sweater," said Kit. "Hospitals always turn up the air conditioning too high."

Hospitals? Bitty? Wait!

"Hey!" I yelled after him, but all I heard was what sounded like my bedroom door closing. Damn.

By the time I dried off, got dressed, and got downstairs, Kit was standing out back with Daddy. Several cats rubbed around his ankles. Most of the furry flock had departed for parts unknown after being fed. As usual. I don't know why my father persists in the belief that having lots of cats keeps rats and mice out of the barn. As far as I know, they all live happily in co-existence. I've seen the rat-holes in the 20 pound bags of cat chow.

"So what's going on?" I asked as soon as I reached them. "Why is Bitty in the hospital? Is she okay?"

"Slow down, tiger," Kit said easily, and smiled at me. "Bitty's fine. She's in the hospital waiting room. Haven't you heard?"

"Heard what? No, I haven't heard anything. I told you, today's my day off."

"It's Miranda Watson," Daddy said, shaking his head. "Someone tried to kill her."

****

Bitty sat in the waiting room of Baptist-DeSoto hospital, where not so long ago she and I had both been taken after being run off the road. Rayna was with her.

"What happened?" I asked as soon as I reached them. On our way to the hospital Kit had told me only the basic details, which was all he knew, that Miranda had been found nearly dead on her living room floor.

"Why are you here? Oh God, Bitty, don't tell me you're the one who found her!"

"Slow down, Trinket. No, I didn't find her. Sit down. You're blocking out all the light hovering there like that."

I sat in one of the stainless steel and padded chairs. "Is she dead?"

"If she was dead," Bitty said, "we'd be at the morgue, not the hospital."

As I sucked in a deep breath intended to fuel a really snarky retort, Rayna said, "She's in ICU. Doctors say it's critical. It's touch and go if she survives or not."

"Good lord. Who hates her badly enough to want to kill her?" I couldn't help asking.

"You mean besides us?" Bitty asked.

Rayna and I both said at the same time, *"Bitty!"*

"Oh for heaven's sake. You know what I mean. She's had something tacky to say about everyone in town at one time or another, and is mean enough to put it in print. It's a wonder she gets away with it like she does. Or that someone hasn't tried to kill her before now."

I was really grateful for my relaxing day. It was obvious Bitty was going to try my patience.

"So," I asked again, "why are you here, Bitty?"

"I brought her," Rayna answered my question. "I wanted company, and your mother said you were out for the day."

"You mean I was your second choice?" Bitty demanded.

Ignoring that, Rayna continued, "I'd thought of something else I wanted to ask Miranda, and since I couldn't get hold of you, I just went on over to ask her. She didn't come to the door, and I remembered about the doorbell being broke, so I started to knock. Well, the door was slightly open and it swung in. Maybe I wouldn't have gone in at all, but a couple of her cats came to the door making a lot of racket, and I noticed one of them had what looked like red paint on its paws. So I . . . I stuck my head inside and called for her. That's when I saw . . . saw Miranda lying on the floor."

She paused for a moment, and her eyes got really wide as if she was seeing it all over again. I leaned forward and put a hand on her arm to reassure her.

"Oh, it was awful, Trinket. She must have put up a really good fight, because her desk was cleared like it had been turned over, and papers were all over the floor. Even the loveseat was pushed down from where it was supposed to be, and her big chair was turned over on its side. And all the blood!"

"So she was shot?" I asked.

"I guess so. There was so much blood, I suppose she must have been. The police got there and they wouldn't say. Then the paramedics came, but I was outside answering questions for the police so didn't hear how she'd gotten hurt so badly."

"Do you know if she was able to say anything?"

Rayna shook her head. "Not that I know of. It didn't look to me as if she was even alive."

"Are you sure she didn't just fall and hurt herself? That might explain the desk and chair being out of place."

"But the loveseat, too? It looked as if there had been a struggle. Still, she could have had some kind of seizure, I guess, and fell and hit her head on something. It's just that the police were asking me an awful lot of questions."

"Like?"

"Like, did I see anyone else at her house, did I know if she had problems with anyone, things like that. You know, things that made it sound as if it wasn't just a fall."

I sat back in the waiting room chair and thought about Miranda. Bitty was right that the columnist had made enemies in town. Then I thought of something else.

"Do you happen to know if she's already sent in her weekly column? You know, the one where she's supposed to tell something big?"

"I have no idea. Why—" Rayna gasped. "You think someone got angry because of something she was going to put in her column?"

"It makes sense. Look how upset we all were because of her silly column. What if she had something really nasty she was going to tell this week? She sure made it sound as if she did."

"If that's true, then maybe whoever she was writing about may have gone to try and talk her out of it—"

"And decided to kill her instead," Bitty finished Rayna's sentence. "It sounds logical to me."

"Despite that," I said, "I think we should see who she wrote about in this week's column."

"What if it's the killer?" Bitty suggested. "I mean, the same person who killed Race and/or Naomi?"

"Surely Miranda wouldn't be so foolish as to keep information like that from the police," Rayna said with a frown.

"Apparently she was stupid enough to tick off somebody capable of killing her," Bitty retorted.

"So did we," I reminded them, and we all got really quiet for a moment. A shiver went down my back. Two people dead, someone tried to kill the three of us, and now this, a gossip columnist attacked in her own home. Someone was desperate, or getting more desperate by the day to keep from getting found out. Who on earth in Holly Springs was demented enough to do all that?

As I looked at my two friends I had the thought that whoever it was, we were way out of their league.

CHAPTER 18

"Are you crazy?" I heard myself ask even though I already knew the answer. "I'm not about to do that!"

We stood in Bitty's kitchen on the afternoon after Miranda Watson was attacked. I'd brought two jars of canned tomatoes that Mama insisted Bitty have, though she'd have no idea how to use. I set them carefully on the countertop.

"Don't be such a chicken, Trinket. Besides, it was your idea and we need you."

"Bitty Hollandale, you should be in Whitfield. I never said we should break in to her house. And I don't believe for a minute that Rayna has agreed to this insanity."

"She said she would if you would. It's the only way we can find out who attacked Miranda. Hush, precious. Mommy will feed you as soon as Aunt Trinket says yes."

"Tell *Precious* not to count on Aunt Trinket for her dinner."

I eyed the pug and Bitty with equal irritation. At least the pug had a good reason for being vocal. Her grunts, growls, and howls sounded almost human. Unlike Bitty.

"It's not as if whoever bonked Miranda on the head will return to the scene of the crime," Bitty said in a patient tone. "Her editor said no column was turned in, her laptop is missing, and Rayna said she was pretty sure she saw some print-outs that looked like her column."

"It could have been last week's column. Or last year's column. Besides, the police have already searched the house and probably taken anything that may point to who attacked her. If she put it in her column, you can bet Lieutenant Maxwell has read it."

"Has it occurred to you that whoever whacked Miranda on the head and tried to strangle her is the same person who shot Race and strangled Naomi?" Bitty paused to put Chen Ling on the kitchen floor. "If Miranda wasn't so fat, she'd probably be dead now. A scarf was wrapped around her neck tight enough to cut off her head, I heard. Of course, that was after she got smacked with a brass paperweight. It's a wonder she didn't lose too much blood to live, but maybe overweight people have more blood. Do you think?"

"You're a ghoul, Bitty. Miranda's lucky to still be alive."

"If you call being in a coma alive. She might come out as a vegetable. Not too much different than before, maybe."

"A cruel ghoul, at that."

Bitty paused. "Well, I suppose you're right. It was unkind of me to say that last. But she really did write some hateful things about people, you know. The punishment fits the crime."

"And someone got mad enough to try and kill her for it. I'd say that's beyond the punishment fitting the crime."

"So, you'll help us tonight?"

"No. I've been on your little investigatory adventures before. You always escape unscathed, and I always end up wounded and smelly."

"Good heavens, Trinket. You make it sound like I plan it that way."

"Not at all. You just have very efficient guardian angels. Mine are always off on a cloud somewhere, not paying the least attention."

Bitty opened an aluminum packet of dog food for Chen Ling and scooped it onto one of her good salad plates. Then she set it on the floor. The pug immediately attacked it with all three of her teeth.

"What happened to her special diet?" I couldn't help asking.

"You know I'm broke now. I have to buy her food off the grocery shelves. Isn't it awful? My poor little Chen Ling."

I rolled my eyes. "Sell a few of her diamond collars and you can buy her enough food for a year."

"Sometimes you can be so unkind. I put the honeymoon cabin up for sale today."

The way she said it told me how much it hurt her to part with it. I felt ashamed of myself for making light of her financial difficulties.

"Oh honey, I'm sorry. I know you hate to sell it."

"Yes. I do, but it has nothing but bad memories for me now. Worse, I know I won't get anywhere near what it's worth. Or what it cost me to build it, anyway. But Jackson Lee seems to think now is the best time to put it on the market, so I did."

"Has he been able to make any headway on those papers you signed?"

"He's negotiating a new deal with the vampires. They're remarkably tenacious for creatures who must live in caskets all day."

"That's never been proven," I said, and couldn't help laughing. "Mrs. Hollandale has been seen in daylight several times."

"Not his sister. Patrice lurks in dark corners like some big, hairy spider waiting on its next meal to stumble into her web. Even at Philip's funeral she stayed inside, if you recall."

"I just remember her stretched out on the church floor and still trying to choke you. I'll give you a point on that one. They may have tricked you this time, but I still have faith in Jackson Lee's ability to get around it somehow."

Bitty bent to pick up Chen Ling's empty dish, then carried it to the sink. There were already dirty dishes piled in it, something I never used to see. Bitty's house had always been neat as a pin. Of course, she had a maid who came to clean several times a week. Now that she was "broke", she did the cleaning herself. With the boys home for the summer, it was obvious housecleaning was getting overwhelming.

I decided to help. Maybe it would take her mind off her circumstances, and off the idiotic scheme her fevered little brain had cooked up for us, too. I had no desire to go off prowling in Miranda Watson's empty house. I'd discovered that there *were* things that go bump in the night.

When I opened her state of the art dishwasher, it was full of clean dishes. It's one of those drawer kinds of dishwashers, where you don't have to stoop over to remove the dishes or put them in. The remodel after the fire was really nice. I started pulling out dishes and handing them to Bitty to put away.

"Just how many people are living here now?" I had to ask. "There are enough dishes to feed an army here."

"Just the boys and some of their friends. Of course, the friends aren't actually living here. They just eat, sleep, and play here."

"Sounds like the same thing to me. Start charging them room and board, and I bet you could afford to rehire your maid."

To my horror, Bitty began to cry. Not loud sobs, just a silent weeping with tears running down her cheeks. I didn't know what to do or say, so I just went and put my arms around her shoulders and held her for a minute.

Chen Ling automatically assumed I was the cause of Bitty's distress and began gnawing at my ankle, so I had to shake my leg to get her off. The determined little beast switched ankles. This time one of her three front fangs got skin instead of denim. I yelped loudly. Bitty jumped back. Chitling barked.

Bitty gave me a wild look, then saw the cause for my yelp and started to laugh. After I inspected my wound and decided I'd live, I began laughing along with her. Maybe not for the same reason, though.

"We're a likely pair," I said. "Both of us are crazy, but not in the same way."

"Normally, I'd argue, but I suspect you're right about that. So. You'll do it?"

"Do what? Break and enter? Risk life and limb for something the police already have? Snoop where someone was almost killed? Risk running into the killer? You betcha. Just let me go home for my flashlight first. I may be late. Don't wait for me."

Bitty frowned. "But you have to go with us, Trinket. I already told Rayna you'd agreed."

"You're kidding—no, of course you're not. Bitty . . . ."

"Don't you understand, Trinket? I have to take control of some part of my life, or I'll go crazy! It's such a hopeless, helpless feeling to have my future in other people's control, even though Jackson Lee is the best, he really is, and I was so stupid to have signed those papers without reading them carefully, but I did and now here I am without money, and people in this town are being stalked by some deranged killer that wants to kill me, too, and well—if I don't *do* something, I'll just go nuts, I really will!"

She stopped to take a breath and I heard myself say, "All right, all right, Bitty, but if I get killed, you have to be the one to tell my daughter. She'll know exactly who to blame. You."

Bitty looked relieved. "Fine. You won't get killed. You always know how to take charge."

"If I always know how to take charge, why am I always the one *not* in charge of these little forays into disaster?"

Bitty was looking me up and down and shaking her head. "You aren't properly dressed for stealth. Your jeans are okay, but that shirt is too bright. You'll have to wear one of mine."

"Are you kidding? One of your shirts won't even reach my navel."

"I have bigger, longer shirts. Or maybe I could borrow one of the boys' jerseys. They have some Dallas Cowboys jerseys in navy blue, I think. Their Ole Miss jerseys are all white with blue—what's the matter. Why are you looking at me like that?"

"Do you realize that what we're about to do is against the law? That we'll be committing a crime by breaking and entering?"

"Don't be silly, Trinket. We won't break anything, and it's not like we intend to burgle the place. Rayna is pretty sure she recognized some of the pages scattered on the floor as what Miranda was working on when y'all went to visit her the other day. A visit that I was not included in, by the way."

She held up a hand. "No, don't feel as if you have to apologize for the oversight. I've gotten over it."

"Good." I didn't add that I had no intention of apologizing.

Bitty turned to look at the antique French clock taking up a huge portion of one wall. "It should be dark in about an hour and a half. That gives us enough time to get you properly dressed and meet Rayna."

"Shouldn't we just meet her at the police station? It would save so much time."

"You can be so droll, Trinket. Come on. We'll pick you out a dark shirt to wear. I think Clayton has one that will fit. Your shoulders are a bit broader than his, but the sleeves are loose so it shouldn't matter."

I kept my opinion on having my shoulders compared to a football player's to myself as we went upstairs. Behind door number one, Clayton's room; clothes were on the floor, the bed, chairs, and hanging from a closet doorknob. An ever-optimistic Bitty went to the large chest of drawers against the far wall, however, and after pawing through several drawers, finally found a clean football jersey. At least, it was supposed to be clean. I wasn't so sure.

"How long has it been since you've washed clothes?" I asked as we proceeded from Clayton's room to Brandon's. "This jersey smells funny."

"Wash clothes?" Bitty sounded a little vague.

"You have a brand new washer and dryer, I happen to know, that does everything but fold them and put them away. They're those really big appliances in the laundry room. You know, that small room off the kitchen."

"The boys do the laundry."

"That explains it."

Music came from Brandon's room, and Bitty tapped on the door until he called for us to come in. I squinted a bit at the loud music, and Brandon must have noticed because he turned down the CD player.

"Hey, Aunt Trinket. What are you and Mama up to now?"

"What makes you think we're up to something?" Bitty asked. "Not that I shouldn't ask you the same thing."

Brandon grinned at her, and reached over to take Heather's hand in his. While he was sprawled on his bed, she sat in a chair at the desk next to him. They were both fully clothed, but he teased, "We were making mad, passionate love, and now you've interrupted us."

Heather pulled her hand away and playfully thumped him on the head. "Your mother is going to hate me if you say things like that."

"No, she won't. She's liberated."

"Be careful," I said. "Mothers are only liberated when it comes to themselves, not to their children."

"Believe it," Bitty said. "Do you have a clean jersey Trinket can wear? Preferably in black? A big one that will fit her wide shoulders."

"Good lord, Bitty, they aren't that wide," I said a bit irritably. "I've been told I have lovely shoulders."

"You shouldn't believe everything a high school gym teacher tells you. Some of those women are very lonely. Ah, here's one that will do much better than Clayton's. The dirty laundry is piling up. Whose turn is it?" Bitty asked as she pulled a jersey out of the closet.

Yawning, Brandon swung his long legs over the side of the bed, stood up and stretched. "Mine. I wash and dry, Clayton folds and puts away. Heather and I have been busy lately, and I kinda forgot."

"I'm going to be polite and trusting and not ask what you've been busy doing. So you can get right to the laundry."

"Heather's a tri-athlete. She's been prepping and I've been helping. I spot her on the weights. Look at her biceps . . . come on, show Mama those muscles, girl."

Heather looked a little flustered, but slid up her short sleeve and flexed what I thought was an impressive bicep. Apparently her slenderness was deceptive. She was just the kind of girl I'd always expected Brandon to bring home one day; pretty, smart, and athletic. He seemed really fond of her, too, something I was sure Bitty had noticed as well.

Since Bitty had been getting in her jibes at my expense, I decided a little payback was due.

"Do you think she's the one?" I nudged Bitty and asked as we went down the hall toward her bedroom.

"Who? One what?"

"Why, the girl Brandon's going to marry. Do you think Heather is the one?"

"Don't get ridiculous, Trinket! He's too young to get married. And even if he wasn't, he certainly wouldn't marry someone like her."

"Why not? What's the matter with her? She seems like just his type."

We had reached Bitty's bedroom, and she turned around and looked at me with narrowed eyes and both hands on her hips. "Just because your Michelle went off and got married, don't think *I'm* ready to be a mother-in-law yet.

"I think you'd be a wonderful mother-in-law. Sort of a cross between Parrish Hollandale and Godzilla."

"Oh lord." Bitty's lips twitched. Then she started laughing, and we both got to laughing so hard we ended up falling across her antique bed and giggling like two girls.

In between bouts of near-hysteria, I wheezed, "Do you remember that old black and white film where Godzilla goes to Tokyo to rescue her baby? That would be you, Bitty. You'd raze half the dorm houses in Oxford to get to your boys."

Bitty sat up on the edge of the bed and wiped her eyes. "So would you. I'd hate to see the two of us on a rampage. I guess it's the maternal instinct thing."

"Or plain meanness. We have a healthy dose of both in our genes."

After a moment, she got up and went to her closet. Bitty's closet is the size of one of the houses I used to rent. In her first remodel, she just appropriated the bedroom next door as her closet, and had the hallway door closed up and the original woodwork reused on the closet door facing. If you didn't know better, you'd think it had always been this way. Bitty hires really good construction people.

She turned on the overhead light; it happens to be a small, really expensive crystal chandelier. The clothes racks are motorized. Bitty presses a button, and the rack hums by at a leisurely pace so she can choose what to wear. Her shoes are on some kind of turn-table with built-in pot lights, arranged by color and style, from bedroom slippers to boots. There are wide, flat drawers that hold her costume jewelry; the expensive stuff is in the safe. Compartments hold her scarves, too. She has silk scarves that cost a fortune, and wool scarves for winter. They're all arranged by season. I've never had enough scarves to arrange by season. Mine are arranged in my sock drawer.

"Do you really think we should stay away from Miranda's house, Trinket?" she called from her closet. I could barely hear her, so got up and went to lean against the doorframe. Her closet looks even bigger close up.

"Good lord, Bitty. Your closet should have its own zip code."

"It is big, isn't it? So, do you truly think we shouldn't do this tonight?"

"Yes. Not that my opinion counts for much."

"Your opinion always counts. I just don't always agree. This is odd . . . I think I'm missing something."

I looked at the closet-boutique and said, "You're kidding. How would you know if you're missing something? You have enough stuff in here to clothe all of Marshall County."

"Everything always stays the same, you know, right in its place. Something's off, and I can't quite tell what it is."

She looked perplexed. I shook my head.

"If the boys have been doing laundry, they probably misplaced something."

She looked startled. "Oh, they don't do *my* laundry, Trinket. I could never allow that. My clothes would be ruined."

"So you still have your clothes cleaned?"

"Not same-day service. I can't afford that. Maybe the cleaners forgot to send back something . . . here. This is out of order. Oh, and my silver Hermés scarf is missing. Hm, I haven't worn that lately. Why would it be gone?"

"It's probably still at the cleaners. You can call tomorrow and ask about it. Now, you were saying that you agree we shouldn't do any breaking and entering tonight?"

"No, I was just wondering if you still feel pessimistic. We can't wait too long, or someone will go in and straighten up and our chance will be gone. Rayna is positive that she saw Miranda's next column, and you said it might name the person who killed Race and Naomi."

"I've reconsidered. If she knew who it was, she would have gone straight to the police."

"Not if they treated her like they treat us, she wouldn't." Bitty pulled an outfit off a padded hanger. "They keep telling us to butt out and stay home. There's some silly law about compromising evidence or something like that. What do you think? Will I blend in with the shadows wearing this?"

She held up a black body suit that looked familiar. I nodded.

"It worked last time we went out skulking. Wear more sensible shoes this time, though. Flats. No high-heeled boots."

"Is that what I wore? I don't remember." She turned back to her closet, found a pair of low-heeled black flats, and shook her head again. "Remind me to call tomorrow about my scarf. I know it's supposed to be here."

I rolled my eyes and yawned. "If we're not wearing orange jumpsuits in jail, I'll remind you. Come on. Let's get this over with. The sooner we find what Rayna says she saw, the better I'll feel. But I still don't know why I always end up doing this kind of thing with you. Have you noticed that in the past few months we've changed into reckless idiots?"

"Honey, the only thing that's really changed is that everyone notices it now."

I couldn't argue with the truth.

****

We met Rayna at the Piggly-Wiggly grocery store. It wasn't the quietest place. Customers drifted in and out, and the tall security lamps sprayed light over the parking area and left the rest dark. From the parking lot we could walk to Miranda's house.

Rayna held one of those long flashlights like the police use. She was dressed a lot like me, with dark denim jeans, sports shoes, and a loose football jersey. She clicked the flashlight on and held it just under her chin so that she looked really spooky. Then she waggled her brows.

"Ready to rumble, Divas?"

"If you're trying to scare me, it worked. Let's go home," I said.

"Let's not," said Bitty. Even in the dim light I could see her determination. "Once we find out just who is trying to kill us, everything will be better. Life will be just like it was before all this started."

I wasn't so sure about that, but if it made Bitty feel better to believe it, I was willing to go along with that premise. I took a deep breath. "Okay, forward march! Only, try to look normal."

Piggly-Wiggly does a thriving business. Customers wore shorts, sleeveless shirts, and sundresses, and still looked hot. We were dressed in black from head to toe.

"You know we'd have a better chance of looking normal if Bitty wasn't dressed as Darth Vader," I commented as we trudged across asphalt.

Rayna gave a nervous laugh. "You think?"

"You're both just jealous because you don't have a leather jumpsuit like mine," said Bitty.

"Most people throw out their clothes from the sixties," I nudged her and said, and she nudged me back with a sharp elbow.

"Most people can't still *wear* their clothes from the sixties."

Rayna laughed, and I did, too. We were all on edge, and teasing one another took some of the jitters away. Not all of them, though. The closer we got to Miranda Watson's darkened house, the higher the hairs on the back of my neck and my arms stood up. I probably looked like a cat, all fluffed out and ready to jump.

We approached the house by the back way. Overgrown bushes almost hid a wire fence that marked the boundaries of the yard. Since the fence was low, I was able to bend the wire down and hop over it with only a little trouble. Rayna managed it as well, and that left Bitty.

She eyed the fence, stuck the toe of her shoe into one of the wire squares, and did her best to get over it. Unfortunately she was too short and her jumpsuit was too tight. All she did was get hung up. The fence was flimsy, one of those ancient livestock wire things that had probably been put up in the thirties. Every time Bitty tried to climb over it, wire sagged and threw her off-balance, and she hung precariously. The back and forth motion of the wire made it look as if Bitty was trying to ride a wild mustang.

Rayna and I tried to help, grabbing her arms to lift so she could get traction with her feet. It didn't help. Bitty is heavier than she looks. And despite her claim of being the same size she was in the sixties, she feels at least twenty pounds heavier.

"Good god, Bitty," I puffed as I strained to keep her aloft, "have you got bricks in your pockets?"

Between wheezes, she retorted, "No . . . pockets!"

"Then your outfit must be made of lead, not leather, Catwoman."

A giggle escaped Rayna as she struggled with Bitty's other arm. The fence post wobbled, the wire vibrated, Bitty weaved back and forth with one leg half over the top. It was a recipe for disaster. I could see it coming, but couldn't stop it.

Rayna and I both tried to hold on to her, but our efforts failed. Leather sleeves slipped through our hands as if greased. Bitty flailed her arms over her head like she was trying to fly, her entire body teetered, her right foot stuck fast in a four inch wire square, her left foot caught on the top, and then she went backward and down.

A loud shriek accompanied her landing in the bushes. So much for stealth.

Next door, a back porch light flashed on. Rayna and I hit the ground.

I have to say, Rayna is a really fast study.

Cupping her hands around her mouth, she meowed like a cat in heat. Obviously, it isn't a sound that's unfamiliar to her. If there were any tomcats within a three mile radius, they were no doubt headed our way. With Bitty flopping around in the bushes and trying to get her foot unstuck from the fence, it probably sounded like a crowd of cats. Pride of cats? That collective noun thing briefly flashed through my mind right before I was smacked on the head with a stick.

"Owww!" I said. Rayna immediately drowned me out with another long moan like a love-starved feline. Bitty hit me with another stick.

"Get me loose!" she hissed, and since I was already crouched on the ground and almost eye-level with her foot, I obliged by yanking off her shoe. It had the desired effect of releasing her, and she disappeared into the tangled undergrowth. There was some thrashing around before she popped into sight again. Still on the other side of the fence, of course. She pressed her face against the wire squares and glared at me. "Not like that!"

"How else was I supposed to get you loose?" I hissed back at her.

"You could have thought of something!"

"I did! And it worked."

Bitty threw a clump of leaves at me and missed.

"Bitty," said Rayna in a whisper, "stop playing around and get over here!"

"I'll go around," I heard Bitty say, then bushes rustled and she disappeared.

Rayna's ruse of being a lovelorn cat must have worked. The porch light next door went out. We were left in the dark again. A dog barked not far away, and I felt the sudden need for a potty break.

Impossible, of course.

In the years of following my ex around the country to random jobs, I had found that with enough training, it's possible for me to go long periods of time without having to visit gas station toilets. Perry believed it vital to get to our destination with as few stops as necessary, although we did have occasional differences of opinion on what constituted necessary.

Thus, I learned that the longer I could wait and the fewer gas stations we had to visit, the less stress I endured. I put that lesson to good use now.

Rayna and I crept toward the back of the house, keeping to the shadows as much as possible. Crickets stopped chirping, then started up when we passed them, and birds muttered sleepily in tree tops. There are a lot of old trees in Holly Springs. Every year a few are lost to wind and storms, but there are still plenty left in the neighborhoods.

Bitty reappeared farther down the fence. Instead of trying to climb over again, she opened the wire gate and stepped through. She met us at the concrete steps leading up to the back door. Twigs and leaves sprouted from her head like horns, and she tried to brush them away with one hand.

"We could have just come through the gate," she whispered sulkily. "I think I got all kinds of creatures in my hair."

"A good wash will get them out," I comforted her. "If the peroxide doesn't kill them first."

"My hair color is natural!" she insisted as she followed us up the back steps.

Rayna turned on the top step and looked at us. "Will you two be quiet? I'd be amazed if the entire neighborhood hasn't heard us by now!"

"Sorry," I said. "Nerves."

Bitty nodded agreement. "We do this."

"Well, please stop! You're making me a nervous wreck."

When Rayna turned back to the door, Bitty and I just looked at each other and shrugged. Apparently not everyone has mine and Bitty's ability to remain cool under pressure. It must be a Truevine talent.

After a few tense moments of feeling around the top of the door frame, Rayna's fingers brushed a key and it tumbled through the air. She managed to catch it before it fell into the flowerbed next to the house.

"How did you know to look up there?" I whispered when we were inside the house.

"Someone has to be feeding her cats. I took a chance." Rayna clicked on the long flashlight and played it around the kitchen. It looked fairly neat. Either someone had been in to tidy it up, or the struggle between Miranda and her assailant hadn't gotten this far. I couldn't help a shudder at the thought of her being attacked so brutally. It must have been a terrible shock.

"Do you think it was someone she knew?" I asked as we tiptoed from the kitchen toward the front rooms. "Surely Miranda wouldn't invite just anyone inside, and certainly not the person she was going to betray in her column. Would she?"

"She can be really smug," Bitty said from behind me. We were creeping single-file down a hallway. "She might have thought she could handle the situation. Or maybe it was someone who didn't have anything at all to do with the other murders, but just took a dislike to something she said."

"I got the impression she intended to publish something startling in her column," said Rayna. She paused at the door to the living room to turn and look at us. "Didn't you, Trinket?"

"Well, yes, but I thought maybe it was just an apology to the Divas. That would have been pretty startling."

Bitty snorted. "It would have been pretty miraculous. Miranda Watson has never apologized to anyone about anything she's put in her nasty little gossip column. She has all the manners of a sump pump. Bless her heart."

The last was added in a "knock on wood" spirit, since Bitty obviously didn't want any bad luck to come back on her for disparaging a woman in a coma.

Rayna swung the flashlight beam toward the living room. "I'll see if I can find those papers I saw, while you two check out the dining room."

I hadn't even thought about bringing a flashlight, and when I looked at Bitty, I saw that she hadn't, either. Rather than admit our lack of foresight, I returned to the kitchen to look for a candle, or matches, or anything that would be better than alerting the neighbors by turning on the lights. As I felt my way along what I thought to be a walnut cabinet, I heard someone right behind me.

"Just wait there, Bitty," I said softly. "I'm looking for a light of some kind."

She didn't answer, but I could hear her breathing as I searched around on the top of the cabinet, then on one of the kitchen counters. I saw where Miranda had one of those old wrought iron match holders hanging on her wall, the dark shape unmistakable even in the dim kitchen light. I reached inside it, but instead of matches, she had a Bic lighter. It would work just as well, I figured.

"I've got something," I said to Bitty as I turned around, but she'd already gone back to the hallway.

When I reached her, she grabbed my wrist. "Where did you go?"

"You know where I went. To get a light. Here. I have a lighter. No candles, though."

"You should have told me. I looked around and you were gone." She shivered. "I think one of the cats is hiding in that doorway. I keep feeling it looking at me."

I flicked the Bic, and we both squinted toward the doorway she mentioned, but the cat was gone. The tiny light flickered and danced right above my thumb. Holding the plastic tab to keep it lit wasn't as easy as I thought it'd be. Every time my thumb slipped, the flame went out and I had to restrike. Still, it was better than no light at all as we made our way into the dining room off the hall and next to the kitchen.

An eerie silence shrouded the house. I wanted to call out to see if Rayna had any luck, but didn't want her to fuss at me again for being loud. Bitty grabbed hold of the back of my football jersey and walked so close behind me she stepped on my heels twice.

Papers were stacked on the dining room table. Several books, a bowl of artificial fruit, a Christmas wreath, vase of wilted flowers, and ceramic statue of a cat cluttered the surface, too. I went to the stack of papers, and held the Bic close enough to make out the words. It was a column from *The South Reporter*, but it wasn't one by Miranda. This one had to do with a ladies' softball team.

"What does it say?" Bitty asked right in my ear as she peered over my shoulder. "Is it the one naming the killer?"

"No, and to be honest, I don't think we're going to find anything like that here. If the police left anything like that behind, they're slipping."

"Maybe they just took one copy of it. That would be all they would need."

"Why would Miranda print out more than one copy? I thought people did all that kind of stuff by the Internet these days, anyway."

"Oh, I don't know. To proof read or something, I suppose. Here. Give me the lighter. I see something on the buffet table."

I passed over the Bic quite gladly. Holding down that plastic tab made my thumb ache. The circle of light it made was small, and while Bitty examined stuff on the buffet, I stood in the dark and waited. A mirror hung over the buffet table, and the flame reflected back in a bright circle that illuminated the leaves and twigs stuck in Bitty's hair. She'd suffered for our cause, I thought to myself with a grin. Usually it's me who ends up with ungodly debris in my hair, on my face, and stuck to the bottom of my shoes. The fates were smiling more kindly on me tonight.

"Trinket," she whispered excitedly, "I think I have it! This is it!"

"What?" I was stunned. This had all seemed like a wild goose chase until now. "Let me see that. Are you sure?"

"As I can be. It has next week's date on it, and here it says . . . oh, let me see . . .."

I made my way around the end of the oval dining room table toward Bitty. She held up the sheet of printer paper, and as she did so, the Bic caught her thumbnail on fire.

Flame shot into the air as her long, curved thumbnail blazed nicely.

"Drop the lighter, Bitty," I couldn't help shouting. "Drop it!"

Bitty dropped the lighter, but her thumbnail still burned. It smelled terrible. She waved her hand frantically in the air, but that only made it burn higher.

"Stop, drop, and roll, Bitty!"

From the next room I heard Rayna telling us to be quiet, but it seemed to me we had a bigger problem on our hands than disturbing the cats. I did the only thing I could think of. I grabbed the vase of flowers from the dining table and dashed the water over Bitty. Of course, the wilted flowers went, too, and daisy petals scattered in her hair and on the dining room rug. The fiery thumb went out, and Bitty just stood there looking at it in the dark as water dripped from her nose and chin, and from the ends of her hair.

Then she said, "At least these are acrylic nails."

Relieved at her calm tone, I nodded. "I'm sure DJ will be glad to work you into her schedule tomorrow."

I heard Bitty sigh. "I've been trying to save money by going once a month. She'll be surprised to see me."

"Where's the Bic?"

"Where's the what?"

"The lighter, Bitty. Did you drop it?"

"Oh. Yes. It's on the floor somewhere—oh, and the paper! It's down there, too. I'll get it."

We both bent at the same time, and in the dark, bumped heads. I put out a hand to steady myself and luckily, found the lighter.

"I've got fire, Bitty, so be careful," I said as I flicked the Bic. It was a good thing I warned her; she was so close her hair would have been in flames if she moved an inch. I held the lighter up a little higher and saw the paper on the wood floor. When I tried to pick it up, it clung soddenly to oak. Uh oh. This was not at all promising.

"Be careful," said Bitty a little anxiously. "I think it got wet."

Flickering light wavered erratically and the Bic went out. I relit it briefly. Enough to see that it was going to take steadier light to accomplish recovery of the paper without ruining it.

"We need Rayna's flashlight. I hope this paper is what we need and all our efforts aren't wasted."

Bitty said thoughtfully, "My leather jumpsuit is shrinking. We better hurry."

"Good lord, Bitty."

She creaked when she stood up, and I giggled like a schoolgirl. I swear, I could almost hear the leather drawing up. It must have been the power of suggestion, because I doubt that small amount of water would have done the trick.

Holding the Bic aloft like Lady Liberty's torch, I led the way down the hall to the living room. I could hear Rayna going through stuff with thumps and thuds. She sounded out of breath.

"Hey," I called softly, "we found it! We found a copy of next week's column in the dining room. Rayna?"

She didn't answer, just kept banging around, and as I got to the open doorway, I saw why. Rayna's flashlight was on the floor, and silhouetted against its beam were two struggling figures. One of them I recognized as Rayna. I had no idea who the other one was. Being quiet didn't seem nearly as important as helping Rayna.

"Hey!" I yelled at the top of my lungs. "Stop it!"

I rushed forward as Bitty asked, "What's going on?"

Thrashing about, both of them seemed to have hold of one another, and I looked frantically around for a weapon. Dust motes hazed the air when I grabbed what I thought was a ceramic statue to hit Rayna's attacker.

The ceramic cat statue bit me and I dropped it. Screeching, it ran out of the living room and down the hallway. I heard Bitty ask again, "What's going on?"

Not bothering to answer, I grabbed a real statue this time. It was a happy Buddha that I cracked over the head of the person struggling with Rayna. The Buddha didn't break and the person didn't collapse, but did let go and stagger a few feet. I followed with the happy Buddha and aimed for the head again. This time, the person turned quickly and thrust the heel of his hand under my chin before I could hit him. I dropped like a sack of flour, still holding on to the statue.

Above me I heard Rayna swearing and saw her sports shoe flash past a few inches above my nose. At least, I think that's what it was. My vision was blurred and it was dark, and the flashlight on the floor was shining directly into my eyes. It could have been anything. Whatever it was, it connected with the bad guy and I heard him grunt. For some reason, the grunt sounded odd. As grunts go.

I could hear Bitty calling from the hallway, "What's going on?"

"Come back here, you coward!" Rayna yelled as the bad guy headed for the front door. "Come on! You wanna fight? We'll fight! Come back here!"

"What's going on?" Bitty yelled.

"Oh, *hell* no!" Rayna shouted. "Get your butt back here!"

The front door swung open and banged back against the wall. I rolled over on my side just in time to see whoever it was escape. Rayna was right behind, and disappeared into the night.

"What's going on?" Bitty demanded loudly.

I moved my jaw from side to side and was gratified that it still worked. The guy had a healthy punch, that was sure.

"Dammit, *what's going on?*" Bitty shrieked.

With Buddha clutched under my arm, I managed to get to my feet. I was woozy but functioning. I leaned against what felt like the loveseat, and finally answered Bitty:

"I hear police sirens."

CHAPTER 19

Some days you're the hammer, some days you're the nail. Bitty, Rayna and I sat at the police station feeling like the nails.

We had been questioned—I thought of it more as interrogation—separately, and then together. Finally the police must have been satisfied with our versions of the story and allowed us our phone calls.

Bitty called Jackson Lee, and Rayna and I decided it would be better for us if we just quietly got a ride back to our cars. The less known about this, the easier it would be for us. We were already facing charges of illegal entry, violating a crime scene, and a few other things that Jackson Lee would sort out.

One thing about Jackson Lee, he can get to the heart of a thing very quickly when he chooses. Once we were in his car, he said, "You ladies are going to end up in jail or dead if you don't stop your amateur snooping. If that's what you want, keep it up."

None of us said anything. We all knew he'd made a very valid point.

It wasn't until he dropped us off at the Piggly-Wiggly that we said anything to each other. We all thanked Jackson Lee profusely, of course, and Bitty paused at his car window to talk to him in a low tone before she joined us.

"Well," I said, "I guess we need to put away our detective badges and whistles."

Rayna nodded. She was still miffed that she hadn't been able to catch the guy who attacked her. He'd just disappeared between the houses. Fortunately, he hadn't hurt her, but she was pretty sure she'd landed a few good blows before he got away.

"I just wish I could have gotten a good look at him," she said now, frowning.

"It was that ski mask. All I could see was that he wasn't real tall and he was pretty skinny," I said in commiseration. "You almost got him, though. Too bad we didn't get what we needed. I guess we'll never know if what Bitty found was it."

Coming up behind us, Bitty said, "Did I hear my name?"

I turned to look at her. "You did. We've decided to hang up our detective hats. We don't seem to be very successful."

"Speak for yourself, Doctor Watson. You may call *me* Mister

Holmes."

"You sound more like Charlie Chan. I hope you don't regard tonight as our crowning achievement."

"Maybe not yours, but then, you left without the prize."

"What on earth are you talking about? We left because the police came and asked us to leave. Not very nicely, either."

Bitty began to unzip the top of her leather jumpsuit. I put up my hands to block the sight. "Oh for heaven's sake, Trinket. I'm not undressing. But, since I don't have any pockets, I had to improvise. Look what I have!"

She produced a folded sheet of paper with a flourish worthy of any operatic diva, and we were immediately impressed.

"You got it!" Rayna said. "Oh Bitty, you're so clever!"

"Aren't I? While you two were chasing shadows, I took the flashlight and went back to the dining room. It took a minute to get it off the floor without tearing it, but I think I got it all. I'm really good at this kind of thing."

"And so modest, too," I said, trying not to roll my eyes.

"Just for that—here, Rayna. You can read it first. Your flashlight still works, right?"

Bitty held the flashlight while Rayna read what she could of the still wet paper. I could tell from her face that it didn't live up to our expectations.

"Damn," she said with a disgusted sigh. "It's a copy of next week's column, all right, but so much of it is wet . . . wait. I know what we can do. Let's take this back to my house. I've watched enough *Forensic Files* to figure out how they dry things and use light to get it to come up better. Maybe I can improvise."

"We *are* mistresses of improvisation," I said hopefully.

"Don't get your hopes up too high," said Rayna. "On TV they use sophisticated equipment that I don't have. And this is laser jet, so it may not come out right. But we can give it a try."

We all trooped over to Rayna's house for our experiment in forensic technology. If it had been something involving duct tape and a fingernail file, I'd have been very helpful. Since it probably involved chemicals and know-how, I would just watch.

When we got there, Rayna's husband Rob was home. She thought it best not to tell him that A: we'd been carted off to jail in a squad car again, or B: what it was we were attempting to do. Not that she'd lie to him if he asked, of course. But unless he asked specifically if we'd been at the jail or had taken evidence from a police-sealed crime scene, there would be time enough later to confess all.

"Hello, ladies," the unsuspecting Rob greeted us cheerfully. "And how is your evening going?"

"Just fine," Bitty lied. "Except we're all thirsty. I don't suppose you have any wine?"

"Ah," said Rob with an eager gleam in his eyes. "Come to the wine cellar and see my latest purchase. It just came in yesterday. An entire case of Beaujolais from California. A new vineyard I wanted to try."

"Delighted," Bitty said promptly, and as she followed Rob from the hotel lobby to the kitchen and cellar door, gave us a wink over her shoulder.

"Clever girl," said Rayna. "Rob's out of the way for at least a half hour. She'll keep him down there talking about wine, while we see what we can do with the paper."

"I didn't know Rob was into wine."

"It's something new. Always something new with him. He's expanding his horizons, he told me. In fact—he's thinking about hiring someone to help him with the insurance investigations he does. That way, when he has to be out investigating fraud, there will be another person to help out here."

"Why don't you write bonds for him? That way you can keep the money in the family."

"Not me. I'm not getting out at two in the morning to bail some drunk out of jail. I like my sleep. Besides, I have my artwork that I prefer. It pays me enough to buy more paints and canvases."

And then some. Rayna has an excellent eye and produces beautiful work. She sold most of it, but still has a few pieces hanging on her walls. I love the colors she uses. Bright greens, reds, yellows and blues, and usually a cat peeking out somewhere in the paintings she keeps.

The infamous Merlin of Chen Ling and mouse-racing fame, curled around her ankles when she went into the kitchen. He's a fat, lovely cat. He's also insistent and a bit spoiled. When his meowing got too loud, Rayna opened a jar of cat treats and gave him a handful. This had the immediate effect of causing several more cats to miraculously appear in the kitchen.

"If you'll keep the cats off the counters," Rayna said, "I'll see what I can do with a light bulb. And some vodka."

"Kinky," I said as I took the jar of cat treats she handed me. "How many cats do I feed?"

"All of them. Just scatter treats on the floor, and they'll take care of the rest."

While I fed the motley assortment of felines, Rayna got to work using a lamp with a bare light bulb. I'm not exactly sure what treatment she gave the paper, but she heated it over the hot bulb until she got the results she wanted.

"Eureka," she said calmly. "We have a few more sentences here. Okay. Here's what it says as far as I can tell: 'What cool blond in our town square had more than a tiny bit of involvement with one of Holly Springs' recently deceased citizens? Readers, I can tell you that law enforcement officials are asking the same questions. Too bad they don't have the same sources I do, because—' and part of that sentence didn't come out, but it picks up here: 'so you will soon know the rest, dear readers. Don't forget, you heard it here first.' There's other stuff in her column, but this is the only part that refers to the murders. So, what do you think?"

"Rose Allgood is definitely a suspect. But that leads to the question—who was the guy who attacked us tonight?"

"I'm not *sure* it was a guy." Rayna opened a cabinet and got out a tumbler. Then she poured a small bit of vodka into it and offered it to me. I shook my head. Straight vodka, even real expensive vodka, is not my thing.

"You think it might be a woman who was in Miranda's house tonight?"

After downing the vodka, she coughed. "That's powerful. Anyway, it may have been. Whoever it was, she's a strong woman if she's not a he. You know what I mean."

I did. I thought about Rose Allgood. She was tall, blond, and could be athletic; it was possible. I squinched up my eyes and tried to visualize her, but all I could remember were the shelves of dildos and her cool stare. Everything else was vague.

"Has it occurred to you that Miranda Watson could be wrong?" I asked after I was out of cat treats and Rayna poured herself another smidgen of vodka. One of the cats got a little aggressive about the lack of more treats, and Rayna shooed it away.

"Constantly. She always thinks she's right, but there have been times when she's wrong."

"Then she could be wrong, now."

"Yep. But I wonder . . ."

"What?"

"Let's sit down and go over everything we know, and what we think we know. It may make more sense on paper."

It seemed like a good idea to me.

We were still on the first fact, Race's murder, when Bitty joined us. She pulled out a kitchen chair and sat down. "He already knows," she said to Rayna. "He's decided to sample his wine for a while before he asks you why you have your head up your ass." She held up a hand. "His words, not mine. I say let him sample quite a while before you talk to him about us going to the Watson house tonight."

"Sounds like a plan," Rayna said after a heartbeat of silence. "Okay, we're making out a list of what we know, what we don't know, and what we need to know. Or really, just putting down things in chronological order."

Bitty looked mildly interested. "I take it the column holds no great revelations."

"Just what we already know from Gaynelle. Now we have to figure out if it's true and if so, how do we prove it."

"Did Gaynelle say how she found out?"

We all looked at each other. Rayna reached for her cordless phone and dialed a number.

"Gaynelle? This is Rayna—yes, I know it's late. No, no one else has been hurt. It *is* important. Now listen. How did you find out Rose Allgood is under suspicion? Uh huh. Uh huh. I see. Okay, thanks. Go back to sleep. Yes, but I'll tell you about it tomorrow. It can wait. G'nite."

"Well?" demanded Bitty when Rayna thumbed the phone's off button and shook her head at us. "What'd she say?"

"She said she heard it from Miranda Watson."

"Oh great," I said. "It all leads back to her. So if she's wrong, then—"

"Then we wasted time and energy tonight," Rayna finished. "Well, let's not waste any more time. Let's see what we can figure out."

We listed Race on one notebook page, Naomi on the flip side, then what we knew related to each under their names. It ended up being a pretty long list, longer than any of us had expected, I was sure.

"Okay," said Rayna, skimming the list under Race's name, "we have Race found dead in Trina and Trisha Madewell's rental cottage. Trina and Trisha both dated him. Trina was once engaged to him. He ended the engagement. Trina has motive. She has opportunity. But it was Naomi's pistol that killed him. Both sisters knew Naomi.

"That brings us to Naomi. She had opportunity and method, but what would have been her motive? She was in love with him by all accounts and expected to marry him.

"So now we go back to Trisha. She had opportunity, but no real motive that I can see, and again, it was Naomi's gun."

Pausing, Rayna looked up at us. "So far so good?"

We nodded affirmation. Rayna can be quite organized in her thinking, which I always thought right brain people couldn't manage. I must be a middle brain person, since I have no creativity and greatly flawed logic.

Continuing, Rayna ticked off the next person on the list, bringing a protest from the suspect herself.

"Hey," Bitty said, "my name shouldn't be on there!"

"I explained to you a little while ago that if we're going to list all possible suspects we have to list *everyone* connected to both the victims, Bitty."

"Yes, but I didn't think you meant me!"

I patted Bitty's arm. "It's okay, honey. Just hear her out."

"As I was saying," Rayna continued, "Bitty dated Race once. While she didn't want to see him again, she had no motive, no opportunity, and no access to Naomi's gun.

"Then we have Cliff Wages, who allegedly sabotaged Race's hot rod. His only motive seems to be greed, although with Race out of the way, he moved up in the NHRA ranks. That might be enough reason to kill, even though it wasn't like Race was that much of a threat to him anymore. Race needed a new sponsor and money to get back into the game. There's no evidence Wages ever met Naomi, though it's possible. I think we can safely rule out Wages.

"That brings us to Rose Allgood. She has money. If it's true that Race jilted her, that would give her motive. No opportunity, no access to Naomi's gun, however. As far as we know, she didn't know Naomi, though it's possible they met since Naomi did go to Carolann's shop pretty often.

"Now, we turn to Naomi's murder. Despite Bitty's suggestion that we include half the high school football team—" She flashed a wry smile up at my dear cousin. "—we've narrowed it down to three suspects.

"One, of course, is Bitty. We've established that she had plenty of motive, but it's doubtful she had opportunity."

"*Doubtful?*" Bitty repeated indignantly. "Don't you mean impossible?"

"I'm approaching this objectively, Bitty. Don't take anything personal. I'm just asking questions the police may—and probably have—asked themselves."

"My phone records show I was on the phone organizing our meeting when she was killed. So I've been cleared."

"There are records that your phone was in use, not that you were the one on it," Rayna corrected, then added, "but I don't think the police believe you're the one who killed Naomi, or you'd already be in jail."

Somewhat pacified, Bitty sat back in the kitchen chair with her arms crossed over her chest. "Oh, we all know that Trina Madewell killed them both."

"It does look that way," Rayna said with a frown, "but if that's true, why drag in Rose Allgood's name?"

"Trina and Miranda obviously had conversations, or that nasty column about the Divas wouldn't have been published," I said. "Maybe Trina told Miranda about Rose just to throw the police off the track."

"But if Miranda went to the police—and remember, she said she didn't—they would have already brought Rose in for questioning, wouldn't they?" Rayna pointed out.

"We have only Miranda's version of that. What if Miranda is the common link in both murders?" I asked.

"Nonsense," said Bitty. "It's Trina. Or Trisha. Most likely Trina is the murderer."

"I didn't mean Miranda is the killer, Bitty. She's just the vehicle the killer is using to spread false information. If not, she wouldn't have been attacked. Maybe the killer thought she'd put together the pieces and intended to go to the police."

"All conjecture," said Rob from the doorway. He carried a bottle of wine and an empty glass. "Let the police handle this. If tonight wasn't reason enough, remember being run off the road."

"Hard to forget," I said. "That's one reason we're so determined to get the guilty person. They've killed twice, and tried to kill four other people, including Miranda."

"Reason enough for you three to stay the hell out of it," said Rob flatly. He put the wine and glass on the kitchen counter, then pulled out a chair and sat at the table next to Rayna. "Believe me, the police are more than capable of solving these murders."

"Before or after someone else gets killed?" Rayna reached across the table and put her hand over Rob's. "Police have legal procedures they have to follow. We don't. We can go places and talk to people who might actually say things they wouldn't say to the cops. You know that."

"I know the police have guns and pepper spray, and none of you do."

"Oh, I do," Bitty said brightly. "I have a gun *and* pepper spray."

Rob rolled his eyes. "That's not as comforting to me as you might think."

"I can shoot. Ask Rayna. I shot up the truck that was chasing us. Maybe I didn't hit the driver, but I did damage. If we could find the truck, I bet we'd find the killer. Let's look out at the Madewell place. They probably have it hidden in a barn or something."

"Hm," said Rob thoughtfully. "Bitty, you just gave me an idea."

"A good idea?"

He grinned. "I hope so. If I do some investigating, will you three promise me you won't go snooping around anywhere?"

"Are you any good?" Bitty asked seriously.

This time I was the one who rolled my eyes. "Bitty, it's what he does for a living. He investigates insurance fraud."

"Oh, I forgot about that. I just usually see him as my bail bondsman."

"For which I thank you," said Rob. "Lately, you've been keeping my bank balance healthy. As nice as that is, I'd like to put an end to your budding career."

"Career? I don't really have a career. Although I have been thinking about going back into real estate. Why would you want to stop me?"

"He's talking about our amateur detective work, Bitty," I said. "Rob is telling us that he'll try to find the black truck for us. If it's at Madewell Courts, as an insurance investigator, he can 'check out a recent claim' so to speak. That gives him a legitimate excuse to go snooping in barns. Am I right, Rob?"

"Right on the nose, Trinket. What do you say, ladies? You retire and let me do the detective work for you?"

"You'll tell us what you find?" Rayna asked.

"As long as you agree that I'm going to tell the police first."

"But then they get all the credit!" Bitty protested.

"Don't mind Bitty," I said. "She's still getting marriage proposals from around the world after all that publicity we got last time. If it wasn't for Jackson Lee, I think she might have accepted the invitation she got from the Shah of Iran."

Bitty glared at me. "You know that guy was really in a Texas prison and not the Shah at all."

I made a face at her. "I'm shocked to hear that."

"Yes," Rayna said, "we all agree that anything you find has to be given to the police first. We would like to be kept in the loop, though. Will you do that much for us?"

Rob leaned over and kissed his wife. "Absolutely. As long as I know you're safe, I will share everything I get."

It was the best deal we could have gotten, I suppose, and really, I wasn't that fond of poking into abandoned buildings after everything that happened a few months ago.

"Want our lists?" I asked Rob, and he reached for the notebook on the table. After looking it over, he nodded.

"Impressive. Your conclusion that the two murders are connected is logical. I'll check out Rose Allgood's past, money trail, anything like that, just to be sure. I have a new software program that can track almost anyone anywhere."

Rayna gave him an exasperated look. "Well, why didn't you tell me this earlier? I could have used it."

He wagged a finger at her. "Hunh uh. I didn't want you getting into any more trouble than you already have. A little knowledge can be a dangerous thing."

Rayna's eyes narrowed. "I think I want to redo our bargain."

"Nope," he said. "We already have an agreement. You keep your end of the deal, and I'll keep mine."

Whistling a cheery tune, he got up from the table. We watched silently until he'd left the kitchen. Then we looked at each other.

"We made a bargain," I reminded. "Let's just see what he comes up with, okay?"

"Fine by me," said Bitty. "I wonder if it's too late to call DJ. I really need to get my thumbnail fixed."

"It's after midnight," said Rayna. "I move we adjourn this meeting of the mentally impaired."

"Seconded," I said.

"Huh?" said Bitty.

I took her arm. "Let's go home. I'll explain on the way."
****

It was an exhausting end to what had started out as a relaxing day. I was amazed we'd packed so much activity into just a few hours. I stopped my car in front of Bitty's house and left the engine running. She looked over at me.

"You're not coming in for a nightcap?"

"I'm too tired. One drink would send me into a coma."

Bitty nodded. In the light that came from her front porch, I could see her frown. "I keep thinking about Miranda being in a coma, and the intruder at her house tonight. It seems like the same person who attacked her, doesn't it?"

"That would be logical. Why?"

"Because that person is still out and about, and if the police had any idea who it was they would have already arrested him or her. Don't you think?"

"Maybe. There has to be probable cause, hard evidence, something besides just suspicion, I suppose. But don't worry about it. You'll be okay. You have a house full of college kids and a Chinese dragon-dog to keep you safe."

"I know. I was thinking about you."

That caught me by surprise. Honestly, I hadn't really thought about someone coming after me. There was no reason. I had absolutely no idea who the killer could be. Maybe Rob's investigation would turn up something the police had overlooked, I didn't know. I just knew that I was tired, dirty from my wallowing about on the floor and in the yard, and ready to bathe and go to bed. I didn't want to think about it anymore tonight.

"I'll be fine, Bitty. I'll lock my car doors and not stop until I get home."

"You should carry a cell phone. Just in case."

"No, thanks. I'm not ready for another monthly bill. Besides, if I had a phone people could call me."

"And you could call people if you have a flat tire."

"My tires are fine. Daddy keeps my car running smoothly, and I have plenty of gas."

Bitty opened the car door. "Okay. I tried. If you won't listen, I can't help you. Remember what my daddy always said: 'Those who will not listen must suffer'."

"I thought it was, 'Those who will not learn must suffer'."

"Both apply."

"Bitty, I'm so proud. You're getting philosophical wisdom at last."

She said something rude and got out of my car. I could hear the leather of her jumpsuit rustle and groan.

"Your vampire suit is creaking," I called to her right before she shut the door. I didn't hear her reply. It was probably for the best.

CHAPTER 20

I got to the intersection of Walthal and Randolph and slowed down
to look at a jogger on the sidewalk. Just in case. One never knows what
killers do in their leisure time, so just to be safe, I locked my car doors.
Then I saw who it was and laughed at myself. Bitty and her silly
admonishment was making me a nervous Nellie. I hit the window button
for the passenger side.

"Can I give you a ride?"

The jogger stuttered to a halt and turned to look at me. She smiled.
"I'm just doing my regular run."

"This late? It's after midnight."

"That's the safest time. Hardly any traffic and everyone's asleep."

"Not everyone," I said. "Ghouls, vampires, me and Bitty are still up.
You sure you don't want a ride?"

"Well . . . ." She hesitated, then nodded. "That would be great, Miz
T. I'm renting a room two blocks over. If it wouldn't be out of your
way?"

"Not at all. I'm going to Cherryhill anyway."

After she got in and shut the door, I glanced at her. She was
breathing a little hard. She had what looked like chalk on her dark jogging
suit. It was one of those Lycra things that fit snugly. Something to do with
aerodynamics, I've been told, but since I'm not into running or any other
kind of fitness program that doesn't involve chocolate, I never paid much
attention.

"You're really into the fitness thing, aren't you," I remarked, and she
nodded.

"As much as I can."

"You need to be careful at night though, seriously. The police
haven't caught the person who killed Race and Naomi."

"Are they close, do you think?"

"Yes, I think they definitely know who it is. They're just trying to
gather enough evidence before they make an arrest. At least, that's what
Rob Rainey says, and he probably knows more than most about it."

"Rob Rainey—I don't think I know him."

"Oh, he's Rayna's husband. You may have met Rayna at Bitty's
house."

"She's one of the Divas?"

"Yes. Rob is an insurance investigator, so he has access to a lot of the same info the police do, as far as running background checks on people."

"Oh. That must come in handy for the Divas, since I know y'all are trying to find the killer, too. I never would have thought so many people would get involved. Usually, it's just the police who do the investigating, not half the town."

I laughed. "That's the way it is in small towns. But you probably already know that. Biloxi isn't that big, though it is a tourist town. Or was until Katrina."

Hurricane Katrina had razed Biloxi pretty thoroughly. It destroyed old antebellum homes like former Confederate President Jefferson Davis's beautiful place right on the main road overlooking the gulf. It also tore up the half-dozen or so casinos, as well as people's homes and lives.

"The casinos are rebuilding. Some are already back in operation. I suppose I could always go back there to work," she said.

"You worked at the casinos?"

"Until Katrina. Then I decided to go back to college, so ended up at Ole Miss. You can let me out at the next corner. I can walk from there. It's only a few houses down."

I stopped on Randolph to let her out.

"You know, Heather," I said as she opened the car door, "I never got your last name."

She turned to smile at me. A street lamp behind her lit up her pale hair. "Lightner," she said. "Heather Ann Lightner."

After she thanked me for giving her a ride, I watched her walk down the side street toward one of the huge homes that had been divided up into a boarding house of sorts. For some reason, an annoying tickle traveled down my spine all the way to my toes. Elusive trivia nagged at me, tidbits of information that might actually form a cohesive solution if I thought about it long enough.

I drove home slowly. It would come to me. I just had to think about it for a while.

****

My brain has an amazing capacity for hiding intriguing pieces of what I consider vital clues when I'm trying to solve a puzzle. But I knew I was on to something. I just wasn't sure what.

I used the method Rayna had used and wrote down everything I could think of on a sheet of ruled paper. Then I went down the list with a pencil and ticked off everything that was either resolved or unrelated.

That left me with hanging pieces of the puzzle. When I asked myself if the answer could involve Heather, it began to make more sense. But did

I dare accuse someone who might be innocent of such heinous crimes as murder? I'd better be sure of myself.

So the next day I called Rob Rainey. At first he didn't want to discuss it with me, but when I told him what I thought, he swore me to secrecy.

"Right off the bat," he said, "we're going to throw out what Bitty's psychic said. Just leave that out of the equation."

"All right, but I can't help but think that she meant Heather when she said there was darkness inside the light. Heather's last name is *Light*ner. Don't you think that's a bit too much of a coincidence?"

Rob sighed. "Trinket, don't get hung up on what a psychic had to say. She could have meant anything. Let's just go with facts, okay?"

For the sake of expediency, and so he wouldn't think I was just as crazy as Bitty, I agreed. "Fine. Have you had any luck finding the black truck?"

"I'll get to that in a minute," he said. "I'll tell you what I've found out so far, but don't tell anyone else yet. Especially my wife. She's obsessed with this craziness, and I don't want her taking any more risks. Or you, for that matter. Will you promise not to go off on your own?"

I thought about it a millisecond, then agreed. "I've discovered I'm not that brave on my own. Or with someone else. I'm good with letting others take the risk and the credit."

Rob laughed. "The credit will go to the Holly Springs Police Department, as it should. All we can do is share what we find with them. They're the ones paid to take the risk, so they can have the credit."

"In your line of work, don't you ever run up against dangerous situations? I mean, like someone getting mad because you've caught them in fraud?"

"Occasionally. Not as much as you might think. Now look, here's what I found out about Rose Allgood. She was born into money, but her father had a big gambling addiction, so by the time she was fourteen, they were living in a shotgun shack on state assistance. Her father died early, and that left Rose, her mother, and another sister. Get this: Rose's younger sister was once engaged to—"

"Race Champion," we both said at the same time.

"Boy, was there any woman in the state of Mississippi he didn't ask to marry him at one time or the other?" I wondered aloud. "Did he ever actually go through with a wedding?"

"Ah, funny you should ask that. Yes, as a matter of fact, he did. In October of 2005, records show he married Dawn Jeannette Hardy. Shortly after they married, Race came back to Holly Springs and filed for a divorce. Since he filed, he's been engaged at least three more times that I can find. Probably more. Every time he got drunk, which is every time he drank, he'd ask whoever he was with to marry him. Most of them said yes, and he apparently didn't know how to tell them he was already married once he sobered up."

"Good lord."

"Some of this I'm just guessing at, of course, but records and facts tell the truth of it." Rob paused. "I'm still trying to track down Dawn Hardy Champion. So far, no luck."

"Do you think she killed Race and Naomi?"

"It's a good bet."

"Which means all my theories just went out the window. Drat. And they were such good theories, too."

Rob chuckled. "Truthfully, until I found that marriage license, I had my alternate theories."

"I'll tell you mine if you tell me yours."

Another deep chuckle, then Rob said, "Well, I was really leaning toward Rose Allgood or her sister. Especially after reading the information collected by you Divas. Rose fits the bill just about perfectly. In fact, I'm still not quite sure she doesn't have something to do with it."

"Well, we have two fairly new arrivals in Holly Springs. One is Rose, and the other is Heather. Both are cool blondes, both lived in Biloxi, but only one of them lived in Biloxi *and* Oxford. After talking to Heather last night, I was almost certain it must be her. For one thing, she's a runner, she's a tri-athlete, she's been working out, and she fits all three qualifications."

"Who set those qualifications?"

I tried to think. Then I remembered. "Race's brother Ronny. He saw a note left on Race's windshield by some girl who'd followed him from the races in Biloxi, to Oxford, and then to Holly Springs. According to Ronny, it spooked Race ."

"Hm. Race didn't seem like the kind of guy easily spooked by a woman. I wonder if it was his wife threatening to out him?"

"That does sound more logical. He went through a lot of women. I can't believe he didn't get caught."

"Apparently, he did," Rob said dryly.

"So true. Have you told the police yet?"

"I'm headed up there in a little bit. I want to get some more info first, and see if I can track down Dawn. It's strange that she seems to have just dropped out of sight. But she can't hide forever, not from my magic software program. In this marvelous age of information, hardly anyone can disappear without a trace."

"Well, that shoots down my retirement plans, I see."

Rob laughed again, a nice sound, and we hung up. I was a bit deflated. I'd really thought Heather had to be the one. She fit all the clues we had. She was an even better candidate than Rose Allgood, with or without her rubber penises. Well, a lot depended upon finding Race's wife. It was possible she had an iron-clad alibi. If so, we'd be back to square one again. And the choice of Rose or Heather as our murderer.

It boggled my mind that a woman could be so cold and cruel as to kill a man, even a current or former husband. Not that there weren't times when I hadn't thought of doing something painful to Perry, of course. Painful, not permanent. It had taken great restraint not to Superglue him to a job. Not that it would have changed him. He'd just have found glue remover, and we'd have been on our way to the next job, state, and town. Ah well. That is behind me now. For which I am very thankful.

I looked at the clock, and it was a little after ten. I had the rest of the day to kill—pardon the pun—so decided to see if my parents needed anything. When I went downstairs, Mama had a small cardboard box filled with things like flour, sugar, canned goods, and inexplicably, toilet paper.

"Take this over to Bitty and the boys," she said. "I know she doesn't think about things like staples."

I gazed at the nice little care package my mother had lovingly packed and shook my head. "It's not that she doesn't think about things like staples, it's that she has no idea what they are. Or how they're used. Except for the Charmin, of course. That she's familiar with. Tell you what. Instead of you going to all this trouble, I'll just take Bitty to Wal-Mart. She's been wanting to go anyway."

Mama thought about it a moment, then agreed. "That's true. The boys would know what to do with sugar and cans of soup, but they may prefer pizza or something else. I'll just bake a couple cakes, maybe make a big pot of chicken and dumplings—or beef stew—for you to take to her later. That would probably be a lot better."

Daddy came in from the yard, mopping sweat off his forehead with an old rag that left streaks of dirt. "Not even eleven yet, and it's hot enough to fry eggs on the porch."

"I'll take mine over easy," I said, and he laughed.

"What's that Brownie has in his mouth?" said Daddy, squinting down at the dog hovering close by my mother's feet. "It's something sparkly . . . here, give it to me. Give it," he said in a sterner voice than I'd heard him use with the little beast.

Brownie must have recognized that tone, because he immediately gulped down the offending object before my father could get it from him.

"Ahhh!" said Daddy. He took Brownie's collar, pried open his jaws, and tried to fish out the item, but the stubborn creature resisted. Mama bent to help. That made the dog even worse. He knew he could count on my mother to baby him.

"Dagnab it," Daddy finally said in disgust, and put one hand atop the kitchen table to help him get to his feet. "He swallowed most of it. Wonder what it is?"

"Let me see," said Mama, now cradling Brownie as if he'd just been attacked by wolves. The dog looked up at her pitifully. His ears were back, his eyes were big, and his front paws dangled over his chest in an attitude of prayer.

I was more amused than irritated, because it was my parents having to deal with him and not me. But then my mother said, "Why, this looks like part of an earring. Where on earth could he have gotten it, I wonder."

Sometimes I can think quickly. I immediately went back upstairs, where I found my bathroom cup on the floor and my treasured earring missing. I looked all around on the tiles, up under the clawfoot tub, the sink, around the toilet, under a wicker chair, a wooden cabinet that holds toiletries, and under the bathroom rug. No sign of it. I knew what that meant.

"He's eaten my earring again," I said when I got back downstairs, and I glared at the offending little beggar until he began to whimper.

Alarmed, my mother looked up at me. "Well, we just have to get him to the vet immediately, of course."

"Don't worry. It's not that big a stone. We'll just have to supervise his daily poop for a while."

"Oh no," said Mama. "He'll need X-rays to make sure it hasn't gotten into an intestinal pocket."

"Into what? I never heard of such a thing. He'll be fine. Really. He's done this before, you know."

"And Dr. Coltrane said we had to keep an eye him, too. The next time it could get lodged somewhere it shouldn't."

When I saw actual tears in my mother's eyes, I surrendered. "Okay, I'll take him by the vet's office. Then I'll take Bitty to Wal-Mart and go back for him. Will that make you feel better?"

Mama nodded. Daddy just shook his head. "I think we need to take that trip to Canada, Anna," he said after a moment. "It's too blamed hot this year."

I was greatly alarmed.

"Oh no, you don't. That means you'd leave me here with the dog and all those cats. If you go to Canada, I'm going to Canada. Don't even *think* about going without me!"

Daddy didn't say anything, but he did look perturbed. Mama got the leash and told me to call her from the vet's and let her know if Brownie was all right. I held my tongue until I got in my car with the culprit. He looked up at me with his ears back and big pleading eyes, and I ended up just telling him I was very disappointed in his behavior. It had worked wonders when my daughter was small, but I didn't hold out much hope that Brownie would care.

Kit greeted me in the examining room with a big grin. "Your mother called. I understand he's ingested jewelry again."

I set Brownie on the stainless steel table. The dog groveled at Kit's side with his tail thumping madly against steel.

"I'm thinking of letting him keep it. Or wear it in his ear. The gold setting is squashed." I wasn't quite ready to admit I'd found the earring, then carelessly left it out for the dog to devour. "It's just the stone. A rather nice emerald."

"I'll take care of him. It may take some time, as I have surgeries scheduled for the next couple hours. Would it be inconvenient for you to come back around four to pick him up?"

I shook my head. "I'm taking Bitty shopping anyway."

"That's great. So she's not worried about money any longer, I take it."

"No, she's still whining about being a poor widow. I'm taking her to Wal-Mart."

"You're kidding."

"I wish. If I'm not here by four-thirty, send out the Mounties. You'll most likely find me curled in a fetal position and sniveling in Housewares."

Kit laughed. "If you survive, I'll treat you and Brownie to dinner tonight. My place."

My toes curled. His place? We'd never been that alone before. Was I ready to take our relationship to the next level? I wasn't sure. Still, maybe a bit of privacy with Kit would be just what I needed.

"You'll have to ask my mother first," I said. When his eyebrows went up, I added, "She won't care if I'm home late, but she will care if Brownie isn't there by curfew."

"I'll promise to keep a close eye on Brownie." He grinned. "And a closer eye on you."

My stomach did that flipping thing again, and my face felt hot. Very hot. I think I said something like, "Sounds good to me" before I left, but I'm not quite sure. All I could hear was my heart racing ninety to nothing.

By the time I reached Bitty's house, I'd regained my composure, if not my nerve. Did I really want to be the one to introduce Bitty Hollandale to a Wal-Mart Superstore? It could go one of two ways: either Bitty would be so horror struck at the lack of brands like Versace or

Giorgio that she would collapse in a cart, or she'd find the aisles and aisles of perfectly useless items like strainers and egg-slicers absolutely necessary to her well-being. Neither option seemed pleasant.

First, I soon discovered, I would have to find Bitty in order to take her to Wal-Mart. Clayton said she'd left about thirty minutes earlier to get a manicure.

"Oh, in that same little shop off Market Street?" I asked.

"No, they moved on the square. Two or three doors from Booker's."

Booker's Hardware has been in the same place since the mid-eighteen hundreds. It still has the same wide plank floors, old wooden cabinets that hold screws, and a lot of the same kind of merchandise. It's a great place to buy a Number 8 washtub or a butter churner, or the newest in chainsaws or drills. I had bought a cute straw hat there at the beginning of summer. It had been partially devoured by Brownie. Maybe I'd get a new hat while I waited on Bitty to get her nails done.

If I'd been brave enough, I would have worn shorts. As it was, I wore a thin cotton shirt and pair of Capri's, and some nice sandals I'd found at Payless shoe store. I felt pretty good despite my rocky start to the day. Dinner with Kit could be very interesting. Maybe I should get my nails done, too. That would be a treat. It had been years since I'd had a manicure, and a millennium since I'd had a pedicure. Not that I could afford either. If only I was broke like Bitty was broke: a tidy nest egg, property, expensive cars, jewelry and clothes, and enough money to buy half of Wal-Mart if she chose.

Of course, she didn't look at it quite that way. Bitty spends money freely on small things, but the large things—like new cars or houses—are only bought after she's haggled some poor car salesman or real estate agent half to death, and they agree to anything she proposes just to get rid of her. It works.

Bitty's constant moaning about money was really just a tantrum of sorts, because Parrish and Patrice Hollandale got one over on her. She can forgive a lot of things, but being tricked is not something Bitty forgives easily.

At any rate, I found Bitty sitting across from her manicurist and chatting away. When she saw me, she waved me over with her free hand.

"Trinket! Come and listen to this. Tell her, DJ. Tell her what you just told me."

DJ held grimly on to Bitty's hand as she worked a form onto her thumb. The sharp scent of chemicals wafted toward me, and I stopped a good yard from them. Acrylic nails must be an art form that's learned only after much practice. I'd tried to do it myself once, and my nails had ended up looking like inch-high shoes on the ends of my fingers. It took me four hours to soak the blasted things off, and I vowed never again to try something so obviously out of my league.

"Sit still, Bitty," I said. "She'll never get you fixed up if you keep moving like that."

"Well, I just can't believe it, and—have you two ever met?"

When we both shook our heads, Bitty made the introductions. "This is my cousin, Trinket Truevine, and Trinket, this is DJ. She's been my manicurist for about two months now, I think."

DJ smiled up at me, and I smiled back. She looked to be in her late twenties or early thirties, and from what I could see, rather tall but not as tall as me, blond, green-eyed, and obviously frazzled by Bitty moving around like a worm on hot concrete.

"It's nice to meet you, DJ," I said, then turned my attention back to Bitty. "I'm here to take you shopping when you're through."

Bitty looked very pleased. "Really? You hate to shop."

"I know. But if I don't take you shopping, Mama is going to send you boxes of stuff you'll have no idea what to do with, and I'll be the one to carry them in and out of the house. This saves me time and unnecessary work."

"So this isn't sympathy shopping."

"Not for me. I have my instructions and a list. As well as a timeline. I have a dinner date this evening."

Bitty pursed her lips. I noted the gleeful gleam in her eyes, and to forestall her saying something I would make her regret, I added, "I'll tell you all about it at lunch."

"Lunch first, then shopping? My, my, aren't we having a good day. Oh, I wanted DJ to tell you what she just told me. Tell her, DJ. Don't leave anything out."

DJ looked chagrined, but managed to flash me a smile while she patted the acrylic goo into the shape of a thumbnail. "Oh, it's not anything. I was just telling Bitty about an incident that happened the same night Miranda Watson got hurt. It didn't connect when I saw it, but afterward, when I heard about her being in a coma and all, I figured it has to be the same man I saw running away."

"Man?" I echoed.

DJ nodded. "I live on the street behind Miranda. I have a rented room there, out back over the garage. Anyway, it was late, right around ten or a bit after that. I went to close my blinds, and my bedroom looks out on that side. I'd heard a lot of cats, so didn't think much of it, but it wasn't too much later that I heard a woman scream. Naturally, I opened my blinds again and looked out. I saw this man dressed all in dark clothes running under the streetlight. Then he came down between the houses and ran right under my window. I got a pretty good look at his face."

"You should have gone to the police immediately!" I said.

"Oh, I called and told them what I saw. They said they'd get back to me."

"Have they?" I asked.

DJ shook her head. "Not yet. They will, I'm sure of it." She began to file Bitty's thumbnail with expert motions.

I chewed on my thoughts for a couple minutes, then asked DJ, "Can you describe this guy to me?"

She paused, her thick nail file poised over Bitty's hand, then said, "I don't know if I should. Not until I tell the police, anyway."

"Oh. Well . . . you're probably right."

My disappointment must have been evident, because she relented a second later and said, "I suppose it won't do any harm, though. He was medium height, I guess right around your height, and fairly slim. When he glanced up at my window I saw he was a white guy, maybe in his late twenties or early thirties. No facial hair, and it looked like he had light eyes. Sort of thin eyebrows, and a squared jaw."

"The police may have an artist draw a sketch."

"Oh, that would be fun," said Bitty, who doesn't like to be left out of any conversation for very long. "I've always thought I'd like to have my sketch done. In chalk, maybe, or even a watercolor."

"I'm sure you will one day," I assured her. "It will be in every post office in the country."

Bitty looked puzzled, while DJ laughed. I rolled my eyes and went a few stores away to buy a new straw hat at Booker's Hardware. It must have been a slow day, since I was the only customer. I prowled the area where straw hats for farmers as well as gardeners are stacked on a high rack, and finally found one I thought wouldn't make me look too silly. A big woman like me has to be careful so as not to look like a giant mushroom, so the brim must be wide but not too wide, and the scarf that holds it onto my head and ties under my chin cannot be a sissy color like pink. I'd look like a deranged Bo Peep if I even tried to wear a frilly hat.

A hat is a necessity in the blistering summer heat of Mississippi. If you intend to be outdoors at all, picking berries or feeding a couple hundred feral cats, then you need to protect your head. I've known people who sunburned their scalps because they wouldn't wear a hat.

At any rate, by the time I'd made my purchase Bitty was done getting her one fingernail replaced, and we walked across the square to Budgie's to get a bite to eat.

"Never go grocery shopping when you're hungry," I advised Bitty, whom I doubted had ever really shopped for groceries at all. She ordered over the phone and had them delivered, or Sharita bought what was needed and put it away. "Especially at a Wal-Mart Superstore. You'd need a flatbed truck to get them home."

Bitty actually looked pleased at the thought of going to Wal-Mart to shop for the week's groceries. "I've never been through the store, just to the produce part to pick up flowers. Oh, and once to the service desk."

"I thought you always ordered your flowers from Jennie's Florist and Gift shop."

"Oh, I do, but there's been a time or two when Jennie's was closed and the Wal-Mart wasn't."

I blinked against the scorching sunlight bouncing off the asphalt curb and found my way blindly to Budgie's front door. Thankfully, the overhang shaded the sidewalk enough that the front window table was in the shadow.

"Where's your sidekick?" I asked, suddenly missing the large growth that Bitty always has stuck to her chest.

"Getting her bath, and nails trimmed."

I shook my head. Even in a financial crisis of monumental proportions, Bitty has her priorities. I wasn't about to complain or point out that people who are really broke do not send their dog off to be bathed when they have two strong college boys home for the summer. Without Chitling, I anticipated a delightfully serene meal.

Since it was so hot, I opted for salad and a fruit plate. Followed by a nice bowl of blackberry cobbler with ice cream on top. Bitty had a chicken breast with vegetable medley and a sorbet for dessert. I eyed her for a moment. She pretended she didn't notice. Then I leaned toward her over the table.

"Are you on a diet?" I whispered loudly enough for the kitchen help in the back to hear.

"Of course not. I don't diet. I can eat anything. I'm just naturally slim. It's my high metabolism."

I sat back. "No, it isn't. You're on a diet. Why?"

She sighed. "You remember my nice black leather jumpsuit?"

"Remember it? You're talking as if it died."

"It has. I thought it was the water making it shrink up and sound like a leaky tire, but when I took it off, I saw half the seams were split. The other half of the seams are almost split."

Bitty looked sad, and I bit my lower lip to keep from laughing out loud. In truth, Bitty looks far too much like Elvira in the thing, but telling her that only incurs argument.

So I said, "I'm sorry to hear that. You can always have it made into a hat."

I could tell she didn't know quite how to take that consolation, so I added, "Ready to brave Wal-Mart?"

"This should be fun," she said, and I shuddered. This should be something, but I wasn't sure the word *fun* would do it justice.

****

About a half hour into our tour of Wal-Mart, I realized I'd created a monster. I spared a moment's sympathy for Doctor Frankenstein, who at least had a more noble quest in mind when he tried to do what God has done perfectly well for the last million—or five thousand—years. The good doctor, however, went too far by mistake. I had created a monster on purpose.

Bitty was enthralled with the bargains she found at every foot along the aisles stretching a football field or two across what had once been cow pasture. I brought her extra carts and took the loaded carts up to the service center to await the end of our shopping excursion. I tried to be at least a little organized and had arranged the carts in order of perishable liability. Frozen foods like ice cream went to the head of the line, while things like crackers, peanuts, and tampons went to the end of the line. Whereas I found it necessary to remind Bitty that she has no or little use for the tampons, she found it obligatory to remind me to mind my own business, that she'd never seen prices this low.

"That's because you only shop at places like Neiman-Marcus," I replied. "You have too much stuff here. You're going to have to sell the Franklin Benz if you keep this up."

Bitty's eyes were a little glazed. She had the look of an armadillo facing off against a logging truck: overmatched but determined to stick it out.

Finally, in desperation, I asked to use her cell phone. She looked surprised but not too suspicious, and I immediately called Jackson Lee.

"We have an emergency situation," I said quietly. "Bring a checkbook and a leash. You'll need both."

"Where are y'all?"

"Wal-Mart Superstore."

There was a moment of shocked silence, then he said, "I'm on my way."

Within fifteen minutes, Jackson Lee had Bitty in hand and was doing his best to explain it was impossible to need all the things she had in six carts. I silently wished him luck, and said aloud that I had to pick up Mama's dog at the vet, and since he was there to help Bitty, I'd just run on.

Jackson Lee spared me a nod and a wave, and I escaped while I could. I'd warned Mama about Bitty's compulsive shopping behavior before; now she'd get the picture.

I was surprised that it wasn't even three o'clock yet, and decided I'd stop by the Delta Inn to tell Rayna what I'd heard from DJ earlier. When I got there, she was just getting into her car. Or Rob's car, the old Jeep she'd been using since hers was wrecked. The insurance company had paid off, but Rayna had not yet decided what kind of vehicle she wanted to buy.

"Hop in," she said to me, and I hesitated. She'd taken off the cover, and the roll bars were all that would be between me and a zillion or so bugs.

"I've got to be at the vet's in an hour. Where are you going?"

"I've got a tip on where to find the black truck. I'm going to check it out. This won't take long."

"Didn't we make a deal with Rob?" I reminded, still uncertain about riding around in an open vehicle on such a hot day.

"Yes, and we kept our end of the bargain. It's been two days, and he's just given the police our collected information."

Still, I hesitated. "Really, it hasn't been quite twenty-four hours yet. Are you sure you want to do this?"

Rayna turned in the seat to look at me. She had her dark hair pulled back into a ponytail, and wore flashy earrings, black sunglasses, a sleeveless blouse, and jeans rolled up to her knees in a wide cuff. I think they call those "boyfriend jeans" or something like that now. Anyway, I could see she was a woman on a mission. Her words confirmed it:

"Rob told me not to worry my pretty little head about finding the truck, that the police would take care of everything."

Oops. Rob had made a big boo-boo. Telling a woman, especially your wife, "not to worry your pretty little head about it" is like waving a red cape at a bull.

I held up one hand. "Wait a minute. Let me get something out of my car." When I returned, I had my purse, sunglasses, and new straw hat with me. Rayna looked a little surprised.

"You're going to wear that hat?"

"Yep. Why?"

She grinned. "You'll see."

We weren't even on Highway 4 before I realized what she meant. Even though I had tied my hat quite securely atop my head by knotting the scarf under my chin, it kept blowing the brim back so that I felt like Klem Kadiddlehopper—an old Red Skelton skit about a rube—and I had to put my hand on top of my head to keep it from sailing off into the universe.

"Are you sure you want to do this?" I shouted over the wind, then gagged when a bug took the scenic route over my teeth and tongue and down my throat. While I coughed and spluttered, Rayna braked at the stop sign on Highway 311.

"I was quite willing to keep our bargain, but Rob made the mistake of treating me like June Cleaver." She shifted into first gear, and we rocketed away down the highway.

I knew what she meant. Some men still get that tinge of condescension in their tones when dealing with "the little lady." It's death to a rational conversation.

"I once put extra starch in Perry's tighty-whiteys for using that tone with me," I managed to yell without ingesting any more flying creatures. "He thought he'd broken something important the first time he sat down in them."

Rayna laughed. Wind whipped some of her hair loose from the ponytail, and then we gathered up speed. Talking was impossible. I held on to the bar built into the Jeep for just that purpose, clenched my lips tightly together, and waited for my new straw hat to disintegrate. It shouldn't take long, I thought.

Having lived in Holly Springs most of her life, Rayna knows all the back roads. I think the roads are really logging trails or dried up creek beds, but the Jeep took them all in stride. My insides were jolted about until I'm sure everything was upside down, but by the time Rayna braked to a halt and I recognized where we were, I forgot all about that.

"Is this where it's hidden?" I whispered in the sudden silence that fell when she switched off the engine.

"So my snooping tells me. We'll see."

"But—this is the Madewell property."

Rayna unfastened her seatbelt. "I know. We came up the back way. See that barn over there?"

I squinted. In the distance, squatting in front of the windbreak of trees I'd noticed on our previous visit, was an old barn. It was weathered gray and dilapidated. The cottages the Madewells rented were probably forty yards or so to one side of it, beyond a high hedge. Even from this angle, the landscaped grounds were very pretty. The grounds where the barn sat were not. Waist-high grass shifted slightly in a desultory breeze, and I was sure there were lots of stinging, biting things lying in wait for us.

"I didn't wear boots," I said. "I have on sandals."

"You'll be fine. I'll walk ahead of you and make a path."

It was very quiet, except for the distant drone of farm machinery, the buzz of bees, and birds rustling about in the bushes that marked the property line. That didn't fool me at all. Snakes don't make much noise.

It's their victims who holler.

"I don't know," I was still saying while she started across the hot gravel road. "I think maybe we should wait."

Rayna stopped and turned to look at me. "Wait on what? Them to move the truck? Rob to get here? The police to show up? Come on, Trinket. All we're going to do is see if it's the truck that Bitty shot all to heck. If it is, I'm taking a picture of it, and we'll go straight to the police station."

"Promise?"

Rayna didn't answer, just started off through the high brown weeds. I heard her mutter something like "Treat *me* like I'm dumb, will you, Robert Rainey, well, I'll show you!" I could either follow or sit in the open Jeep. Winged things buzzed around me, occasionally landing on my arm or face. It didn't take long for me to decide that sitting in the hot sun and slapping myself had lost all charm, and I got out of the Jeep.

The thing about meadows is they're filled with all sorts of interesting species of insect, reptile, and grass. Some of the grass is quite sharp. I admit wild flowers, like Black-eyed Susans, Queen Anne's Lace, and Indian Paintbrush, are nice. Not so nice are the thorns and nettles that freely mix with said flowers.

By the time I caught up with Rayna, I was bleeding, hot, sticky, and out of breath. My thin cotton blouse stuck to my back, my hair straggled in front of my eyes, and my new straw hat did little to keep the sun from broiling my brain. Also, I was pretty sure I'd seen a rat. I have a thing about rats. Recent close experience has not alleviated this flaw in my relationship with all God's creatures.

"Shh," said Rayna when I tripped over a hump of dirt and fell against her. "Just in case the barn isn't empty."

"Empty of what?" I whispered a little frantically. "Rats? Do you think there are rats in there?"

Rayna motioned me to silence. I grabbed hold of her shirttail. If there was to be a confrontation of the rodent kind, I had no scruples about immediate desertion, and she'd be an excellent rat-distraction. As the saying goes, I didn't have to outrun a rat; I just had to outrun Rayna.

Right in front of the barn there was a clear patch of ground and what looked like tire tracks. Of course, the tracks could have been from any kind of vehicle, but they were pretty wide. A truck of some kind, surely. Tractor tires aren't as wide. Unless you get up into the combine or picker range, and I doubted anyone would put such an expensive piece of equipment into this rickety old barn. It looked like it might just collapse into the weeds at any minute.

Some of the boards were missing in places, but the double doors were barred and latched. A huge padlock hung from a chain. I nudged Rayna.

"It's locked."

She turned to look at me. "You think?"

I decided it was just the heat and tension that made her cranky, so I nodded. "If we can't get in—"

"What makes you think we can't get in?" she interrupted.

"Uh, that lock?"

She pointed to missing boards. "You go that way around the barn, and I'll go this way, and there's probably enough space somewhere for one of us to get through."

"If there's a space big enough for *me* to get through, there's a space big enough for something I don't want to mess with to get through," I said, but since I was talking to the empty spot where Rayna had been an instant before, I surrendered to the inevitable.

Of course, the weeds were really high right next to the barn, and I found myself taking giant steps just to navigate. Crickets wheezed lazily in the high grass. Carpenter bees droned above my head, drilling holes into the old wood for their high-rise dwellings. Mainly, I tried to focus on where my next step would put me.

Sandals are not meant for tramping through rough areas. Sticks slid between my toes, briars and burrs pricked my tender ankles and legs, and I was so busy watching for snake or rat holes that I forgot about other stuff and walked into a gigantic spiderweb. It was as big as one of those orb spiders that rival tarantulas, I swear it was. A bird could have been trapped in that thing.

Luckily, I remembered not to scream and just made some harsh, grunting sounds of panic. I stood still and panted like a dog for a moment. Sweat ran down my face, neck, and armpits. I could forget about going to dinner at Kit's unless I ran myself through the local carwash first. I smelled like a goat.

So far, the only opening wider than the span of my hand had been above my head. Some windows near the top were open for ventilation, but most of the lower windows were boarded up. A huge hole near the footings held murky water, and in the shade of the wall, the mosquitoes rose in a swarm. I could actually hear them buzzing. I think they were talking about me, because a moment later, a squadron torpedoed me. I ran, swatting at the damn things with both hands and my hat. A few kamikaze insects dive-bombed me before I could get out into the sun again. Blood-sucking critters. Like vampires, the light of day burns them to a crisp. A hot day, anyway.

From my new vantage point, I saw an opening in the wall near the rear of the barn that just might accommodate someone my size. If I could get far enough inside to see if a black truck with chrome and bullet-holes was hidden there, our mission would be accomplished, and we could get out of this haven for all things that bite and sting.

It took a little huffing and puffing, but I squeezed my svelte, stinky body through broken boards and inside. Not much light illuminated the space, but as my eyes adjusted to the shadows—and I took off my sunglasses—I saw a banged up black truck sitting smack dab in the middle of the main barn area. The front bumper dangled, and several holes punched the windshield and hood.

At first, I was elated. Then, the cold realization struck me that Trina and Trisha Madewell, either both or singly, had killed Race Champion. And if the truck was theirs, as it must be, they'd also tried to kill Bitty, Rayna and me. That made me mad. What on earth was worth killing a human being over?

A sense of urgency rose up in me, drowning out my righteous rage. I had to find Rayna. Now that we knew where the truck was, we needed to get the hell out of Dodge. She could take her photo, and we would hightail it back to town.

Unhappily, I discovered that getting out between those loose boards was not as easy as getting in had been. Rusty nails stuck out at odd angles. I risked tetanus if I tried to leave that way. I turned around to study my surroundings. Slanted light came in from several places, so there had to be another way out. I hoped. Maybe Rayna had already gotten in, taken her picture, and waited outside for me.

Standing in dusty gloom that smelled like stale hay and dried manure, I debated taking a chance of calling for her. Madewell Courts wasn't that close, but if someone had noticed the Jeep, they might come looking to see who was nosing about. I hem-hawed around for several precious moments, then took a deep breath.

"Rayna," I called as loudly as I dared. "Can you hear me?"

No answer. Nothing but the whine of insects and droning of carpenter bees filled the musty silence. I crept forward to see if there was another opening. If not, I would just have to squeeze back through the way I'd come, rusty nails and all.

Straw littered the hard packed dirt floor. It rustled under my feet, and a long stick of it stuck right between my toes. I muttered something profane and lifted my foot to get it out. That put me off-balance, and before I knew it I smacked hard against the dirt floor. Dust rose up in a cloud, straw chaff and god only knows what else, and I sneezed. Twice.

Then I had a coughing fit. I got to my knees and did my best to muffle it. I looked up and around, and since there was still no sign of

Rayna, decided I'd have to go back out the way I'd gotten in. My options were rather limited.

Really, I thought to myself as I trudged back through dried up cow patties and hay dust, *I do the stupidest things. Now I'll have to go home and shower before I go to Kit's for dinner, and then listen to Mama ask me a dozen questions about what we have planned for the evening.*

Whatever else I might have groused to myself about was cut short by my abrupt descent into some kind of trough dug into the ground. Once more I ate dirt and spit out stuff I didn't want to think about. I sat up, swearing so badly that I figured I'd have to show up for the next Atonement Day at the United Methodist church.

When I heard a noise right behind me, I half-turned, afraid I might see a rat or worse. But I saw nothing but stars when something hit me hard in the head. It knocked me silly, and I went sprawling again. While I lay on my back looking up at the open beams of rafters and trying to regain my bearings, I heard what sounded like hundreds of birds circling above me. Then there was a flash and sizzle.

My last thought for a while was that God had heard me swearing and hit me with a lightning bolt. Then oblivion.

CHAPTER 21

Sometimes it pays to listen in church. I woke up to total darkness and figured I had died and gone to hell. It was just a matter of time before I smelled brimstone and got poked with a pitchfork. I began to feel rather sorry for myself. It wasn't as if I hadn't *tried* to be good most of the time. Half of the time. Some of the time. I was just a weak sinner. Now I faced an eternity of fire, and worse—a family reunion.

"Be still," a voice in the darkness said, and I sucked in hot air and dirt.

"Cousin Letty? Is that you?"

"No, you idiot. It's me. Rayna."

"Ohhh, I'm so sorry you're dead, too."

"What?"

"Aren't we dead?"

"Not yet," she retorted. "Be still. You're just making it stuffier in here. We don't want to run out of air before someone finds us."

I ran all that through my thought processes, which were admittedly a bit slow. My head hurt, my eyes hurt, and I had a million bites that itched like crazy. Rayna must be wrong. We had to be in hell.

What she'd just said finally struck home.

"Air? Why would we run out of air?"

Rayna's hand closed on my arm, though she could have been going for my throat. It was really dark.

"We're in some kind of storm cellar, I think."

My life flashed before my eyes. Not again!

"Are there rats? I think I hear rats . . . did you hear that? It sounds like a rat. Did it squeak?"

Rayna made a sighing sound. "Get a grip, Trinket. As far as I know, there are no rats in here."

"How do you know we're in a cellar?"

"Because when you were dumped in on top of me, I caught a glimpse of light and rafters. We might be under the barn."

A wave of panic swamped me. I began to shake uncontrollably. I babbled things in some unknown language. I gasped for air and clawed at the roof, and when I couldn't find it in the dark, I smacked my hands against the sides of our cellar. They were damp.

Rayna grabbed me and shook me. "Trinket, snap out of it!"

It wasn't until she held me tightly in a bear hug that I got calm. She began to say over and over again that she was so sorry she'd made me come with her, until finally I dredged up enough sense to say fairly articulately, "It's okay, Rayna. Really."

She made a sniffling sound. I squeezed her hands to let her know everything was all right now. I'd recovered somewhat.

Silence fell again, and I did my best not to think about rats, or cellars, or death. It would be too easy to lose my tenuous grip on control.

After a few minutes went by in which we were both lost in our own thoughts, she said quietly, "I know how difficult this must be for you, especially after . . . after last time. I am so sorry, Trinket."

"This isn't your fault, Rayna. I came willingly."

A sigh, and then, "Well, Rob warned us."

"And I'm sure he'll make it a point to remind us of that, too."

"If I ever see him again."

"Listen, if there's anything I learned from my last similar experience, it's don't give up. Panic is acceptable. Surrender is not."

She laughed softly. "No, neither one of us is the kind to give up."

"Right." I took a deep breath. "So, after you tell me how we got in here, maybe we can figure a way to get out of here."

"I wish I knew." I felt her shrug. "One minute I was walking down the side of the barn looking for a way in, and the next thing I know, something hit me between my shoulder blades, my body started to twitch, and I passed out. I'm thinking it might have been some kind of stun gun."

I nodded, realized she couldn't see me in the dark, and said, "That sounds logical. If hitting people with stun guns can be considered logical. Of course, whoever did this only had to wait a couple of minutes and I'm sure I'd have obligingly knocked myself out and saved them the trouble. There are a lot of unexpected things on barn floors."

"Any idea who is behind this?"

"Most likely the same person who shot Race, strangled Naomi, put Miranda into a coma, and tried to run us off the road. I don't suppose you caught a glimpse of who stunned you, or heard him speak?"

"No. I can't even tell you if it was man or a woman." Rayna paused, then added, "but if it was a woman, it must be a fairly strong woman."

"You know, I thought I had it figured out. I was sure Heather was the one who's gone on a homicidal marathon."

"Heather?"

"Brandon Caldwell's girlfriend from Ole Miss. She's Miss Tri-athlete and goes to the gym to train. I saw her jogging last night and gave her a ride."

"Why would she want to kill Race and Naomi? Did she even know them?"

"I have no idea. But remember at the wake, when Ronny said someone had been leaving notes on Race's truck, and she'd followed him from Biloxi, to Oxford, and to Holly Springs? Heather fits that description pretty well. Better even than Rose Allgood."

"My money was on Rose," said Rayna.

"And Bitty's money is on Trina Madewell. Which brings us to the fact we're on the Madewell property where we found the black truck that tried to run us off the road, and now we've been attacked and stuck in a cellar. That doesn't look good for either of the Madewell sisters."

"What I'm wondering now is, why are we still alive?"

That question put a knot in my knickers, and I thought about it for a minute. Why indeed? So far the killer or killers had been successful in murder and near-murder. Why leave us alive?

Finally I said slowly, "Well, there are a couple of explanations I can come up with for us still being here. None of them are especially pleasant. Which do you want first?"

"Surprise me."

"Okay. Here are my theories. The best situation would be if the killer has no intention of finishing us off, but intends to leave us here while she gets out of town. That's the best because it means we aren't facing sudden death, but the downside is, what if no one finds us?"

"A cheery thought," Rayna said glumly. "Next?"

"Next. . . maybe the killer intends to come back and finish us off."

After a deep silence, she said, "Well, that's pretty brutal."

"Yes. We can hope for the first theory to be correct."

"Why leave us alive, though? If the killer meant to do us in, wouldn't she have just done it already?"

"Not necessarily," I said. "What if the killer ran out of time? Even Trina or Trisha Madewell wouldn't want anyone up at the house or in one of the cottages to hear a gun."

"In other words, we need to find a way out of here pretty damn quick."

"Yep. No point in waiting around to find out what our killer has in mind. Any idea how deep we are?"

"I'd say about ten feet down. I think there must have been a ladder at one time, but all I've been able to feel are rotting pieces of wood. And slugs."

"Eww." I thought about it, and then asked, "How tall are you?"

"About five seven. That's what's on my driver's license. Why?"

"I'm five nine. You can stand on my shoulders and see if you're able to reach the trapdoor or whatever's up there."

"I don't know . . . you think that will work?"

"I think we have to try something, whether it works or not. If it doesn't work, we can think of something else. I thought about hollering, but—"

"That may bring the killer back to finish the job," Rayna finished my thought. "I get it. Okay. This would be a lot easier if we could see each other."

"Then again, if I look like I feel, it's probably best we can't see. I'm sure I look quite terrifying."

Rayna gave a shaky little laugh. "All right. Here goes."

We both managed to get to our feet, but it took a couple minutes to feel our way around the cellar. It felt more like a shaft of some kind instead of a root cellar or proper cellar. It occurred to me that I'd spent far too much of my time in deep, dark holes since I'd come back to Holly Springs. I should really do something about that. Just as soon as we got out of here, I would turn over a new leaf.

After a few tries at boosting Rayna up toward the top, we figured out it'd be a lot easier if she just climbed me like a tree and stood on my shoulders.

"Boots off first, please," I said, and Rayna mumbled something about already having lost one of them, but I heard her pulling at the leather laces of the other.

"Ready," she said, and I turned and braced myself against the damp wall. It was cool to the touch and slightly slimy, and I didn't even want to guess at what might be on the blasted thing.

Rayna felt her way up my back. Her hands cupped my shoulders, pressed down at the same time as she dug her toes into my braced legs, then she clambered up me like a monkey. She's heavier than she looks. I think I said something like "Oof!" a couple times, but not loud enough for her to hear.

In my younger years, we girls used to play cheerleader a lot. Some of us actually were cheerleaders, but the rest of us just liked learning the steps of their dances and how to form human pyramids. So my years as a pyramid base helped out in a time of need. Go figure. Who would have thought it?

Once I got my balance pretty good, I held on to Rayna's feet and cautiously took a step away from the wall. I felt her wobble, and once she gasped and jerked, and I think had to brace herself against the wall. We slowly, slowly, got to where she thought the top door should be. My muscles strained, and the weight on my shoulders got heavier by the second, it seemed. I had my knees locked, and hoped they didn't give way.

If they did, she would drop like a sack of wet sand.

"Steady now," she whispered. "I think I've got it . . . right here . . . there's some kind of latch—wait. I have it . . . I think. Damn! Splinters."

A crack of light suddenly pierced the darkness. If I hadn't been holding so tight to Rayna I would have clapped my hands in glee. Then it disappeared.

"Damn . . . thing is . . . heavy," Rayna panted. I heard her scrabbling at the wooden door again, and again a thin spear of light briefly illuminated the blackness. This time the door stayed open long enough for us to catch a glimpse of barn walls.

"We need to prop it open with something," I said, and she agreed.

"Let me down. I'll use some of those ladder pieces."

That sounded good. My shoulders were really aching.

She half climbed, half jumped down, and we both slid down the wall to sit on the floor for a few minutes, resting and thinking.

"I've got some wood pieces here that might be strong enough to prop it open," she said finally, and we got to our feet.

We repeated the entire thing again, a bit faster this time since we'd had already done it once. I had to hold one of the wood pieces in a hand braced against the wall so she could get up on my shoulders without banging me in the head with it.

This time the light through the cracked opening was a lot dimmer. I had no idea how long we'd been in this hole, but it must be close to dark now. Rayna stuck the first piece of wood into the crack to hold the door open, then took the other from my hand to use it, too.

"See anything?" I asked.

"Walls. Rafters. The undercarriage of a car . . . no, truck. Damn. I think we're in a hole under that black truck!"

It seemed impossible. How had someone gotten us under the truck without moving it? Or had they moved it after tossing us down here like garbage?

Rayna came down again, and we thought for a few minutes about what to do next. If we were under the truck, getting out would be impossible. I didn't see how we could manage it without getting the door completely open.

"Didn't Rob say he knew where the truck was?" I asked. "If he does, then maybe he has an eye on it right now."

"He didn't have an eye on it earlier—Trinket! The Jeep! Rob's Jeep is out on the road, and if someone recognizes it and wonders why it's there, or if there's been trouble of some kind, then they'll call the police. Don't you think?"

"It's possible, I guess." I slumped against the wall, dispirited and out of ideas. "It's also possible that whoever stuck us in here has moved it somewhere."

"Oh. Well. At least we have a little bit of light in here," Rayna said.

"Not for long. People must miss us soon, you know. I was supposed to pick up Brownie at the vet's, then we were going to dinner at Kit's, and I know my mother is probably fit to be tied that Brownie got left. She'll be ringing phones all over Marshall County before long, if she hasn't already."

"Who knows when Rob will realize I'm missing," Rayna said, sounding tired. "I think he went over to Leflore County to check up on a claimant or something. Of course, he could be home by now and irritated that he can't find me. The animals are probably all over him wanting their dinner." She sniffled. "And he doesn't even know that Merlin isn't eating like he should, and Jinx has to have his pills tonight or his allergies will come back . . ."

Time passed in silence, each of us drowning in self-pity. The light through the crack faded until it was gone and we were in almost total darkness. I figured there had to be a light on in the barn somewhere, or it would be pitch black again. Maybe the killer left it on for later. That would mean he or she meant to return tonight. It was a scary thought. No. It was a *terrifying* thought.

"Rayna?" I said after a while had gone by. "Are you awake?"

"Afraid so."

"Don't you think the police should have already checked this barn? I mean, after we were almost run down within minutes of leaving here, they should have at least come out here to look around."

"Maybe they did. Maybe the truck wasn't here then. Maybe the driver was clever enough to hide it somewhere else, figuring on bringing it back here after the police had already searched the barn."

"Yeah. I guess that sounds reasonable. But still . . . that's taking a terrible chance. I talked to Rob earlier and he was going to tell me about the truck, but we got sidetracked and he never did."

"Knowing Rob, that was by design and not chance. He's devious that way. It comes with his job description." Her feet scuffed across the floor, and I felt her shiver. "I sure do miss his devious little self."

I scooted closer. As stuffy and close as it was in the hole, at least there were no mosquitoes. "Rayna, I've been thinking . . . we need to have a plan when the killer comes back to . . . to get us."

"Are you kidding? It will be like shooting ducks in a barrel. What can we do?"

"If Trina and Trisha are the killers, and we assume they must be, one or the other or both of them, then they won't want our bodies to be found here, will they? It doesn't make sense. They could always claim they were being blamed by someone else, but I don't think they'd get away with it. So they'll have to hide our . . . our bodies somewhere else."

"What are you getting at?"

"Just this—I doubt either or both of them could easily carry around the dead weight of corpses. Hang with me a minute," I added quickly when she made a distressed sound. "So they'll probably take us to wherever it is they plan to kill us. I think we can take them."

"You mean you and me against Trina and Trisha. Hm. I like it. Yes, I think you're right, Trinket. For one thing, we're in better shape. Yes, we are. For another thing, we have desperation on our side."

That was true enough. I nodded, then I realized she couldn't see me.

"Okay, I'll take Trina because she's the biggest and I'm the biggest, and you go for Trisha. Give it everything you've got."

"How do you think they'll get us out of here? Should we come out fighting or wait?"

"Probably a ladder of some kind. We'll wait until we're out of this hole and can move around. We'll have to distract them somehow."

"What if it's not the Madewell sisters?"

"Then it will be Rose Allgood and I *know* we can take her. Or Heather Lightner, and that will be two against one."

"And if it turns out to be a man?"

"There's no man on our suspect list."

"That doesn't mean there can't be one."

I had to admit that was true. "But it's not very likely," I added. "And I hope not, because we'd need a weapon, and we don't have anything but rotting wood scraps."

"And my camera."

"Your camera—Rayna, that's perfect! Does it have a flash?"

"Of course it does."

"That's what we'll do, then. When we get out of this hole and they aren't expecting it, pop your flash right in one of their eyes. Even if you only startle one of them, it will give us an advantage. Think you can do it?"

"Sure. And if nothing else, they'll have lovely photos as keepsake souvenirs of their murderous spree."

Despite the stuffy heat in the hole, I shivered. That might be a bit too close to the truth for my liking.

****

It must have been way past midnight when we heard noises in the barn. Rayna and I had several contingency plans worked out for all possibilities.

Except there were two killers, and one of them was a man. That blew all my theories to the moon, and worse—it made it even more difficult to implement our escape plans.

At first we heard the truck start up. Exhaust fumes poured down into the hole and we nearly choked. The engine sounded horrible, which wasn't surprising since it had a few bullet holes in it. Tires crunched over straw and litter, and it moved slowly off the trapdoor. Debris showered down on us as someone lifted the planks Rayna had propped up. If they noticed our efforts, they didn't care.

A flashlight beam blasted against our eyes, momentarily blinding us. A man's voice said, "I have a gun and I know how to shoot. No funny stuff or you're dead where you sit."

Nothing could have made me move at that moment. I was petrified wood. Rayna gave a little groan and was silent. We sat like caged monkeys while a steel sliding ladder lowered into the hole, nearly crunching my right foot.

"One at a time," the gruff voice came again. "Climb up. You. Big girl. You come up first."

Big girl? That could only mean me, and I rather resented the term. Yet I was in no position to take noticeable offense. I wiped my sweaty palms on my Capri's and grabbed hold of the ladder sides.

"Play it by ear," I whispered to Rayna. "Stick with what we can."

"Hey! No talking! Just git your ass up here!"

He sounded irritated, so I scaled the ladder as best I could after having sat in a hot, musty hole for several hours. My heart pounded against my rib cage, and my mouth was so dry I couldn't have worked up enough saliva to stick out my tongue if I'd wanted. I had no idea who I'd see when I got to the top.

Someone, his partner I assumed, kept the flashlight in my eyes so I could hardly see. I put up a hand to block it, and the man grabbed my wrist and yanked it hard behind me.

Now, I'm not used to being manhandled. Whatever his faults, Perry had never in all our years of marriage laid a hand on me in anger. Not only that, but the wrist this man grabbed was the one that had been damaged in the car accident several weeks earlier. It was sore, and my reaction was swift and involuntary.

"Ow!"

I pushed back with my free hand, catching him by surprise and knocking him off-balance. He stumbled into his partner who let out a squeal like an enraged sow and swung at him with the flashlight. All this I saw in the space of a half second, I think. I started to run toward the now open double doors. A muffled sound like a hollow whistle darted past my ear, and a chunk of the old wooden door splintered before I reached it. I came to an abrupt stop.

"Next bullet goes in your back," the man said, and I believed him. "Now git back here!"

I turned and walked slowly back across the barn floor. My knees were weak and my heart still hammered painfully against my chest. I felt faint. I wondered what he'd do if I keeled over at his feet. Probably shoot me while I lay there, I decided.

This time he held the gun up to my head and told me to put my arms behind my back and stand still. I did, even though I had no plan for this contingency. At last I'd gotten a brief look at him. I had absolutely no idea who he was. He didn't look the least bit familiar.

He was a lot taller than me, which made him pretty darn tall, and he had heavy features and thick shoulders, and wore tight faded jeans, a tee shirt with NHRA on it, and a baseball cap that said John Deere right above the brim.

"Gimme that scarf you got on," he said to his partner, and she protested.

"No! I like this scarf. It cost a lot of money. Use something else."

"Gimme the damn scarf, Dawn. Won't be long until you got plenty of money to buy you another one. Now give it here."

"Damn you, Cliff. You should have brought the rope like I told you to do."

"Woman, I ain't gonna stand here arguing with you all night. We got stuff to do after we git rid of these two, now hand it over!"

Cliff? Dawn? My mind churned with possibilities. I should know those names, I knew I should. Yet I couldn't pin down where or why. Nothing came to me. My brain was so numb with dread I could barely think.

Whatever scarf the woman didn't want to part with, she ended up doing so, and it was ripped in two by the man she called Cliff. I wanted her to come out from behind the flashlight so I could get a look at her, but she stayed back in the shadows, even though she kept whining about the silver scarf.

"It's expensive, Cliff, really expensive."

"What the hell. You didn't pay for it anyway."

"No, but I'd have to pay a lot to replace it."

The man snorted. "It's a wonder you ain't got caught taking stuff off your clients like you do."

"Those rich bitches don't ever miss it. And don't worry about what *I* do."

"Stupid risks, Dawn. There's been too much at stake for you to go and take such dumbass chances."

"Well, it's worked out hasn't it? Just this last bit, and I can get out of this town and sit back and collect my money."

Cliff knotted the scarf around my wrists and yanked hard to be sure it wouldn't come loose. Then he said, "What do you mean *your* money. It's *our* money."

"The policy is in my name, don't forget."

"And I took most of the risks. Don't *you* forget."

"Well . . . you weren't alone. And this is almost over with anyway."

"Yeah? Keep in mind that we're both in this together, sweetheart. If I go down, you go with me."

He jerked me around and shoved me toward the woman. "Hold on to this one. I'll git the other one up from the hole, and we can git out of here."

He talked about Rayna and me like we were inanimate objects, just loose ends that needed tidying up. It was not only infuriating, it was terrifying. But while the two of them had been arguing, my brain had kicked out random bits of information. Things began to click into place, and I wasn't that surprised when the woman pulled me over beside her and I recognized her.

"Well," I said as calmly as I could under the circumstances, "we meet again. What a coincidence."

She lifted a brow and just looked at me for a minute. Then she said, "You should have stayed home and not gone snooping where you had no business."

"Dawn—or should I call you DJ? You know you won't get away with this."

She rolled her eyes. "Yeah, yeah, yeah. That's what you think. It's gone perfect except for a few bumps in the road." She laughed at that, and my eyes narrowed.

"I suppose you thought it was funny when we ran off the road into the gully?"

"A lot funnier than that firepower your bitch of a cousin was throwing at me. I never thought someone like her would have the guts to do that."

"You'd be quite amazed at Bitty's talents."

Dawn snorted. "Her talent is spending money and talking a blue streak. That's all the talent she has. That's all any of you bored rich people do."

"Rich? Me? I wish."

"Right. Look, just keep your mouth shut, okay? I don't want to hear anymore out of you. This isn't the time to swap war stories."

I had a feeling hers would far outmatch mine.

Cliff, who must be the same Cliff who'd tried to kill Race Champion on the track, pulled Rayna off the ladder and gave her the same treatment he'd given me, turning her around and tying her hands behind her back.

Rayna looked from him to Dawn without recognition. I decided introductions were in order.

"Rayna, this is Cliff Wages, and I'm pretty sure this charming young lady is Dawn Jeannette Hardy. Race Champion's wife."

A look of shock crossed Rayna's face. "But I don't understand . . . why are you two doing this? Race is dead, so—oh. Of course. Insurance money."

"Bingo," Cliff said dryly. "You win the prize puzzle. Now git over here by your friend. We're going to take a little trip."

I exchanged glances with Rayna. We didn't seem to have much choice. My throat got pretty tight and my eyes stung, but I kept my head held high. I wasn't about to cower in front of these criminals. Not yet, anyway. I was pretty sure that would come later.

With Cliff and Dawn behind us, we were shoved toward the doors and the truck waiting outside. I half-turned to look at Dawn.

"Tell me, why did you run us off the road? We weren't even close to knowing about you."

"I thought Bitty recognized me. I was staying in one of the cottages and had started out the door when I saw y'all coming across the yard. I just didn't want anyone to put me at the scene."

"But if you were registered under your real name—okay, I assume you weren't. You took some pretty big risks, you know. Cliff is right. It could have blown up in your face. Why stay at Madewell Courts right under Trina and Trisha's noses?"

"It was the easiest way to get to Race. Only he had that stupid bimbo he'd gotten engaged to with him, and it nearly ruined everything. I'd told him to meet me here to discuss our divorce." She laughed. "I guess he'd forgotten to tell her he was married. When I showed up, she got mad as spit and pulled a gun on him. It scared the life out of me for a minute, until he took the gun away from her and got shot in the shoulder for his trouble."

"And you finished the job," Rayna said. "I wonder why she didn't tell the police about you?"

"Money is an amazing bargaining chip. I told her if she'd just be quiet, I'd give her some money. Of course, Race was still alive then, and he was all for a quick divorce.. It wasn't 'til she left that I shot that lying, cheating bastard between the eyes. He deserved it, too."

"But Naomi? Did she deserve to die?" I couldn't help asking.

Dawn got impatient. "Naomi was an airhead. An idiot. The only reason Race was with her was because she was supposed to inherit a lot of money from Bitty's ex. That was a crock, and I knew it. Race and his damned hot rods. That's what he cared most about, those stupid cars."

"Hey," Cliff said, and she shot him a fierce look.

"If it wasn't for you messing up, he'd have died in that race and we wouldn't have had to do all this. But no, you said you knew what you were doing. Now look, we've had to cover our tracks from Day One. I've had to do it all."

Cliff jerked to a stop and grabbed me by my hair. "I'm the one who killed Naomi, and I'm tired of listening to you bitch. Let's just git rid of these two now and to hell with the rest. Stick 'em in the truck, and let the cops sort it out."

"Don't be stupid!" Dawn snapped. "We have to do it right. I don't want to be looking over my shoulder the rest of my life."

Off balance from the way Cliff had hold of my hair, I looked up at him. "Better listen to her, Cliff."

He stuck the gun up by my face. "I'm not listening to neither one of you! Got that? I don't take orders from women!"

Just when I thought I was about to be blown to kingdom come, a voice I didn't recognize said from about three feet behind us, "Put down the gun, Wages. Now!"

It was a decidedly male voice, and he didn't sound at all friendly. My head was pulled sideways, and I couldn't see anything but Dawn's face in the dim light. Her eyes got really wide, especially when another voice said, "We've got six rifles pointed at the both of you, and if you don't let go of both those women I'm giving the sharpshooters the okay. Put down your weapons, put your hands over your heads, and go to your knees on the ground."

For a moment I thought Cliff would refuse. His grip on me tightened, he tensed, and I waited for the bullet.

Then he shoved me away, threw down his gun, cussed a blue streak, and put his hands over his head. I caught my balance before I careened into Rayna, and we both took off running toward the uniformed officers bunched on the other side of the ruined truck.

I have never in my life been so glad to see police waiting on me.

CHAPTER 22

"Weren't you scared?"

I looked at the women seated out on Bitty's front porch. Rayna and I had been unofficially crowned queens of the Divas, and now that we were partially recovered from our harrowing brush with death, we held court like royalty.

"Terrified," I replied promptly.

Rayna said, "Petrified."

Even though it had happened a few weeks before, there were moments when I broke out into a cold sweat just remembering it. Today, however, was intended to banish the memory. Or at least relegate it to a lower place on the roster of events in my life. If I let it constantly shadow me, then the two criminals would still have control. I'm way too stubborn for that.

All the Divas were there: Gaynelle, Cady Lee, Cindy, Sandra, Marcy—having safely delivered her baby—Deelight, and our newest two members, Carolann Barnett and Rose Allgood. While we were still shy a member, Bitty had been overruled and we also had a guest.

Miranda Watson had unexpectedly come out of her coma and done so well that she'd been released from the hospital the previous week. During her stay, she had also lost nearly forty pounds and said she felt better than she ever had before. Rayna had suggested inviting her to join us at our first Diva meeting since all the murders, and so she'd shown up fifteen minutes earlier. To Bitty's chagrin and my amusement, Miranda had also brought along her new pet: a miniature pink pig.

"They're quite expensive," she repeated several times, "and the only one I could find was in Oregon. I've been on the waiting list for a while. It's a Stewart pig."

While I wasn't quite sure what a Stewart pig was, or what made them expensive except that they were so little, I said, "She's cute, Miranda. She's about the same size as Chen Ling—and looks very much like her, don't you think?

"I certainly do *not*," Bitty answered instead. "Chen Ling has a pedigree."

"Really," said Miranda. "So does Chitling."

Bitty nearly turned purple. I stuck my face in my martini glass to keep from laughing too loud. Most of the Divas followed suit. Miranda Watson smiled broadly. It was obvious she was having a good time bursting Bitty's little bubbles. Bless her heart.

"So how do you think your new job will affect your weekly column in *The South Reporter?*" asked Cindy Nelson.

Miranda touched the wide brim of her flowery hat in a primping gesture. "Oh, I expect to be able to handle both well. If not for Michael Donahue reading my exposé on the people who murdered poor Naomi Spencer and recommending me to his editor, I'm sure I wouldn't have gotten the position. He's such a wonderful journalist, you know."

Bitty, who still hasn't quite forgiven the reporter from the Memphis *Commercial Appeal* newspaper for reprinting the photo of her in a story on the fire at her house last month, muttered something under her breath. I didn't even try to catch it. It was probably X-rated.

Instead, I smiled to myself and sucked in a deep breath of rain-washed fresh air. It was as if I couldn't get enough of being outdoors lately. After sitting for hours in that dank, dark hole, being indoors seemed confining. Rayna had admitted to having some of the same reaction as well. We were both very aware of how lucky we were to be alive. It could have so easily ended tragically.

It did end for Cliff Wages and Dawn Jeanette Hardy. As Jackson Lee says, they're both so far under the jail they're having to pipe in daylight. Just as it should be. Neither one of them has the remorse of a billy goat. Killing one person for money and the other for convenience takes a coldness of character that should be incarcerated for life. I hope that's what they both get, too, life in prison without parole. By the time they get to trial, the prosecutors will have an airtight case against them. The Holly Springs Police Department collected tons of evidence like fibers from clothes, partial prints, even DNA.

Leaning close to me, Rayna said, "I fear Bitty may explode soon if Miranda keeps on calling her pig *Precious.*"

"Well," I replied, "it's said that the greatest form of flattery is imitation."

"Oh, my god. Do we really want a Bitty-clone?"

In unison we said, "NO!"

"One is more than enough," I added fervently. "I feel like an idiot wearing this get-up she insisted we all wear, and if I wasn't just dying to see what kind of product demonstration Rose is doing later, I'd take off this damn dress and hat and put on my tee shirt and shorts."

Rayna giggled. "We're all supposed to look like our favorite flowers. How'm I doing?"

I eyed her. "You're a chrysanthemum?"

"Close. Indian Paintbrush."

"It's the brown and orange that threw me off. I should have looked at your hat. I can see the blossoms around the crown."

"Your favorite flower is the red rose," she said, and I nodded.

"I'm an easy one. Red dress, red roses stuck in my hat, voila!"

"Bitty is a forget-me-not. I only know that because she told me. I thought at first she was supposed to be a blueberry."

We laughed at our own wit and spent a moment or two trying to figure out if Gaynelle was supposed to be a jonquil or a yellow rose. Miranda Watson had come as an entire bouquet. She said she loved them all and couldn't choose.

Bitty had gone all out for this Diva day. She'd ordered flowers from Jennie's and had Sharita prepare petit-fours with tiny frosting flower buds on each one, and our place settings at her dining room table each held an old-fashioned nosegay. The salad contained dandelions and pansies, and there was rose-hip tea and dandelion tea as well.

Brandon and Clayton acted as our waiters, and the boys did their jobs with a dose of wry humor.

"Mama said it would help build our character to know how to do these things," said Clayton solemnly when he brought me another chocolate martini. "Just in case we ever have to supplement our trust funds."

I took a sip of my delicious martini, briefly closed my eyes in ecstasy, and said, "I hope you have other avenues of employment in mind, as well. Although you could surely make a good living as a bartender. I can't believe these things are so good."

Beside me, Rayna agreed, "Our two favorite things at a Diva meeting: chocolate and alcohol."

"I wonder what's in it that makes it taste so good," I mused.

"Crème de cacao, vodka, cocoa powder, a tiny chocolate kiss in the bottom, and some ice. Easy as pie," Clayton said with a grin. "The white chocolate martini has Lady Godiva white chocolate liqueur, if you want to try that."

"I don't want to spoil myself too much all at once. Maybe after we eat," I said. "Oh, and Clayton, I'm staying overnight, so just keep them coming, will you?"

He laughed and lowered the big silver tray loaded with chocolate martinis to the next Diva on my other side, who happened to be Cady Lee Forsythe. "Are these swizzle sticks chocolate, too?" she cooed as she helped herself. "I'm in heaven!"

There's something deliciously decadent about sitting out on a porch in the cooler air of evening, especially dressed to the nines, wearing a big floppy hat and imbibing an exotic drink. I felt very relaxed, and very Southern.

Miranda Watson pulled a chair over closer to Rayna and me and settled into it with her pig in the billowing folds of her flowery dress. "Well, I must say, these Diva meetings are much tamer than I've been led to believe. Maybe I do owe you ladies a retraction, after all."

I smiled sweetly at her. "Dear lady, if you can still say that when you leave, then you've left too early."

Rayna sucked on her swizzle stick and nodded agreement. Her hat brim flapped slightly over her face. "Miranda, is your pig wearing a flower?"

"Why yes. It's supposed to match mine, but I wasn't paying attention and she ate part of it. That's why it's mostly leaves now. Do you think I should put another one in her ribbon?"

"Well, this is a tea party of sorts, and we're supposed to be festooned with beauty, so why not? You know, I don't think I've ever seen a prettier pig. Really, I don't think I have," I said.

I meant it, too. There was something quite endearing about that little pink face, with her Miss Piggy nose and long eyelashes, and the bright blue ribbon she wore around her neck that was supposed to have flowers.

Miranda beamed happily and sucked down most of her chocolate martini. Yes, it was going quite nicely. There had been no disasters yet, although I was well aware we had plenty of time left in the day for that to happen.

It may have been the martinis, but I felt the tension and horror of the past weeks float away on the evening breeze. Sunlight still gilded the tops of the houses across the street and slanted across Bitty's front lawn, but up there on the porch it was cooled by ceiling fans and Mother Nature. My short-sleeve red dress was a nice linen blend, and my hat was one of Mama's old ones that I'd decorated for the occasion. The only thing missing was my emerald earrings.

Daddy had done poop duty and recovered the stone for me, but I just hadn't been able to bring myself to have it reset yet. One day. For now, I had put it away in the top of my chest of drawers for safety from Brownie. Until he learns to push a chair up to the side and open the drawer, it should be secure.

Carolann Barnett and Rose Allgood wandered over from the other side of the porch, and when Cady Lee got up to talk to Sandra Dobson, Carolann took her place in the white wicker rocking chair. Flamboyant as ever, she wore a brilliant green dress that would have been in fashion in the 1960s, a wide-brimmed floppy hat festooned with what looked like three dozen cat turds, but I learned were pussy willow pods instead, and high-top granny boots. The hat sat atop her head at an odd angle; I figured because her mane of thick hair would not be tamed. It rioted out from under the confines of the hat like a brush fire.

Rose, on the other hand, wore a simple white sheath on her tall, angular body, and her chic cloche hat held a single peace lily. Rather classy, I thought. It was hard now to believe I'd once thought her a possible killer. She may be quiet, but her wit is dry and quite sharp at times. It still amazes me that she sells sex toys for a living. What a world.

Rayna looked up at her. "My husband Rob tells me you have your own company, and you worked your way up from the warehouse."

Rose nodded. "It's a novelty company. Of course, we aren't traded yet on the stock exchange, but we will be one day." A faint smile curved her mouth. "It's not all about fur-lined handcuffs, you know. My company produces campaign buttons, prizes for grocery store machines, things like that. I've been looking for a place to build our new factory."

"And?" Rayna prompted.

"And I think I've found it," Rose said. "There's an empty building that used to house a toy manufacturer, and it's right on the railroad. It may suit my purposes nicely."

"Isn't that exciting?" Carolann put in. "A lot of new jobs in town."

"New jobs, more employees, more families, more real estate sales, grocery store sales . . . it should help the local economy, too."

I was fascinated. "Are you going to manufacture . . . fur-lined handcuffs, too?"

This time Rose actually grinned. "It would be cheaper to produce my own line of products, yes."

The ladies committee at the local Methodist church would faint dead away when they learned that rubber penises, complete with vibrating speeds up to Supermax, would be manufactured right here in their own home town, I thought, and grinned back at Rose. I was beginning to like her. Hopefully, she would never find out that she'd been a key suspect in two murders. At least, among the more amateur detectives—those not paid for their opinions, nor were their conclusions actively sought or wanted. By the local police, anyway.

Late afternoon turned into twilight shades of deep purple, indigo, and crimson, and Bitty turned on the porch lights. Not regular porch lights, of course. These are lovely crystal chandeliers made for exterior sites.

Mrs. Tyree walked over from next door when we got too loud, but instead of complaining, she accepted Bitty's invitation to join us. I wasn't at all certain how that would work out later when the festivities really began, but fortunately, Mrs. Tyree has only a short distance to flee at the first sign of chaos. Her walker may impede her speed, but she's been Bitty's neighbor for a long time and no doubt can handle almost anything.

I'd gone inside to the powder room when I bumped into Deelight Tillman on my way back to the front porch. "Violets?" I guessed, and she smiled a little crookedly and nodded.

"Red roses, right?"

We clinked martini glasses in a salute to our respective homage to flowers. I was beginning to appreciate Bitty's side-trip into the absurd. It was entertaining to guess all the different botanical representatives. Or maybe deep down I'm reverting to childhood and playing dress-up. While I'd never been that feminine as a child, I enjoyed getting in touch with my imaginative side. Bitty may be right. Playing princess is fun. Of course, she does it all the time and takes it to the extreme in even her daily life.

"A little bird told me you and Doctor Kit Coltrane are a hot and heavy item," said Deelight.

"Bitty's no little bird. She's a turkey buzzard."

Deelight laughed. "Well, is it true?"

I tried an enigmatic smile. "Maybe."

"Um. Lucky you."

"Aren't I?"

"So, tell me about the arrests. I never did get all the details about who did what to whom, and why and when."

"It's a little complicated, so I'll try to boil it down to the basics. Race Champion married Dawn Hardy back in 2005. They stayed together until he figured out she wasn't going to support him and his hot rod career, and she realized he didn't intend to give up his other hobby of collecting girlfriends—which took about ten minutes—and then split. I think he took another woman on his honeymoon. Neither one of them bothered to get a divorce.

"Fast forward a few years, and Dawn bumped into her husband again at—of all things—a hot rod race. By that time she was dating Cliff Wages, an arch-rival of Race's. A merry time was not had by all. Apparently, racing hot rods can be very expensive. Cliff and Dawn concocted a scheme where she would inherit a lot of money. He planned to invest in his career of wrecking pricey hot rods, and she planned to invest in herself. I do not think either of them play well with others.

"At any rate, Cliff was supposed to do something to Race's car so it would crash at an important turn on the track, and Dawn would inherit money through a life insurance policy she'd prudently purchased on her husband. That didn't work out so well since Race survived. That's when they went to Plan B."

"Shooting him," Deelight put in.

"Right. Only, how to do that without being caught was vital to their plans. That's when Dawn came up with the idea to have Race meet her at Madewell Courts to 'discuss' their divorce. She'd been leaving him notes threatening to out him to Naomi as well as a couple other ladies he was engaged to—he seemed to be very flexible in his contingency plans himself—and if he didn't want her to ruin his little games, he'd better sign papers."

"Did she really intend to divorce him?"

"Lord, no. If she had, she'd lose her chance at collecting insurance money as his wife and beneficiary. Of course, Race had no idea she had a policy on him, or I'm sure he never would have agreed to meet her at the Madewell cottage. But he did, and to his utter surprise, who should track him down but Naomi? She was furious with him, thinking he'd continued his affair with Trina. He hadn't. He'd started dating Trisha, but Naomi didn't know that. And Trisha didn't know Race had checked into the cottage, because Dawn had made the reservations under a false name. It was Dawn's intention that Trina or Trisha be blamed for Race's murder, but when Trina went in and surprised him with Naomi, that worked even better. Naomi and her mother both seem to have a penchant for toting around guns, and Naomi got so mad she pulled her pistol on Race." I paused to sip my martini before continuing.

"He got it away from her, but in the process was shot in the shoulder. It was just a flesh wound, nothing major. Naomi took off like a bat, leaving behind her gun and fiancé who was very much alive. That's when Dawn came in, picked up the pistol and shot him right between the eyes."

"That is so cold-blooded," said Deelight, and I agreed.

"I could have understood it more if she'd been in love with him and caught him cheating on her, but for money? There's no excuse for that."

Deelight nodded. "What I don't understand, though, is why Dawn killed Naomi. I mean, the police had arrested her for the murder, so why didn't Dawn just leave it alone?"

"Because the police are pretty clever. They figured Naomi might be a little, shall we say, intellectually challenged, but she wouldn't go to the trouble of wiping her fingerprints off a registered gun and leaving it behind at the scene."

"Ah, and of course Dawn wiped it down to remove her own prints, then left it behind so Naomi would get the blame."

"Precisely." I stepped back as Clayton came through with the heavy silver tray full of empty glasses. "How's it going out there?" I asked him.

He gave me a wild look. "Good god. One of those women pinched me on the butt. I think it's getting too rowdy."

"Wait a half hour, and if Mrs. Tyree isn't hitting on you yet, you'll know you've got a bit of time to make your escape." I laughed when he flinched.

"Mama said we have to leave once y'all sit down to eat. She doesn't want us exposed to too much fun."

"Believe me, whatever Bitty has planned, you'll be glad you weren't exposed."

"*Waiter!*" I heard someone yell from the porch. It sounded like Cady Lee. She gets a certain tone in her voice after the third drink. "Where are our matching waiters with the drinks?"

"I believe one of our delicate Southern magnolia blossoms is calling for you," I said to Clayton.

Shaking his head, he pushed his way through martini-drinking flowers and into the kitchen for refills. Deelight and I laughed.

"Such nice boys," she observed.

"They'll grow up. Brandon is already dating one girl a little too steady for Bitty. I think she'd like to keep them in college for the next ten or twenty years."

"Heather Lightner," Deelight said. "She seems like a nice girl, though."

I didn't mention that I'd suspected her of murder. "I'm sure she is."

"So, back to what we were discussing, why did those two decide to kill Naomi? And try to kill Miranda Watson? It still doesn't make much sense to me."

"Murder never makes sense. Dawn attacked Miranda when she figured out Naomi had confided in her, but Cliff decided to kill Naomi when Dawn began worrying about whether or not Naomi might have seen her at Madewell Courts. Dawn wanted no connection between her and Race. Not until she got out of town and collected the insurance money. If Naomi got scared and told that Dawn had been there, it might have blown the alibi she had already established. Cliff was sure the promise of money would keep Naomi quiet until they could do something about her."

"So Naomi knew Dawn had been in the cottage?"

"Naomi wasn't as dumb as most people think. I guess that includes me. While she didn't see Dawn in the cottage, she did see her walking across the grounds. Dawn, as her alternate personality DJ, did Naomi's nails. So she knew Naomi would recognize her, and once everything came out about the insurance and her being married to Race, she would figure things out. But Naomi surprised her. Race had *told* her he was meeting DJ to sign divorce papers. Naomi put two and two together pretty fast, and decided that if Dawn wanted to avoid investigation, she'd have to pay for it."

"And that's when they killed her. Do you think Naomi would really have taken money from the people who killed her fiancé?"

"I don't know. Maybe. Or maybe she thought she'd turn them in to the police. A tape recorder was found in the cabin where she was murdered, and it had Naomi's prints on it. The tape, of course, was gone."

"She was expecting trouble, then."

"I think she was expecting Dawn to show up, not Cliff. She probably felt she could handle a woman, but Cliff was too much for her. He strangled her and left her there on the bed."

"And of course, that's when we found her." Deelight shook her head. "Poor Naomi. And her poor mother. I'm so glad you and Rayna solved the case, even though the police got the credit."

"Well . . . let's just say we may have solved the case, but it was by sheer accident. Thank heavens the police were way ahead of us. They'd already located the truck that ran us off the road, but did a stake-out to see who'd left it there. When Dawn and Cliff came back for it, the cops followed them to the Madewell's barn, where they'd intended to leave it to incriminate Trina and Trisha. The killers had gone back to their original Plan A, once they'd gotten rid of Naomi."

"Okay, here's where it gets murky for me. Why leave their own truck there?"

"It was a stolen truck. Cliff stole it in Alabama and drove it up here. He didn't want anyone to recognize him, and stayed hidden until time to plant the truck as evidence against Trina and Trisha."

"If the cops knew all that, why did they wait? Why didn't they arrest them a lot earlier? They could have killed other people, too. Like you!"

"It has to do with evidence. The more the better. The cops were watching them and wouldn't have let them actually kill anyone, I guess. Not if they could help it. That's how they knew we were at the Madewell barn. Rob recognized his Jeep on the road and called it in. The police decided to wait until Cliff and Dawn returned to take them down." I shook my head. "When I think of all those hours we spent sitting in that hole and thinking we were about to be killed, I could do some damage to Rob Rainey. But, as he pointed out, if we hadn't been foolish enough to go there looking for trouble, we wouldn't have found it."

"So Rob's working for the police now?"

"No, not really. He used to be in law enforcement before he decided to write bail bonds and run his own insurance investigation company. Since his wife was involved, Marcus Stone let him go on the stake-out and take-down."

"I bet you and Rayna were glad to see the police!"

"Girl, you know it. I was sure we were about to be killed."

"How can those two killers plead Not Guilty, I want to know? That's disgraceful. And with all the evidence against them!"

"Our criminal justice system guards against injustice, but sometimes I think they can take things too far. Still, for the innocent, it's necessary to make verdicts beyond any reasonable doubt."

I was about to add there could be no reasonable doubt about their guilt, when I heard a familiar yapping interspersed with what sounded like pig squeals. Deelight and I looked at each other and headed for the front porch.

By the time we got there, Bitty and Miranda were in a scuffle on the porch with a pug and a pig. Try to say that three times, really fast. Anyway, Bitty got Chen Ling up and held her, while Miranda managed to rescue Chitling. It turned out the pig had tried to nibble on the pug's flowery collar, and Chen Ling had tried to nibble on Chitling. As far as I was concerned, it was a match made in heaven. Two squash-faced greedy creatures on the hunt at the same time. What fun.

Bitty, looking a little out of breath but determined, lifted her dainty little hand and rang a bell. "Dinner is about to be served," she called above the din of half-inebriated Divas and the recovering pug and pig. "Please go to the dining room and be seated in the chair that has your name on the place card."

"Place cards?" I echoed. "My, my, how fancy. I wonder if there's one for the pug and the pig, too."

Rayna came up beside me and chuckled at my remark. "Bitty really is putting on the dog for us, isn't she?"

"And the pig," I reminded. "Don't forget the pig."

We all laughed at that, but quietly so Bitty wouldn't hear. She'd gone to a lot of trouble, and we wouldn't want her to think we were making fun of her. Especially since she already felt left out. I think she hated that she'd missed being in that dilapidated old barn with Rayna and me. Not that she wanted to go through hours of sitting in a black hole, but she does love the attention we got afterward.

And of course, she's scolded me several times for leaving her at the Wal-Mart Superstore with six carts of merchandise and Jackson Lee. I understand that while the managers at Wal-Mart have extended Bitty an open invitation to return and shop any time she likes, Jackson Lee has threatened severe reprisals if she accepts. He was wise enough not to actually *forbid* her to go, of course, but said he wanted to be with her if she does so he can help load the carts. Oh, and he also tacked on the warning that one more such shopping trip might result in a devastating depletion of ready funds in her play money account. It's not really play money. It's the money she plays with, and Bitty has great respect for not being too foolish now that they've reached a tentative agreement with Parrish and Patrice Hollandale regarding the settlement money. While the alimony checks will cease, the settlement funds increased exponentially so Bitty doesn't have to worry about being broke, and Parrish and Patrice don't have to think about Bitty after the payout. There can be peace in our lifetimes after all.

I also happen to know Bitty wrote a generous check to Sukey Spencer and had Jackson Lee give it to her to help pay for Naomi's funeral expenses. In lieu of Bitty showing up for the funeral, Sukey was most happy to accept it, I'm sure. But I'm not supposed to know about that. Bitty doesn't want it known that she felt any guilt at all over the way both she and Philip treated Naomi. After all, Naomi was under-age when the senator began his affair with her. Young girls are often swayed by older men with money and power.

Dinner was absolutely delicious, and everything went much more smoothly than I'd expected given that Chen Ling and Chitling were at the table, too. None of the Divas seemed to mind. It's amazing what the properties of chocolate martinis can do.

After we ate, we progressed from the dining room into the living room, where Rose Allgood had set up a table with quite a few interesting items on it. It was something to see, I can tell you. Too bad Mrs. Tyree had left before dinner. Her reaction would have been most interesting, I'm sure.

While Brandon and Clayton had defected when we sat down at the dining table, Sharita Stone and one of her nieces served coffee and tea while Divas settled into comfy chairs or the un-comfy, antique, horsehair-stuffed settee that Bitty loves.

Rose moved to stand in front of the table, and a hush fell over the room. We all waited with eager attention to see which item she'd select, and what she would say.

There were gasps of astonishment—and some of delight and probably dismay—when Rose said that our gracious hostess, one Bitty Hollandale, had purchased all the items on display as gifts for the assemblage. Only she didn't say it quite that way. Her style of salesmanship or showmanship or whatever you want to call it is blunt without being obnoxious or offensive. Her matter-of-fact tone is absent of any prurience, and that makes the presentation less embarrassing. Not that it would have mattered.

We giggled like sixth grade girls, and even Gaynelle Bishop cupped her mouth and hooted, "Show us the really big one!"

Chen Ling gazed at the rows of items with greedy interest, no doubt choosing the one she wanted to chew on, while Chitling the pig seemed more intrigued by the flowers of Miranda's souvenir nosegay. Really, Bitty had truly gone all out for this meeting. I anticipated a run on the table once Rose finished her presentation and invited Divas to choose their preference among the displayed gifts, but that was before her announcement.

Smiling a little, her hands clasped in front of her as if she was giving a book report or reciting a poem, Rose said, "Now ladies, for the *piéce dé resistance* of the evening, our final items are being modeled for us by these gentlemen from a group of performers known as The Chippendales. You'll note that each model wears a different garment, and each garment is created of tasty flavors such as peppermint, honey, cherry, and vanilla. The ingredients are natural, as well as including artificial preservatives, of course."

Well, of course. My eyes bulged and my tongue fell out so far it hit the bottom of my martini glass when three well-oiled models with ropes of muscles and taut, tanned skin walked barefoot into the living room. They strode across Bitty's antique Turkish rug like lithe, graceful animals wearing nothing but edible underwear in three different styles. There was *nothing* artificial about these guys.

Somewhere, someone had turned on some music, and the low, throbbing beat kept time with the pulses of one dozen Divas, a pug and a pig. The latter two for far different reasons, I'm sure.

I think Rose added a few words about the styles of their bikini underwear, but I'm a little fuzzy about that. It really didn't seem to matter to me that much. Or to anyone else there. Except maybe the male models. They looked a bit edgy when new mother Marcy Porter gave out with a wolf whistle and cry of "Yeah, baby, *show* me!" but kept smiling and parading down the aisle between the settee, antique chairs, and gaping women.

Then, as one of them passed by the settee where Bitty sat with Chen Ling on her lap, the pug could take no more. Before Bitty could stop her, the dog leaped down and lunged toward the nearest model. I never was sure if Chen Ling wanted to taste the edible underwear or play with the . . . shall we say, *real thing*, but there was a high-pitched male scream, a flurry of activity involving several Divas—including Nurse Sandra—offers of immediate and extensive female assistance, and the model disappeared under nurturing hands and multi-colored flowers. His counterparts looked on but offered little practical advice other than *"Run!"* before they were also required to demonstrate just how edible is thong underwear.

As Miranda Watson reported the next week in her weekly gossip column with *The South Reporter,* however, "No more shall be said here. · What happens with the Divas, stays with the Divas."

Mrs. Tyree will never know what she missed.

The Divas' Debut
Book One

DIXIE DIVAS

Where their adventures in high

heels began . . .

CHAPTER 1

If not for long-dead Civil War Generals Ulysses S. Grant, Nathan Bedford Forrest, and a pot of chicken and dumplings, Bitty Hollandale would never have been charged with murder. Of course, if the mule hadn't eaten the chicken and dumplings, that would have helped a lot, too.

My name is Eureka Truevine, but my family and friends all call me Trinket. Except for my ex-husband, who's been known to call me a few other names. That's one of the reasons I left him and came home to take care of my parents who are in their second adolescence, having missed out on their first one for reasons of survival.

We live at Cherryhill in Mississippi, three miles outside of Holly Springs and forty-five minutes down 78 Highway southeast from Memphis, Tennessee. My father— Edward Wellford Truevine— inherited the house from my grandparents around fifty years ago. It wasn't in great shape when he got it, but over the years he's put money, time, and his own craftsmanship into it, and now it's on the Holly Springs Historic Register.

Every April, Holly Springs has an annual pilgrimage tour of restored antebellum homes, with pretty girls and women in hoop skirts and high button shoes. Men and boys in Confederate uniforms stand sentry with old family Sharpshooters and cavalry swords, neither of which could do much harm to a marshmallow. It's a big event that draws people from all over the country and gives purpose to the lives of more than a few elderly matrons and historical buffs.

This year, Bitty Hollandale cooked up a big pot of chicken and dumplings to take to Mr. Sanders, who lives in an old house off Highway 7 that the local historical society has been trying to get on the historic register for decades. Sherman Sanders is known for his fondness of chicken and dumplings, and Bitty meant to convince him to put his house on the tour. It'd been built in 1832 and kept in remarkably good shape. Most of the original furniture is in most of the original places, with most of the original wallpaper and carpets still in their original places. The only modern renovations have been electricity and what's discreetly referred to as a water closet. It's enough to make any Southerner drool with envy and avarice.

"Go with me, Trinket," Bitty said to me that day in February. "It'd be such a feather in my cap to get the Sanders house on our tour."

I looked over at my parents. My father was dressed in plaid golfing pants and a red striped shirt, and my mother wore a red cable knit sweater and a plaid skirt. Under the kitchen table at their feet lay their little brown dog, appropriately named Little Brown Dog and called Brownie. He wore a red plaid sweater. They all like to coordinate.

"I don't know," I said doubtfully to Bitty. "I'm not sure what our plans are for the day."

What I really meant was I wasn't at all sure leaving my parents alone would be wise. Since I've come home, I've noticed they have a tendency to pretend they're sixteen again. While their libidos may be, their bodies are still mid-seventies. The doctor assures me it's fine, but I worry about them. Daddy's had an angioplasty, and Mama has occasional lapses of memory. But otherwise, they're probably in better shape than Bitty and me.

Bitty, like me, is fifty-one, a little on the plump side, and divorced. But she's lived in Holly Springs all her life, while I haven't come back to live since I married and followed my husband to random jobs around the country. Bitty and I have been close since we were six years old and she rode over on her pony to invite me to a swimming party. As I then had a love for anything to do with horses, she fast became my best friend. Besides that, she's my first cousin. I've got other cousins in the area, but over the years we've lost touch and haven't gotten around to getting reacquainted.

Bitty knows everyone. I've only been back a couple of months and am still struggling to reacquaint myself with old friends. Some people I remember from my childhood, but many have been forgotten over the years. Besides, the shock of finding my parents so different from how I remembered them in my childhood still hasn't faded enough to encourage more shocks of the same kind.

"They'll be just fine," Bitty assured me. She knew what made me hesitate. "Uncle Eddie and Aunt Anna can do without you for an hour."

"Maybe you're right." I studied Mama and Daddy. They played gin rummy with a pack of cards that looked as if they'd survived the Blitzkrieg. "Will you two be okay if I run an errand with Bitty?" I asked in a loud enough voice to catch their attention.

"Gin!" my mother shouted triumphantly, or what passes for a shout with her. She's petite, with flawless ivory skin that's never seen a blemish or freckle, bright blue eyes, and stylishly short silver hair that used to be blond. Next to my father, who's over six-four in his stockinged feet, she looks like a child's doll. My father has brown eyes and the kind of skin that looks like he works in the sun. He wears a neatly trimmed mustache, his once dark brown hair is still thick, but has been white since a family tragedy in the late sixties. He reminds me of an older Rhett Butler. Since I'm using *Gone With the Wind* references, my mother reminds me of Melanie Wilkes, with just enough Scarlett O'Hara thrown in to keep her interesting. And unpredictable.

I, on the other hand, am more like Scarlett's sister Suellen, with just enough of Mammy's pragmatic optimism to keep me from being a complete cynic and whiner. I inherited my father's height, my grandmother's tendency toward weight gain, and auburn hair and green eyes no one can explain. I like to think I'm a throwback to my mother's Scotch-Irish ancestry.

"We'll be fine if your mother will stop cheating at cards," my father said.

Mama just smiled. "I'm not cheating, Eddie. I'm just good enough to win."

Daddy shook his head. "You've got to be cheating. No one beats me at gin."

"Except me."

"So," I said again, a little louder, "you'll both be fine for a little while, right?"

My mother looked at me with surprise. "Of course, sugar," she said. "We're always fine."

Bitty and I went out to her car. Bitty's real name is Elisabeth, but it got shortened to Bitty when she was born and the name stuck. Anyone who calls her Elisabeth is a stranger or works for the government. Bitty is one of those females who attract men like state taxpayers' money lures politicians. On her, a little extra weight settles in the form of voluptuous curves. About five-two in her Prada pumps, she has blond hair, china blue eyes, a complexion like a California girl, and a laugh that'd make even Scrooge smile. If she wasn't my best friend, I'd probably be jealous.

"I wish you'd drive a bigger car," I complained once I'd wedged myself into her flashy red sports car that smelled of chicken and dumplings. "I always feel like a giant in this thing."

Bitty shifted the car into gear and we lurched forward. "You are a giant."

"I am not. I'm statuesque. Five-nine is not that tall for a woman. Though I admit I could lose twenty pounds and not miss it."

Gears ground and I winced as we pulled out of the driveway onto the road that leads to Highway 311. One of the things Bitty got in her last— and fourth— divorce was a lot of money that she's found new and interesting ways to spend. I got ulcers from my one and only divorce. Those aren't bankable. My only child, however, a married daughter, makes up for everything.

It was one of those February days that promise good weather isn't so far away. Yellow daffodils and tufts of crocus bloomed in yards and outlined empty spaces where houses had once been. Some fields had already been plowed in preparation for spring planting. A few puffy clouds skimmed across a bright blue sky, and sunlight through the Miata's windshield heated the car. I rolled down my window and inhaled essence of Mississippi. It was cool, familiar, and very nice.

"So what are you going to do with yourself, Trinket?"

I looked over at Bitty. "What do you mean?"

"You've been home almost three months now. A doctor just bought Easthaven. Want me to introduce you?"

"Good Lord, no. I don't want another man in my life."

"He's a podiatrist. Think of how useful that could be. And Easthaven is one of the nicest houses in Holly Springs."

"My feet are fine. And Cherryhill suits me right now." Bitty ground another gear and I checked my seatbelt. Undaunted by my lack of interest, she went right on talking.

"Think of the future. Once your parents are gone, God forbid, you'll be all alone in that big ole rambling house. Is that what you want?"

"Dear Lord, yes. Not that I want my parents gone, but living alone doesn't bother me. I'm used to it. Perry traveled a lot."

"Whatever possessed you to marry a man named Percival, anyway? It sounds like a name out of Chaucer's medieval romances."

"His mother read a lot. Besides, with a name like Eureka Truevine, that's not a stone I felt I should throw."

Bitty nodded. "That's true enough. Percival and Eureka Berryman.

Good thing his last name isn't Berry. Then he'd be Perry Berry."

We laughed. It's funny what appeals to middle-aged women past their prime but not their youthfulness. There's a sense of freedom in being beyond some expectations.

When we pulled up into the rutted driveway of The Cedars where Sherman Sanders lives in voluntary isolation and bachelorhood, he was sitting on his colonnaded front porch, serenely rocking with a shotgun across his lap. He stood up, a small man with wizened features, bowed legs, and a nose that juts out like a ship's prow. He wore faded blue overalls, muddy boots that had long ago lost any kind of shape, a flannel shirt that had seen better days, and a straw hat that looked like something big had taken a bite out of one side. A bone-thin black and tan hound lay beside the rocking chair, and when Sanders nudged it with his boot, the old dog struggled to its feet and bayed in the opposite direction. Sherman Sanders casually brought up the shotgun. It pointed straight at Bitty's car. He obviously had better eyesight than his hound.

"Don't mind the shotgun," Bitty said when I made a squeaking sound. "He doesn't shoot women. Usually."

"Dear Lord," I got out in that squeaky tone. "Who does he usually shoot?"

Bitty opened her car door and stuck her head out. She waved her hand and called, "Yoo hoo, Mr. Sanders, it's Bitty Hollandale. You remember me?"

Sanders aimed a stream of brown spit at the dirt in front of the house and nodded. "Yep. I 'member you. You're that pesky female that's been worryin' the hell out of me 'bout my house."

One thing about Bitty, she never lets minor obstacles deter her from her goal.

She smiled real big. "That's right. I brought you something."

Sanders shifted the wad of tobacco in his mouth to his other cheek. "Don't need nuthin'. Might as well go on back home. I ain't in'trested in my house bein' on no stupid damn tour with a bunch of strangers walkin' through it and gawkin' at everything."

I didn't much blame him, but I didn't say that to Bitty.

"Oh, you'll like this," she said, and started to put both feet out of the car to reach in the back for the pot of chicken and dumplings. Unfortunately, she'd forgotten to take the car out of gear or set the brake. The Miata bucked forward. Off-guard, Bitty pitched out of the car like a sack of cornmeal and sprawled face-first onto red dirt. Luckily, she was wearing a pantsuit and not a skirt, but her rear end stuck up in the air like a generous red wool flag. The car coughed, died, and made an annoying buzzing sound.

Sherman Sanders cackled so loud his hound started to bark again, turning its head in all different directions just in case the mysterious noise was dangerous. While Mr. Sanders slapped his thigh and cackled, I set the brake, took the keys out of the ignition to stop the buzzing, then got out and went over to see if Bitty was hurt.

"Are you okay?" I asked anxiously, but could tell she was just more mad than anything else. She sat up and brushed dirt and gravel from her face, palms, and the front of her pants.

"Damn car. I keep forgetting it's got a clutch. Look at my pants. I just got them out of the cleaners, too. Give me a hand up, will you?"

I did and she turned back to Mr. Sanders. "As I was saying, you'll like this, Mr. Sanders. It's your favorite."

Bitty has always been quite resilient.

"Oh my, where *are* my manners?" she said then, and gave me a push forward. "Mr. Sanders, this is my cousin, Trinket Truevine from over at Cherryhill."

I managed a polite smile and "How do you do" while keeping an eye on the shotgun, but a still chortling Sanders looked like what I often call, "ain't right," meaning not right in the head.

Bitty pulled out the big aluminum pot where she'd secured it behind the driver's seat, and marched relentlessly up to the porch. When she set it down on the white-painted hickory planks, the hound immediately found it irresistible. Its nose seemed to be the only one of the five senses still working efficiently.

"Sit, Tuck," Mr. Sanders said, again with another nudge, and the dog reluctantly squatted on its back haunches with nose in the air and sniffing furiously. Sanders leaned forward. "What you got in that pot?"

Bitty smiled. "Chicken and dumplings. Homemade, of course."

I could see Sanders wavering. The shotgun lowered, the bowed legs quivered, and I swear that his nose twitched just like his hound's.

"Huh. Reckon you intend to bribe me with those, do you."

"I sure do." Bitty's smile got bigger. She lifted the lid and a thin curl of steam wafted up. "Fresh, too. Just made early this morning. They have to sit a little bit to let the dumplings soak up all that broth, of course."

"Young hen?"

"Two. And White Lily flour cut with shortening and rolled out to a quarter inch."

While they discussed the intricacies of dumplings, I looked around. The white painted house has a chimney at each end; old brick covered with ivy at one end, bare wisteria limbs on the other chimney. Windows go all the way to porch level on the front, with green shutters that can be closed in stormy or cold weather. Elongated S-hooks have the patina of age on them, but still look in good working order. A lantern hangs from the center of the porch, and electrical wire covered with conduit pipes painted white run along the porch's edge to make a sharp right angle beside the double front door, and then run parallel above the footings of the house and around the corner. One of the front doors was open, the screen shut. The closed door has one of those old-fashioned bells that have to be twisted to make a noise. It's a bright, polished brass. Everything about the house promises loving attention, while the front yard looks like goats live in it. No grass. Just red dirt, ruts, and gigantic cedar trees with furrowed gray trunks splintery with age.

"Reckon you can come in if you want," I heard Sanders say, and I looked over at Bitty. I thought she might faint. Her face had the dazed expression of someone in a spiritual trance.

Her voice shook a little when she said faintly, "Why, Mr. Sanders, we'd love to come in. Wouldn't we, Trinket?"

I looked at the shotgun. I wasn't so sure.

"Uh..."

"Come on, Tuck," Sanders said, and opened the screen door for us. "He don't bite, but I ain't of a mind to leave him out here with that pot."

The hound didn't worry me. When it'd drooled over the chicken and dumplings, I'd seen that it had no front teeth. Mr. Sanders, however, seemed to have all of his teeth but not all of his marbles. Maybe it was the odd glint in his eyes, or the way he kept cackling like an old hen.

Reluctantly, I followed Bitty and Sanders into the house. It has that smell old houses have of meals long eaten, people long past, memories long gone. It isn't a bad smell. It's actually very comforting. Furniture gleamed dully, smelling like lemony beeswax. Bitty paused in the entrance hall and took in a deep breath. She was obviously having a religious experience.

As if afraid to wake the saints of old houses, she whispered, "Beautiful. Just beautiful!"

I have to admit she's right. Oval-framed photographs of family members in garments a hundred and forty years old hang on walls. The walnut mantel over the fireplace holds more old photos in small frames, a chunky bronze statue of a soldier on a horse, and a pair of crystal candlesticks. A low fire burned behind solid brass andirons. The front room is filled with antiques, and just a glimpse into the dining room across the foyer promised more treasures in the heavy furniture and wide sideboards against two walls.

Since I don't know that much about antiques or old houses, I followed along as Mr. Sanders gave us the royal tour. Bitty kept clasping her hands in front of her face as if praying, and murmured in rapture while we looked at huge old beds with wooden canopies and mosquito netting, cedar wardrobes that go all the way to the ceiling and still hold clothes from the 1800s, and gilded mirrors with a mottled tinge betraying their age. Carpets laid over bare heartpine floors look as if they hadn't been walked on in years.

By the time the tour was over, Bitty had almost convinced Sanders to allow his house to be put on the historic register and added to the tour. He still had reservations and muttered about turning his home into a circus, but had definitely wavered. Bitty really is good. She should sell real estate or run for Congress.

When we got down to the foyer again with Tuck tagging along at our heels, Bitty picked up a bronze statue from a small parquet table. "This is General Grant, isn't it?" she asked.

For the historically uninformed, General Grant was a Civil War general who burned and slashed his way across Mississippi in 1862, but spared most of Holly Springs. Legend says it was because the ladies were so pretty and treated him to nightly piano concerts, but historical fact has a different version.

Ulysses Sherman Sanders was named in honor of Generals Grant and Sherman, since his family had taken possession of The Cedars right after the war when taxes were high and Confederate income non-existent. As Yankees, they were not enthusiastically welcomed into the community. A few generations have gone by since then and hostilities have ceased for the most part, even if not been completely forgotten by some.

Sanders bristled at any hint of censure in Bitty's question. "That's right; it's a statue of General Grant. Got a problem with that?"

"Heavens no. General Grant was an absolute gentleman while he and his troops stayed in Holly Springs, though I can't say the same for all his soldiers. With some exceptions, of course," she added hastily, apparently remembering that Sherman Sanders' ancestor had been one of those Union soldiers. "This statue's very heavy. Is it weighted?"

Sanders nodded. "I reckon so. Probably because it'd be top heavy otherwise, what with the general liftin' his sword like that."

Bitty smiled and set it down carefully. "I'll be back in a day or two to discuss what needs to be done before the tour. Even though The Cedars hasn't yet been put on the historic register, we can fill out the paperwork and submit it. I don't think there'll be any problem at all. You've done such a wonderful job taking care of this house. I honestly don't think there's another house in Marshall County that's been kept up nearly this well. Most need extensive renovations."

Sanders puffed up his chest. He still held his shotgun, but just by the barrel now. I hoped that was a good sign.

Tuck suddenly barked and rushed toward the open screen door, making me jump. We all looked outside. Something big and brown had its head stuck in the pot of chicken and dumplings. Before Bitty or I could move, Sanders started to cussing, and banged out the screen door and took a shot at the aluminum pot. Rock salt pellets pinged against metal, and the mule made a strangled sound and took off down the rutted drive wearing the pot up to its eyeballs and shedding chicken and dumplings behind it. Tuck immediately took advantage of this unexpected windfall, and the pot-blinded mule ran into a tree. The impact knocked it backwards so that it sat on its haunches blinking dumplings from its eyes while the liberated pot rolled across the yard. Tuck greedily and happily worked the path the pot had taken, slurping loudly. The mule got up and shook itself free of dumplings, obviously unharmed. And unfazed.

Bitty and I just stood there transfixed by the entire thing. Mr. Sanders heaved a disgusted sigh.

"Blamed mule," he said. "I swear it's part goat. Ate half my hat last week."

Roused from temporary astonishment, Bitty said brightly, "Well, I'll just have to cook you up another big batch of chicken and dumplings. Don't worry about the pot. I have another one at home."

We were halfway back to Cherryhill before we started laughing. Bitty had to pull over to the side of the road so we wouldn't wreck. Finally I wiped tears from my eyes and tried to keep from snorting through my nose. I have a tendency to do that when I'm hysterical with laughter.

"Is putting this house on the tour worth another pot of chicken and dumplings?" I asked as soon as I was snort-free.

Bitty nodded. "As many as it takes. I'll just have to buy more ingredients and take them over to Sharita's house."

"You fraud. Someone else cooked them for you?"

"Good Lord, Trinket, you know I can't cook. If I'd cooked them we'd have been shot, stuffed, and mounted over that magnificent walnut mantel. Did you see it? All those gorgeous hunting scenes carved into the wood... I thought I'd pass out from pure pleasure."

Bitty and I have different values in many ways. While I appreciate antiques and old houses and generations of custom, it's more in an abstract kind of way. Bitty has obviously made it her reason for living. There are different ways of handling divorce and that empty feeling you get even if the relationship degenerated into nastiness and you're happy to see the last of him. My divorce was pretty straightforward. Bitty's last divorce made waves throughout the entire state.

Bitty let me off in front of my house. "I'm going shopping for new shoes," she said, and tooled on down our circular drive with a happy wave of her hand. I smiled and shook my head. Now there's a woman who knows how to cope.

Mama and Daddy had gone from playing gin to planning a cruise. Pamphlets were spread over the kitchen table. Something familiar smelling simmered on the stove, and afternoon light made cozy patterns on the walls and floor. Brownie slept in a patch of sunshine. He's a beagle-dachshund mix with long legs, a short body, a dachshund head and coloring, and a beagle's loud bay. He can be heard three counties over when he scents a squirrel. He's also neurotic.

"Where are you going?" I asked my parents when I'd hung my sweater on a coat hook beside the back door and stood looking over Daddy's shoulder at the array of pamphlets.

"I was thinking we'd enjoy rafting down the Colorado River. But your mother wants to take the Delta Queen down to New Orleans. They have a cruise in March this year. It's usually June before the cruises start, but it's been chartered just for us retired postal employees."

Mama looked up. "I thought it'd be nice to travel down the river like those old gamblers used to do. Do you remember *Maverick*? Not the movie. The old TV show. James Garner always did well. I have a feeling I might be just as lucky."

"Huh," Daddy said. "You just think you're a card shark now because you beat me at gin."

"Three times," Mama said with a big smile.

I thought it best not to interfere. "What's for supper?" I asked instead.

"Chicken and dumplings."

My parents just looked at me as if I'd lost my mind when I started laughing, and I heard Mama say to Daddy in a low tone, "Hormones. Must be The Change."

Virginia Brown

About Virginia Brown

Mississippi writer Virginia Brown is the award-winning author of fifty novels in the romance and mystery genres. Visit her at www.bellbridgebooks.com and at her Live Journal blog.

LaVergne, TN USA
30 October 2010
202801LV00006B/4/P